ENTANGLEMENT

QUANTUM AND OTHERWISE

ENTA

ENTANGLEMENT

QUANTUM AND OTHERWISE

NGLE

JOHN K DANENBARGER

MENT
A NOVEL

STORMBLOCK

Entanglement—Quantum and Otherwise
StormBlock Publishing, Ottawa, Kansas

© 2019, by John K Danenbarger

Editing by Rebecca Heyman, Leslie Busby, Erik Hane, Laura Chasen, and Daniel Burgess
Cover design by Richard Ljoenes
Interior layout by Vinnie Kinsella

ISBN: 978-0-578-45037-7

Publisher's Cataloging-in-Publication data

Names: Danenbarger, John K., author.
Title: Entanglement—quantum and otherwise / John K. Danenbarger.
Description: Ottawa, KS: StormBlock Publishing, 2019.
Identifiers: LCCN: 2021902740 | ISBN: 978-0-578-55503-4 (Hardcover) |
    978-0-578-45037-7 (pbk.) | 9781982782412 (audio)
Subjects: LCSH Crime--Fiction. | Space and time--Fiction. | Psychological
    fiction. | Thriller. | BISAC FICTION / General | FICTION / Thrillers /
    Psychological
Classification: LCC PS3604.A515 E58 2019 | DDC 813.6--dc23

CONTENTS

PART 1

The Bony-Eared Assfish, *Symbolum mortis*, the only known member of its genus, lives at darkest, funereal depths of the oceans.

PROLOGUE

PRESENT DAY 2044 CE

GLACIAL ICE. LAYERED. THICK. FORMING AFTER THE BEWILDERING STORM IN HER head and creeping up her spine. The courier's delivery from Joe Tink lies like a white patch of snow on her desk. Being alone in her office, she doesn't have to explain to anyone why she is waiting for it to melt. But it doesn't. Finally, with curiosity spreading like hoarfrost, she feels forced to open this unwarranted denunciatory thing in front of her. To decide if she should leave.

Your father is dead.

That's it? She's vexed. Almost angry. What's with this couriered letter? He could just as easily have called her from Bangor. Always had. They were close, weren't they? Closer than normal.

Besides, she had long hoped her father would kill himself.

But, Joe wrote more. Pages and pages.

This late-September afternoon, in some sort of unfamiliar circuitous telepathy, Geena has been thinking about Joe—*Pickled Tink Joe*—more than usual. She was reminded of him earlier by two different women in her Kansas City office asking Geena about the fall season back in New England, presuming that she knew all about New England and its leaves.

You know, Geena, how beautiful it must be!

With Geena's children out of the nest and her ex a near-forgotten fugitive from marriage, she had moved to a smaller apartment in Prairie Village, west of Kansas City, to live alone, but rarely feeling alone. Her two boys, or more probably their spouses, dependably call about visiting her with the grandchildren during holidays, and neighbors in the building complex drop in daily to see if she *needs anything*.

While early on in younger years if she had lived there in Prairie Village—if she would have had time to think—she might have found this neighborly spontaneity a bothersome lack of privacy. Now, in her fifties, she loves this place and the midwestern populace who go nowhere. No New Englander had ever seemed as outgoing and optimistic as these Kansas busybodies. And, although Geena found that the religious tethering of the Bible Belt could be a nuisance, she has several local social friends who are comfortably unbridled and who distract Geena from her shrouded pathos, often recruiting her into playing bridge on Sunday afternoons and in occasional local tournaments.

Geena would never tell any one of these people, or anyone else for that matter, how she had grown up seeing the fall season as death-and-dying. Invariably depressing. Kansas is nosy neighbors, but still, New England is the epitome of fall presenting itself in all its dispiriting glory. In New England she had thought she smelled the dying in the rotting leaves, and she had heard death's unambiguous footsteps in Maine's ice and snow, inwardly cringing with the sound of each bone-crushing footfall in the long, dark winters.

Or maybe not. Maybe the winters are not the reason at all. Maine reminds her, in overkill, of the past, the shivers of buried darkness, ruining sleep. Anguish, grief, agony. Words that mean nothing compared to the reality.

Thus, many years ago, when offered a full-time position after temping in Kansas City during college, she decided to continue living in Kansas, away from New England. Geena is running her own construction consulting business, her towering height underscoring her authoritative presence, both for her few employees and for her clients. She has made sure her office staff have only seen her as a stoic engineer, a just but distant boss. Thus, the arrival of Joe's letter forces her to leave the office as if struck by a sudden illness, which is, in fact, substantially true. She has escaped—not remembering the drive home—to hide her soul in the bedroom corner with her mother's memories, in the few things she has kept: the cushioned chair—a maudlin carver chair she would never have bought—and the dorm-room lamp, as stringent as its droll Ikea name, that her mother bought Geena years ago.

Lost in the bedroom corner to scrutinize this bewildering letter, she doesn't remember having ever screamed before, but at the end of this letter, she has screamed. Now crying quietly, the soft reverberations of her emotional outburst, Geena feels a punishing sensation sweeping harshly over her with the intensity of a squalid wind, a punishment for all things hidden inside her.

Her kids are gone. Her ex is ex. Her parents are dead. Brother Davis is halfway around the globe. Joe, her only real friend, has forsaken her.

She and her brother are all who are left. Geena fears with fair certainty that her brother is also a murderer, that he has probably murdered at least one person, maybe more. Maybe. No, probably. Undeniably probably. Still, she regards him as her real brother, right now even more so, no matter family blood and all. She has loved him, despite her brother's cruel childhood tales, since age five or six because her mother told her to, and because her mother was everything Geena wanted to be.

Different from her father. She's crying, but not for him.

She tries to beat back the tears, to scrutinize why she is crying, but the emotion packed in her neural network that she had carried deep-frozen from Maine has liquified into a cold ocean. She sits transfixed, timelessly floating on that ocean—shards of pain from the deep—until she is slowly impelled, as only the castigation of loneliness can do, to form a determination.

The brusque taste of salt and of untenably bitter copper pervade her mouth and bring her to an awareness of the room. Blinking to try to clear her eyes, at length she gets up and, still blurry-eyed, walks slowly to the kitchen. Plucking a Kleenex from the box on the counter, she methodically wipes away the remaining tears and pats dry her cheeks, not yet aware of the black smears. Habitually she sets water for tea on the stove.

Murderer!

The word repeatedly disrupts her disordered thoughts until the teakettle's encroaching high-pitched whistle sounds its alarm.

She turns off the flame. No time for tea. No time for self-pity. Her mind is made up. Joe has written that he cannot, would not, could not make himself inform Davis about their father Kevin's death. Geena has decided she has to face Davis, to tell him personally.

Unintentionally, she exhales, "Oh, Joe." The sound surprises her and makes her body shake as she can no longer control her desolation, intensely aware that Joe was the only reason she never felt lonely. Joe's shocking desertion has evanesced into worry. Taking time off from work for her trip to see Davis in Norway, she will stop in Maine first, to see what she can discover about Joe, to tie up any loose ends. Fill in the gaps, maybe. That's her decision. Daunting. No, fucking terrifying.

Like the knock at the door.

BACK THEN

1. BETH

PURIFICATION

SIXTY YEARS AGO IN 1984, BEFORE BETH MET KEVIN NUSS AND BEFORE DAUGH-ter Geena was born, Beth Sturgess survived two years on prostitution, a dark, drug-filled period from which she escaped with herpes as the only permanent vestige. As a chubby sixteen-year-old, she had run away from her Newburyport, Massachusetts, home from her parents, Rob and Nor, who were so psychologically needy themselves that they had nothing to offer to each other, let alone to their daughter.

Two years later in the spring of 1986, she was discovered under an office building's porch in Provincetown in an emaciated, cata-tonic state by a strong young man about her age who carried her home on his back to his one-room apartment, brought her back to consciousness, fed her warm nourishment, and got her examined and somewhat cleaned up by a doctor.

While she was semiconscious, he had managed somehow to wash her old jeans, thrown away the rag she had been wearing for a shirt and bought her a new white blouse. He even bought her new white socks, but she still had her old leather high-top boots and worn-out underwear. She awoke smelling her own putrid body. He had never dared to touch her to get the sizes, or to attempt to wash her. But once she had showered, she saw he had made such a good guess that the lingerie he bought and left for her on the bed board fit just fine, and was, in fact, quite stylish.

How guilty she felt. What kind of person was this? He must have spent money that he didn't have. The first time she tried to close the squeaky, barely private door to the toilet and creepy shower, she realized that his studio apartment was so basic that he must be dirt poor. The kitchen and bathroom sink were one; the furnishings were comprised of a springless single bed and a threadbare, plaid chair leaking its stuffing beside a metal gooseneck floor lamp—all ready to assault anyone with dust allergies.

But when she first awoke and sat up in the bed, what struck her most were all the piles and shelves of books, to the extent that her first question had been to ask if he was running a used book business. And she was startled by his oddly formal way of speaking, as if he were quoting someone.

"I have to chuckle," he said. "But it is a bit embarrassing. I will have to clean all this up one day, I suppose. I spend everything I earn on books, used books mind you. I just like to read. Reading is my drug. Sorry to say it that way. Not criticizing you. I'm not innocent in the drug-use arena, but I eventually found it more appealing to escape through reading. I figure I can make some use of it sometime if I can ever get out of here.

"But I forgot to ask you your name."

"Beth," she said.

"Do you have a last name?"

"Not one I am so proud of." She paused. "Sturgess."

"Well, I'm Joe. Joe Tink."

She looked at him incredulously.

"I know. You don't believe me. My father's name was Tinkerman, but I hated my father. And, my friends all called me Tink, so I adopted it."

He was smiling. "And it fits well with how I like to describe myself…that I was born in a pickle jar and am so gay I'm pickled Tink."

She felt her muddled mind slowly think about that for quite a while, and then asked, "What do you do?"

"I'm a stripper."

Compared to Beth, he was short, but he was bullishly muscular. At the moment she was only pale skin and bones under a mop of unwashed, tangled, nondescript brownish hair. He was obviously a weight lifter who spent time on the beach plying his tan. She guessed he needed to have a perfect body if he was going to show it off. Otherwise, her sense about him was vague. Maybe it was the hard dark-brown eyes. She couldn't read his face. He showed no embarrassment about being a stripper; it was just a statement of fact.

As she scanned the room like a trapped animal, she said, "I'm sorry I'm taking your bed. I don't deserve this. I don't even know why you brought me here. It doesn't look like you're going to torture and kill me."

This time Joe laughed until tears made him get up from his chair to get some toilet paper to dry his eyes. Sitting again before he spoke, he said, "Thanks for the laugh. I don't have any such plan. Or any plan."

"But why'd you bother?" she asked. She couldn't see the humor, but was less afraid.

He hesitated, got up again, and washed his hands. Without turning around, he said, "I saw my mother die."

"If you can tell me where I am, I'll get out of your way." She began to cry out of relief, from guilt, from frailty, from loneliness. He didn't ask why.

* * *

Through all her guilt of taking advantage of young Joe, she knew she had no choice but to let him help her recover her strength. She couldn't help him pay for the food she ate, but she tried to neaten up his books and to clean dishes, the bathroom, the floor while he slept. But most of the time, she was too weak. She stayed in bed while he slept most of the day in the chair, when he wasn't reading. He would disappear late at night. She heard him return sometime after the sun was up.

In the dark, she tried not to want to die, the way she always felt in her withdrawal periods when the money was gone—when she couldn't buy a fix—when it would feel best to die. She would shake. But somehow he had given her hope. He had given her something that she couldn't explain. Sanity maybe. Kindness.

Conversation was sporadic, mostly because she didn't know what to say to him.

One afternoon with three books in her hands, she asked, "What're these books about?"

He was chopping vegetables near the sink and didn't turn to look at her. "Which ones do you mean?"

"These have the titles like *The Man Who Never Died*, *The Labor Wars*, and, uh, what's this one? *A Covert Life*."

Looking at his body language from the back, she could see him smile. "Well, I'm kind of a leftist, at least, by American standards. I believe human life has a value and shouldn't be left to suffer and die. I read stuff about it."

As she placed the books on a shelf in the corner, she said, "You're a stripper. I never knew men did that. Where do you work?"

"This is Provincetown. You don't know about Provincetown?"

"No, what about it?"

"How did you get here?"

"I don't know."

"Why did you come here?"

"I don't know. I don't remember anything about that. That's terrible, isn't it?"

"My dear." He had turned to look at her. "You are why I read these books."

* * *

Joe had acquaintances, a couple named Linda and Gerry, who were willing to take Beth on board their forty-two-foot cruiser on their sail to Bermuda.

They met in the late morning at the White Porch Inn off to the left along the street from Joe's apartment. Joe had simply said they were going to meet some of his friends.

After normal polite greetings and the coffee orders were delivered to the table by a smiling young multipierced and densely tattooed girl, they all, Joe, Beth, Linda, and a Swiss guy that nobody bothered to introduce, looked down in silence seemingly meditating, but, as Beth soon discovered, they were instead just waiting in deference for Gerry to speak. It seemed like he had to work up to a speech with great effort. She couldn't tell if he was slow mentally or shy.

Without any introductory explanation and without looking at her, Gerry finally ejected, "Joe suggested that you could do the cooking and galley work onboard the *Adventure*."

His voice was much more feminine than Beth had expected. She waited. On board what? The Adventure? A train? A ship? "Galley" meant it was a boat or a plane, right? With nothing more forthcoming, she wanted to say something to encourage him to explain, but couldn't think what. Maybe he was actually slow. Finally, not knowing exactly to what she was agreeing, she said, "Sure. Whatever."

To her it was whatever; it was not a choice. Boat, train, bus, airplane, or horse and buggy? What else should she do?

In the next two days, Linda helped her with buying more sets of underwear and a pair of sneakers, which, Linda said, were to protect the boat deck from the old boots. Beth felt that short Linda, with her fake, thin smile—and nose-singeing halitosis—always seemed to be talking down to Beth. She overheard Linda tell Gerry that she thought Beth would be trouble on board because she was too tall. It wasn't what she said; it was how she put the emphasis on *trouble* that bothered Beth.

For Beth, Linda was one of those women sporting long straight deliberately grey hair with straight chopped-off bangs as an intellectual trademark and who were just a little too good for everyone else or, for that matter, to eat meat. Her voice even seemed to twist witchy to Beth. Gerry, lithe in his young age, was more distant, but he seemed unassuming to Beth—not pompous and definitely a man of few words. She sensed something hidden.

"I'm going to cry," Beth said to Joe when early morning on day ten, it was time to board. "How do I thank you?"

"Just be well," he said.

"Will I ever see you again?"

"Maybe, on your return. I hope so."

"How can I pay you back?"

"You have paid me back by living."

"But…" She paused. "I'm scared. Bermuda? I've never been on the ocean."

Joe stood quietly looking at her for a moment, then said, "You'll be fine. They've done this trip many times. You'll be safe and well taken care of. Bon voyage. Really. I'm jealous. I guess what I mean is, you will love it."

When the boat began to move, she began hunting through her pockets, her bag, everywhere for something to calm her fear. She cried as quietly as she could, sitting below in her designated little forward cabin while the others prepared whatever they prepared. Her space had a bunkbed, a teak cabinet for hanging clothes, and two teak drawers. She found no drugs, not even a remnant, in her pockets. She had no money, but when she unpacked her new (Linda-purchased) little canvas bag to put things away, she found one thousand dollars in odd bills folded in the side pocket.

One thousand dollars cash—tens, fifties, even a few fives and ones—out of nowhere. Should she try to thank Linda and Gerry for putting it there? It didn't make sense for them to be secretly giving her cash, and for what possible reason? And Joe? Joe couldn't afford to stop stripping in Provincetown. If he had that kind of money to give away, he would have left long ago.

She hunted through her cabin and the bowhead to find a secret place to hide the money, deciding, for now, that the metal sink support strap in the roof of the cabinet in the bathroom had enough space with a little bending to let her press in the rolled bills.

In addition to Linda, Gerry, and Beth, the young Swiss man, Carl, said he was helping crew in order to accrue sailing hours for his captain's credentials.

He spoke with a low masculine tone in perfectly nuanced English. "I want to own a boat, but Swiss law requires a boat owner to have a captain's license. Every hour I spend sailing will qualify toward a Swiss captain's license."

Beth struggled with the thought that Switzerland had no ocean, but realized…duh…like an idiot, lakes floated boats, too, and was glad she kept that thought to herself.

While they had lunch the first day, he told her, "I own a security company in Zurich based on personal protection of business clients and important politicians from kidnappings and assaults. We drive around in little Smart cars. They're great because they are cheap and still have a kind of status."

Beth began to imagine that he must think of himself as a sort of fantasy superhero. She had to admire Carl for his seeming ability at fixing anything and everything, and all with an enthusiasm which she primarily took as gratefulness for the sailing opportunity, but also as part of his innate hyper personality.

He was muscular and agile, with perfect Germanic facial features—bright blue eyes, perfect teeth. His short stature made him even more capable at managing the boat's movement. He thought nothing of climbing the mast to fix the faulty light connection as the yacht dipped and swayed, amplifying the motion at the top where he hugged the mast as he dangled from a strap like some well-practiced circus performer. It seemed to Beth that, as opposed to her, he was always doing practical work and useful things.

He picked up after himself with such preciseness that Beth was shamed into neatness herself. She wanted to ask him, just not yet, what that quarter-sized medallion was he wore around his neck with a fine gold chain. She began to hypothesize that the captain's license was just one more badge he wanted to pin on the hero outfit he wore while he leapt tall Swiss buildings, if they had such things.

Beth felt guilty for being just a favor-granted ride while everyone else seemed to have a real purpose onboard. She felt she would have to try to earn her place, but she felt she couldn't and wouldn't be able to find important work to do. Work at what? Setting out microwaved Kraft macaroni-and-cheese, sorting garbage, and rinsing plastic dishes was hardly work compared to the constant activity the others were doing steering, adjusting sails, and fixing this or that, all important stuff she couldn't understand.

Then almost immediately, the seasickness began. She would have felt guiltier for getting sick except she was not alone. Carl, the superman, could not withstand every attack on the human senses either. A previous storm, perhaps a hurricane for all she knew, had roiled the sea during the week before they left. Already the first day, the ocean's residual undulations, as high as multistory buildings, made the boat rise and fall and churn like an insignificant insect floating in some ungodly giant's snifter of swirling cognac, getting everyone except Gerry so seasick that he had to sail for thirty hours alone at the helm.

The next evening, the ocean had calmed. They all were feeling better and Gerry had slept some. Gerry explained, "Soon we'll be entering a giant eddy along the edge of the Gulf Stream."

"Gulf Stream? Is that...?" Beth began to ask.

He didn't wait for her question. He was obviously not nearly so reticent to speak when it concerned the ocean. Or maybe he felt it was a necessity. His voice was not only feminine, but velvety.

"The Gulf Stream is like a giant hot river without solid banks to keep it in place. So along the edges, these giant whirlpools get created with their own weather system and move along the edges of the river, so to speak. It is impossible to know exactly when we will hit one, but I think that the mass of black sky on the horizon up there in front of us is probably the eddy's weather system."

It was the longest string of sentences Beth had heard from him. And it frightened her, like maybe he was nervous about this thing they were approaching, even if he didn't sound nervous.

The sudden soft wall of the eddy's fog was so dense that even the water either side of the boat was invisible and silent. Entering the darkness, they lost the little bit of wind they had. For Beth it was an even more frightening and ghostly sensation to enter total blackness and silent calm, being all too reminiscent of the diverting narcotic smog of her near past.

Gerry said, "Because we don't have any wind, we're being dragged south and east by the currents. We can't use the sextant or LORAN, so the only way I know where we are and what's happening is from a little dead reckoning and experience, but after a few hours, the eddy will spit us out into the sunshine again."

Gerry was actually speaking without prompting. She had no way of understanding the navigation stuff, but he sounded confident and she was glad to hear about the coming sunshine. Then Gerry calmly told a story which he must have thought would comfort Beth.

"Because the ancients had, like us now, no sense of motion, no light, no stars to guide them, when finally, they came back into the sun- or starlight and they saw that they had moved great distances, the ancients could only imagine that some sort of spirit had lifted them to an unknown location and they were thankful that those spirits were gentle and benign enough not to drop them off the edge of the earth."

Still frightened, Beth was wrapped in the silent darkness of unwavering anxiety. After what seemed like an eternity to her, but was about five hours, they suddenly came out of the dark fog into the sunshine and the wind of the steaming Gulf Stream. She felt an exhilarating damp heat that she imagined was like a Finnish sauna and had to strip down, along with everyone else, to a minimum of clothing.

Then that night came the storm, while Beth was below sorting out the garbage and crushing the plastic containers. In the middle of the Gulf Stream, because the darkness disguised the approaching front, a wall of wind hit the boat without warning like a bulldozer, so hard and suddenly that Beth was sure the whole yacht was tipping over. Below deck, she was thrown against the galley cabinets and fell to the floor, while food, dishes, books, and loose items flew off their places, banging and crashing in coordinated chaos. She heard shouts and commands above, the clanking of unknown metal parts, the zipping sound of fast-moving rope, and the whole cabin shuddering. As she slid on the slanted deck to the cabin bench, she held onto it with all her strength. She screamed, being sure it must have to do with the Bermuda Triangle and that she was going to die.

No doubt hearing her cries, Carl had come down from the deck to the main cabin to sit beside her on the cushioned bench and spoke with a soft confidence. Carl, the army ant of strength and practicality, was a perfect gentleman to Beth. Maybe he acted so polite and courteous because he really had a true love back in Zurich, as he said he did. He always asked Beth first if she needed to use the toilet, "the head" she learned to call it, or the shower before he would go in. He let her have the privacy and comfort of the forward cabin while he slept, or attempted to sleep, on the main cabin bench, which had no lee cloth or harness. Therefore, not tied and without bunk edges to keep him in place, he frequently got dumped on the floor in the middle of his respite by the listing yacht. Sometimes he slept on deck where he could hold onto a railing or two.

Maybe she was not attractive to him, but, during the storm, she would have folded up in his arms if he had offered. She needed to be held. She thought he must know. She was pale, afraid, and asked not to be alone.

"It's okay, Beth. This is a well-designed sloop. Sailboats don't tip over and especially this one; you just have to adjust the sails accordingly and sometimes a sharp wind sneaks up on you. Right now the wind is blowing the opposite direction of the flow of the Gulf Stream so the waves feel a bit rougher than normal, but with a good captain like Gerry, this sloop has no problem dealing with such weather."

The yacht had righted a bit, but was still clattering and clanging from the blasting wind, making Carl yell to be heard. "To me this is just fun; it is not dangerous. I work with danger, so I know. I teach my clients how to handle guns. I teach them about how to stay safe by showing them how to be as invisible and anonymous as possible, how to drive cars defensively, and how to defend themselves in the worst case. These are wealthy clients with families who can be targets for ransom."

His deliberate confident talk about other dangers distracted Beth and she knew that was his purpose. She had been treated with such careful concern, first from Joe and now from Carl. She would never ask in a hundred years, but it made her want to be held by a real person, someone she knew.

Thirty minutes later as the front passed, they were in quiet waters, heavy rain, and a constant wind that continued all night.

Once they had finished crossing the broad, hot current of the Gulf Stream, the ocean water temperature cooled a bit and the color changed from the black cold water with which she was familiar north of the Gulf Stream to a soothing warm tropical blue water like she had seen in pictures.

Small white birds, seemingly lost and tired, began resting on the boom, and pods of grinning dolphins hunted and swam sometimes in herds of hundreds, toying with the boat by surfing in the bow wave. The enormity of the ocean's quiet offered a tranquility she would never again know.

For the next three nights, the cloudless sky was only a faded light, exposing a distant ocean horizon. The susurrus of water near the hull sparkled like Fourth of July sparklers with the miniature flashes of algae aerated by the boat's passage. As she lay on the deck at night, she picked out the satellites, the airplanes, a few comets (or meteors? Which was which?), and once each night, some large cruise ship would display its lights as it crept along the surface of the earth's curvature.

She felt the sky was wrapping her with a magnificence that her conscious mind could never describe. The stars lit an open sky, so open and endless that once it gave her an unspeakable foreboding that at any moment a superhuman leviathan with stale tentacles would reach down from that openness to violate her. But it was only for one horrifying minute.

During the day, she sometimes tried to save the ill-fated flying fish that, after gloriously escaping through the air from some unseen underwater predator, would at times land, not back in the vast ocean, but, against all odds, on the oak surface of their deck.

On the third day, a huge white ghost in the form of an albino whale surfaced so close to the yacht where she was lying that the horrid smell of its rotten fish breath made her gag. The yacht was on autopilot and the others were below deck. She was even afraid to yell for them to come see. Here she was alone with a white presence of such magnificence and magnitude, tilting its body to stare directly at her with one huge, deep, brooding pupil, evaluating her significance, deciding whether to let her exist, and then fading away without a sound making Beth feel like something remarkable had happened, an approbation of sorts, an epiphany, an awakening. She felt her body molt a soiled veneer.

After grimy years on drugs, the five-day-and-night sail to Bermuda was an adventure in purity and grace, with sunrises and sunsets she had never previously valued, alien ocean voices in the boat's wake, and tuna leaping from the surface in sea-serpent formation. The ocean light and an all-night twilight, all added details, minutiae, concepts, and emotions that had previously never been in her realm of comprehension.

Then one early evening after sundown, Gerry pointed toward the horizon where Beth could see a bright light floating on the water and said, "That is Bermuda."

"It looks like a ship," she said.

"Yes, but it's the lights of Bermuda about thirty-six hours away."

She stared in silence at the light. "It looks so close."

"Lots of things are deceptive on the ocean," he said.

Beth thought that was a strange thing to say.

Nearing land the next day, she heard Gerry communicating over the radio with some Bermudian official office and heard him say his boat's name, *Adventure,* and the names of those on board, how many, and how many would be leaving onboard with him. She couldn't hear all the details, but that's when she understood Carl would be flying home from Bermuda. She heard her own name, too, but didn't catch the context.

In Bermuda, after surrendering their passports at the customs wharf, they rented a slip at Hamilton's Royal Bermuda Yacht Club, where everyone except Gerry showered in the club's storage cellar with the sail rigging and cockroaches since the royal showers and toilets upstairs were for members only. But the friendly black staff made Beth feel she belonged.

Because her mind continued to sway with the waves for another day, it was a blissful feeling to have solid ground under her feet again.

On day two, Linda, Carl, and Beth walked the streets in central Hamilton, which, according to Gerry, were monitored by police cameras and that any drug trade caught on camera meant immediate "slammer" time. No judge, no jury.

She felt a vague, sad empathy for the prisoners. In the split second that a mind can revive and relive a drug-filled history, she felt the terror of her trip to Mexico, to Ciudad Juarez. Somebody had fixed a plane ticket and a passport for her, the same one she had with her now, in fact, with the same horrible picture that would not let her completely escape her history. All she had had to do was follow instructions. Swallow some bags of shit and shit them out later. Trip paid. And then she had had money to survive. And then she had had drugs to survive, the drugs to help her forget.

During the three days of luxury docking at the foremost Bermuda yacht club, Gerry always seemed to be off on his own. Beth tagged along with Linda and took in the touristy part of Hamilton along the main street. On day four, they had to move out, Gerry said, because the annual Newport Bermuda racing boats' arrival was scheduled, which would mean sleek racers sailing in with tired sweaty crews, hundreds of colored pennants and flags, horns blaring loud fanfares, exhibitionist captains bragging about their boats, and lots of champagne spraying and man bonding.

Gerry, with the help of Linda and Carl, moved the boat to St. Georges Island, docking in the bay with the stern toward a stone seawall in what, Gerry explained, was Bermuda tradition, making Beth learn to take quick steps on a narrow plank between boat and wall in order to get on land. From there, leaving Gerry behind to fiddle with things on the boat, she walked with Linda and Carl to a magnificently clean coral beach, incongruously named Tobacco Bay, strictly regulated so that cigarettes were not allowed on the beach, along with straws, small snacks, and other potential trash.

Later that day hurrying back on board, she certainly didn't mean to walk in on Carl. She just needed the head, and she wasn't thinking, but there he was with his erection in his hand looking at her like a guilty child. Carl had shown her consideration and concern, and now she had caught him in the most humiliating circumstance possible.

Worse, she was caught in her own turmoil. How often she had had to fake it with naked men, to make them feel like she wanted their sexual desire. It wasn't she who was in shock; she was simply confused. Confused because her initial reaction, her hard-learned instinct was an internal hate and an external mask. But she had always been drugged and, although still a teenager, maybe now a part of her brain was no longer missing as it was then.

Before it had always been a stranger, a thing, not a person; now it was Carl. Carl wasn't encroaching on anything or violating her life. She was intruding on his, and yet her only experience had been the opposite, the wrong way.

But here was Carl, the gentleman Carl, with his dick in his hand. And frozen. Frozen hard. This thought suddenly made her laugh. She laughed. She really laughed. A laugh she had forgotten, one that started nervously high on a shallow inner shelf but now exploded from deep inside her making her feel wonderfully happy.

And he laughed. And they laughed and laughed until they were both leaning on each other, their heads together in tears.

Carl wrapped his right arm around her and said in a whisper, "Let's go in your cabin."

For the first time he had his hands on her body, hands that had never felt so good, so perfect. Hands that had been so respectful now wanting to touch her skin in a way she felt was right.

"No," she said. "No."

Tears burst into her eyes. She would love to feel his body next to hers. She would love his hands all over her body. She had lost all need to use the toilet. She felt only the tingling electric greatness of a sexual yearning she had never felt, never allowed herself to feel. And she wanted to feel it. But she had to protect him from her dirty past; she couldn't tell him about her herpes. Not now. Not ever. He was leaving tomorrow. What a horrible gift to attach to him and to send home with him to his love. He would hate her forever.

She moved her hands down his body, keeping him from moving as he would understand where her hands were moving. She knew how to paralyze him.

It didn't really make sense, but Beth had to say something. "No, we don't have time. We don't know when they will come back."

She moved her right hand down to his penis, carefully wrapping her fingers around it, knowing exactly where to touch, where to move her encircling, encouraging fingers. And he was responding, not moving, but his penis was growing, returning to its previous hardness. As she knelt in front of him, he took her arm gently in his hand and made her stop.

He said, "Wait. Wait one moment. Please."

She let go, confused. Was he putting on a condom? Did he have diseases, too?

Turning quickly, he opened the Colgate toothpaste tube on the sink, put a dab of toothpaste on his finger, wet it under the faucet, and within seconds had rubbed it quickly and completely onto his penis until the whiteness of the toothpaste was gone. It was the first time she noticed that he was missing a fingertip on his left hand and a scar on his lower abdomen as if he had been subject to a hernia operation.

Then he said, "Sorry. So sorry to stop you. Now, it won't taste bad."

What was this? A hundred thoughts shot through Beth's head. How perfectly Swiss of him to clean himself; no American had ever, would ever do that. Or was he just strange? Did he always do that? How incredibly experienced was he at having women blowing him? He had his love in Zurich. Maybe a wife. Maybe hundreds of other women. He was older than she was. Was this too…? She couldn't think *too* what.

She began hating herself for her thoughts, her diseased self, as she so wanted to climb in next to him, feel his warmth, keep him warm, to make him care for her because she offered every part of herself. But that was not possible, or at least, for him not right. *What am I thinking? Too much? Too much what?* After the nightmares of prostitution that she had experienced, what could be too much?

She reached up and gently wrapped her fingers around his penis again, guiding it to her mouth, curious. This was weird. Was she supposed to thank him?

He shuddered and placed his hands on the sides of her head, caressing her. He was right. His penis was like a fantasy, almost illusory. She didn't know how many ugly, foul-tasting and smelling penises—rods, she called them—she had put in her mouth, stupidly disregarding any idea of disease and somehow miraculously avoiding all of them except herpes. It was not anything she ever wanted to count, recount, or remember. She had managed to cover the loathing, the vulgarity with her mind swimming in one drug or scrambled in another. Whatever she could find, whenever.

Now she was abstemious or maybe even clean. He was beautiful. This was someone she knew, and felt something extraordinary for. Did she dare say loved? This was a penis, not some brutal punishment for being who she had become. It was the first time she had ever wanted to hold a penis in her mouth to just feel his heartbeat. This time, the only time ever, she wanted this man, the one she was now embracing in her head, the one embracing her head, any way she could have him, to come in her, to share part of him in her.

Carefully, she removed his penis from her mouth and began to move her cupped hand over the sensitive edge of the head. Softly, but with certainty, knowing that the evenness, the repeated, even motion was what he needed. She knew every man was different, each one having a special pressure, speed, and rhythm, and she knew her repulsion each time previously had forced every one of them to take over and to use his own hand.

Carl would have his special need, too. But unlike all the others, she wanted to sense his need, feel for it. Do it for him. Just for him.

The next day he was gone; silently up and off to the airport before she awoke. She had wanted to know—maybe not ask, but at least sense—if he hated her, or maybe could he not hate her for saying no, not letting him have her whole body. But he was gone. Flown away to Switzerland. She had no address, and, in fact, no name. Carl who? Carl who! How could she have not asked his name? If he had died, she would, at least, know where he was, or was not. She would know his name.

She cried in her cabin, telling Gerry she was sick. She could ask Gerry or Linda for his name, but not now; she would have to ask when she was less in pain. Then under her pillow that night, she found his medallion, the medallion he had worn every day. He had left it for her and her tears refracted the moonlight into the colors of her emotions.

The very next day, Wednesday, day seven, she had thought to ask for Carl's name. The weather was perfectly Bermudian, sunny, cool sea breeze, the peeping sounds of terns, and calming ocean ripples against the sea wall. But something was different that morning. Gerry seemed distracted as he suggested that she take a walk to the store for milk and maybe some fruit. It had always been Linda who did the food shopping. He handed her much too much spend-money explaining she should take her time and could give him the leftover money when she got back. Linda stayed in her cabin. Beth thought they must have had an argument.

On returning from shopping to the seawall, she found the cruiser was gone. Unable to stop herself, she emitted a yelp like an abandoned dog. For an endless sinking moment, she was lost again.

2. JOE

THE PRIEST

JOE KNEW HOW THE FOOT TRAFFIC MOVED SO HE COULD ENTERTAIN HIMSELF AND manage to eat his late breakfast simultaneously.

Most visitors arriving in Provincetown, either by ferry from Boston or up the Cape Cod peninsula by car and parking their cars in the large asphalt lot by the docks, walk in on Ryder Street Extension. In the summer, Provincetown is jammed literally day and night with tourists, beachgoers, and summer boarders.

Today, being a warm Sunday in the summer of 1988, Provincetown was clogged with all ages, shapes, and sizes of beings, the majority of whom were day-trippers, incalculable numbers of children, and dogs. Circling these masses were swarms of sharp-eyed, fearless seagulls, outsmarting the dogs for the tiniest edible scraps dropped mostly by the children.

At Mojo's, in the first building from the parking lot on the corner along Ryder Extension, a man was sitting alone in Mojo's outside eating area facing the parking lot. Mojo's was quiet despite all the passing foot traffic along the street, because the tourists at this time in the middle of the afternoon just wanted to hurry farther in along Commercial Street with all the honkytonk shops to find souvenirs and ice cream, which Mojo's, a greasy spoon, didn't offer.

And he was sitting right beside Joe's normal place. The thin man was somewhere in his late twenties, perhaps. His dark-brown curly hair was long, down to his shoulders with his widow's peak emphasized by the curls dangling down his forehead. The most notable things, Joe noticed, were his dark shirt and pants, which were completely out of place in the summer heat, until Joe noticed his white collar. But because the guy was sitting still, elbows on the bench table, with his face in his hands, his face and collar were difficult to see, giving Joe the impression that the man was tired or had a headache or, maybe, that he was crying.

Joe, having discovered Mojo's back in his first days since arriving in Provincetown, had not bothered to look around for other places for his breakfast because he liked Mojo's homemade fries, even if he knew they were bad for him. But now in this dark shift of his life, the fries gave him one small pleasure and so he couldn't really care if they killed him.

Tired and having no desire to speak to anyone more than necessary, Joe hesitated to sit in his regular place for his afternoon breakfast, this place now being right next to the priest with no other outdoor choices, but it was just too hot to sit inside.

Joe showered this morning as he always had to after being on stage, and his hair was so short, he didn't need to comb it. He was just a bit afraid of how his clothes smelled, since he had thrown on an old white t-shirt and some well-used jeans, not really caring and certainly not expecting to sit so close to anyone.

Each afternoon for the weeks he had lived in Provincetown, Joe had eaten here while entertaining himself watching the families enter and exit their cars and pickups in the parking lot across the street and then funneling their way up Ryder Extension. He even questioned himself as to why he liked to watch the people so much, but he suspected it was probably a combination of loneliness and having no family anymore.

The priest had no food or drink in front of him, so Joe also wondered if his plate of eggs, toast, and fries he was holding was going to disturb the guy. *Hey, fuck it. This ain't the Ritz.* As Joe climbed over the bench to sit, the guy didn't twitch, continuing to sit with his face buried. Joe decided the guy was concentrating on praying hard for something and, all in all, it was better for Joe to ignore the guy as best he could, but it felt weird sitting so close to someone who didn't seem to know Joe even existed.

Joe forked the over-easy eggs onto one of the two pieces of dry toast, saving the second piece and the fries to last. After finishing off this first part of his food, he decided to get a refill on his coffee. Joe thought this might be a test of the priest's hunger, what with a tempting pile of the world's best french fries sitting unguarded next to him. Like the apple in Eden?

But, as Joe expected, he saw no movement in the man during the time Joe was up and moving in and out of the café. Finally, as Joe's re-entry rocked the bench a bit upon settling back in place, the priest uncovered his face to look out over the parking lot with wet eyes. A quick glance told Joe subconsciously that the young man smiled often because his narrow squinting eyes already had a smile crease.

Without turning to look at the man, Joe said, "Sorry to bother your prayers, Father."

The man didn't respond immediately. But as he continued to stare forward, he finally said in a soft voice, "I wasn't praying." Another pause. "There is no God."

Joe became wary, immediately glad he was in a public place. He stuffed four fries in his mouth in rapid succession to avoid the need to speak. In Provincetown, the town of *fruits* and *nuts*, you never knew what to expect. This guy might just have been an oddball in costume and maybe dangerous or drunk or hiding some unpleasantry. But, of course, he could just have been terribly depressed.

Then the priest said, "Sorry. That was a dumb thing to say." He paused again. Then pointing a little to the left on the street, he said, "See that blood spot on the asphalt?"

Joe could see some spots, which could have been spilled cola or water or just shadows. In fact, the more he looked, the more spots he saw on the asphalt; Joe wondered which one? Was this where God died?

"That was where my dog was killed this morning."

Dog. God. He was close. Joe had almost laughed thinking of the cartoon he had seen of a man standing at the Pearly Gates who was just discovering that man had spelled God backwards. To keep a straight face, Joe looked harder at the street and then at the man and said, "Sorry about that. What happened?"

It seemed the priest had to make himself say it. "Run over by a car. Not the driver's fault. Stupid dog saw me and ran in front of the car."

"Oh, that is too bad. I wondered. I was thinking you must be really sad about something."

"Yeah, he was my friend and companion, I guess like all dogs are…I mean, as pets. He was just a puppy."

Joe stuffed more fries in his mouth.

After waiting for an enormously fat, sweaty, and loud-talking couple to waddle their way past on the sidewalk, the priest said, "But my sadness is more about the totality of things. Ironically, I had just concluded that there is no God and this morning, I had decided finally to give up the priesthood which is sad in itself. Then it's as if God decides to punish me by killing my dog." A pause. "Except I know that isn't true."

Joe wanted him to finish his thought. Go on. It isn't true because…? Even if Joe was an atheist, he expected this man to have a different reason, and the guy spoke just like a preacher.

To prod the priest on a bit, Joe said, "Maybe some sort of omen?"

The priest smiled a bit and said, "You believe in omens?"

Taken aback, Joe said, "Well, no. Not me, but…"

"But you asked for some reason."

Instinctively, Joe liked the man, the man's demeanor, something about him. "You got me." Joe said, "Well, truthfully, I was wondering what you thought." Pointing to his plate, Joe said, "You want a fry?"

After a few seconds, looking crestfallen, the priest, waving off the fries, said, "What I think is that I am a joke and a fake."

Joe noticed his own reaction. He was pretty sure a cartoonist might illustrate his surprise with a huge question mark above Joe's head. But he didn't try to respond. What could he possibly say? It was time to finish off the food on his plate.

"It's not because my dog was killed that I say it. Through long consideration, I have, over time, come to understand man's creation of religions with all the need for stories to protect against the absurd. I realize that religions, poets, and writers bridge the gap between reality and that absurdity and that is good in every way possible. But I can no longer pretend that I am one of those bridges, at least, the religious one. And now I'm faking it and I'm scared because I don't know what to do next." Wistfully, he said, "Maybe I can be the poet."

This guy was going to be a gabber. Joe felt his brain go from sleepy grey to a lighter, more aware grey; there was something interesting happening here. Not knowing what else to say, Joe said, "Yeah, why not? I read somewhere just what you said. That the gap between our belief and what is real is only expressed by poets and writers."

"It's hard to eat poetry."

After swallowing his last bite, Joe said, "I'm not a poet and I am not religious, but I would think the church would help you somehow, if you asked."

The priest smiled and said, "Or they might throw me out the door, and I could become a stripper."

Joe's mouth opened, gaping. He could only stare at the man in shocked silence.

Smiling still, the priest said, "I recognized you from the strip club. I think your name is Joe." Holding out his hand, the man said with a smile, "I'm James. James Bond. No! Sorry! Wrong James. I'm James

Fredrick. It might have been Fredrickson at one time, but somebody cut it short way back in the jungles of history."

Joe, still in astonishment and staring at the man's face, shook hands loosely without a word.

James said, "Don't act so shocked. You're famous."

The man's face had a likeable warm radiance even if he seemed to look out of the top of his squinting blue eyes, eyes which most people might use to scold a child. Joe's major doubt about the guy was that he seemed to speak in stilted sentences, in a tone like he was quoting something or someone.

Incredulous, Joe said, "Infamous, I think is the word. You have been at the place I work?" Then he didn't know what to say.

"I know. Sounds odd. What's a priest doing at a strip club? And my answer is, of course, theoretically, why not? If I were recruiting for the church, what better place to hunt for lonely souls?"

Joe sipped on his coffee, and while staring out toward the parking lot, he began breaking up the second piece of toast and tossing it out on the pavement for the gulls, all the while trying to arrange in his tired mind what this man was saying into something coherent, and believable.

With no response from Joe, James continued. "But that's not the reason I've gone to the strip club. As I said, I don't give a shit about the church any more. I've seen the light, so to speak. I am a curious person trying to figure out everything.

"I probably should have never tried to become a priest. Let me tell you, I was a bad kid," he said. "Luckily, I didn't kill anybody, but I might have tried; I don't even know. Unconscious or drugged. That tells you everything. I was born and grew up in Detroit because my father had a big dump truck, hiring out his dumpy service to the construction business.

"I decided at an early age to try to be a writer, and I wrote and never got my books published since, of course, nobody wanted to read my trash…terrible stories. I was such a poor student in high school that, well, I learned to pick the lock on the principal's office, so that I could sneak in and erase bad stuff on my reports."

Joe began to sweat from both liking the guy and hating him; he never stopped talking.

The priest continued and continued, talking about his hair, an old art teacher, starting a gay club in Detroit, selling drugs on the street, and how sad his life had been working for his father.

He took a breath after, "But I kept writing stuff." Seeing Joe staring out toward the ocean, James asked, "Am I boring you?"

"No, no! By no means," Joe said, somewhat meaning it. The guy's talking let Joe be silent, to think, and to watch the pedestrians. "Please, go on."

Joe liked that the guy was so open, taking it as a compliment, but was beginning to worry this might get to be so personal that it was just too much information, and that Joe couldn't escape if the guy wouldn't shut up. But still there was something about this guy.

On a roll, it seemed, James continued. Without pause, he told about how, together with George, his old love in Detroit, he became a priest, or rather thought he became one. How he had been influenced by his mother and bamboozled by the teacher priest.

"But that's when George and I blew up and we went our separate ways. And now, although I know lots of people, I am alone."

The guy finally took a pause. Still staring toward the parking lot, Joe said, almost afraid to ask for fear of another sermon, "So what are you doing here, I mean, in P-town?"

"I gravitated here after I began to get bad vibes from the church about my being openly gay. You were supposed to hide it, even though I suspect the majority of priests are gay. For a while, that was okay, I thought. I met people. But then my mind began working on the whole doohickey. Now, once again, never completing anything, I'm stopping what I started. I won't bore you with the rest.

"Besides, Joe, that's enough about me. What's your story? I know damn well you are not looking to continue being a professional stripper."

"Why not?"

"Because…. No, you tell me why not."

"Why not? Why not. I haven't thought about it. My mother died about six months ago. At my mother's request, I buried her far from my guinea father, who had died a year before that. I sold the house and came here for purgatory, I guess, until I figure things out."

"You are definitely a survivor," James said. "You inspire me."

Annoyed, Joe wondered what this priest was trying to put over on him. He wanted to say it was bullshit—that James was bullshitting him. Joe was certainly no model to be emulated, and his face must have shown it.

Without any response from Joe, James said, "No, seriously. You are a survivor; no one has given you any golden key to the future." He paused to look at his watch. "Oops! I hate to break this off, but I have to go bury a dog."

Even though Joe had some skeptical alarms ringing, he and James decided to meet the next afternoon, this time on the beach walking and talking, during which Joe decided to trust the guy. They talked about most everything, especially dreams. Eventually, Joe felt he could risk telling his newfound friend about young Beth, about Joe's loneliness and need for love, and about his crimes, because James was also an admitted degenerate. And, sure enough, James didn't condemn Joe's actions or disparage him, and Joe's enchantment with James grew.

They agreed that they were both broken souls who had found themselves scraping a bottom—each in their own barrel—but that they had helped each other become aware. Such a discovering made Joe, at least, begin to think it was time to make a change. It was no sudden light, but began as a dim awareness in the back of his head that his life must change, yet, with no skill or talent, he could see no future narrative in any way, shape, or form that would allow that small cognizance to brighten. And he didn't want to just continue as a thief.

After more conversations on the beach in the following days, Joe hated to see the guy leave, but could reluctantly give nothing but encouragement as James decided to leave to go to the University of Michigan, which had previously offered him financial support, to study science and philosophy, his idea to become a teaching professor.

James, once again, thanked Joe for being a real friend, maybe his first. Joe and James obviously liked each other in more ways than just friendship, but they never had time to show that physical love before James left. In the nearest days after James left, Joe got more depressed and lonely as his deep human instinct for social contact had been awakened. He had been left behind. Alone. As this state of loneliness, confusion, and yearning continued over days and weeks, Joe met with trouble or, he might even have admitted, created misfortune for himself.

Later and luckily, not sure if James was quoting someone or not, Joe got what seemed a magical note from James:

We dream of the better times. If we did not believe this, life would be unbearable. The moment in the future is what keeps us going. That moment is at an unknown time.

And, as if James had godly powers, it was on just that day of receiving this message that Professor Martin Case tripped not-so-accidently over Joe on the beach.

3. BETH

LOST IN BERMUDA

BETH'S IMMEDIATE THOUGHT WAS THAT SOMEONE HAD DISAPPROVED OF HER LIAISON with Carl. Maybe Carl himself had been so upset and hated her so much that he told them to get rid of her.

Then a young white girl, much too formally outfitted in a lacy white dress and who had obviously been sitting on the seawall waiting for Beth to arrive, approached Beth holding Beth's belongings in the yellow canvas bag.

"You are Beth?" she asked in what seemed to Beth a very deep voice for a young frail thing.

Beth couldn't determine the girl's age. Ten, twelve, fourteen?

"My mother asked me to wait for you. You are supposed to live with us." Holding up the yellow bag, she said, "This is your bag." Then she laughed a short staccato laugh like a skidding car tire. The girl spoke as if the lines were memorized, almost put on, and something about the laugh was tense. "Please follow me."

Beth said, "No wait." She searched every niche, pocket, and corner of the bag and her clothing, deeply and secretly in distress, hunting for the money, hoping above hope that it was in there somewhere. But it was not. Why would it be? She hid it exactly for that reason, so no one would find it. And now a thousand dollars was on the vanished boat, to be found some day by who knows?

"Listen," she said to the girl. "Where did the boat go? When did it leave?"

The girl said, "He told me not to tell."

Beth was completely baffled as she kept asking, but couldn't get any meaningful information from the girl as she led Beth along the wall a few hundred feet farther, toward a woman dressed in a ruffled turquoise dress who was sitting in a wooden lawn chair. The woman seemed not to notice their approach and, startled, dropped her book on the ground as she fought her way out of the chair. The young girl introduced the woman as *my mother.*

"Hello, Beth. My name is Georgia. My daughter here is Cynthia." She spoke with a British tone.

Cynthia discharged a pair of skid laughs.

"My husband, Jason, and I would like to invite you to stay with us if you care to help us around the house, maybe do some grocery shopping for us. We could use the help for as long as you care to stay."

She paused, maybe waiting for Beth's reaction. Beth couldn't make herself speak. The woman said, "So? What do you think?"

This was all so weird; Beth still wasn't sure what to say. She wasn't sure if she should ask about the boat, to tell about the money. She couldn't tell if this was real or maybe even dangerous. First she was abandoned on an island, and now she was getting picked up by strangers.

The woman seemed harmless enough, if strange. She was as tall as Beth, dark tanned, and somewhere in her late fifties, it seemed, but the wrinkles from the sun were perhaps misleading. Her strained voice and general nervous uncertainty were off-putting, but then their little daughter with a cherub's face was smiling and watching all this.

Before Beth could say anything, the mother said, "Cynthia, help Beth with her grocery bag. I'm sorry. I didn't explain that your friends Linda and Gerry arranged this stay before you left the United States. If they hadn't, you could not have stayed in Bermuda."

So they had meant to abandon her here all along, take her to another country and dump her. Why didn't anyone care to ask her, or at least tell her what they were planning? Once again Beth was left with no choice. Not that the offer wasn't okay. What other choice was there anyway? Swim home? Home? What home? This was a beautiful place. But she swore to herself that she would never again let herself be herded and dumped. She was suddenly embarrassed for not answering.

"Oh, thank you," she said. "That is so nice of you. I don't know what to say."

"Good," said the woman. She picked up her book and handed it to her daughter to carry. "Then that's settled. Let me just fold up this stupid chair."

She seemed not to understand how the chair folded. Even Beth could see how it worked but she was afraid to say anything. Her only thought was, "No wonder she wants some help around the house."

Georgia drove a huge hearse, a monstrosity of embarrassing blackness, to a nearby place, so close that they could have walked, called Tucker's Town. Up a side street among luxurious houses and into a long cement driveway, they parked behind a large, two-story, looming white house. In Beth's mind, the house, like the car, was like an oversized cartoon drawing that she felt had been throbbing and now was frozen in place in one expansive throb. It struck Beth that maybe everything needed to be oversized to be fortification against Georgia's klutziness.

The yard had a flourishing variation of flowering green shrubbery surrounding a lawn perfectly mowed and trimmed by, she learned later, a team of yard help.

Georgia said, "Leave the groceries. I want to show you the front. Cynthia, tell Hanna to get the stuff out of the car."

They walked around the front to enter. She saw a straight gravel path from the street to the door on which was a sign that said "Hutchins." They had money from somewhere. Beth had a bad feeling, the feeling of make-believe, complete with deception and fraudulence.

Cynthia, carrying the canvas bag, led Beth with Georgia behind her to a room where it was obvious Beth was to stay.

With a dispirited look on her face, Georgia said, "This used to be a nursery."

And that was it. No explaining whether that meant it had been Cynthia's or some dead or long-gone child's. There would be a lot she was never told and was too afraid to ask. But she consoled herself with the thought that all of this was temporary, so she didn't need to know; it wasn't her business to know.

Georgia said, "Leave your stuff. Let's go meet my husband."

The luxurious interior had so many rooms and enjoining hallways, Beth just hoped she could find her way back to the room. As they passed through the house, Beth tried to remember the doors, turns, portraits and pictures, dark hall tables with embroidered runners, and throw rugs on the dark hardwood floor like dropped bread crumbs that would help her find her way back. Finally, entering a small office with built-in bookcases filled with knicknacks more than books, they found an elderly gentleman that could have been Georgia's father.

"Jason, this is Beth. She will be staying with us for a while."

"Hello, Beth. Welcome to Hutchins," the man said.

From his cold but gentlemanly demeanor, the way he spoke, his groomed thick grey hair, and the way he held himself, Beth judged this man to be the source of the money. A banker maybe? A retired banker, probably. She didn't discover then what he did, but she did get surprised by his flatulence. It was constant and so common she soon discovered that no one in the household seemed to notice it; it was just taken as an ever-recurring noise like an irreparable squeaky floor.

* * *

"Mother asked me to teach you how to ride the scooter."

"Oh, you scared me!" Beth, in her shorts and sneakers that Linda had bought her, had been taking a break sitting in the cabana by the pool behind the house and hadn't heard Cynthia coming up on her. Cynthia's deep monotone made Beth a bit nervous anyway, being so incongruent with the little girl image.

Cynthia simply repeated, "Mother says you need to learn to ride the scooter if you're going to do shopping," followed by the staccato skid laugh. Handing Beth a small, shiny-black box Cynthia held in her hands like an offering, she said, "And she said to give you this phone." Another monosyllabic skid.

Beth stared at the thing that looked like some sort of walkie-talkie, antenna and all, with *Motorola Micro T.A.C.* printed on it. "But what is this thing?"

Cynthia said, after another laugh, "It really is a phone. My brother brought it back from the United States. Said it was the first one and cost three thousand dollars." Another skid sound.

"And your mother wants me to use this chunky thing?"

Cynthia said quickly, "Well, why not? She doesn't know how."

Finally picking it out of Cynthia's hands with her thumb and forefinger, Beth said, "Thank you, Cynthia. Now I won't be so lost."

Beth suspected that this was Cynthia's idea, but Beth was again uncertain what she should do or what to believe. She could certainly have empathy with Cynthia's mother. The thing looked complicated. It was best just to put it away somewhere so she didn't damage or lose it. She couldn't imagine why she would ever use it.

Thinking she should try to get to know Cynthia better, Beth asked, "So what are you studying? What do you want to be when you grow up?"

Without a second's hesitation, Cynthia answered, "I want to start a rock band called A Band on House. Our first title and performance will be called *Abandon House* by A Band on House. I will be the lead singer."

The answer was so quick and the tone so solemn that Beth didn't know how seriously to take it. Was she trying to be funny? She seemed dead serious. How could someone with such a monotone voice manage to sing?

It didn't seem right to ask how old she was, so Beth simply said, "That's nice. Let's go look at that scooter."

Beth had never tried to ride a motor scooter or a motor anything before, just a bike. But she had seen that this was the way many Bermudians traveled, so if they could, so could she. After a few instructions from Cynthia and some beginner's mistakes, Beth was able to use it with a bit of pride, even if she burned her bare leg once on the exhaust bringing tears to her eyes.

She learned her way around Hamilton by trial and error as Georgia's guidance from the kitchen was doubtful, certainly about what was left, right, or how many blocks' distance. Georgia would give her a shopping list and, upon giving her some money, told her each and every time, like some unprecedented good news, that whatever she could save was hers to keep. Beth never felt this woman could ever, in a billion years, be any help in finding the lost money on the boat.

The areas where she had walked earlier were not where the locals shopped. She learned to shop on the back streets of Hamilton away from the Front Street jacked-up pricing on plastic souvenirs and fancy jewelry and away from the cruise ship landing areas. But fruit, vegetables, and food in general on the island nation was expensive and the family gave her so little shopping money that, even on the back streets, the expensive island economy didn't allow her to save enough to fly back to New England.

Today the island light had a feel of artistic joy with the brightly colored flowers supporting the mood—flowers and greenery she, growing up, had never seen. She had heard an artist once say how today felt when he said the colors are so real you can feel them.

On the way to the grocery, she stopped the scooter to have a closer look at a garden, one she had passed several times before where new flowers just seemed to pop up every day.

"That's called a Golden Chalice," someone said from behind the hedge.

Startled, Beth said, "I'm sorry. I just had to look at it closer."

A black woman, dressed in a bright blue, sweeping gown, stepped closer and smiled. "Good afternoon. Nothing to apologize for, my dear. Flowers were made to be admired."

"It is so beautiful."

"It is quite common here on the island. Where are you from, my dear?"

"Well, I'm living here now, but was originally from Massachusetts."

"And what brought you here?"

Beth studied the woman, judging her to be one of the most beautiful people she had ever seen. Her hair, perfect skin, bright eyes filled with kindly laughter made her some striking romantic middle-aged movie star. She also seemed genuinely interested in Beth with an amicable warmth that gave Beth a good feeling about her. It was not the first time she had felt this way meeting people here, or, at least, meeting the blacks. The British descendants, on the other hand, seemed so closed, so reticent, and often looked at her more as a victim, while the blacks she had met were affectionate and open.

"I guess I am here by mistake," Beth said. "I was sort of brought here."

"You are a slave?"

"No, no, I…" Beth answered quickly with an embarrassed nip of laughter. Then she didn't know what to say. Maybe that is exactly what she was. "I'm staying at the Hutchins." She hoped that meant something to the woman.

The woman frowned and said, "Oh, yes. I see. Down the country. What is your name, my dear?"

"Beth. Beth Sturgess."

"Well, Beth, my name is Florenz. You can call me Florie. I see you have the most common bike burn festering on your leg. You want to come in and have a cup of tea? I will find something for your leg."

"I have time. Yes. Thank you." Beth felt an abashed flush, feeling she had accepted much too fast. The woman said nothing, and just turned expecting Beth to follow. This woman's home was obviously of another status than where Beth lived. The yard was full of flowers and flowering bushes, but neither the shrubs nor the grass was as perfectly trimmed. The house was neat, tiny, and sparsely furnished with bamboo and plastic furniture.

Beth sat down at the small Formica table in the cramped kitchen, smelling of cinnamon and herbs, while Florie put water in a tea kettle from a pump by the sink.

"So," said Florie, "what do you do over at the Hutchins?"

"I do their shopping and help with the housework. They have a lady who comes over daily to cook and clean. I do a bit of stuff with her." Beth paused a moment to see if Florie had a comment. "It seems like the father doesn't lift a finger and the mother in the family, Georgia, is useless, more or less. She seems lost most of the time."

Still getting no comment, she continued, "They have a young girl, Cynthia, who doesn't go to school, but a woman, a tutor or something, comes over daily and teaches her."

Finally, Florie said, "A daughter, huh? Is that what she is now?"

Now Beth felt wings flapping in her head like when a magician uncovers a bird. "Yes, I mean, what do you mean?"

Florie looked Beth in the eye with a somewhat surprised expression. "You never noticed?"

"I'm sorry but noticed what?"

"Well, sometimes she's a girl and sometimes he's a boy."

"Who?"

"Our little friend Cynthia. That's who we are talking about, right?"

Beth was still unable to get the point. "You mean they have two children? I've never seen but one."

Florie laughed a loud, deep black laugh. "You are innocent, my dear."

"No. No, I am not. Absolutely not. But…"

"Okay, my dear, I guess you have not seen her change. Sometimes *Cynthia*, if that's her name now, is not Cynthia; she may sometimes be Tom or Frederick. I don't know when or how he decides. Maybe the mother decides, I don't know."

Beth was quiet as she let her mind absorb the realization.

"It's okay, dear. You didn't know. They are, shall I say, an odd family. You've never had any trouble with them, have you?"

"Trouble? What kind of trouble?"

"Well, nothing. Nothing at all. If there is no trouble, there is no trouble. But I would like to know if they are paying you anything. That is, if you don't mind telling me."

"They give me money to go grocery shopping for them. Whatever I can save, I can keep."

"And? Are you able to save anything?"

"Only pennies. They give me two hundred dollars for the week to buy food. I usually spend about one hundred ninety-five or six, and then I have to tip the poor baggers."

"Ah, so you are a slave." Florie smiled. "This kind of thing went out with the coal mine company store."

Beth looked down at her hands, opening and closing them. Florie was right, but, so?

"You do your shopping back o'town?"

"Excuse me, where?"

"In the back streets?"

"Oh, yeah, as much as I can. I even buy veggies along the road at the stalls and, if I can, I stock up on Saturday morning at the farmers' market. But they make me get British stuff at the Supermart, like smoked salmon, scones, and British tea."

"Okay, honey. I can help you do a little better, but you aren't going to get rich even with my help. Let me find something for that leg."

From that day on, Beth spent more and more time with Florie. As the weeks passed, Beth learned that the official cultural traditions performed on the island were British, like the Queen's Birthday holiday with a meretricious parade and loud twenty-one-gun salute on Hamilton's Front Street.

She liked better the black Bermudians, both because they were more open and friendly and because they were beautiful, kind, helpful, and laid-back. She smirked at the toothy Brits who wore ridiculous Bermuda shorts with the knee-high socks, wide-brimmed canvas hats and who thought they were stylish.

One day Beth mentioned to Florie the odd thing that was repeatedly happening.

"At night, almost every night, I hear quiet footsteps stop outside my bedroom door. At first, I thought it could be Georgia checking up on me until I heard the familiar…uh…the sound."

"The sound?"

"Well, yeah, Mr. Hutchins has a problem with gas."

"Oh, he farts," Florie said smiling wryly.

"Yes, all the time. I am not even sure he knows he is doing it." She paused. "The first night I asked who it was, but nobody answered and I sensed the person left. Of course, I listened harder next time and heard his noise. And each night it has been the same. Jason standing outside my door. Nothing more. But I have started to become afraid; it is so weird."

The day after Beth had told Florie, they agreed to meet on Hamilton's back streets at four o'clock in front of a place called Cora. The weather was even hot for Bermuda, which usually had the sea breeze, but not today.

Florie said, "We're going to drop in here at the club. I have some friends for you to meet."

"The club?"

"Well, it isn't the Mid Ocean. It's our club."

They entered what to Beth seemed to be from the outside just a regular bar named Cora. But inside it was soon evident that she was the only white woman in a dark place tightly packed with black women talking and drinking in a room not much bigger than her bedroom. The heat was worse inside with all the bodies and, with no circulating air, the smell of sweaty bodies was unbearable. Beth knew that these women were probably more used to the heat, so she dared not think to comment.

As they worked their way through the people, women turned and greeted her.

"Hey bye."

"A longtail. Where you to?"

Beth just kept saying, "Hello," while Florie repeatedly said, "She's from away. She's my ace girl." It was all friendly and polite, if confusing to Beth.

In the corner of the room, sitting at a small round table were two women who seemed to be expecting Beth and Florie to sit with them.

To the women, Florie said, "This is Beth."

One of the women, lissome and catlike, stood up, smiling, to greet Beth. "Hello, Beth. I'm Ruth and this elderly lady here is Sister Sue." Sister Sue, wrinkled and silently staring straight ahead at nothing, seemed as ancient as a rocky beach and almost as large.

"Let's get you something to drink. You like rum?"

"Well, I don't know...I..."

"Don't worry about it. I'll have Fairy over here fix you a nice one. It's on me."

As Ruth moved toward the bar, the other women seemed to take it as a signal to leave and the room quickly became quiet as the women exited the bar in rapid succession.

Once they had arranged their chairs and Beth had her drink, Ruth said, "Don't worry about the drink you won't get hot."

"Ruth means you won't get drunk," Florie explained.

"Yeah, that's what I mean, but you could get half hot." Ruth let out a quick laughing snort.

Beth said, "Did all these people leave because I came in? Maybe I'm not supposed to be here."

The three others began laughing.

Florie said, "No, dear. These two ladies are the head of the club and I asked for a private meeting with them so we could talk a bit."

"That was nice," Beth said. "But I don't want to be any trouble."

Florie nodded toward Ruth who was looking back at Florie.

Ruth said, "Well, trouble is what we are here to discuss with you."

Beth was confused. "Trouble? Am I in trouble? Did I do something wrong?"

"Take it easy," said Ruth. "We are here to take care of you. You are Florenz's friend and she says you need a little, shall we say, information."

Suddenly, the older lady, Sister Sue, spoke for the first time. She yelled, in fact, so Beth figured she must be hard of hearing. "Is this the girl what live down the country at Tucker's?"

"Yes, Sister Sue, this be her," said Ruth in a louder voice.

"The Hutchins house?"

"Yes, Sister Sue."

"It's a hot one today, a Sally Bassett," Sister Sue said.

Ruth smiled, nodded, and said to Beth, "When Sister Sue says it's a Sally Bassett, it…is…hot! I tell you! Woo!"

Beth could smell Sister Sue's old breath. She smiled and said, "Yes, Sister Sue, it is hot in here."

Looking directly at Beth as best she could with her yellow cataract eyes, Sister Sue said, "Well, child, where there is so much money there must be something out of kilter. I think that the white man there should be in a terrible fix. That man there says that women need help into automobiles, and a strong arm over mud puddles, and to have the best place to sit. He talk like a gentleman. And, oh yes, he may help any woman into automobiles, and over mud puddles, and give them any best place. To make them very sorry after.

"I heard that man there, he even say women have as much rights as men!

"When he eats with the devil, does he speak like he is the friend of Jesus? Where did his Jesus come from? This man and his father and his grandfather had nothing to do with Jesus Christ. Jesus ain't no friend o' that man.

"But what's all this here talking about? Things that oughtn't be. You get out of that house, girl. Obliged to you for hearing me, child, and now I ain't got no more to say."

They were all silent. Beth had no idea what Sister Sue had said or meant. Get out of the house?

Looking at Beth's puzzled expression, Ruth said, "Well, Sister Sue here is from the old Progressive Group time. She's seen lots of bad stuff and she knows pretty much all the history of slavery and all the death that has been. And she knows about your Mr. Jason Hutchins and his father and his father's father.

"What she knows, Beth. That's your name, right? I forget names so often." Beth nodded. "What she knows is that all the money he has is from slave trade starting back at the beginning three hundred years ago and up to now. He's not the man you think."

Beth said, "But slavery's over, right?"

Grimacing, Ruth said, "Officially. Back in the sixties, Sister Sue's secret Progressive Group along with Reverend Tweed broke up the segregation at the theaters and schools and public places. But the power is still with the money, and your man's got plenty of both. All he's missing is a conscience."

"Okay, but…"

Ruth broke her off. "Listen, child. That ain't what we brought you here to say. Sister Sue is right. You gotta get out of that house. Mr. Jason is a dangerous man. He's probably raped more women than we could count if we was Einstein. He rapes mostly black women when he can, but he ain't choosy."

Beth sat still while, beginning with the very top of her head, the oppressive heat of the room dissipated and ice crept down over her body. "I don't get why...I mean, you know...if it's true, so why doesn't he get arrested?"

"Beth," said Florie. "Ruth just told you. He has all the power and influence anyone could want. No one can touch him."

Ruth said, "And how was it you think you got to stay here...I mean, here in Bermuda...without any permission or papers?"

Beth could barely speak. She whispered, "I don't know. They arranged it."

"Who they?" said Ruth.

"The people with the boat. How I got here."

"And do you know who that was?"

"Gerry. And Linda. Friends."

"Friends?" said Ruth.

"Friends of a friend. I think."

"Sister Sue knows who Gerry is." Ruth paused as if she were uncertain how to say something, her mouth opening and closing. "Gerry is Mr. Slave Owner's son, Gerry Hutchins."

Beth's mind emptied of all rational thought as the dread flooded in. The words tonged Beth's mind as she realized she was the sacrificial lamb delivered on a plate. *Dear Dad, here is your next delicacy.* He had even moved the boat closer to the house. Gripped with dread and panic, she realized she still had to return to that house.

Suddenly, after three months on the island with the approaching threat of hurricane season, she had a much greater threat, immediate and tangible and yet imponderable and impalpable. She had to leave any way she could, and as secretly as she could, for fear that her leaving would trigger an attack from the serial rapist. She was in danger; the women had made it clear that the most terrifying, ever-present incubus was waiting to descend any moment.

At least, compared to them, she had a choice.

"Hello, Mother. It's me."

"Beth. Is that you?"

"Yes, Mother."

"Where are you?"

"I'm in Bermuda."

"Bermuda! What are you doing in Bermuda? How did you get there?"

"An international phone call is too short to explain now, Mother. I need your immediate help." There was silence on the other end which Beth had expected. "I just need a ticket to get to Boston. Delta Airlines has one for two-sixty-two one way. Can you buy that for me so I can get home?"

"Home. Where's home after all this time?"

"Mother, will you or will you not?"

Florie said she would check the Western Union desk as often as she could, as Beth couldn't be oddly running out of the house over and over during the day, but she improvised a trip to get back her passport.

For the next days and nights waiting for her mother's money transfer, the most nebulous noise in the house during the day frightened Beth and, during the night, woke her. She was sure that her pending escape would be discovered by some indicative mistake she might make and then the raving monster would come crashing through her bedroom door.

Beth had met Jason Hutchins only a few times during her weeks in the house, once or twice in the kitchen and a few times in the yard. It always involved a short greeting and nothing more. Now during these days, she never saw him and had not heard him standing outside her door since she decided to escape, making her intensely nervous about his present location and his intentions.

As the nights and the days ran together, it seemed the evil was present in the room, hovering, ready to swoop down, and the omniscient evil would, of course, know the money was coming and lunge just before the money arrived, because he knew. He could see that she had made a long-distance call.

She was sure that Nor, her mother, was being slow on purpose. Or she had run into problems getting the money from her father, Rob, or had been true to herself as "Ig-Nor" and even forgotten. Beth tried to show calm, especially toward Cynthia, who Beth in her paranoia was sure was spying on her.

Finally, after three days and nights, at ten in the morning on the fourth day, Florie signaled that the money had arrived and to pick it up, and she said she would take the bus to the airport to meet Beth at the Delta Airline ticket desk and would try to reserve the ticket before Beth came with the money. As if she were shopping, Beth took the scooter, not caring where she might have to leave it.

The Delta ticket agent said their flight 316 was fully booked, but that Beth was first on the standby list.

At the gate where she couldn't go farther, Florie smiled and said, "You'll be fine now. Come to visit me."

Beth's body was shaking, with tears dripping off her chin. "What if I don't get on board?"

"Then you come to stay with me 'til tomorrow."

"Oh, Florie, I'm so scared. I don't want to go anywhere except away from here. I'll sleep on a bench here and be first in line tomorrow."

Florie put her arms around Beth and said, "You know you have a home here. Don't forget me."

"Forget you! Forget you! How would I ever?" She began crying so hard she couldn't speak.

"Stop it, honey. You gotta go." She pushed Beth toward the gate.

As Beth went through the gate, her brain was swimming around the thought of sleeping unprotected on a bench at the airport, exposed. They would start looking for the motor bike and discover where she was. But no way was she going back into that house or even Florie's house or out on the street.

For a moment she wished she had that walkie-talkie phone thing, but it was hidden in her room at the house. She had figured the thing out; she had used it to call her mother. But then, who would she call here? Florie had no phone. The police? A picture ran through her head of trying to dial the phone while she was being attacked. She saw herself throwing something like a brick in Jason Hutchins's face.

Where was it safe from an omnipresent monster? Of course, she might not be safer at the airport, but maybe guards protected the airport. She hoped.

Just then the announcement came: "The boarding of Delta flight 316 is delayed. Technical problems we expect to have corrected soon."

Beth had been unable to find a seat in the area where now all the passengers were impatiently waiting to board. She was standing against the wall when she saw Jason Hutchins across the waiting area. He was just standing there, staring at her. Her legs wanted to fail her, but the wall's friction and a small edge protruding from the wall kept her from dropping to the floor.

Behind and around him were masses of black slaves, some crawling, some bent in pain under his feet. The delusion stopped as quickly as it began; the slaves were just other passengers, part of the masses of people waiting everywhere.

But Jason Hutchins was not a delusion; he was standing there. He had seen her, and was glowering at her. Was he the one delaying the plane? Stopping it from taking off so that he could keep her from escaping? He had all the power and the money in Bermuda they said. Was he arranging for the airline to take her off the waiting list?

The flight began boarding.

"Parents with small children may now proceed to boarding."

Beth envisioned grabbing a small child and dragging it, scream-ing and crying, on board as hers. Why do they get to go first? They take way too much time. The plane is already late. She had no watch and surprisingly she could not find a clock in the waiting area, but then why did she need to know?

"Boarding First Class and Diamond Club Members."

Why was he standing there, sometimes looking at her, sometimes not? Now she noticed that he was not in the boarding area; he was outside behind some previously undetected glass wall. He wasn't looking at her anymore, was he? He was waiting for something. Waiting to see if she got on board? Waiting to see if he had killed her ticket so he could politely offer her a nightmare ride home?

"Boarding rows twenty-four through forty."

Oh, please let me on board. She felt a constant ache from the mid-dle of her grinding stomach. *Don't let him throw me off.*

How could a plane take so long to load passengers? She had flown only that once to Mexico in her life and, at that time, was not sober, so she didn't remember just how it all worked. It didn't seem that it took forever that time, like now. Sure, they all could afford to be slow; they had all the time in the world. They had their tickets. They were not being stalked by a rapist.

"All remaining passengers with seat reservations may now board."

As dumb as the thought could be, she considered injuring some straggling passenger to be sure a seat was left empty.

Then she saw that Jason had turned away, that he had been waiting for his personal driver, or at least, the person she had seen pick him up at home one day. Like creeping mud, she slowly real-ized Jason had been away and not in the house during the time she was waiting for her mother's money. That's why he was here at the airport.

But he had seen her and had been glaring at her like some wild animal. Since he had seen her here now, was he hurrying to prevent her from leaving?

Then it dawned on her from the way other people were preening themselves that the lighting had made the glass one-way. He had been looking at his own reflection. He had not seen her and was not cancelling her ticket or blocking the flight.

"Beth Sturgess, please come to the ticket counter."

Deep in a reverie of relief, she almost didn't hear it. Then at the realization that they were broadcasting her name everywhere, she panicked. He knew. They were calling her up to the counter to cancel her ticket, to tell her she had to leave the airport, that she could not go, that she could not board the plane to Boston.

They were looking at her there, staring solemnly, the lone waiting passenger. They screamed her name again on the ceiling public speakers so loudly that the earth must have heard it, and she was sure Jason had heard her name again and was smiling. In the knowledge that he was all powerful, she was sure he was blocking her ticket. So even if he had not seen her, he knew. He had rushed to stop her.

She studied the faces of the two women behind the counter for some indication. Their expressions were irritated, or maybe they were looking grim and sorry because of what they had to tell her. How would they tell her?

Sorry, miss, the flight is full. You are not allowed to fly on any plane.

Sorry, miss, Jason Hutchins has a ride for you.

She moved as if her legs were wading and pushing through deep water up to the counter to meet her ruinous fate.

* * *

Looking back on it, she knew that she must have been delusional from the exhaustion. They took her ticket and told her to hurry up and board. They had frowned at her because she had just stood by the wall, not coming forward to get her ticket. The plane was already late. She walked so slowly. Hurry.

Jason Hutchins had been there, hadn't he? But that was it. Pure chance. On the plane, she slept for the first time in three days.

Her mother picked her up at Logan airport without a word or a hug. During the hours traveling north in the car to her parents' house in Newburyport, looking out the window at the huge land area paved over with lanes of asphalt lined with steel girders, steel tower structures with power lines in the fields disrupting the sky, noticing the contrast between the ocean and the car's rude vibrations against the road's rigidity, and hearing the nonsense on the radio, she knew she was a different person. Of course she was. To her, everything done to the earth by its dominant land animal was now ugly. Necessary maybe, but ugly.

In Bermuda, as Beth had bathed in the cordiality of the blacks and the sun, she had found herself smiling more and more. She was becoming a human with a new will and defiance that had been intravenously fed back into her body by people who had withstood death, abuse, and enslavement as much as she had, and who were all mothered by the ocean, and to whom Beth was a child of the sea.

When she did return to the house now after three years, she was unprepared for her parents' continued stories of self-pity. She had forgotten how they were, Rob and Nor, in their endless self-pity, or maybe she had just hoped for a maturing introspection in them also. But sorrowfully she found it had been a pitiful and foolish hope, and only brought to mind how she spoke of them back then, not as father and mother, but bitterly as *Neither Rob Nor Give a Shit*. They never asked about her story and she never told it.

She did tell her story to Kevin Nuss.

4. KEVIN

DETECTIVES CAN'T BE CHOOSERS

KEVIN NUSS HAD A STUBBORN STREAK, WHICH SOME MIGHT HAVE ATTRIBUTED TO HIS being born under the primal zodiac sign of wolverine, but Kevin knew that wolverines—the animal—have other, less savory innate traits.

From when he was a kid, Kevin always wanted to be a cop; never a doubt. This defined view of his future, with no war and no draft to interrupt the transition from school, allowed him to become a cop much earlier than most others in policing. His noncommunicative parents reared him more with example—bad example—than words and culminated in his first murder.

His father worked as the handyman and grease monkey in the local Weetabix cereal factory, his mother often fixed other people's clothes, and Kevin and his brother Jake both odd-jobbed it after school to bring in a little more money. His little sister Mag was just Mag and she needed hovering protection.

The toughest part of his life was that his father, Andy, was a drunk—not a mean drunk—just an incurable alcoholic. But, if by the word *mean*, one thinks of running off from Kevin's mother, older brother, younger sister, and from Kevin at irregular intervals and disappearing for days, then his father was mean and thoughtless.

His mother, Marjorie, had converted from Lutheran to Catholic after she found it difficult to find a Lutheran church around the area when they moved to tiny Clinton, Massachusetts, to be nearer Andy's job. And because she liked the ceremony better, especially the mystical Latin, she complained to the family at the dinner table more than once when the church cut out the Latin about the time she joined. But she said she liked the confessional and the support the down-to-earth priest offered her.

"Why're you crying, Mother?" It took Kevin some minutes standing in the kitchen doorway to get up the nerve to ask. This was not a family that discussed emotions, and he was not sure what she might do or say.

She had been stitching some clothing for a neighbor or somebody, but now her hands were still as she sat bent over the kitchen table. She looked up, first without looking at him, seemingly unable to see anything through her tears. She quietly picked up a napkin from the table and gently dried her eyes, after which she turned her head slowly, weaving back and forth like a cobra to focus on Kevin.

"It's nothing, my dear," she said. "Don't you have some homework?"

He was only thirteen, but he was not going to accept her answer; he did not budge from the doorway.

She said, "Your father and I just have a little dispute."

Then he climbed into his secret hideaway in the living room behind the built-in bookcase. He felt safe there in the dark. No one else in the house knew about this place, or even if Jake did, no one was skinny enough to fit there except Kevin, not even his brother. Often he would spend hours in the blackness creating stories about disputes and whispering them to himself—forming his thoughts—many times crying, now and then wondering how many dead bodies could fit back there.

Other times, alone in the house, he would sit at the piano and teach himself to play as the music changed everything for him. People would tell him that he had a natural talent, but for him, it was just an escape, to cover the anguish.

Looking back, Kevin could see that his mother knew Andy was running off with some woman named Ruby or maybe it was not always Ruby, and that Marjorie knew that Andy had some secret place he went. Watching quietly, Kevin had observed his mother as she learned Andy had managed to construct himself a secret hideaway out of the materials he pillaged from the Weetabix factory. Where this devil's haven was exactly, she bewailed loudly for three years that she didn't know. Because it was a small town, Kevin thought her yowling alone in the kitchen while Andy was away was because maybe she didn't want to know where this place might be. But Kevin's pain grew even more when she finally couldn't avoid knowing because someone, one of Marjorie's sewing customers, was unconcerned enough to tell her. It made it so real for her that Marjorie lost her voice.

And even if Kevin felt it was stupid that his mother's Catholicism would not let her divorce Andy, even worse, it couldn't stop her from punishing herself for marrying and living with such a sinner and with such pain. He knew that his mother's voice was her most important attribute, not for singing, but for the readings she loved to perform gratis for community gatherings and the schools at Christmas and Easter.

He had wanted to be proud of her back then because she had felt that history and culture were priority number one for her young, mesmerized audiences. Or maybe because she was a happier person, she never preached religion or read from the Bible in the readings. The readings were always some literary bit that she felt was profound from some such thing as a Hemingway novel, the history of Rome, or the fairytales of Scandinavia. And he was proud that she was locally famous and well regarded for that. But her self-destruction not only made her lose her voice, but eventually lose Kevin, too.

As a young tween, Kevin still listened to his father, Andy, relating how he had learned from his wealthy Irish parents that he should be a benefit to society however he might choose, and so should his boys. So to Kevin's short-lived delight, Andy initiated a boy scout troop, number 1510 based on the town's zip code (and at Kevin's suggestion, called The Wolverines), planning to hold regular Monday evening meetings in the basement of the Presbyterian church when Kevin was twelve and Jake was fourteen. Looking back on it, Kevin saw that, by making this effort, Andy must have held a faint, benign hope he might force himself to bond with his two sons while the boys were scouts and he was the den leader.

* * *

"Hey, Kevin, where's your dad?"

Kevin heard this awkward question on more Monday Scout Nights than not. For some reason they never seemed to ask his brother Jake, as far as he could tell. Did the other boys know something about Jake that he didn't?

Kevin had some concept of what his father was doing, but learned to protect himself instantly, to encase his mind, and to practice self-preservation by leading the troop himself. He guided the other boys into their scout projects, earnestly helping them to earn their merit badges through his talented capability to explain and his ability to demonstrate with authority how to be prepared—to tie the knots, to salute, to pack a backpack, and other *neato* scout stuff.

And twice each summer for three years, when the troop needed to earn other badges by pitching tents, starting a fire with flint, and cooking with the basics over a campfire during a weekend field trip, Kevin had covered for his father who would lie drunkenly unconscious in his tent both days. For Kevin, Andy's tent was a screaming shame-pit, surely drawing every other scout's focused attention; it might as well have had sirens with flaming red flags.

But if Kevin could occupy the other boys' days with hikes and lessons for merit badges (or *merick badges* as the younger scouts called them), maybe they wouldn't think about Andy's absence so much; maybe the boys would think that Andy had asked his sons to lead the activities. Consequently, both he and Jake racked up the merit badges and rapidly became Eagle Scouts. Kevin even attained one unique badge for music, earned for creating and constructing a fiddle.

The Wolverines scout troop dissipated in the third summer, because of two deaths. Andy was found dead in his tent. Apparently, he died from being so drunk that he drowned from his own vodka bottle, which, while suspiciously stuffed down his throat, no one cared to scrutinize, even if rumored suspicions were soon to become rampant of the wrong person, since the actual murderer was beyond suspicion.

* * *

Obviously, Kevin loved his brother, but the two never talked to each other about the gnawing problem of their father's behavior, the tiger crouching in their house. Kevin's and Jake's feelings about it were a mute subject. So Kevin was caught in one more insidious nightmare when his brother committed suicide at age eighteen without warning or explanation, so shortly after his father's death that the suspicion for Andy's death from those who bothered with such rumors, unbeknownst to Kevin at the time, fell on Jake. And Boy Scout Troop 1510 became a memory. Good for some, nightmarish for others.

In the following year, Kevin remembered little Mag asked exactly three different times, always when he least expected it, "Why did Jake die?"

"The tiger got him, Eagle Scout and everything," Kevin would say. He regretted ever after that he had not known what else to say to her.

He was relieved that she graduated from high school, and that she moved into a communal group of women to live like a nun. The others in the commune said she was doing fine, but he repeatedly found it was hard to communicate with her as she didn't always make sense and, each time he spoke with her, it only reminded him of the past he wanted to erase. At least she didn't kill herself.

With his father's death, his mother, who had been silent for five years, began to speak again. Although she didn't do as many readings because she didn't have the same powerful voice, she filled direct requests from friends to do readings to small gatherings.

Kevin was glad for his mother. Maybe she could forgive his father, but it was too late for him. Kevin had learned the hard way that he had to take care of himself first, learning to suppress the past by training his mind, making the stoicism in him even more unable to reach his emotions or to speak of himself or even think of his feelings, for fear some vulnerability—or secret—sealed inside him might seep out like nameless ooze. Instead, he became an entertaining story-teller so that no one would think to notice his armor of introversion and fractured conscience.

Growing up in isolated Clinton, Massachusetts, he had heard the story that just down the road a mile or so, in the now-abandoned village center, ironically called Devilsville—or maybe the name came later, he didn't know—the villagers had killed a couple to stop a relationship, a relationship of which the village disapproved. This story was an inspiration for him to become a storyteller and to become a detective, even if he had doubts whether he could qualify as a cop according to his teachers since he was, like some retard, left-handed.

His expressed thoughts about religion and family were by the book, so-to-speak inside the box, yet he was attracted to people who had broader, even unconventional views of family, the earth, the universe, and religion. He presented himself as boring, letting people have that impression, even believing it himself.

He figured that he needed this image to be good at his future detective job. He was not going to be a patrolman for the rest of his life. Detective was his goal and, if he were going to be a dick (which he embarrassingly learned to avoid saying), he needed as complete an understanding of human behavior as he could get.

What his teachers considered daydreaming was his boredom. Because he was all too often far off in another world, he had been a D-student. The teachers passed him mostly out of pity or were actually afraid to flunk him, he discovered later, because some teachers wanted to get rid of him because of something indefinable in the young boy and feared him.

But he did learn one big word from English class: *Obstreperous*. It became his word. It stuck in his head, just like the word from science class he remembered, *Bony-Eared Assfish,* because it sounded hilarious.

* * *

Now more than a year had passed since Kevin had spontaneously, and with humongous satisfaction, fixed his father problem, coolly and calmly, without being discovered. Strangely humongous, however. Strange because, after all, it had been his father. Eerily satisfying, not because he got away with it; it was the *fixing* that had been satisfying.

Okay, he had to admit to himself, this delighted contentment had been perplexing back then. The feeling had been so something. So peculiar. Complicated. Could he say thrilling?

His drunken father's struggle and waking eyes staring in disbelief haunted Kevin for a while, but his teenage mind had worked around it by reiterating that he had helped his brother and his mother, and by burying, along with his father, the question—*Had he actually enjoyed the killing?*

Back when Kevin could only sense the sins of his father, Kevin had worshiped his brother for all the great times growing up—building a tree house together, the secret clubroom they created between them up in the storage room above his grandmother's garage, and timing the races down the laundry chute at home from the third floor to the basement until Jake eventually grew to where he didn't fit in the chute anymore. They knew every corner and hidden nook in the two large houses, their grandmother's and their parents', both built on grandfather's bank fortune.

But this summer at age sixteen, Kevin was preoccupied with why Jake had died. Why had Jake committed suicide? The guilty memory of Jake and the fishing incident had germinated and, for the eight years since, ideas of retribution had intermittently chipped and chiseled at Kevin's days and nights. But now adding to the desire for revenge was the unanswerable question of how much had Kevin's mistake influenced his brother to kill himself this year. Each time he thought about it, Kevin could not decide if anything would make up for his stupid mistake.

This fateful year, Kevin had spent his time and especially this summer organizing much of his activity around his envisioned future as police detective, and mourning over Jake's death at the same time. All the time. So Kevin had planned today's expedition in meticulous detail, except that it didn't happen that way, the way he had planned. Instead of being just reconnaissance, it became a surprising accomplishment with a thousand lucky parts, except for his hand getting infected from his fall (off my bike, Mom).

Lucky, indeed. No fingerprints were found, just a little untraceable blood on a piece of canvas. He had not been seen by Leon Duprey's family or noticed by anyone else in town. The whole operation had taken only one hour and forty minutes, from home and back again.

Kevin had decided that it was time to act—to figure out what retaliation he could take, like maybe some serious prank—like maybe dumping a truckload of dead fish in Leon Duprey's car, if he had a car or if fish came in truckloads. But Kevin would decide on something once he knew more about Leon Duprey.

All he knew was that Leon Duprey had not been in school for two years, quitting at age fifteen, probably to work somewhere, Kevin assumed. Over several days, by innocuously asking his neighborhood acquaintances, Kevin had covertly been able to get the jerk's address in a rural area on Clam Road out on the southeast edge of town.

Bicycling around small Clinton was no problem, but then Kevin had been glad the address was near a familiar road in case he needed to make a fast exit. He had just needed to choose the right day and time when he had the excuse to be out of the house for an indefinite while, unchallenged and maybe even essentially unnoticed by anyone here or there. So today right after one o'clock, with his mother in one of her frequent silent modes, sewing in the kitchen, and people in general back at work, Kevin chose this windy, sunny August afternoon.

To avoid any comments from his mother about being dressed all in black, even to his socks, on such a warm, cloudless summer day, he yelled from the front hall where she could not see him. "Mom, I'm going over to Jimmy Foster's."

In her rediscovered voice, so foggy and weak that Kevin could barely hear her, she responded as he hoped. "Who's Jimmy Foster?"

"He's a new...well, his family is a new family and a few of us are going over to say hello."

"That's nice," she croaked.

Before she could say anything more, although he doubted she would, Kevin escaped out the door with a fading "Yeah. I'm late. See ya, Mom."

Now all he had to do was pedal over to explore this rarely visited side of town, the first thing on his list being to learn Leon Duprey's schedule. But discovery was one thing; that's what detectives do. His biggest problem could be getting caught by Leon Duprey or any cohort around there. His second biggest problem, less dangerous, could be not finding Leon Duprey at all. Maybe he wouldn't be visible, outside or even at home.

But Leon Duprey had been there.

* * *

Of all the stories he had in him about his brother, Kevin's clearest and most disconcerting memory was when, at about age eight, he and Jake went fishing up at the little pond next to the Blader lake. The fishing wasn't really Jake's choice. It was the weekend and their mother announced that the kids needed to get out of the house and said, "Jake, take your brother fishing."

"Aw, Mom, do I gotta? I'm supposed to go down to Eugene's."

"Eugene is not somebody you should be with."

"Why not?"

"'Cause I said so, that's why."

And that did it. Mother had decided and that was the decision. But Kevin felt really, really guilty, because his brother really didn't want to go fishing and, even less, he really didn't want his little brother tagging along. Personally, Kevin could have been just as happy to follow Jake over to Eugene's, but that option would have been even worse, according to Jake.

Jake knew just where to dig up some worms in the field behind the house. He told Kevin to put them with some dirt in the tomato sauce can Jake had instructed Kevin to get out of the stinking garbage can. Kevin hated touching the worms and hoped Jake would put the poor, slimy things on Kevin's hook.

So once the two got all their stuff together, Jake made Kevin carry the heavy tackle box with the worms inside and Kevin's rod for the forty-minute walk to the pond, while Jake just carried his own rod. But that was okay with Kevin. Kevin was with his big brother, who knew everything about fishing, putting worms on hooks, and all that stuff.

And Jake did put a worm on Kevin's hook after telling Kevin how useless he was. Then Jake showed him how to pick the seeds out of the sunflowers and eat them. This little pond probably didn't have more than minnow-sized sunfish in it, but for Kevin it was the neatest place on earth. It was hidden by the tall sunflowers and weeds from the road and from the big lake where all the older guys went. And it was shady and cool and quiet. Really quiet, until Leon Duprey and his buddy Sammy came along.

Leon Duprey at age nine was the meanest, worst bully on earth and just the far-off sight of him scared Kevin something awful. Leon Duprey would throw crabapples at Kevin or hit guys with sticks just to make them cry. There wasn't much for Kevin to do other than run like hell. Jake was a year older than Leon Duprey and could take care of the situation.

At least, that's what Kevin thought. That was his first lesson in big mistakes and his guilt made Kevin feel this mistake was part of the reason for what later happened to Jake. Even years later, Kevin remembered this time, painfully, like it was yesterday.

Kevin had run up to the road, not crying, but whining and grunting, out of wind, really worried these bullies were right behind him. So when Jake came out of the weeds about five minutes later, Kevin first thought it was them and almost ran.

Climbing slowly up to the road, Jake looked mad and said, "You little shit, you ran away."

Kevin stood there frozen and said, "Yeah. Leon Duprey was coming."

Jake said, "You coulda helped. Usually, you're as slow as a dead sloth, but no, not this time. You shot off like a goosed pig. You know what they did? They took your pole and mine and threw them and the tackle box in the water."

Kevin was thunderstruck. "But you were bigger."

"You little idiot. You left me alone. You coulda helped me. Together we mighta stopped them."

"Really?"

That's all Kevin could get out of his mouth. The whole picture of the scene was that his brother had wanted him. His brother had thought he could be of use. Really? And Kevin always wondered what happened to the can of worms.

It was eight years later that Leon Duprey died, smashed in the head with a brick, or so the evidence analyzed by the Massachusetts Bureau of Investigation seemed to show in that the brick itself was missing. The local police never found the killer, but always suspected Leon's pal Sammy, although he proved he was thirty-nine miles away in Athol and the bloodstains on a piece of canvas and the roof were not his.

* * *

Today, the streets on the way to Leon Duprey's house were quiet, especially Clam Road. No traffic. No neighbors. From the road, Kevin found the neglected small, one-story wooden frame house, set back into the woods. A sweaty, wrinkly-looking thing, peeling its dirty white skin, exposing horizontal strips of dark meaty wood. Worn car tracks in the dirt led some hundred feet from the road up to the right of the house, but no car. Nobody out front.

The woods on the left were perfect for approaching the house unseen—perfect—except for the wind. The rustling in the trees made it difficult for Kevin to hear who else might be lurking in the woods. After he leaned his bike on a tree hidden from the road, he waded slowly through the undergrowth, trying not to step on twigs, and stopping every few steps to listen, checking to be sure Leon Duprey wasn't going to leap out from behind a tree.

No one leaped out.

Working his way through the trees and plotting his escape route at the same time, Kevin was able to circle around to the back of the house where he saw a weedy, flat, brown area and, on the north side in front of him, a creaky-creepy shed with hints of red paint and an oddly slanted roof—high in front, low in back. Creepy, because who knew what was in the shed? Torture victims? Stolen goods?

The larger, more practical question now was the *creaky* part. Would the shed hold Kevin's weight? Upon seeing the shed, Kevin had immediately decided that, if he could climb on top of it, he would have a perfect view of the yard and the house. From the woods, he had no chance of hearing anything except shouts, while the shed roof would also let him see more into the house. Since, at the moment, no one was in view, he could at least check out the possibility of climbing up on the roof from the hidden back side of the shed.

Keeping the shed between him and any view from the house as he approached from the woods, his hopes grew stronger upon seeing that the unkept area behind the shed was littered and stacked with old tires and a wood pallet, all potentially useful for constructing a stairway to his perfect surveillance perch.

The wind, carrying alternate smells of oil and sewer, made Kevin nervous, and made him jump when a gust suddenly rattled the shack's tin roof. But then he realized that the rattling and the general wind noise would helpfully cover his own noise as he moved the pallet and the tires against the back wall to create some sort of climbing arrangement.

He had seen, or more likely hoped, that the slant of the roof was perfect for hiding as he peeked over the edge to shadow Leon Duprey and his criminal friends and family. It struck Kevin that he had never thought about Leon Duprey even having a family, since he seemed like some mistaken creation from the netherworld, the recurring wafts of sewer-smell confirming it.

Kevin muttered under his breath, "Get real, Kevin. Stick to the job."

As quick and easy as moving the pallet and stacking the tires had been, like they were just placed there for his use, Kevin was dripping with sweat. Sure, it was hot, and his nerves and black clothes weren't exactly helping him stay cool either. But he didn't know hot until he climbed up to the roof, where he met two unexpected problems.

The lesser of the two problems was that the bricks on the roof, which had been placed there to keep the corrugated tin from blowing away, could easily slide down the slant, making suspicious noises if he shook the panels while climbing up on them or moving around too much.

But, secondly and immediately worse, the tin burned his fingers; it was hot enough to fry eggs.

With all the day's plan working out so perfectly for him so far, detective-in-training Kevin was not about to give up on his progress in order to try to luck out finding a less hot and sunny day. Even if he learned nothing this time around, the spy nest would be ready for his next watch. Detectives can't be choosers. And the warm oily stink in the wind certainly confirmed that, too.

Besides, in this hot weather, Leon Duprey's being outside would hopefully be more probable. Of course, most likely all Kevin could and would learn from watching the house and the yard would only be Leon Duprey's comings and goings, but that was something.

First, he needed to solve the hot tin roof problem. His heart lifted when, upon scanning the junk strewn on the ground behind him, he spotted a dirty, ragged canvas tarp, overgrown and half-buried under some skeletal rusty metal parts of discarded machinery.

The bad news was that, to pull the canvas loose, he would have to step out from behind the shed and be in full view of the house.

He peeked gingerly around the corner of the shed at the house, but could see no one in the dirty, dark windows. On the other hand, how could he know for sure? Maybe they could see out even if he could not see in much. He leaned his back against the shed to think; he had to decide. Who knew when he would have a new chance? Should he just watch from the woods? Give up?

No.

With nobody in the yard, no car, everything quiet in the house, it was now or never.

With one more wary, long inspection of the house and not seeing the slightest movement, he high-stepped through the weeds. Stumbling on a half-buried cable, he fell—cutting his hand on some hard object—jumped back to his feet, and began pulling at the tarp. It loosened quickly, much more quickly than he had anticipated or had hoped, making him nearly fall over backwards. And luckily, the large piece of the rotted canvas that ripped loose was the right size to fit nicely under Kevin on the roof.

He quickly leaped back behind the shed dragging the canvas. As his body trembled uncontrollably, he realized that he had been holding his breath the whole time he was in sight of the house, as if that would help. He was disgusted with himself for such an emotional, uncool reaction.

"Clear your mind, detective," he said in a whisper. "Calm down."

He inspected his cut right hand. No big deal. Not bleeding much. He refused to let it hamper him. After the long pause, he shook the remaining dirt off the canvas and climbed up his makeshift stairway construction, using his left hand to help climb while holding the tarp in the painful hand, the gusts of wind making the canvas tug at his grip. Then, waiting for a break in the wind, Kevin swung the tarp up onto the roof with both hands. The tarp smelled oily and Kevin realized he would be dirty and shitty smelling after lying on it. He would have to find an excuse to tell his mother. But there it was, landing perfectly, and now only needing a brick or two to hold it in place.

He leaned forward and grabbed the closest brick, holding the tarp in place with his bleeding hand.

A male voice below him said, "Hey, fuckhead, what do you think you're doing?"

Kevin froze. Even after how-many years, Kevin knew immediately it was Leon Duprey's voice, risen from hell. The bastard himself. Because of the wind, Kevin had not heard the footsteps or any approaching noise. Now Leon Duprey was right there below him, a bit to the right and sounding just as ghoulish as Kevin remembered.

Kevin didn't answer. Didn't turn. Had he been seen from the house? Had he missed a car arriving? But these questions were a waste of brainpower. Oddly, he felt no fear. He just listened and plotted.

"I said, what do you think you're doing, asshole? Get the fuck down from there or I'll beat your fucking ass, and probably will anyway, you little shit."

Kevin's conclusion: Leon Duprey was alone. Kevin gripped the red brick harder in his left hand. His mind concentrated with a clear focus. Like a spider in its web sensing the vibrations, Kevin felt his makeshift stairway being grabbed.

As a hopeful distraction, he helped the wind lift the canvas, making it flap noisily off the tin roof. Then instantly, all in one motion—slow motion in Kevin's mind—he slid the brick off the roof, twisted to his right, and threw the brick side-arm with a groaning strength he didn't know he had at Leon Duprey's face.

The brick seemed to travel forever the few feet to Leon Duprey's head, and finally, when it struck with a loud but dull snap, the brick continued traveling into his head, the force knocking Leon Duprey backwards, an odd cry coming from his mouth as his body began its descent. Reflecting and refracting in the sunlight, blood exploded in the air like an assorted cloud of flapping insects fleeing from a predator, spurting away.

In precise detail, Kevin watched Leon Duprey's body thud to the ground, silently bounce once, and the wet brick bounce farther a foot or two. In the ensuing seconds, time was neither short nor eternal.

But then when everything, even the wind, was still, Kevin again began to breathe. Knowing he should leave immediately and quickly back through the woods, he picked up the brick. Leon Duprey was dead. Kevin didn't know what he should have felt, but he felt relief and an intoxicating ecstasy.

In triumphant exhilaration as he ran, he said to the trees, "I am the wolverine."

PART 2

The quantum physics equations that govern reality don't tell us which way time flows and are just as valid for time streaming into the past as they are for time streaming into the future. Time, the human construct, exists only where you are, flowing in one direction.

—JAMES FREDRICK

+/- TWENTY YEARS LATER

2010 CE

1. MARTIN

GETTING UNTANGLED

"I KNOW IT SOUNDS OUTRIGHT LUDICROUS, BUT, AS MUCH AS I CAN BE, I AM SURE that the future of mankind will be influenced by what I have solved." He walked to the door. "I have to go."

Martin's whole night needed to go, to walk out that door. This would be the last time. He thought he might even be experiencing some guilt for having trysts with a hairdresser, while Joe, faithful for these twenty years, was back in Boston. When Martin woke up, immediately after trying to establish where he was, he noticed the bedroom stunk of halitosis and hairspray, singeing his nostrils and making him rub his nose so as not to sneeze. Martin's legs were tangled up in the bedsheet, which just added to his irritation at having no way to sneak out of the apartment. Besides, he needed the bathroom. Oh, how he regretted being here in this situation.

In previous times he had always thought how, for a hairdresser, this wasn't such a bad apartment—large, sunny, and open, with modern appliances. So he had to assume that the hairdresser must have some sort of deal with the modish-salon shop owner, his shop being just below, where the hairdresser worked and with whom Martin got his greying locks trimmed once a month.

Actually, he knew his thoughts of immediate escape were fatuous; no way could he just leave. He needed a shower, a shave, and to fix himself for the meeting at ten in the Hawthorne Hotel bar before the Tuesday Rotary lunch where he was the speaker. He would give his public presentation package which he had done a zillion times before, for which he had asked to be allotted a whole two hours to speak, rather than the normal Rotary Club twenty minutes. The club fulsomely flattered him as a quasi-famous physicist and had invited the city's high school kids to attend, so he could feel he was not just speaking to the benumbed ears of a few elderly business members.

He would win their hearts telling them how he liked Salem and loved to dine out on his regular visits here because he felt it was the town of great restaurants, quite the opposite of snobby, rich little Marblehead, of which blue-collar Salemites were so envious, and where, although just across the bay, he found no serious restaurant.

And he planned to tell the story he had picked up one day on the ferry between Salem and Boston, a humorously derogatory story about how, back when the peninsula was discovered and named by the British, the word for peninsula was "head." The white rocks protruding up from the ocean around the peninsula were deemed to be marble, and thus the name Marblehead. The big mistake was that the rocks were actually only covered with bird excrement. Therefore, the story concludes, the town should have been called "Shithead." He knew they would love it if he could tell it with a straight face.

Yesterday, as usual, he had left his Volvo at home in South Boston because the Salem ferry made it so easy for him to think about something other than traffic, plus he enjoyed the pleasant fifteen-minute walk from the ferry dock through the shanty part of Salem to the hotel.

At his favorite restaurant, the Lyceum, where Alexander Graham Bell (he liked to relate) famously tested his prototype phone, Martin and the hairdresser had met last night and driven to the flat in the hairdresser's sputtering VW bug. So, through nobody's fault but his own, Martin would have to face his hairdresser to say this was it. No more. Hairdresser was one thing, but discovering that the hairdresser was a student at the college where Martin taught a course was another.

When Martin got out of the shower stall, the hairdresser-alias-student was sitting half-asleep, unromantically naked on the toilet next to the shower. They didn't speak until breakfast.

"I have to go," Martin said. He didn't sit down at the kitchen table. NPR morning news was on in the background. He smelled warm fragrant tisane. For the first time the warmth of the kitchen with its wood and bare-brick design prompted memories, sending a momentary stab of regret that he would not be returning.

"Nothing? No breakfast? I got the toast all toasted," the hairdresser-student said.

"No, I've got to go. But I need to explain to you something. A very difficult something."

"Uh oh."

"You have to understand that, since you told me you were a student at Salem State, things are different."

He realized just at that moment that he had never bothered, even after multiple encounters, to learn the hairdresser's name. He must have heard the name, but they had always just arranged things during the salon visits. Not much point now, he thought.

"Yeah, I knew that was going to happen."

"But it is more than just that. This may be something that will mean nothing to you, but I don't just come up here from Boston to get my hair done. Whether you knew it or not, I teach a mathematics class once a week while most of my work is in Boston at MIT researching and investigating quantum physics. You know about quantum physics? Quantum physics is an inexact bit of mathematics. Well, more than a bit. I'm trying to prove our existence, and it is my life."

"You sure you don't want some toast? I have some homemade peach preserves."

"Listen to me, I think...I mean, I really believe that I have solved one of the most difficult pieces of the quantum physics puzzle and am about to publish the paper announcing it. It may well revolutionize the whole thought process concerning this science. It could even give us a key to stop global warming."

"So how does that relate?"

He thought that question would normally deserve an explanation of the connection between his theory and global warming, if it had been anyone else. But suddenly Martin was aware that his overoptimistic explain-anything-to-anybody teacher feature, the pontificator, had once again, as all too often it did, tried fallaciously draping its glory around him.

Instead, he said, "If my reputation is hurt by any sort of scandal, the paper may not be taken so seriously. I can care for you all I want, but this is above us—more than us—far more important than our relationship or anything about us. It may change every concept we humans have."

"Are you sure you don't want to eat something? I can drive you back to the hotel."

Martin knew he was not able to explain any more, anything that would have any perceptible meaning or create any clarity for the hairdresser-student. So he determinedly opened the door, shut it quietly behind him, and more or less trotted down the stairs and out of the building.

The air smelled fresh. Sea air. It was a perfectly pleasant day in Salem, and the twenty-minute walk along Lafayette Street would offer time to regret that, instead of staying in his room at the hotel, he had let himself be tempted to stay overnight again with someone he knew ahead of time he had to dump.

The tree-lined sidewalk that passed in front of the hair salon was a mile-something stretch between the state college and downtown Salem. The street was quiet this early morning, except for a few cars outside the sleepy coffee shop just across the road from the salon.

Despite the sidewalk being well-trafficked most days with college students walking to and from classes, the varying maintenance of the walkway, wholly reliant on the property owners' obedience of the ordinances, normally required less-flexible pedestrians to watch where they were stepping.

However, as always, Martin looked up, reflexively searching the sky for attacking seagulls. Sometime back when he was a child, although not recalling how old he was or with whom, he had walked along a dirt pathway on some island bird sanctuary off the Massachusetts coast and was nightmarishly attacked by great black-backed gulls. The monstrous birds flew at him so aggressively, so close, sometimes even hitting him, that he was sure they would peck out his eyes and rip out his hair. The adults said they had been warned that it was nesting season and that the birds might want to protect their nests, but no one seemed to have an idea of what that meant and what to expect. Martin was terrified. He and all the others retreated, finding it too intimidating to continue.

Ever since then, any time he walked on any sort of path, the vision of the attacking-bird tumult returned. But, of course, he knew better. There was no reason or logic to this anxiety, other than a childhood scare, but he had to work consciously to cut it short.

Today to calm himself, he assimilated his present surroundings: some dull-colored chickadees acrobatically digging at all angles into the tree bark, a squirrel couple with quivering tails executing short, quick dance routines on the grass, and innumerable sparrows chaotically hip-hop hunting and chirping encouragement to each other while searching for terrestrial delicacies. His séance with nature abruptly ended when he stumbled on a sidewalk brick.

He fell so clumsily that he felt embarrassed, and like a cat that has just fallen off a chair, he looked around to see if anyone had seen him fall. His mood changed. He felt wretched. A repetitive thought kept cycling through his mind.

Martin, you are a mathematician and a physicist, but a poor judge of human beings.

He tried to comfort himself with the conclusion that it was not possible to be both practical and theoretical.

He brushed off his pant leg with his hand. His overnight stay made him put on the same fine clothes that he had worn last night for dinner with the dress socks and thin-soled loafers. He was just not dressed for this walk. The uneven bricks were not only damaging the shoes but hurting his feet.

And moral? Was he moral? Maybe morality doesn't apply. No, Martin, you are one immoral bastard. An intelligent bastard? A bastard that might save the earth? Or just a bastard?

A good scotch at the bar might resolve that question.

2. ELLEN

ENTANGLEMENT TANGO

"Entanglement," he answered.

Ellen couldn't tell whether she should laugh. In their first few minutes of meeting in the bar at the hotel, she had just asked what exactly Martin, the professor, was working on at the moment. He was working on hair?

"Entanglement is a subject?" she asked. She had certainly had problems with tangles.

"Well, in quantum physics we have a few mysteries and this entanglement part is one for sure. We are constantly looking for a singular mathematical formula for the universe, a unified theory. The mathematics of the unified theory breeds coincidence and the formulae that come the closest to a unified theory have always seemed to hatch new problems.

"The math has generated theories of a parallel universe, ten parallel universes, and even eleven or many more. But the newest weird thing seems to be entanglement."

She looked at him as maybe a puppy might, a nervous puppy at that, enthralled and anticipatory, not sure when to bark. Wiping the bar surface unnecessarily with a cloth, acting like she was doing her job, helped unknot a brain cramp.

She said, "They have quantum physics courses at Salem State, Professor?"

"No. No. I am just an adjunct math professor here in Salem. And my name is Martin…Martin Case. Call me Martin. And your name was Ellen?"

He was wearing things she could never afford, a silk light green turtleneck under a luxurious sports jacket of some brand she would never know. His youthfulness was contradicted by his greying combed-over hair looking like it was styled in the early 1900s. He didn't use his manicured hands except to scratch the short hair on the back of his head; everything about him was cerebral.

His huge, broad, dimpled smile that's all perfect upper teeth below a flawlessly groomed Chevron mustache was shockingly handsome, but his deep blue eyes were distracting her because the black pupils varied in size as he thought and made her feel she was too near the event horizon of these black holes without being capable of analyzing the content. She found him alarmingly disturbing as his eyes seemed to gloss over a veiled realm.

He made her become all too aware of how she looked, forcing her to put a camera on herself, her myopic grey-green eyes, froggishly oversized when her ugly thick glasses weren't slipping down a pointed nose, her neck-long dark hair greying around the fringes, her piano hands, her thin body taller than his, and even becoming aware of how she tended to stick out her tongue while she thought. He didn't have to see how poorly she dressed because she was covered in her required hotel white bar jacket.

And he didn't know how vain she was. Even at her self-perceived late age, her late start on life at age forty-seven, she still hadn't learned the pitfalls of vanity. Knowing he was coming today, she stupidly didn't wear her comfortable sneakers. Now standing all morning in heels and no socks was killing her. Her feet hurt and her back ached and, while she was behind the bar, he couldn't even see her feet. Vanity was a woman's punishment for being born.

He produced something magnetic, but not magnetism. Unlike the poles of a magnet, one attracting and one repelling, his magnet produced bipolar presence without attraction. She knew she must just acclimate to his looks or she wouldn't be paying him for edification, or anything she could use.

"I'm Ellen," she said. "Ellen McKinnon." She gave him her maiden name even if she was still stuck with Lodovico, an old marriage cognomen remnant of a not-so-distant divorce.

Distrait, he hardly seemed to register her words. "My real love is at MIT's labs where I'm a research professor." He didn't pause, but she could hear in the formal inflexion that he was practicing his standard presentation to be given at lunch.

"Entanglement, as a part of quantum physics, tells us that two particles can be directly connected even across vast distances. Tests have been done showing that two particles more than one kilometer apart are somehow connected to each other. It defies any logic.

"This theory has been extended to other fields by some who like to call it Quantum Biology as a way to explain how birds find their way in migration. You can sort of look at it another way as two unconnected people being mysteriously connected, who, although miles apart, dance the same dance, and, when they crash into each other, they get all tangled up in each other. I can't explain it better than that since we know so little.

"But I will take another Scotch on the rocks, and then we need to discuss what you hired me for, your thesis." He held out his glass. "As someone said, work is the curse of the drinking classes."

Her mind always demanded some mindless response. She said, "Bartending is the curse of the sockless classes."

She was immediately embarrassed. He had no way of understanding something so irrelevant and inane, and she turned away to fix his drink.

Luckily, the hotel's bar control was slack enough that she could sneak him his addiction. She had immediately understood that most of the reason he agreed to help her with her paper was not the money; it was the free booze. She now knew why he insisted on meeting at the hotel bar while she was on duty.

Actually, today she hoped the alcohol would protect him from her neophyte cold. The cold was just a preliminary tickle but it was making her feel shaky and fragile, and, along with the feet and back discomfort, sorrowfully not so bright. At least the cold blocked the bar's recurring smell of old beer, which was constantly bilking any cleaning attempts, as much as she had tried. Maybe her normal nose was just oversensitive.

At this time of day, just before lunch, the bar was at its quietest, a room resting from the harsh commotion of its evenings. She was there more or less to be sure it was open for the straggling midmorning coffee drinkers and, thus she had time to work on her thesis. And she didn't really care if her tutor had bad habits as long as such a prominent professor was willing to tutor her on the art of thesis writing.

After he took a nip at his drink, he said, "So you want to write about fish."

Pushing her glasses back in place and looking around, acting like she was doing her duty controlling the needs of other guests, helped her gather her disobliging thoughts. His extreme attractiveness was distracting enough, but also she felt odd correcting a prominent professor. She knew he was highly specialized and maybe that was the excuse for his ignorance, or maybe he was teasing her.

"Not fish," she said. "Cetaceans. You know, dolphins, whales. Sea mammals. These are highly intelligent animals that have evolved over tens of millions of years, before apes and us humans."

"Evolved from what? Fish?" He smiled.

Her nose was still working; he smelled of alcohol and expensive perfume. Now she can't tell if he was drunk or joking with her. "Oh, come on, professor."

"Martin," he said.

"Okay, Martin. You know better than that. But I will tell you they evolved from a land animal about the size of a ferret in the area of what is now Pakistan. And they sort of split off into a couple directions. One version developed into a sea animal eventually becoming dolphins and whales, while another became a land animal like hippopotami." She paused deciding whether to spring her joke. "And a third group split off and became Pakistanis." She watched his expression.

He smiled. "Very funny."

Okay, he had a sense of humor, at least. A human side.

"So what makes these swimming mammals worth a doctoral thesis?"

"As I said, these living beings have been around for more than eons and they talk among themselves. We have yet to understand their language. But I have a theory about it based on the enormous number of studies and recordings that have been done. In fact, I am certain that I have found the key to the dolphins' communication."

He seemed to sink inside his head into some sort of surreptitious, deep deliberation. She started to feel uneasy. He didn't like the subject? Was he deciding to leave?

Breaking out of his trance, he took another sip at his drink and said, "Okay, let's start."

The interior of Salem's Hawthorne Hotel was neither here nor there when it came to style, being perhaps in a sort of anguished hesitation, waiting to become interesting. The hotel's attempt at Federal style was replicated in the lobby with a pair of Martha Washington chairs, also called lolling chairs, with upholstered tall backs and arms, criticized at the time of their creation for the manners they suggested, since Puritan industriousness and purpose were so highly valued, especially over sitting around in cushiony chairs.

But the other chairs and settees of that time would have been much too stark and fragile for a hotel, especially in the dining room or this bar where Ellen was working. The white paneled ceiling and chandeliers countered the bar's dark red walls. Heavy chestnut-colored drapes, dark green wall-to-wall rug, the thick yellow tablecloths, and upholstered dining chairs all dampened the sound of the few scarcely noticed visitors spread in the room.

She had been hired at the Massachusetts Woods Hole NOAA lab on the promise she would finish her doctoral thesis. Working mornings here at the hotel helped foot the tutoring by Professor Martin Case on Tuesdays, and, of course, a few freebies from the bar was, obviously, enticing him, maybe reducing his fee.

She and Professor Case worked across the bar in low voices on the thesis structure, but at the third and fourth Scotch, his attention began to stray and he wanted to talk about himself. He obviously believed in himself, she guessed with good reason, or maybe it was because he believed in himself that he had become so accomplished.

But then he dumbfounded her.

He said, "I want your opinion on something personal."

With doubt gushing out like an unfiltered faucet, she said, "Okay."

"In fact, I have two questions for you, but they are related."

Continued misgivings, "Okay."

"Do you look at me as an unkind, untrustworthy person?"

Did he really expect a truthful answer? It was a question with one answer. "No."

"I can't explain to you why I ask that, but I should tell you that I have been together with my partner for close to eighteen years now."

Panic began tearing up Ellen's insides like a rat clawing in her chest. He was going to tell her that he was gay and what did she think about that.

"We have a good life. I earn most of the income and he does most of the housework and daily chores at which I would fail miserably. He is kind, loving, ever attentive." He paused.

She didn't know what to assume. What was his point? This was not leading where she expected. She couldn't look at his face, and saying anything seemed inappropriate. She picked up a dish towel and gave the bar surface another slow, circular, unnecessary wipe.

"So in my travels, we usually travel together, to let him get out of the house, to see the world. We've traveled to Europe several times both for business and pleasure. And he thanks me for it. Like the surprise plan he has for my birthday on Thursday."

"Happy birthday."

"Thanks."

Again he paused. He sipped his empty glass. "Oh, while I think about it, I'll be unreachable the rest of the week because of this surprise."

And again, she remained silent. She didn't offer him more to drink.

"But at the university, I met another person who claims to love me. Young, smart. Most of all, he smiles and makes me feel good just being in his presence." He had become tense. "Maybe I'm doing the wrong thing telling you this…"

"Yes, you are. Yes, you are," Ellen thought.

"…but I have to ask someone. I am a scientist and not very good at people.

"This new person is exciting, but I know it is because he's new. Not especially handsome, but young and enthusiastic. If I would put them in the same room, at a table in front of me, and I looked from one to the other, I'd love both for what they are, for what they have done for me."

She glanced at him out of the corner of her eye. Suddenly he looked up at her, making her jump out of her skin.

He said, "I don't know what to do. What should I do?"

She wanted to say, "Go drown yourself."

He wanted her opinion? She had so many smudges—faces she had erased and no longer remembered—each blurred memory pressing a despairing weight on her body. It wasn't like she woke up in the middle of the night each time, knowing an affair was over; she always knew it just when he would walk into the room from the bathroom while she was lying naked in bed. She would even try to let herself be seduced, but the wetness would dry up in the middle of intercourse and the story would repeat itself. He would stop, roll off onto his back, and each one of them, with reproachful desolation, would say, "What's wrong?"

And with the same anticipatory intonation, each one would never want the relationship to end, continually and repeatedly asking with the same droning optimism for another chance; she always had to end it with quiet, painful determination. Finally, after too many, she just stopped hoping and looking.

Now with the professor's question, she was like a broken bird on a perch; in disbelief, she couldn't blink. Her beak couldn't smile or show emotion; it could only open and close, but nothing came out. Why was this person asking her? Her of all people. She who had failed so miserably at human relationships; she who married a monster who destroyed her life. She was not the person to ask. She was just not. She had no right to judge anyone.

She figured he was drunk. She had created another antagonistic creature. Okay, she hadn't created him, but she gave him the injection he had needed to morph and attack. She needed to leave, to get away from him, but she was stuck working behind the bar for another hour.

The chirps, farts, thuds, knocks, creaking hinges, monkey squeaks, rapid clicks of dolphin sounds from her cell phone interrupted the silence, making her smile.

"Excuse me a second," she said.

Her newfound son was calling. Even with the hours of talking, she felt she hardly knew him, but during their conversations, his intensity always got to her, so much so that she felt a sort of nervous buzzing inside her after they had spoken. Every time. She supposed that's why she liked calling him by his choice of nickname, Cricket.

Now, it was urgent that he speak with her. But not on the phone.

3. KEVIN

THAT FRIDAY MORNING

KEVIN WAS PRACTICING HIS HONED ABILITY TO CATNAP—UNTIL HIS LIFE CHANGED. This morning, as he sat in his police cruiser parked in the woods, he had been in his half-dozing-half-aware zone—allowing him to be aware of the woods around him while reiterating the story of meeting Beth and how they had jumped in the sack every chance they got.

Kevin had tired of the drudgery of being a cop in Massachusetts, and more so, the futureless grind his fellow cops felt about their work. The police union had been strong for years and the benefits were good. Along the way (when the police union, after some historically tough battles, was finally strong enough), some prospective governor, in order to get the union's political backing, had promised to fulfill the union's laziest, most extravagant wish, making it mandatory for a policeman to be on duty for any roadwork and to be paid overtime for standing around scratching his nuts. No governor since had dared touch that agreement.

Kevin had scruples that would, to all appearances, defy his shrouded depths. For police to demand flagmen jobs with a cop's overtime pay, rubbed him as morally wrong and he saw it in the miserable attitude of the whole force. How could anyone rather be a flagman than a policeman, and laugh behind the scenes anytime the subject came up? He tolerated it for seven years before applying for a job he found open in Bangor, Maine. His moral indignation, although not erasing it, abetted obfuscation of the disturbing turmoil of the depravity deep inside him.

As an adult, Kevin's voice seemed forced out of a paper bag and made him sound like a thug, but his slight build belied that image. Even his service hat seemed oversized and he was sure it made him look more like a comical Barney Fife he had seen on reruns than a policeman. He just tried not to wear his uniform hat when he could get away with it.

He seldom spoke and seldom, if ever, raised his voice, unaware of how his bass voice and dead-level, tacit calm involuntarily placed him into an authoritative position. Early on he was often amazed when people did what he asked. He learned to allow himself to be underestimated, using it to his advantage.

After Kevin moved and began working out of Bangor, he didn't think like an unconcerned Mainer; he was another kind of stoic. He consciously analyzed everything to discover what the easiest solution was to control the situation or solve the problems that might arise, to plot, and to avoid discovery—with avoiding discovery permeating his total being. This quiet, even personality only convinced Beth, who many people, including Kevin himself, thought was above him, that the two belonged together.

Kevin learned Beth's dark history from her, but now, unrecognizable to anyone who might have seen her in Bermuda, Beth, five years older, was commanding, beautiful, confident, and outgoing, and, in fact, dominated her surroundings. Of the two, Kevin felt she was the face, the communicator.

Unlike many of her peers who were sucked in by uniforms, especially in her world of uniforms, Beth said that wasn't what drew her to Kevin. When she met him out of uniform that time in Bangor, she said she was in love with him before she even knew. And later, she said, because of his straightforward, solid, faithful nature, she had confirmed that this was no fluke.

Reminiscing today reminded Kevin of meeting her, who, in the meantime since her return from Bermuda, had studied and, attaining the qualifications to become an emergency medical technician, began doing ambulance runs out of Worcester, Massachusetts. She had a purpose. She was good. Then on a first-aid training conference in Bangor, back in October 1997, around Halloween, she had gone out for dinner by chance the same beautiful night as Kevin.

In The Taste of India restaurant that night, she with her new-found friend Susie and two other nurses had sat at the next table, where Kevin sat with three cop drinking-buddies. The room of ten tables was full, but the atmosphere had been pleasantly subdued as he sat himself.

Kevin had often observed that it only took one loud person in a restaurant to make the whole room echo as each person had to speak over the loudest voice to be heard, one louder voice stacking on another. Now he regretfully saw that this one obstreperous person sat at his own table. Rick, not only the biggest of the four guys, but the loudest, had a voice that couldn't whisper.

"Hey, guys, you seen the table behind me? Filled with babes in just the right number."

Kevin was disconcerted, not just that the women at the table could hear Rick, but so could the whole restaurant. Kevin had sometimes conjectured that there was a connection between dumb and loud. He saw how the muscle boys in the gym were always yelling to each other even when they were two feet apart and he had always wanted to put up a sign in the gym saying, "Danger! Too much muscle makes you deaf."

Roger with the thick eyebrows, who sat on Kevin's left, seemed to be anticipating pouncing on any opportunity with the girls as his leg began shaking like a scratching dog and vibrating the whole table.

Funny, goofy-looking Henry, sitting with his back to the women said, "Roger, calm down. Down boy."

"Hey, waiter," Rick bellowed. "Bring us a round of Bud Light." Referring to the Calcutta beer that they had been drinking, he said, "This India stuff doesn't hack it." Turning in his chair, he said, "You girls want a beer or something?"

While Henry made a mouth-twisting funny face and Roger grinned, Kevin, head bowed, looked out of the corners of his eyes to study how people reacted.

The women at the table looked at each other as if to figure out whether to even respond and, if so, who?

Kevin glanced around the room and saw that people had stopped whatever they were doing—eating, talking, reading—and seemed to be waiting for the reaction.

Forced to give an answer, one of the women said, "No, thanks," and, although they tried to restart their previous conversation, they were deterred by the sense that the whole restaurant was silently listening.

"Well, that went over well," Rick said loudly.

Kevin knew, when the beers came, Rick was not going to get any quieter, but he was at a loss as to what he could do to stave off embarrassment, other than get up and leave. He sneaked a quick look at Beth who, to his astonishment, was smiling at him. He tried to look away, but couldn't. He felt out of place and extrinsic; she was the most beautiful woman in the room. Then she raised her wine glass and gave a small nod.

Roger's heavy eyebrows lifted as he said, "Hey, Kevin, I saw that. Tell her your Halloween story."

If there had been a rug, Kevin felt he would have belonged under it, but only after he stained that rug with Roger's blood. Why would he suddenly tell her the Halloween story?

Rick said loudly, "I'll tell a Halloween story."

Kevin sensed a roomful of gritted teeth.

Rick said, "So this couple dresses up in Halloween costumes. He dresses up as a big ugly bug and she dresses up as a nipple, so they could go out ticking and teating." He looked around the table, hopefully, but the whole room had gone silent.

Then Beth said in a louder voice than necessary, "Hey, girls, you want to hear what a nine-one-one call sounds like in Maine?"

Kevin could almost see the guys' ears perk up in unison. The women at Beth's table giggled. One of them said, "Sure."

"Okay." In a singsong Beth said, "One ringie-dingie! Two ringie-dingies! *Nine-one-one Emergency Help. What is your problem?*" She lowered her tone to sound masculine. "The voice on the other end, sounding like he is in huge pain, says *Can you send emergency help?*" Singsong voice again. "The 911 operator says, *Yes, I can.*"

Kevin was taken by her ability to change voices, use the right timing, and keep a straight face. She had paused to let the subsequent silence sink in, until somebody off in a corner seemed to get it and laughed.

Then she said, "The caller screams *Please, hurry! Call me an ambulance. The 911 operator says, Okay, you're an ambulance.*"

The women laughed; the guys groaned. Kevin observed.

Then Henry and Rick chimed in. "Yeah, so Kevin, we all want to hear your Halloween story." And now suddenly, so did the women at the next table.

Now he was sure the whole room was listening. The worst was that he not only loved to tell the story, but with Beth telling a joke and he having consumed enough beer to luckily snaffle the horse of his horse sense, the encouragement made him blurt out, "Okay, okay."

There was sparse applause around the room.

He didn't stand up, but the room went silent in anticipation of a Halloween ghost story.

Basking in the room's attention, Rick in his non-whisper said to the room, "This is a great story."

"Shut up, Rick," Henry said.

Kevin began. "Okay, okay, I don't know if this story is true, but this is what I know. There's this abandoned center or maybe you'd call it a community down the road from where I used to live in Massachusetts called Devilsville."

"Yeah! Devilsville!" Rick barked.

There were some *shushes* around the room. Somebody in the room said, "Stand up."

The new order of beer came. The crowd was getting into it. Kevin glanced at Beth. He flushed, but he pushed his chair back, going along with it, just so that he could see Beth better. She smiled broadly at him. He gave her a quick, almost indiscernible grin.

He said, "Some clever scientist, a biologist or something, had learned to read messages in DNA like history records."

Kevin's heart was racing as she seemed to be so focused on him—not hearing him—just holding him in her visual grip.

"He could read them in insects, animals, and humans."

Like you are reading me, he thought.

"So, somehow, he had heard the story about an old murder in Devilsville, and because it was a place that had been long abandoned and isolated enough, he thought historical stuff might be preserved in the bugs and things living there now and the people who had lived there before."

Kevin realized that the distraction of Beth's beauty was screwing up his storytelling. He would have gone into detail and acting it out a bit as he knew he could easily transmit fear into the listeners, but now he just wanted to hurry through it. To sit down. To concentrate on Beth.

"As he, the scientist guy, collected flies and hunted down some people who used to live there and checked their DNA, a story began to show up. For him, it was like reading an old rotten manuscript with holes in it, like the Dead Sea Scrolls, or something. But the story he found was about two people who had fallen in love and wanted to marry and live together."

"Aaaw! Cute." Kevin heard a female voice behind him say.

"But the local people did not approve of this relationship..."

Rick emoted a hammy dejected sigh.

"...maybe because of jealousy or maybe it was a gay couple or something. It wasn't clear from the DNA. The disapproving villagers spread horrible stories about these two, which, like all gossip, just got worse, and became so horrible that the whole village turned against them.

"Then one day the villagers had a big feast at the church. Everybody came to the field behind the church except this outcast couple. It turns out, the same somebody that had arranged the feast had murdered the couple and cooked them in a stew which the whole village ate."

Groans circled the room. Kevin glanced at Beth again. His words seemed to come from somewhere else. His mind was talking to her.

"It was not clear whether the villagers knew what they were eating, but since the story spread through the DNA of everything and everyone the way it did. The flies had feasted too. The scientist was able to detect the same DNA remnants of the victims in the flies as in the families of the past locals. It was probable that everyone knew the main ingredient."

A wave of grimacing sounds rippled around the room, except for Beth, who just looked at Kevin with a grin on her face. And they stared at each other like the room was empty.

It was at that moment that Beth and Kevin somehow transmitted the desire to leave the Indian restaurant, to vanish, without explanation or finishing the story, if there was more to tell. And, importantly, out of gratitude, he consciously erased his antagonism toward Roger.

In the following weeks and months, he, who had barely experienced anything other than touching a girl's body at a chaperoned high school dance, got the lesson of his life in pleasure. And Beth, who had no inhibitions any longer, was now in a dream world of loving the person with whom she was, as she liked to call it, petting the cat. She would climax uncontrollably, almost at his touch, but often thirteen, fourteen, fifteen times, something that she had never done once before in her two years of self-loathing not so many years earlier, and which Kevin had never known was possible.

And what struck Kevin the most, he who had always felt he owed respect to almost anyone—except the chosen few—was the startling inappropriateness of leaving his buddies at the restaurant, taking Beth home, and, without either one of them speaking, jumping into bed. Both knew it was right and never had to explain it to each other, nor did either of them feel the need to excuse himself to their restaurant acquaintances, who were, after all, just acquaintances in a new environment.

More seriously Kevin and Beth were in love, first in the obvious thralls of Eros and now later each in their own way. Beth's agape love still seemed oceanic. Kevin grew into it over the years steeped by Beth's adoring immersion in blind devotion.

Early in their relationship, Beth had told him her story, not asking for pity, but for praising the people who had helped her and to be sure he would still want to be with her with such an immoral past. Although her herpes seemed to have regressed, she had told him about that, too. He had found both her and her story mystifying and exciting and had become even more convinced that he wanted to spend the future getting to know her. He told her a redacted version of his past, but her love made her think he had told her everything.

She was only happy to move from Massachusetts as far from her family as possible. And worse yet, inexplicably because she remembered nothing about that time, local rumors about her prostitution had begun to arise around her childhood home. To her delight, because of the need for personnel at the Eastern Maine Medical Center in Bangor, she could demand to follow Kevin's shift schedule so they could have a life together.

Beth felt no affinity to anyone, neither there in Bangor nor back in Newburyport. So when they married at the city hall in Bangor led by a baggy-panted female JP smelling unshowered and of cheap cigarettes, Beth invited no one but Florie to attend but who declined, lacking the finances to make such a trip. Instead, Florie sent a tourist book about Bermuda with a pressed Golden Chalice bloom and a newspaper obituary about the death of Jason Hutchins.

Kevin just invited his three drinking buddies. Both he and Beth were hoping to be able one day to thank Joe, whoever he was, for being her savior.

* * *

Kevin knew that the incongruity of his State Trooper Impala cruiser, sitting this Friday morning like one more discarded piece of junk in the Maine woods, might have been construed in so many ways by an observer. Was he on watch to catch a clandestine drug deal? Was he part of a drug deal? After all, he was too far off the road to set a speed trap. But he didn't care.

Kevin's eyes were almost closed and his young thin face had a solemn grin. With his crew-cut head at an odd angle, over and over he would begin to snore and then his head would jerk up again. In his waking moments, he had noticed the sparrows had accepted his presence, leading the way for other birds and a squirrel and even a young moose, smelling the salt in the car's paint, gave the car a close inspection. He thought that his squeaking vibrant snoring or quick movements would have scared the animals, but they seemed to understand it was just a small moving part of this stationary aberration.

After a night of beer and watching the Celtics, Kevin was doing his well-practiced napping, having often napped while on duty. Being the noob, he got the worst shifts, so he had learned how to sneak some sleep, even though today, for the first time, he was on day shift. Consequently, he had forgotten to roll down the windows for air. And now the suffocating heat and his own breath stench began to disgust him. The stale air made him open all the windows, immediately eliminating the possibility of any further napping as Maine's giant mosquitoes began their sibilating bloodthirsty invasion.

Trying to wake up fully while waving and slapping at the annoying bugs, he regretted that he had to stop his daydreaming. He loved to reminisce, in fact to dwell often, on Beth.

But now…

In his old age, under completely different circumstances, Kevin would think back on the next minutes and how he had not been, by any means, a theorist. But if he had been, a foreign conception for him this morning might have been that, if for some reason he had decided to climb on top of his car and had fallen off here in the woods, he could well have hurt himself. But if time was also dimension, could he have fallen off time and hurt himself? By going through this enigma and possessing a bit of introspection, being a theorist perhaps, Kevin will muse, might have prepared him for what was about to happen.

Squinting at his watch, he saw that he should be getting back out on the road, but he put it off just a few more seconds, executing a potentially bug-trapping yawn, in an attempt to better wake up. Suddenly, just as Kevin was starting the car to get back out on Route 52, the short hair on his neck rose and fear turned strands of his crewcut grey. Instinct took over; he, the young stoic, was immediately all cop.

Kevin had heard an explosive crash of such enormity it could be nothing other than a head-on vehicle collision on nearby Route 52 from which he had exited to take his nap and now had planned to return.

He had been in enough situations that he knew what happened in his mind during an emergency. Although some people go blank, panic, and forget the details, Kevin's mind slowed everything down to where fractions of seconds became minutes, and his mind analyzed each tick of a microsecond and packed them into the hippocampus of his brain.

And so, he saw a crushed red pickup truck, seemingly ignoring gravity, rolling end-over-end toward him. His accelerated mind's first thought was to wonder if he would be blocked in, on the wrong side of the truck. His whole future was suddenly thundering toward him in the form of this pickup truck's destruction, and his planned future was about to be destroyed with no good explanation in any report as to why he had been on the wrong side of this vehicle when he should have been arriving at the accident scene, after the fact, from the road. There would be no way to explain how he got here. No promotions. No detective. No money for Beth.

The pickup continued thundering toward him like the animation of a bouncing toy, end-over-end and, according to his intuitive visual measurement, would land, no doubt, exactly on top of his cruiser. He calmly decided that if he died now, he deserved it.

One more bounce closer. Would Beth miss him? Or would she think he was an idiot because he had been napping? At this millisecond, the Ford pickup (he could see the emblem) was descending on top of him.

He did not blink. He was serene. He would die in peace, without fear, die with an acceptance of his fate. No religious sentiment that transforms death from a normal fact of daily life into an awful nightmare passed through his mind. Someone older might have looked at death as a relief from the diminishment of old age, but for him, death meant nothing to him at that moment, only that Beth might miss him.

Someone who still had a specific minute section of his brain less touched by childhood anger and bitterness, and had not defensibly grown a sealed impermeable shell around that small temporo-parietal junction, might have felt regret for vengeful murders.

A flicker of darkness. He was on both sides. Another flicker. He was on both sides of the red pickup. The flicker extended to seconds and it was perfectly clear to him that both he and his car were on both sides of the descending wreck at the same time for one moment. At that moment he was infinite.

And then he was past the wreck—on the highway side, his car untouched—where he should have been. How that could be possible no longer mattered to him. But that's what he remembered.

4. CRICKET

THAT FRIDAY MORNING

SITTING ON THE EDGE OF THE MARINA FUEL DOCK FEELING THE COLD GREEN OF THE dark ocean while eating an early morning breakfast of questionable nutrition from the hotel up the road, I can't help but savor how it is a thousand times better than sanatorium food.

Meanwhile in anticipation of his imminent arrival, I create my mother's story, letting my mind run through the scene the way I think he must have experienced it:

The ice pick held under his chin was drawing blood, dripping on his best shirt. He tipped his head back, as far as he could, to try to stop the fucking pain. And he thinks he actually felt something that he had never experienced. Fear. Probably.

Here he was, sitting parked in his new little Daewoo that evening outside the house in Salem, Mass, listening to the news of planes crashing into the World Trade Center. The streets are empty because people are hunching at home to get more news.

A black-clothed, masked figure, from what he could see in the mirror, slips in the back door behind him and, before he can think, immediately drops a restrainer around him and jabs the goddamn point of an ice pick into his chin.

Click! A mechanical male voice close to his ear says, "Sit very still or I will jam this ice pick so deep into your skull, if you are not dead, you will wish you were. Get it?"

Nodding is not the move he should make. He got it all right. He smells something, but his mind can't think what it is right now.

Click! The voice goes on. "Since you cannot seem to understand, I am here to explain to you how you will act with your son and your ex for the future. If you do not follow my instructions, you will again wish you were dead."

Above the car radio he can distinguish a faint mechanical hum.

"Number one. You will stop seeing your son.

"Second. You will pay support of two thousand five hundred dollars per month to your ex's bank account to support him and her until your ex writes a note that she does not need the money anymore.

"Have you understood?" Click!

He tightens his body against the restraint to avoid nodding and to help release the hellish pain of the whole fucking thing. He smelled moth balls. That's what it was.

Click! "Any failure to follow this will have consequences. Do not ever try to contact your ex again."

He hears the hum and nervous breathing next to his ear.

"Do not try to call the police. They will only laugh at you."

With the final click of some mechanism, the asshole leaves the car, leaving the door open, and disappears, releasing the restrainer, which was simply a blanket sewn into a band, locking him defenselessly in place while the invader steps on it behind the seat. Simple. Smart. Yeah, is he pissed!

Other than lifting off the band and shutting off the radio to have silence, he didn't want to move for some time. How long? Long enough to get blood on all his clothes, the car seat, and the floor. Long enough to wonder who it might have been. The breathing seemed feminine.

The ex-cunt herself didn't have it in her.

It is not perfect weather today, not for sailors, I mean. Hot, cloudy. Super humid. Not a wisp of wind. Even the clouds are motionless. A smooth ocean, which, of course, makes it easy for the docking process that most powerboaters flub.

Here, along the coast of New England, the seafarers who have survived the dark ocean's treachery have derisively baptized coastal islands with names like Misery, The Graves, and Coffin Rock. The ocean's impenetrable currents of madness are part of me, I think because my brother got locked away.

Jim, a retired freighter captain, and I pretty much run this marina on the tip of New Hampshire for the hotel owners up the road. Most regulars don't know my real name, because…I think Jim started it. No, maybe I called him "Jiminy" first, so he called me "Cricket," it doesn't matter; the two of us are known as Jiminy and Cricket.

He handles the money stuff; I handle the people stuff. I have summer boaters, fall sailors, beer socializers, and sometimes occasional daughters of the yacht owners, who without much competition, gravitate to me, discard their inhibitions by the romantic sea, and love my poetry describing my darkest thoughts, letting me escape them.

Mostly, I go out of my way to deal with people and their sailing vessels within the tight quarters of the docks and, out to sea within the tighter quarters of their boats and their minds. I've been told that my imagination is spectacular and that my stories are mesmerizing. This studied, purposeful extroversion outside of my head puts a lid on what's in it, until Mama sends me a link to Sunday's obituary for my grandmother—the abused one—by her son, my father.

Last week Jiminy mentioned something that I had missed. That, on his way up to Penobscot Bay past Portland, it has become a habit the last three weeks for someone named Dan Lodovico to stop at our marina in Wentworth to gas up his yacht, a British-made Fairline Targa 52-foot thing with two inboard 615-horsepower Volvo engines.

It's Friday and normally I'm on, but I told Jiminy that I had arranged to hitch a ride on this yacht up to Portland and that I would take care of the docking and fueling procedure for Mr. Lodovico today, then return this evening.

I emphasized Portland so Jiminy would swear that's what I said.

The stifling early morning is so quiet that I think I can hear the yacht's low rumble coming an hour away. But then, of course, Jiminy has warned me of the arrival because Lodovico always makes sure that he follows protocol by reporting his vessel's whereabouts.

As he pulls up to the fuel dock, I stand ready expecting him to look toady with long, dark full hair, a picture I guess I must have built through time. Actually, he is quite handsome or maybe, on second thought, self-important looking, standing like he has back problems, rigid in his East Coast sailing outfit—tan slacks, white shirt, two-tone leather boat shoes, and obligatory yellow sweater, which he surely, in New England fashion, ties around his neck when at the bar. But then again I think he's too old to be hanging around in bars.

Being the day it is, he isn't wearing sunglasses, and thus, the kind-looking old gentleman image that might have been, disappears when I see his eyes. His hair is unknowable since he is wearing a Red Sox baseball cap, which I hate, because, regrettably, so am I.

He's definitely organized. He has the fenders out and, having the midline ready, he tosses it to me. I cleat it to the dock, and I see that he has both a bow and a stern line ready within reach. I use the stern line.

He shuts down the motors, lifting the oppressing, growling sound blanket.

"Welcome, Mr. Lodovico. Fill 'er up?"

"You know who I am?" He frowns, sort of. The eyes are black holes. And then he smiles broadly.

Careful, Cricket, what you say.

I start the diesel filling since he doesn't stop me. "Of course. You are a regular here."

"I don't think I'm that regular." His smile is disarming.

I say, "Hey *Deliverance*. That's quite a name for a motor yacht. Usually a guy names the lady after his lady."

No response.

"Tell you what," I say. "I'd like to go below to check your filters. Permission to board?" I put my hand on the stern rail, tapping a finger to the pinging rhythm of the diesel pump, ready to pull myself aboard via the swim platform.

"What are you going to do?" He presents the faint frown again about a second and then back to the friendly face.

"Like I said, check your filters."

He seems doubtful. "Yeah, okay."

As he glowers at me with shadowed eyes under the cap's bill, I feel like a lab rat working my way from the aft swim platform, up steps, through the sun deck, to the center cockpit, and like that rat, without greeting him, I scurry down the companionway steps using the handrails.

I survey the impeccably clean, orderly, or better said, sterile cold white fiberglass salon, teak floor, red plastic cabinet doors, a teak door to the aft cabin and, by the steps, the door I enter to the engine room. I play solitaire on my phone for about five minutes, and come back up.

"Mr. Lodovico," I say. "You had junk in your fuel lines." I hold up a picture I had prepared on my phone. "I've cleaned your filters, but something's probably in your tanks. Dirty diesel maybe. It could be no problem, but I have a suggestion."

"Oh?" He avoids looking straight at me. More like focuses on my T-shirt. Inspecting the NOAA logo? Or wondering, correctly, if I slept in it?

"Yeah, I need to get up to Portland and you might need my services. I know these Volvo engines frontwards and backwards. I'll do a trade-off. You take me with you and I will service your boat for nothing if something happens along the way."

He is silent for a moment. With a hint of a facial expression, he says, "But I'm not going to Portland." He almost sounds sorry.

"You're headed for Penobscot, right?"

"Penobscot. How'd you know I was going to Penobscot?" His glaring intensity is disturbing, as it is a leaping double-flip-with-a-half-twist from his smile.

"We hear your reports. You are a careful, responsible captain, Mr. Lodovico."

"I don't have time to detour into Portland, sorry."

"Oh, you don't have to," I say. "You can drop me off anywhere in the bay or up the river. My girl said she would rather pick me up there than drive all the way down here. And, importantly, for you, I can check on your engines."

"I've never had a problem before." Again he avoids looking at me.

"Lucky you," I say. I wait. I sense doubt.

Don't look desperate, Cricket.

"Do what you want. I sure would appreciate your help, though. And so would my girl." Again I wait.

The rat now has a bird of prey scrutinizing him in silence.

"My name is actually *Ludo*vico, not Lodovico."

So you changed the pronunciation of your name? Big fucking deal.

"Oh, sorry about that. Maybe they got it wrong in the office here."

"That's okay." Again, while staring at me and stretching the doubt, he unburies, "Okay, you can come."

"I'll bring us some beer and snacks," I say, as calmly as my exhilaration will allow me.

As I climb back onto the dock, he says matter-of-factly, "I'm in a hurry, and I don't drink while I'm sailing."

"Well, that's proper and correct of you, Mr. *Ludo*vico. I prepared some stuff just in case. I got my backpack right here." I drop my backpack on his deck, idiotically hoping it will keep him from running off without me. "And I'm ready to go when you are, as soon as you're all tanked up." I have the thought that I was ready a little too fast. Too enthusiastic. He doesn't seem to notice.

"It's hot, huh?" I say.

He doesn't smile. His eyes are practically the only clue that he has real emotions. "Yeah, it's cooler out a bit."

"So why the trip up to Maine?"

"Escape."

The diesel pump pinging punctuates the awkward silence.

"What's your name again?" he asks me. Back to the smile.

"Cricket. Everybody calls me Cricket."

What's with this again bit?

"What's your real name?"

"Eric."

"And your last name?"

"Larsen," I lie. "Norwegian background, three generations ago they came over to America...hungry."

The pinging stops.

"Okay. Your tanks are full." I screw on the cap and inspect the meter. "That'll be one thousand four hundred and thirty."

He has wandered down to the lower deck prepared to hand me his Visa card, so I run the fifty-some feet over to Jiminy in the office shed. Luckily the card reader works. Later, I realize Jiminy greets me, but my brain's too full of crap to hear. I still have this irrational fear that Lodovico will change his mind and run off without me even if I have his card *and* he is tied to the fuel dock.

I see he has changed his name spelling even on his card. Sticking it in my back pocket, I trot back sweating like a banshee in the damp heat. I will not be smelling like flowers.

He's back in the cockpit. I untie the center line and throw it on board. To let the bow drift out for easier exit, I pull the stern line a bit before climbing aboard. He turns the key and the twin engines' grumbling roar shocks the nature out of the air.

I give him a grin as I hand back his card. Up close I get a whiff of his charm when he gives me the singular masculine nod covering both "Thanks for getting the yacht pointed in the right direction" and relief at getting his credit card back.

I immediately hold up my backpack and point below to show I need to put the pack down in the cabin. As he begins swinging the brute away from the fuel dock, his head nods permission while the eyes don't.

As I descend the steps, I have to shake my head. He is one difficult character to read. If I didn't know. Thinking about it, why he even let me on board is kind of strange, but, having no backup plan, I'm lucky my little emotional plea worked on someone like him.

While I'm below, I recheck what I need, pulling all the items out, one by one, placing them on the galley's red Formica countertop, making sure I forgot nothing. Two plastic grocery bags to wrap my pants and socks, sea socks, swim trunks, Ziploc, a small glass jar with scallops, and one can of Heineken.

In about two hours, I will need to begin. Timing is everything, but I think I have it figured pretty well. The harbor is 110 nautical miles up the coast. We will average 20 to 30 knots. So we have little over a three-hour trip.

I place everything back into the bag in the right order. God, when have I ever kept order in anything? But this time...this once...yes. I need to stay cool; no distractions.

I control the galley dish situation, check how the microwave works, go up on deck, neaten up the stern line, and sit in the social area behind the cockpit to wait...away from him. Even if he has his autopilot programed and could, thus, be free to socialize, I have understood that any communication between us has to squeak through a narrow hole.

Once he feels that the yacht's speed and direction are set, he wanders below to use the head or whatever he thinks he needs to do. I sit as calm as a leopard, looking out over the glassy water, the receding shoreline, and the grey sky, as if it were all interesting.

My brain's film camera goes to work:

Forward little shit. This kid has pushed his way on board, no doubt about that.

Eric Larsen, a brown-eyed, sneaky-looking young man…tall, lanky, with no way of looking him up on the internet with such a common name.

The cap doesn't hide the kid's hair. Unkept, dark, greasy, and worse was the beard. What kind of kid has a beard these days? Probably gay.

Unemployable. Okay on the docks. Marina workers were always sort of lazy leftovers, into drugs probably, couldn't be so skinny otherwise.

The biggest hesitation about letting this kid on board is his obvious sloppiness. He could dirty up things fast…maybe even try to smoke something…burn a hole somewhere. Look how he just dropped his backpack on the floor, but not much else out of order below except the remnants of his repulsive body odor. Probably why he's called a dirty bug.

The more I think about it, the more I regret saying yes to the little tick. But, done is done.

He is right about the air being cooler out to sea a bit. Once we get away from the land, the summer heat wall ends abruptly and the cold northern sea air grabs hold. He's put on a fancy-brand white sailing jacket. Offered nothing, I use the folded blanket he has on the seats to keep warm.

I try to put my mind on hold by looking for the dogfish that feed and breed on the glassy surface. The air seems cooler and the clouds thicker as we travel north.

But my curiosity keeps growing and I have to pee. Dumping the blanket, I wander forward, passing close in front of him, thinking it will get his attention. But, sitting on the side bench in the cockpit looking at his tablet thingy, he doesn't bother to look up.

"Excuse me, Mr. Ludovico, but I was admiring your boat…or should I say, yacht." He looks halfway up, at my belt, I guess. "I know it's a really expensive toy. Are you a doctor, or something?"

He begins with the annoyed eyes, but the flattery sinks in enough to uncloak the smile. After a pause, he says, "No, I'm in banking."

"Oh, wow," I say. "You must be high up in the ranks, right?"

"Well, sort of." He hesitates. "I help nonprofit trusts handle their money."

"God! You must feel good about helping those nonprofits to grow. That's important and a nice thing."

As the birdbrain puffs up his feathers, he says casually, "Yeah, it's rewarding if you do it right."

"Well, you must be doing it right." Indicating the boat, I say, "Just look at this thing."

Most normal people would want to continue talking about themselves and their successes, but he goes back to his reading like we never spoke. Chopped off, I wander on down to the head, flabbergasted by how his mind works.

5. JOE

THAT FRIDAY MORNING

BEFORE THEY LEAVE, JOE JUST HAD TO HAVE ONE MORE LOOK AT THE DEAD THING in the water.

Martin said, "Come on, honey, let's go. I don't want to be late."

"Do you know, Martin, I read that Matinicus Rock, a small uninhabited island about twenty miles off Penobscot Bay here, is the only known North American nesting site of the puffin?"

"That's great, Joe, but we gotta go."

Joe was not sure why Martin was so worried about the time. It was only a four-hour drive home. It was terribly early. They didn't even have to stop along the way to deliver the keys.

While walking along the cliff edge, Joe sang loudly,

"I'm coming. I'm coming.

For my head is bending low.

I hear Professor Martin calling

Ol' gay Joe."

Getting no response, Joe shouted, "Okay, I'm coming, Professor. Just a minute."

He had to see what happened. Last night, after Martin went to sleep, Joe had wandered outside to think. A dead something-or-other had been there in last night's dim light, reminding him of a big white belly or the reflection of a wet colorless moon in the water. He really was curious this morning what the hell it had been. But, as he scanned the water's edge and along the boat dock, he could tell that it was gone. Washed away. Or eaten by something.

While he stared down at the shoreline, his irritation at having to leave this place so early got to him.

He mumbled aloud to himself, with a yearning loudness that he hoped Martin could hear or, at least, sense. "So where's the big birthday plan? We just lock up the cabin that I went out of my way arranging, to find someplace special and different for your birthday from our dangerous Provincetown summer house. I go through Angie's List in detail for hours and find this beautiful place on the Maine shoreline at Orcutt Cove in Penobscot Bay. Wednesday we're late arriving, and, after one measly day, you are eager to get home to Boston by eight p.m. No sweat. Early or late, so? Good choice, Joe.

"No sweat, Professor," he yelled. "No sweat! I'm coming!"

So something had died. Just died and vanished. Is that the way it is? That something exists and then doesn't?

The peeps of a few terns interrupted the ocean's rhythmic foamy rippling against the stony shore, sounding like frying hash browns in a greasy spoon. The only life he could see now were dragonflies and damselflies. The smell of petrichor painted his nostrils.

He felt ugly. He had worked so hard to be in shape, to keep his goatee well-trimmed and to reduce his underbite. He cultivated a full mustache, had kept his dark hair beautifully coiffed and trimmed to be presentable when they were out together. Did Martin even notice his finely toned body anymore?

Last night, late into the night, they had spent talking. Joe, in his reading, often expounded on a subject to such a degree that Martin, the professor, had to admit that he had not put his mind to that matter. In fact, to Joe, because of Martin's narrow focus, Martin seemed ignorant of many things. They had begun talking about Paris and their multiple trips there.

"So, Martin, why do you think Paris drew writers, artists, and creative minds from around the western world through time?"

Martin had been half-asleep in his overstuffed chair and didn't seem to care to answer.

Joe had continued. "You remember when we visited the Dali exposition? We saw a governess or primary teacher telling stories to these little kids about Dali and his art. The look on the kids' faces; they were enthralled. I said at the time that in America the kids would be running around the show wild, pissing everyone off. But the French kids were sitting captivated and getting culture pumped into their blood as tiny tots…into their DNA like tiny dots. Am I a poet or what?"

Martin still had his eyes open.

Joe said, "And why did the ignorant murderers choose Paris to indiscriminately shoot to kill? I know they mistakenly wanted to start a Muslin uprising. But these poor victims are dead and gone. Dead for no reason. So why do you think the Medici supported artists and left such a cultural treasure trove in Italy and around Europe?"

Scooting back in his chair a bit, Martin said, "Okay, I am not sure what the connection is between killing people and the Medici. Were you checking to see if I was awake?"

"*Were* awake," Joe corrected.

"Oh, come on. Enough with the grammar examination. First you are wrong and secondly I was listening. Usually, you just throw in 'Your mother wears army boots' to see if I'm listening."

"So?" Joe said.

Frowning, Martin replied, "My mother wears army boots."

"No, I mean, so why would the Medici blow their fortune on culture?"

Martin said, "I suppose it was part of their culture, their DNA as you said. And what else were they going to do with all that money?"

Joe said, "What do Americans today do with all their money? There are people in America who are just as rich, but they don't patronize sculptors. You have a few people like the guy Ludovico, who owns this place we're renting. He is one huge philanthropist. You ever heard of the guy?

"I got curious when I saw this stunning place listed for rent. He's the kind of guy you wish all rich people were. He gives a huge percentage of his money for practical use like school building and health facilities all over the world.

"You're right that we are missing the cultural indoctrination at birth. But more than that and besides that, the Medici did not want to be forgotten. Notice that we, present-day people, still talk about the Medicis in a favorable manner despite their money and their cruelty like never will happen with the Koch brothers."

Martin fell asleep on the sofa.

Now today, Joe noticed that Martin had changed his clothes and was looking his most handsome in a tight black T-shirt, cherry-red silk Bermudas, and his best Italian loafers without socks. The curves of Martins lips still made Joe's spine tingle. Now he had never felt so plain, or maybe downright hideous.

"Are you talking to yourself down there? Joe, I don't want to be late. I've locked up. I've put the key under the mat for Ludovico. Let's go."

Feeling, but not hearing, the notes of a chipping woodchuck or the chirping sparrows. Feeling, but not noticing, the uneven earth under his L.L.Bean boots, Joe trudged slowly up the slanting wilderness landscape the fifty feet to the car.

He was shorter than Martin and, although brawny, he had the feeling of being diminutive, and at the same time, he had never felt so heavy, so tired. He said, "Did you put the key under the mat for Ludovico?"

Martin said, "I already told you that. Let's go!"

Joe had already packed the travel bag in the trunk of Martin's Volvo C-70 convertible, and, as usual, Joe drove. They both agreed that too often Martin goes off into another world and forgets that he's driving.

They were silent for the hour it takes to reach Belfast.

Martin, still irritated, said, "Have you ever considered how much time a person spends not using his brain? Especially waiting for another person who has locked you in place with a late arrival, making you wait? That person leaves you in a vacuum unable to add anything to your life or your mind except annoyance."

Joe did not answer, well aware of the scolding; heard it before and before that. As he drove out of Belfast Center, Joe said, "Sorry, Martin, for being so quiet. I think I am just sad to leave. Now I see I've taken a wrong turn."

"What?"

"Yeah, I missed the intersection with the route three turn-off. Now we're on route fifty-two."

"So turn around."

"Nah, come on. Use your GPS on the phone. I'm sure there's a road back to three."

Martin groaned. "There's no signal up here, dummy. We are in never-never land for phone connection; you know that. So turn around."

"Come on. We've got time. We'll find a sign to three and in the meantime, we'll see some real Maine countryside."

"You mean yard refrigerators?"

They drove along through Martin's silent annoyance until Joe said, "I saw an osprey grab a bird out of the air this morning. It took the little thing, screaming, back to its nest to be torn apart and eaten."

"Nice," Martin said, sarcastically.

"It makes you think. What the hell? Here is this beautiful, admirable osprey, a hawk that's a bit rare, protected, that rips apart its living food."

Martin said, "At least it's fresh."

"You're sick. How can you even say something like that?"

Martin was silent for a while. "You know that I have a hard time taking life and death as something different or, for that matter, significant. Perhaps even real."

"Why? Because you study the universe? That makes us nothing?"

"It doesn't make us nothing. There is a huge difference between 'nothing' and 'insignificant.' In our insignificance, we can know and love each other. You give my life a purpose and an importance."

Joe smiled the corner-mouth smile of skepticism.

Martin continued. "If it wasn't for you, I feel all of my work would be for naught. My work points out that we are insignificant creatures in a giant collection of universes, while the tactile and emotional relationship we share lets me, and I hope you, know that I have some sort of significance."

Again, silence. Joe said, "What am I supposed to say?"

"That you love me, that we are together, and that it means something to you."

"This is cornier than usual. What's going on?"

"Nothing different," Martin said. "Just seldom expressed. How do we learn to express our feelings when we have had to put on an act since we were children? It becomes second nature to hide who we really are. Unlike any other animal.

"Someone said once that a cat is like a libertarian; thinking that it's the center of the universe, acting like it is completely independent and yet it is absolutely dependent. But a house cat is a cat and, comfortable in its own skin, acts like a cat. You and I have had to grow up the opposite. Our way of being, homosexuality, required complete loneliness, an imitation of others to hide our true selves, and not knowing how we should act.

"So how can we learn to express our feelings when we have never done it before? When is the time? When the emotions are bare? Unless some predator has torn apart its food and we have seen the basics of life."

Joe felt there was an answer to this, but he knew that Martin has an attitude. Not what one might call a bad attitude; more like a problem. Martin's attitude was that the only thing to do with good advice is to pass it on. It was never any use to Martin.

But Martin told Joe once in a weak moment that he, Martin, felt that he was too handsome, a victim of his own looks. As a result, he was always under suspicion. Obviously, it wasn't clear to people who were around him day-to-day that he was gay. He complained that he was unfairly accused by women—jealous women, he assumed—of womanizing, of deception, of flirtation, of degrading harassment of women with the slightest twist of his language or look in his eyes.

He had been told by one woman that her mother had warned her against him, to watch out for Martin. It had Martin stumped as to why, but it must have been a combination of eye and body language. Maybe he was too handsome and, therefore somehow implicitly untrustworthy. He was left a victim of his own appearance.

Then in that same moment of weakness, Martin said that maybe, he had misjudged himself and actually he was a pompous, arrogant dandy. But he concluded that he was unable to "fix" this, and besides he was attracted to men.

And worse yet, he was weak and obsessed. He was drawn to the unknown, the exotic, the mystery of a man, not knowing why or who this person was, but feeling that he could make that person adapt to his needs. Each affair began with doubt of its perfection, but he *knew* he could make it work. Each relationship fell apart. Joe was his longest.

Today Martin's first-time-ever sermon about love had alarms ringing in Joe's ears. The discomfort was so huge that he felt he'd better change the subject. Joe waited a few seconds and said, "Multi-universes. Explain that to me."

Martin tipped his head to one side in a gesture of uncertainty, if Joe was serious or maybe how to ever explain it to Joe. Or even if to try. "How can I explain it to you when I don't completely under-stand it myself?"

"So why do you believe there is more than one universe, as you say?"

"It is not so much a belief. It is what the math tells us has to exist if string theory exists. And string theory is not proven, but answers many of the mathematical uncertainties of a unified theory of the whole kit and caboodle."

"And so?"

"And so nothing."

Joe said, "So we are nothing?"

"That's not what I meant. I meant that after the unified theory is found—one single math formula that explains everything—we will know nothing, expect nothing…cannot, at this time, even guess."

"Why do you bother?"

Martin began to answer, stopped, and began again. "You're asking for my thesis. It's a long and complicated piece of work that I will be presenting next month. Why do you think I'm in a hurry to get back?

"I wouldn't attempt to explain it to you now, but I would say that it may be so revolutionary, so important that it will affect mankind's future in such a positive way that even I, the skeptic, have hope for the future."

"That big? What happens if you die before next month?"

Martin turned in the car seat toward Joe. "That's an odd question."

Joe said, "Not so odd. If this is going to change mankind, it is quite risky for you to be anywhere but in a bulletproof bubble. Is it on a computer file somewhere? Does anyone else have access to your material?"

Martin was quiet for a moment. "You know, in actual fact, I have not put any thought into that. It is highly encrypted on my computer in such a way that even the most clever MIT hacker is not supposed to be able to steal my material until I publish it. Let's just hope I manage another month." He laughed.

They were silent again.

Joe asked, "So can't you give me, the plebian neophyte, a summation?"

"I would just say that, instead of using some manmade religion to cover the unknowns, I have worked to discover how it all is. Big Bang does not answer it all by far. What about before? And before that?"

"Yeah, and so?"

"And so, that is where I am going."

They were quiet, listening to the wind as it roared past their ears, which Joe found annoying, but he knew Martin loved having the top down for some reason, probably just because, and Joe agreed, it looked cool the way Martin's hair blows. But Joe missed everything else. Nature. What about the animal sounds, the aroma of wild-flowers, and, not least, hearing the silence?

Attempting to cheer things up, Joe said, "I noticed that stars, con-stellations, and black holes get Latin names."

Martin glanced at Joe. "Yeah, a lot of the time."

"Well," said Joe with a grin, "I have a few names for black holes that maybe you discover."

Martin frowned. "I'm not an astronomer."

"How about Rectum or Anus? Wouldn't they be perfectly fitting Latin names for black holes?"

Martin tried to keep himself from grinning but said nothing.

"Or, as you discover more, you have Esophagus, and Uterus."

"Okay, enough," said Martin. "I have other things to think about."

To Martin, Joe said, "While we were up here, I was hoping for some intemperance and debauchery, so to speak. But I noticed none of that happened."

Martin frowned. "I don't understand."

"Something else you won't understand is that I hoped we could have our corn ground while we were up here. Also called horizontal refreshment. We didn't."

Joe paused, looking off into the woods just long enough to worry Martin about Joe's straying off the road.

"You know, as we were leaving, I looked for something in the water that had been there the night before. It was white, about the size of, I don't know, a big dog? A little dog? Anyway, a dog."

"And was it a dog?" Martin asked.

"What you may not understand is that I have no purpose. I had you to care for because you cared for me, but I sense that has changed. I can die as nothing, a zero, as most people do, and they are either happy because they live in a fantasy world or they are unhappy wondering why they bother with it all. We all die, so why not make death have a purpose?"

Yelling above the passing wind, Martin said, "You are not making sense."

"You must know what it is like to be nothing like anyone else; as lonely as a pig in a den of lions. You know I am not the least bit religious, but the happiest I had ever been, before meeting you, was sitting across from a queer priest in a P-town bar and knowing that he and I were equally lonely. But, at least, we were together lonely.

"But then the time shovel comes up behind us and cleans out our past where we once belonged, changing and erasing some of our identity."

6. ELLEN

THAT FRIDAY

"I'M COMING. I'M COMING."

As she passes over the Piscataqua River expansion bridge headed north into Maine, Ellen finds herself yelling in frustration over the motor and wind noise of the NOAA pickup they let her borrow. Windows down. No air conditioning. Just the hot engine pushing hotter air into the cabin and the smell of motor oil penetrating and tormenting her now-feverish cold. The gears require double-clutching; the pedals are just metal knobs bruising her feet.

Christ! Even her glasses are filthy with greasy fingerprints because she has to constantly push them up—no time to stop and clean them all the time.

"I hate glasses. I hate glaaaaasses!"

Talking aloud—even shouting—to herself somehow helps blunt the stabbings of guilt for her starting late—helps to push regret out of her direct line of sight. At least, a little.

The day is hot. How hot?

"How would I know? NOAA can't even afford a radio. How about just a little music?"

She doesn't actually remember, but her intense hatred of pickup trucks is not helping her mood, arising from her real mother abandoning Ellen as a toddler in her mother's pickup, time and time again. Ellen was too young back then for her to remember specifics now, but she does remember being taken away from her mother, being

127

sent to different homes, back to her mother, and then to a horrible number of more homes before she—at the age of six—met someone who cared enough for her that Ellen couldn't abuse and manipulate them with her tirades created by an amalgamation of her frustration and intelligence.

But now, driving this truck, years zero to six are subconsciously punching at her brain as this thing she is driving ignites the horrible memories. Even if she can't remember, the immediate discomfort tells her that she does.

* * *

Ellen's infant screams resound in her head: *Mama? Where are you? Mama?* And all she could do was cry herself to sleep in the shadowy pickup cabin alone on the plastic seat that smelled like Mama's vomit and sweat. Ellen can't remember how Mama looked, but that smell and the torment she remembers is now an ache in the back of her neck and the core of her gut.

Unsuccessful at trying not to shit herself, she got whacked for taking off her clothes while she was locked in the truck cabin, trying instinctively to rid herself of the stink and the mess. Shadows passed the truck in the night and ghostly faces peered in the windows, making her stop crying in trembling fear.

* * *

Today the intense heat, the horrible truck, and her fear of what Cricket is about to do make her yell at each of the cars she passes. Luckily the cars are few and far between. Right now, she yells at the old Buick in front of her, "Why do you farmers have to be on the road? Drive, you jerk! Get out of first gear! Jerkface!"

And her glasses need cleaning so badly.

* * *

And what year did she decide her foster parents, Rachel and Edgar, were unequivocally stupid? It was somewhere around 1990; she was in her early twenties or maybe exactly twenty. It wasn't the teenage thing when teenagers know everything and everyone else is stupid. She definitely had been through that period, too, when a part of her undeveloped brain kept her from filtering disfigured information. She fed into it and she would just regurgitate whatever. And "whatever" was all anyone needed to know as far as she was concerned.

Then the droll church psalms began to burrow into her spine.

"Rolly, polly, wholly. Good lord all flighty. God had three purses, wholly emm-pe-tee."

Her rebellious mindset probably started right there, sitting in the Presbyterian church pews, where she was forced to go every Sunday with dim-witted Rachel and Edgar and a senile grandmother, making up new words to the incessantly repetitive boring psalms. When was that? Early teens?

"You will not continue with this unholy nonsense," Edgar demanded. Ellen was sitting at the dining table for the Sunday greasy brunch. "I heard the blasphemous things you were doing and saying during church. If you continue with that, the Lord will not forgive you."

Ellen had begun to sift some of the dogma Edgar preached at home, somewhere along the line, as her literature and history classes began to give her wonderful information, interesting factoids, useful data. She loved school for all the reasons that freed her from the daily dump that Edgar poured on the family.

Ellen asked, "Forgive me for...?"

No response.

She was not letting it go this time. "Forgive me for what? Tell me, Edgar." She had stopped calling him Dad a short time back; she didn't consider him her father any longer. "You are so ignorant that you don't even know who John Locke or Pierce Bayle were, let alone that they and tons of other people were already questioning your dopey Christianity, way back in 1785."

Foster-mother Rachel exploded in her usual excessive lacrimation with a shriek and ran off to the bedroom.

"You are only a teenager," was ever his only response to anything he didn't like. And then he would hit Ellen where it hurt most—but didn't show. Rachel was probably the instigator, signaling when it was time to beat Ellen by shrieking and disappearing. Rachel knew he would hit Ellen, but Rachel always made a point of not being in the room when he did it, which was more and more often as Ellen rebelled.

But Ellen had no conscious awareness at that time about how her foster parents were smothering her. It was not until they wanted to pull her out of school, to homeschool her, that she began to wonder.

At first, she thought that might be a great idea. She was pregnant and she imagined that the students' opinion of her morality would decline in direct proportion to her increasing body size, but then it began to dawn on her that this house with its small rooms would become even smaller. The ugly flowered wallpaper would spill its ugly on her, and the cheap furniture would, like a vice, clamp around her, bruising her already-bruised body and squeezing the life fluids out of her and her unborn child.

On top of that, she would be trapped into listening to more of Edgar's ignorance of the world and the beatings would be more frequent. And she would actually be protecting them from the shame of having a pregnant teen daughter.

If Edgar was going to hurt her, she needed to try to skewer him where it hurt.

"You know what I have discovered, Edgar? I have discovered, Edgar, that ninety percent of all abortions are performed on Christian teenagers. You know why, Edgar? For two reasons. One is that kids like me, Edgar, don't have a clue about sex because you want to keep me barefoot and ignorant. Like Rachel."

He acted like he was not listening, wandering off to the bathroom and shutting the door.

She shouted through the door. "And the second reason, Edgar, that ninety percent of *ALL* abortions are done on Christian teenagers, is because their parents want to hide that their little angel is not perfect. She has been out fucking, Edgar. For that reason, Edgar, I am going to have this child and I am going to school whether you like it or not."

He flushed the toilet. And, of course, he followed her into her bedroom and he did his usual "You are only a teenager and you will do what we say." And he did his whacking on her where the marks wouldn't show.

But she was prepared for that response because she had spoken to the school principal, and yes, although worried about the principal's reaction to her pregnancy, she was less worried about him than about Edgar. She had shown the marks to the principal. That's when, exactly at that time, her predilection for school and enthusiasm for study became cemented and she became the nerd she is.

Edgar and Rachel did not succeed because the city of Lowell would not allow them to pull her out of school and they even threatened to remove Ellen from the house because Edgar was beating her. Why did they only threaten? Had she asked them not to remove her? She didn't remember, but she probably had a strong fear of living in some sort of orphanage with a bunch of ragged, wretched things. Eating porridge.

Some students, or maybe all of them, looked askance at her. She felt that some of the girls played interested and asked about her pregnancy just to find some salacious piece of crap to gossip about, but that was not much different from before. She was never part of the in-crowd, never part of anything. But the teachers liked her, and studying and reading abated the pain and helped her to know that she was not alone in being alone—or, at least, to try to feel that way.

The child was taken away. She knew it was a boy, but she had never discovered where he went. She never got to hold him. She never got to name him. She learned something unknowable that year. *Unknowable* because she still didn't know what it was, other than that her whole view of everything and everyone changed, and she became a self-conscious, phenomenological loner, first sad and insular, then indignant, angry, and isolated as any disjunct nation. And she confirmed that, if she concentrated on learning, studying gave her an inner peace of some sort.

And when Edgar and Rachel tried to stop her from going on to the University of Massachusetts despite a full scholarship, her brain filter had developed to the point that she was able to step outside of herself and them, to see the fact of the matter: Not only were they ignorant; they were hopelessly stupid. What made her sad was that, no matter how she had tried, there was no way they could know they were stupid, because they were stupid.

Because she finally realized that she could not change them, she became, instead, moderately grateful. Grateful, despite the beatings (which had stopped), because they had been willing to adopt her, saving her from graduating to a complete Charles Dickens waif, and grateful that she was *only* adopted and not part of their gene pool.

* * *

After tailgating and flashing her lights at the car in front of her, she finally manages to get the old pickup truck past the car. She screams again at him, "Jerk head!" But immediately she realizes that this is not like her and she feels embarrassed and her head hurts more each time she yells.

* * *

But later she discovered that she did have stupid genes in her, perhaps from Edgar after all, dripping off him as he pounded them into her. She tried to tell herself unconvincingly that it was not a brain abscess, an absent physical chunk of her brain, just ignorance. This ignorance caused by her past seclusion resulted in her marrying a man whose hidden and premeditated agenda she could not recognize while, at the same time, he viscerally knew she was a perfect victim because she had no experience with men, or, for that matter, with human judgement.

She married a grifter. A chiseler.

Stupid was as stupid does. The scammer quickly began wrapping his invisible, sordid appendages around her as he grabbed at the most minuscule scraps of information about her past mistakes upon which he could build a convincing story of how useless and worthless she was, never touching her physically, only hammering her mind at every opportunity. If he had physically struck her, she might have had a chance to understand and maybe even leave him.

But first he wanted a child with her to seem normal and to leash her to him. For the longest time, she had thought that her single hope of happiness could have been a son she almost produced in her relationship with this controlling master of thievery and grieving. This boy would have been brilliant, someone who would love her and she would love him with every cell and neuron. He would have been unique and his brilliance would have lifted her soul and would have gotten her back into wanting to learn, back into nerdiness, back into wanting to live, and wanting to teach and nurture him, her son, her only light in an absence of light.

In his young years, she would have taken him with her on a NASA mission. They would be test objects for how a mother and son are affected by space travel and she would say something wise to him, like *We will never again experience anything this exciting and wonderful or we will die, and both things are exactly the same.*

But she crashed back to earth when she realized that this boy would have instinctively tried to love his father, too, and that this boy would have had no hope whatsoever of understanding that his father would not—and, in fact, could not—love him and, would, in fact, reject him.

Soon after the miscarriage, even while she was still in the hospital, the grifter's mental depravity began to enfold her. Knowing she was weak and literally in a vulnerable state, he had her sign some mystery papers which signed away to him all her marital rights to anything and everything, including everything she had owned and possessed before she met him.

Her mind no longer functioned rationally, other than to tell herself that she must be guilty of deficiency—wanting for whatever vague characteristic she must lack. With her lack of comprehension of being repeatedly molested mentally and why he was doing it, she could only cry—cry when she was alone in the kitchen, cry when she was in the shower, cry when she was between the grocery shelves. And cry when she was left on the street without a thing.

Her scholarship helped; her job helped. Threatening him with an icepick didn't; he just laughed. But she didn't think about that anymore, because she had found her long-lost son, the one she had given away long ago. He, now a young man, had looked for her and they had met.

* * *

Exiting the turnpike earlier and now also Route 295, she hopes this new back road is the one he said. Forcing this garbage heap of a truck to move faster, the guilt and overwhelming need to protect her regained son has now evolved into what she knows is a mistake.

And now a mistake too late to retract. A horrible mistake she can only regret. And as many times as she has called, he wouldn't answer the phone. Once again, she is feeling helpless, alone, and forsaken.

The heat and the motor noise are clawing at her own sanity. Being late makes it worse. Taking the back roads, she hopes also avoids speed traps. But then maybe the speed traps are more likely on the back roads; who knows about Maine? Maybe their enforcement is different from Massachusetts.

Who knew Maine was so big? It seems to go on forever. He has already signaled that he has begun the end. She should be there, stopping him.

"It's my fault. I started late. It's my fault!" She hates that she's left-handed and has not driven a stick for years. Can't this thing go any faster? It drives like a bus. No, a boat. Like shit.

She had called her ex to find out. This victim with the same name is not her ex.

She yells, "Please stop. Please stop. Please wait for me, my darling son. I will be there soon. Let him be! Let him be!"

Bursting into tears makes it even harder to see. Even him—even her ex is not his father. She had lied; she wanted her son to have a father.

But she didn't lie about the dolphins; the dolphins are talking. This cetacean discovery will bring honor and fortune, she is sure.

Her yelling, her cold, the heat, the oily smell have given her a headache. She says softly, "I will take care of you. I promise."

Louder she sings, "Holy! Holy! HOOOLY! Lord God all flighty!"

A flock of gulls and ravens are fighting over their rights to some roadkill.

Fucking birds!

"God…!"

7. JOE

THAT FRIDAY

MARTIN WAS GETTING A BIT FRUSTRATED AND IRRITATED. "WHAT THE HELL IS A time shovel?"

Joe didn't hesitate. "How do I know? It just comes and makes you forget. It buries crap on top of your memories. If there were no shovel covering the pain, we wouldn't want to plow ahead. Then it digs your grave and you are no more.

"Sometimes we work to push the crap aside to find certain times...the beautiful moments. Like when I met you. Or better said, when you found me on the beach and you took me in as your friend and lover. Before that, I was unnoticed, cataleptic, and near the heart of wild. Finding you had to be the real happiness floating magically in my future. Love. Safety. A place to be. This had to be happiness. But the shovel heaped on trash along the way.

"And there is something else that makes us alone. It has nothing to do with parthenogenesis. It has nothing, or very little, to do with being gay. Yeah, I felt it earlier maybe, but I had my mother. Then she died and asked not to be buried next to my guinea bigot father. But I am a bit jealous of the ignorant, like my mother, who can wrap themselves in a religion.

"I asked you to try to be up here in Maine with me to celebrate your birthday because we seem to be under threat from someone there in Provincetown. And besides I hoped to be alone with you instead of in busy P-town and all the town-bonding of the queens.

137

"Sure, I have an affinity to P-town. That is where you found me, but during the time I was there before you, I was alone most of the time. I couldn't relate to the world. My one joy during that time was rescuing a destroyed young woman, helping her come back to life.

"Helping her was a great distraction. When I was helping her, it was during a very strenuous time, which turned out to be even more outrageously frightening. I sent her off with someone on what I thought was going to be a dream for her, but that someone ended up being a nightmare."

"She was a nightmare?"

"No!" Joe said loudly. After a pause, he said, "It doesn't matter. I was just blathering. Forget it."

"Jesus, Joe. Get to the point."

"What did I see in the water? It was my soul. It has long been lost in the longing to know you. I brought you up here to discuss our getting married. If you die, I have nothing. No money. No place to return. Even your crowd fakes their friendship with me. Your moneyed society is a false support to me who will show acceptance only for as long as we two are the perfectly happy couple. I can't go back to my bigoted environment of bowling balls, beer, and ball caps on backwards. There is no belonging for me."

Both Joe and Martin screamed something simultaneously as a red pickup truck sped around the bend in the road. Someone was in the wrong lane.

8. CRICKET

THAT FRIDAY

AS WE PASS OVER THE WATER'S DEPTHS, I KNOW, LURKING BELOW US, A MEGALODON or some giant cephalopod may suddenly decide to drag us, in an instant, down to a concealed lightless fissure in the earth's crust. I try to turn off my head. Dreading the approaching hours and minutes, I picture the coming sequence over and over. Ninety minutes.

Excruciatingly slowly, the minutes finally pass.

Here we go, Mama.

Unceremoniously I defrock myself of the blanket again and step into the cockpit.

"I think I should check those filters."

"What?" He is still on the cockpit side-bench looking at something on his tablet gizmo, or pretending to. He doesn't want to look up from the screen.

"I think I should check those filters."

"Is this really necessary? I'm really in a hurry."

"It is just a matter of minutes and, if your engines stop, it will take even longer to get there."

He injects me with a bothered glare, gets up, and pulls back the throttle handle. The sound of no motors is shocking.

"And what is it you want to do?" he says. Again, the assassin eyes.

"Remember you had dirty fuel. It's time to check if things are okay. It seems your engines are running a little warm," I say, bluffing, vaguely pointing at his dash. "You need to cut the motors completely. We're okay out here. There's no wind."

"Mind if I come watch what you're doing so I know what to do next time?"

Oh, sure, just what I want. But, at least, he is talking to me.

To keep him from coming down to check on my work, I say, "You should know how to change filters, but I need to work fast. I can show you when we arrive or next time you come to the marina. If you can keep an eye on our drift from the current, I'll be back in a jiffy."

Squinting with doubt, but acquiescing, he kills the engines and I go below. The first thing I do is dump the jar of bacon-wrapped scallops on a plate and stick it in the microwave for about 60 seconds while I open the Heineken.

"I made us a snack," I say as I hand him the plate and the beer through the companionway door.

Oh, Mama, I hope he doesn't notice my hands are shaking.

He's standing right at the door as if he were still planning on coming down. Good timing. "Enjoy yourself while I check out the situation."

To my amazement, his face shows an emotion: a surprised look. He puts on his broadest smile, and takes both things with the intent seemingly to imbibe.

"You're a regular saving angel. The ocean makes you hungry. You're not such a bad kid after all," he says with a sincerity I didn't know he had in him.

"Sorry," slips out of me.

I duck back down below before he can re-decide, or seem too human. I bang around the engine room making working sounds for about ten minutes, bothered by this sudden surge of personality and half expecting him to call me up on deck to tell me how good the food was.

Wait just a bit longer.

I see Mother has tried to call a hundred times and written lots of messages, but I don't have time. I force one more game of solitaire on myself, then climb back up on deck.

A quick inspection tells me that he even drank the beer. Now I can only wait and see. I say, "The filters needed a little help, but weren't too bad. Let me take the dish down to the galley and let's get out of here. Start the engines, Pops."

I don't try to see his facial expression at my insolence. I dash down the steps, place the plate and the can quietly on the floor, text Mama, and take my time coming back.

Hold your excitement, Cricket.

Once again, it is time to sit and wait.

Pops? What is that about? Is he mocking me? The kid didn't even fold the blanket back up. The cockroach, or whatever his gross nickname is, has something strangely familiar about him.

Glad for the snack. Strange, but good. Even got me drinking a beer. Forgetting to stock the fridge in the hurry to get away. Losing my cool. Not good. Not good at all, Dan. You'll lose a lot more if you don't keep cool; she is progressing.

Deliverance. *It's the perfect name. From one cunt to another.*

Just seconds after he gets us moving and the autopilot set, he begins wiping his mouth with the back of his hand and with increasing frequency. I try not to grin. I need to be sure.

When he begins shaking his hand in the air like his hand is falling asleep, I know I have him. It has not even been five minutes.

"Are you okay?" I yell. I get up and move forward a bit. Too excited.

Not turning toward me nor speaking, he continues shaking his hand, but harder and more often. When he begins stamping his feet, I move again. This particular yacht has a pair of captain chairs beside each other which allows me to slip into the seat to his right.

I say, "You're not looking so great. I'm glad you are sitting down."

"Deliverance!" he yells.

"You're losing it, Pops. I think it's time to tell you that paralytic shellfish poisoning is caused by eating shellfish contaminated with dinoflagellate algae, which produce toxins a thousand times more potent than cyanide. Unfortunately, I'm happy to tell you, there is no antidote for these toxins.

"I was able to secure perfectly poisonous specimens from the NOAA labs in Woods Hole where I now work, where I do a little night watch. Okay, why am I making up this NOAA story? So, hey, your old ex works there."

I try to see his facial expression to be able to tell if he is comprehending what I am telling him. It is hard to tell, but I think I see a glimpse of fear. He is past controlling his body or he would surely attack me.

"I don't want you to die. Just yet. I have so much to tell you."

I stand up presumably to check on our position, but mostly because I'm wound up and to let him stew a bit about his situation. Then back to the chair.

"In the half hour before we get to Penobscot, I'll tell you a story, Pops. You want to hear a story? It's about you, so you probably want to hear it. People love to hear stories about themselves, unless, of course, they are at funerals.

"You want to know why I call you 'Pops'? Okay, you have never seen me, but that's not your fault. Mama kindly asked you not to, as she held an ice pick under your chin. I can see the scars." I bend in front of him looking for where the scars should be, but the angle of his head is wrong. I point anyway, watching carefully for any flicker of reaction. "Right there."

His body is shaking, from anger or poison, I don't know, but his eyes are blank, like a blind man? I snatch off his baseball cap and throw it overboard. His appearance changes from marauder to a half-bald pitiful geezer with a fringe of grey hair. For a second in the back of my mind, from the pictures she has shown me, the lack of hair distracts me. But I'm on. The rage feels beautiful. A flood of intense glory. Finally!

"So what do sheep know when they see a wolf in sheep's clothing, Pops? No more than when humans see you, the monster, in human skin…a monster without a conscience. No one knows until it's too late.

"So my brother couldn't grasp why you rejected him. Mama said that you would never hold him, not even touch him as a baby or small child. You took away his toys so he wouldn't ruin them by playing with them. Playing with his own toys!

"Mama told me that when she tries to tell anyone what a cruel asshole you are, they think she must be exaggerating.

"Anyone looking at you cannot see that you have the lateral frontal pole prefrontal cortex missing from your head. Are you impressed I would know that, Pops? How do I know such things? Because I knew Mama could not just be bitter, stupid, wrong.

"Who could believe you would never visit your son in the hospital, or just send him away when you decided it was too difficult to be a parent. It literally drove him nuts. You, and you alone, drove him into the loony bin."

Mama, I am here.

"You manipulated Mama because that is what psychopaths do as, in her own mind, she filled in the gaps you were missing, until she couldn't anymore. She, the beautiful woman that she is, wanted to love you but you simply dumped her after stealing everything that was hers, leaving her penniless and desperate. I wish she had stuck the ice pick deep into your pretext of a heart.

"You paid for a while, but then the payments stopped. I don't know when; she wouldn't tell me.

"Mama worked, studied, tutored my brother. She got her doctorate and was hired at the Woods Hole NOAA, and she never complained, except to wish you were dead. In her dark moments through the years, that is all she would ever say. She wished you were dead.

"Even so, when I discovered you were dropping by to visit the marina, it still took me a while to convince her to help. Not because she is too forgiving, but because she was afraid for me. She was even afraid there might be more than one Dan Lodovico.

I am not there, Mama. I am here.

"You are a terrible excuse for a human being. You are a predator, so much so that even your own mother was afraid of you. Your mother, my poor, not-so-bright grandmother, went to her lonely death defending your abuse and neglect.

"So, Pops, since no normal human can believe what Mama says, I came to the conclusion that the only cure for your destructive nature is to make sure that you no longer exist. That Mama gets her wish. That you are dead. And the earth will be better for it."

Although the boat is finding its way with the autopilot, I need to get there before he dies. I push the throttle to full. Pop's neck is no longer supporting his head, and I smell that his underpants have taken a horrible beating, so I push him off the chair. What a mistake that is. He falls to the deck and throws up. As he lies on the floor with fucking vomit everywhere, I can see he is still breathing, and twitching.

At high speed, the churning water, the wind flogging my ears, and the motors all seem so loud. I shout. "You were a lowly bank teller. No way did you earn the money to afford the gas for this thing, let alone for this million-dollar monstrosity. You either stole the money from the bank or, more probably, from women like my mother…and your own mother."

I lean to starboard and demonstratively throw my cap overboard, both because it will be in the way and because now I hate it. While there is time, I lift myself over and around him and go below to change my clothes, shoes, Ziploc my phone, wrap my pants in the bags.

The scallop plate is still on the floor where I put it. The beer can has rolled somewhere. They'll say, poor guy, he got poisoned. The jar, I need to dump now out on the ocean; I don't want to poison the harbor by any chance. That harbor is a treasure trove of lobsters.

As I climb the steps, the thought of Pop's vomit polluting the bay flickers through my mind, but what am I going to do?

9. KEVIN

THAT FRIDAY

THEY ALL GATHERED BY THE CRUMPLED VOLVO. THE CAR'S RADIO, SWITCHED ON BY some fluke in the collision, was blaring rock music announced with a flourish of bravado as the new hot single "Abandon House."

He, Kevin, still pale as a ghost, had no developed eschatology, no abstract judgements about the inexplicable near-death experience minutes ago. In fact, his mind was so muddled he hardly recognized Beth and was surprised to see her, even though he knew she was on duty.

Slowly endeavoring to describe the situation to her, to the other ambulance staff, and to the fat patrolman Bob Gaines also from Maine's Troop E over the loud music from the car radio, he did not try, or think about trying, to explain why he smelled of vomit or why he was wet from tears.

He hoped they could not see that he had wet his pants. He was so numb that he had hardly been able to speak, let alone yell over the blasting radio. He didn't tell them that the tears were not from sadness, but instead from relief, relief at being alive. They would never understand; not even Beth would understand. He certainly did not.

He couldn't shut his eyes without seeing crawling swarms of insects—ants, maybe—and torrents of images he didn't want to see. Now to patrolman Gaines all he could manage to say was "I have never seen, never thought I would ever see, such a mess." He closed his eyes again only to see the descending red truck and quickly opened them again. He no longer feared death.

The EMTs turned to the task of getting the injured, unconscious driver to the hospital.

Bob Gaines shook his bulging balding head. "Yeah, me neither. I thought I'd seen the worst on another code three when an ambulance driver herself was killed because some idiot didn't mind the siren and pulled right in front of the ambulance at an intersection. And then, you know what? The car driver made a run for it. Left the dying ambulance driver to crawl to radio for help before she died. Some people are just fucking disgusting.

"But this. How do two people get so completely…two people welded together? I'd say they joined giblets. It's gonna be hard to know who's who. And then that driver of that ragtop Volvo is alive! It don't seem possible."

Kevin felt anger at the sad irony of Gaines saying some people are just fucking disgusting. He was revolted by the man's ambulance story; it could have been Beth. He looked up in the sky, only to see the gulls circling above, anticipating their next mealtime.

Both stood jacketless and with sweat-stained shirts from the oppressive heat, gravely watching the ambulance EMTs expertly pull the driver's broken body out of the Volvo, judiciously place and tie his body to a stretcher, and load him into the ambulance. A paramedic in the ambulance began work even before the doors closed.

As its red light flashes were suddenly amplified by the deafening siren, Kevin realized he forgot about Beth's leaving in the ambulance and felt an intense precipitous loss. It was all he could do to not start crying again. Dead bodies were what he continually tried to reject in order to stay rational, but now, standing here, he was in some altered, vulnerable perplexity, vulnerable to change and to never change again, becoming his permanent state in which human death enters his soul like a dark worm. And, although he could not know it and would never admit it, he will conjecture later that Beth's proximity might have saved him.

The second ambulance crew began inspecting and appraising the crushed bodies lying on the asphalt. The Volvo's radio was still blaring its tumultuous musical disorder.

Bob Gaines reconfirmed that he was indeed witless saying, "Okay, guys, did you bring a mop?"

Kevin got a lump in his throat. In unison, the two paramedics stopped examining the bodies. The one member closer to the trooper stood up and turned without a smile. The distended face, his eyes, the size of the man made Kevin glad he was farther away. For him the uneasy silent tension between the two dragged on too long.

Finally, after no exchange of words, Gaines turned and said to Kevin, "I guess we better get down to work again. I took pictures and called the tow company. I'll go look in the car to see if there's any I.D. and turn off that goddamn radio. It'll be hard for the family to I.D. them two. Hope she ain't nobody's mother who's gotta I.D. 'er. You wanna check the truck? Oh, and you got a tape in your car we can measure with?"

Gaines, seeing Kevin was not listening or moving and, instead, was seemingly mesmerized by the EMTs' work on the bodies, said, "How are we gonna report that mess on the road?"

Kevin, like some doomed prey, was absently frozen for a moment, then slowly shook his head. He had this uneasy sensation that he knew one of the dead on the ground. But how could he? They were unrecognizable. His mind ordinarily never dwelled on such uncertainties, but everything was just screwy right now.

Breaking out of his trance and without any unnecessary body movement, slowly but with a disturbing stab of pain in his left arm, Kevin pulled his phone from his shirt pocket.

Sticking out his tongue as he always did when he concentrated, he punched his phone with his left index finger. "Can you speak?"

Beth said, "This guy's going to live. I don't know how he got so lucky. Lots of broken bones, but, we use enough duct tape, he'll be fine."

"Who is he?"

"Joe Tinkerman. Was on his license. I hate to say it, but I think it's Joe Tink, that guy I was telling you about."

Kevin saw that Gaines had walked off. "Beth, who's the big ugly medic working in the other ambulance?"

She said, "Oh you mean Frankenstein. He's a really nice guy. His real name is Frank Stern, and he thinks Frankenstein is a comical nickname. Why do you ask?"

"No special reason. Just curious."

After he hung up and had no one else to ask, he spoke to his phone again. "Okay, Google. What is the word for a messy predicament?"

Google said, "Entanglement."

10. MARTIN

THAT FRIDAY?

WALKING UP A GRAVEL PATH OR BEST DESCRIBED AS A STRIP OF DARK, SHARP ROCKS, Martin with Joe beside him is walking toward a gloomy structure, apparently made of wood beams, set back towards some interchangeable forest area. *Presumably* wooden because it is not entirely clear to Martin how this building is structured. Martin wishes he had worn socks as the gravel is stabbing the soles of his feet through his thin, fancy Italian loafers.

And species-less birds are attacking him, large black and white birds hitting, clawing, and stabbing him with their beaks, making him bleed. The screaming bird sounds seem not only out of sync, but seem not to match the birds. Martin should be in pain, but he's not. He is afraid, but continues walking toward the structure.

After entering through a large heavy, weightless door, Martin hears the sound of a train, but only that faraway sound before you can be sure that it actually is a train. He is not sure why they are here, and, at first, thinks it might be to buy socks.

The interior is at best rustic, at worst, filthy. Certainly not appetizing. Neon signs hang on the walls with no specific message. He feels something is missing and the indeterminate nature of the interior puts Martin in a state of doubt that he does not recognize in himself. Usually he is interested in being particularly aware of his surroundings. It's not that he couldn't see how it all might look; he just can't seem to care.

Most apparent are two obese women sitting at shorter ends of a small rectangular table. To their left is a lunch counter lined with immovable floor-mounted round, red vinyl–covered stools, the kind seen in drugstores when he was growing up. It is hard for Martin to think of anything else than the enormous corpulence of the two women—one facing them, the other with her back to the door.

Martin remembers suddenly that Joe is with him when the one fat woman facing them looks up and glares at Joe and Martin as they enter. Now he understands what is missing. The smell. These fat sweaty women should smell like the ones toward which he always felt such an abhorrence, but he senses nothing. No odors whatsoever.

The women are speaking to each other using gibberish like from some child's movie script. Martin hears nonsensical snippets: "Wunllagable. Professor mumpsimus. Grog blossom. Meletē thana-tou. Grei."

Martin whispers to Joe, "Friendly atmosphere."

Joe doesn't respond.

Martin is left with a vast contradiction, not a disquieting incon-sistency. The whole feeling is of calm, even of satisfaction, of deep comfort or maybe passiveness.

He says to Joe, "Why are we here?"

And then he notices Ellen in the room. Somehow he doesn't ques-tion her manifestation even with its illogic. He hears nothing, not even her breathing. He again notices the background roar.

"Hello, Ellen."

She doesn't respond. It's as if she were in a sound-deadened box as he feels the sound of his voice drop to the floor. He senses that she doesn't know he is there, but presumes, being in such proxim-ity, she must.

The woman facing them begins to work her enormous body out of the chair with such a struggle that Martin is surprised by the complete lack of human sounds of exertion and the absence of any scraping sound of the chair. Once up, she waddles into a kitchen area to her right that Martin had previously not noticed. After a time, she returns, squeezing her even more monstrous body sideways through the doorway, with a menu in her bulging fat hand but with fingers that look like lobster legs, and drops it in front of him on the countertop.

The menu, a grease-stained sheet, contains a short list of the usual expected sock choices: some knee-highs, some thick hiking, some argyle, several solid black or boringly brown. No prices. Martin, feeling no need to pick it up, spends some absurd amount of time trying to work out the reasons for such a short list of items. He concludes and determines repeatedly that it had to be the rural supply limitation, until he suddenly realizes Joe is no longer beside him.

He quickly turns to scour the room but sees only the back of the enormously fat woman still sitting unmoving and larger than before with a stomach so corpulent that, sagging between her legs, it is resting on the floor. For the first time he realizes she is naked.

For some reason he has not expected Ellen still to be there, but she is, dressed in the white bar jacket as he had last seen her at the hotel, and the fat lady is still talking to her but he can't hear her words.

His first thought is that Joe has gone to the restroom without saying anything. Standing behind the fat lady at the table, Martin asks, "Excuse me, but where can I find some socks?" He becomes confused about why he could not ask about Joe.

The answer is slow in coming. It is as if their voices need to transverse some cosmic vacuum. The fat woman's voice is deep, loud, the booming kind that he knows is from a fat woman without looking at her. The responding voice is close, closer than she is.

"Vis scire?"

He watches Ellen expecting her to notice him, to want to know his answer. And should he look at the fat, naked monstrosity in the chair or even answer her when her voice is right in him? He takes the question to be rhetorical.

In his head, he hears her say, "Tu mortuus es."

"I am dead," he repeats with indifference. He does recognize that this is a disruption of the social structure familiar to him. Death for Martin is far too intertwined with everything that gave meaning to his life for him to feel any specific emotion.

The voice continues.

But your mind is able to process billions of thoughts in our split second together. Time is being buckled for you. You know that you have passed into another universe and would like to show science the proof. How you got here could be some sort of proof of the unified theory with the speed of your particles accelerating you into this new universe.

Now Martin is completely aware that he is speaking to himself. For Martin, his death proves the graviton transfer to a parallel universe, a Brane Three maybe, but he can no longer prove it to the living. He knows this episode can last as long as he wants because time is not part of this very universe.

Joe's last words had been, "I know you no longer love me."

Martin begins to feel loss. Not his personal loss, but the loss of knowledge that might have saved the mammal man from himself. Martin feels certain it must be inherent in mankind to require self-destruction as each time the empowered ignorant mindlessly killed off the intelligentsia, the world lost unknown information, creation, salvation.

Martin says, "But Ellen is here. But not here."

The noise of the invisible train is now louder, repetitively rhythmic like a rusty escalator or maybe a loop of an early Velvet Underground live concert. Is it voices he hears? As the sound intensifies, the unmistakable thunder of multiple metal wheels is recognizable, but without any Doppler effect and, with only the metallic resonance, he has no way of knowing how to or if he should move out of its way. Besides, his feet hurt. He still wishes he had socks.

The jarring, clanging roar is rapidly becoming louder, becoming earsplitting and nothing else. And everything. Deafening. *Nothing* else and perfectly everything.

11. CRICKET

THAT FRIDAY

As we near the magnificent bay, I start to cry.

"Fuck! I can't see shit."

I slow the boat down to two or three knots and quickly go grab the blanket to wipe my eyes. It's one p.m. The sun is still hidden in the summer sky. With the water and the shoreline in shadows, the whole bay seems darker than I remember it. Shadows and light of Rembrandt.

The water's beautifully still, the air surprisingly cool so near land. The mirror reflection of the Maine shoreline rocks and conifers on the water's surface is disturbed sporadically by a few creatures, both over and under the water, nabbing bugs off the surface. The thought of this machine disrupting the bay's serenity seems like rape.

According to my research, the least populated shoreline on the bay is just before Fort Point Light, even if it has always seemed to me that there is no population *anywhere* along the shore. But the state park location, I hope, will help reduce the probability of witnesses to a maximum.

With the slowing of the boat, I can smell green—the moss and trees—but with a tinge of vomit.

"Goddamn it, Pops, you are ruining this place already, and now the flies are arriving." Swatting futilely in the air, I say, "Hey, Pops, we slow down and the mosquitoes start swarming. You have the flies;

157

I got the mosquitoes. Up here the bugs are just murder." *Do crickets laugh or cry?* "Wow! My humor surpasses me."

Here come the fucking tears again.

Why can't I stop crying? Because I killed my brother? My fantasy brother? I have erased him, Mama. This time, Mama, I am here; not in the dark closet facing the wall. Forgive me. I'm getting my sticks together. Really I am. Now, Mama, this is my time to help you.

"You know, Pops, I have no way of knowing if you have any official bank account for me to inherit. I think not. But if there is any, I'm giving it back to my mother."

The GPS reads we are just outside Fort Point ledge. A lone red marker buoy warns us to stay away.

"Right now, though, I need to throw you down the steps."

I pull the throttle back a click to neutral.

"I loathe even the thought of the idea that there could be part of you in me. I want you to drown. I'm dumping you down the stairs to drown when I break open this boat, and I'm hoping falling down the steps gives you pain."

I study his twitching half-fetal posture on the cockpit floor, tipping my head to see how I can best handle his weight and to avoid the crap he has regurgitated. I decide to turn him on his back and to pull his legs around toward the companionway.

As I pull on his legs, he begins making sounds which are not recognizable for a man, or even a human. Dog sounds maybe. A dog wanting attention? A dog in pain, I think. I hope.

Can you hear it, Mama?

Once I get his feet to hang over the edge of the companionway, I step over him, bend over his head to lift him under his shoulders. The stench is unbearable. I have to back off to take a deep breath and to try not to breathe while I lift and push him.

Then I vomit. It all hits me. The smell. His uncontrolled bowels and bladder stains. The flies. The splotchy multicolored urp on his white jacket. The cockpit's exaggerated rocking of the boat. The pale light-green color of his skin. Mostly, the idea of a dead or dying man in front of me.

The only food I had in me is now on and around him. Traces of me are everywhere. Another mess. But I don't have time to even think to clean it up.

I feel like a used condom, but I still have to move his puke-coated carcass. Luckily, it turns out to be fairly easy. His frame is still pliable and smaller than what I expect. With a couple of new inhales, pushing, and breath holding, I'm able to let go and watch him slide down the steps to the lower deck floor.

Happily, he seems to crack his head a couple times on the steps, and as his feet hit the floor, the weight of his head folds him like a melting marshmallow, slowly tipping him to the right, and finally thumping on the floor, landing him on his side, curled on the floor like a soft turd, and the piece of shit that he is. I hope to see that he is still breathing, but it's hard to tell. With all the distractions, I forgot to check for scars.

As I kick his lost shoe down the steps, I yell, "My mother was ashamed for even letting you touch her. I hope you are still breathing. I want you to suffer, slowly, you bastard.

"Fuck!" I yell as I forget and step back into the slippery goop on the floor. "I hate you for everything!"

I should feel happy right now, shouldn't I? Later. Maybe later. Is it fear or guilt clawing at my gut, offering me no options? Stop crying. Keep the lid on, Cricket, or you're done.

The edge of the hidden underwater rock ledge by its mere invisibility strikes fear in most sailors who enter this bay. The depth meter is not much use since the edge of the underwater rock shelf drops so sharply that it can't be seen until I hit it. I am going to have to feel my way.

I am not at all sure just how deep the rock shelf is in certain areas. I'm not sure if this craft will float long enough with a hole in the hull for me to get off. Now suddenly, I'm not so sure about anything except that I can't stop now. Mama is waiting.

As your mother would say, Mama, "There'll be no Thanksgiving with a half-baked turkey."

There is a subtle current caused by the Penobscot River. I test how to set the throttle to move the boat just a knot or two faster than the current, circle around, and take a very slight angle toward the shore.

I'm moving so slowly that it seems I'm never going to hit anything. I am far past the red danger marker. Distances on water are deceptive.

At this speed the motors sound like a muffled laundromat, quiet enough that I can hear the water rippling on the hull between the screeches of the gulls, who seem to be complaining that I'm breaching their territory, or maybe they're just hoping for garbage.

"Do you know why they are not called seagulls, Pops? You don't know, do you? Here they're *not* seagulls because they are flying over the bay. They are bay-gulls, Pops. Bagels. Get it? Oh shit! Crunch!" I yell down the steps. "There it is, Pops. You hear that? That's your superyacht feeling death."

Sweat's burning my eyes. I try to steer more parallel to the edge to scrape along it, listening and feeling the horrible grating and crunching sound tearing on the fiberglass hull, right up through my spine.

The depth of the rock shelf seems to vary, but I feel good about it just here. This yacht model has a fraction over three-and-a-half-foot draft. I'm hitting higher on the port side somewhere, which means that the ledge is only two to three feet deep, right here anyway. I feel that I can wade ashore fairly easily, not having to swim too far with a backpack. Perfect. I hope. Maybe.

But I can't fart around. Someone can show up anytime. Ramming the rocks and leaving the motors running in gear will echo like civil war out over the harbor, probably attracting the whole State of Maine *and* Vermont.

Okay, dumbshit, somehow you have to get off this monster.

I envision jumping from the deck into shallow water and breaking a leg or hitting a sharp edge or getting trapped between the hull and the rocks. Or even worse, landing in deep water and being too exhausted to get over the edge of the shelf.

I'm scared, Mama. Will you love me if I die?

I mark the trees on the shoreline as guidance for the immediate return trip to the hidden ledge. I turn the boat to starboard and once I'm out and away some hundred feet, swinging around, I turn on the autopilot, setting it for those trees. Grabbing my backpack, holding my breath, I throttle the engine to full, and rush to brace my back against the companionway wall.

The end is coming, Mama.

It all happens much faster than I'm expecting. Trying to avoid the vomit, I have almost no time to sit before impact. I bang my head hard against the cockpit wall.

The sound of rock meeting fiberglass is not what a yacht owner wants to hear, even if the water muffles the screech of fiberglass hull crushing against sharp edges of rock. The whole boat jerks up and leans to the right. Then it lets go and moves again, twisting to starboard, and the bow rises whale-like out of the water. The roaring engines continue to push with all their horses, causing a continuous cacophony of plastic against solid rock, and swinging and wagging the boat like it is desperately hungry and angrily gnawing at the rock for nourishment.

It's difficult to stand up. The angle of the boat. The least bit of rocking hull is exaggerated high in the cabin. The whack on the wall has made my head throb and hard to think. Dizzy, on my knees, bracing myself, it takes several attempts to put on my backpack.

Needing to silence the noise flooding the whole harbor, I struggle to stand on the slanted surface, holding on to what grips are possible to reach the dash while trying not to slip on the stomach crud.

Suddenly, thankfully, the engines, unable to find water to cool themselves, cough and choke simultaneously to a stop, opening the door to grateful calm and stopping the seismic movements. I switch off the autopilot, and, as I adjust the throttle for investigators to find a realistic speed setting, I try to see if water is filling the salon, but afraid to go down to check for scars.

One scan of my situation tells me my only real exit is off the swim platform, now mostly submerged in the water. I descend the deck's sloping obstacle course and lower myself into the water. Icy water. Fucking icy.

Dog paddling, I hide low in the water and move away from the boat to circle back toward the shore.

After I guess that I must have crossed over into the shallow water, I try touching the bottom with a foot. Weeds. Sludge. Lobsters. Stuff on the bottom I can't see. Stuff that's never been stepped on. It is a shallow never-never land.

And, Jesus, the water is cold—the brack water of a cold river from the Canadian mountains mixed with a northern ocean that, somehow, lobsters love. I hadn't thought about how much colder the water would be in Maine. Keep moving, fuckhead. Swim.

The impenetrable dark water surface threatens. Bad things go through my mind. I still have so far to the shore. Rocks. Trees. Warmth. They seem oppressively distant.

With living things nipping at my legs protesting my presence, leeches maybe, I stand to rest and try to warm myself in the air. Immediately swarming striped deer flies, their slanted eyes painted to exude suffering, appear from some invisible hellish netherworld, circling to decide where nipping raw flesh out of my body will be most painful and forcing me back into the freezing water.

I hear shouting on the park shore. Crouched low in the water, it's hard to see far, but I think I hear the distant hum of boat motors, or is it the flies? The shore seems remote and the longer it takes to get there, the greater the chance I'm fucked, the greater the threat of the water's dominion.

Dog paddling. The only way to move effectively. But each time some underwater entity scrapes my body, I'm now sure it is some animal, an eel maybe, about to sink its teeth into me, to taste me and to start a feeding frenzy.

A small shift in the weather causes a breeze over the harbor, rippling the water ever so slightly, killing the shoreline reflection, and making its refuge seem more unreachable. I'm disturbing this place, and it is messing with me. The wrinkled water is hiding its primordial revenge. Humans don't belong here; they have never been here; they aren't welcome here.

My waterlogged pack is heavy. More and more often I drop to my knees into the bottom slime as the pitiless sea siphons off my energy. The whole thing is, I don't know, cold. I can't feel my legs.

I whisper to the sea. "I didn't mean to poison you. Leave me alone. I don't want to be here either." Just breathing is hard.

The shore is close now. On my knees, I peel off my backpack with immeasurable effort and throw it toward the shore as hard as I can, but it doesn't reach.

In the middle of the rippling rings spreading out from where it lands, my father's head, rising from under the surface, staring and disparaging, his thick hair in horrifying Medusa disarray, says, *Ludo*vico?"

As the darkness wraps its warmth around me, I see Mama next to me in a dazzling window with watery shadows of a thousand prowling Bony-Eared Assfish.

She says, "Did you see the scars?"

A stranger, wearing a baseball cap, begins obscuring the view like tears.

No, Mama. I didn't. I did not see them.

Raging currents rip regret's leeches out of my chest as the megalodon arrives.

PART 3

Should solitude be a candle, I would choose darkness.

—Joe Tink

THE FOLLOWING YEARS

1. KEVIN

TELLING A STORY

WE HAVE A BANK ROBBERY AND A MURDER WAS HOW HE WOULD LIKE TO START THE story. In fact, Kevin often just repeated that sentence out of nowhere with it popping into his head like some song lyric.

He had quite a story to tell, if he felt like it. Storytelling put order in the chaos he so often felt. He loved to tell stories, but with this story it was a problem, that is, feeling like it, because he had to worry. He had to be extremely careful, depending on the listener. Other stories he could never tell; this one he could. Mostly. He wanted to tell this one completely, or essentially so, once at least. Maybe to Joe. Maybe to one of the other cops. Maybe at a Thanksgiving dinner with the family, but then the family thing was unrealistic.

First, it seemed the family gathering never happened anymore with Kevin's odd hours, and with everyone off doing their own thing, and, worse yet, he might let the cat out of the bag.

Kevin's habit of listening to the world news on the police radio started the whole process. It was springtime and the snow had just melted in Bangor. Work was easier for both Beth and him when they didn't have to fight the ice and snow to get around, she in the ambulance and he in his police cruiser. And the Spring weather also reduced the number of accidents, so he had more time to listen to the police radio.

The news item was ignored by most news agencies, both television and radio, and certainly the bloggers and print press. So when he picked it up on police circuits, he almost ignored it, too, as one more of the thousands of headlines throughout the world beaming into his station. But when he heard the words Switzerland and bank robbery, something subconsciously made him retain the thought in the back of his mind.

About a week passed by before he remembered to mention it to Beth.

It wasn't every day they had breakfast together at the kitchen counter because their odd shift hours, although mostly simultaneous, most often excluded time for a breakfast.

This breakfast with Beth on that Saturday morning while chewing on an English muffin, he said, "You remember…?" He coughed.

Beth had laughed and said, "That's what you get for trying to talk with your mouth full."

After clearing his throat with some coffee, he said to her, "You remember that Swiss guy you told me you met on the boat to Bermuda, I don't know, maybe five or six years ago?"

Beth immediately woke up. It seemed that question hit her like a descending microburst. She told him later that, unlike the boat's frightening violence back then, this question launched a mix of terror and a warm wind of great memories, recollections of the most crucial time in her life. And for him to notice the radio report and to remember it as only a few years ago when it had been, in fact, twenty-four years, made her think that he understood how important it had been to her.

"Yes, Kevin. Of course, I remember." She said it slowly, trying not to sound too interested or alarmed at what he might say. She had told him later that she had tried to keep her smile, but that if human ears were like cats' and could perk, then hers did.

"Well," he said, telling it the way he had first understood it, "I heard on the police notices that there was a very unusual bank robbery in Switzerland… some city…Zurich, I think it was. So I thought of your guy from the boat, the tough guy guarding the important rich people and I thought probably he knew about it. It was big news over there."

There are some odd details he remembered as he was talking to her then. Their black English cat, Shadow, complained from the floor right then, interrupting things. Beth's tall body let her easily lift the back of her chair with one hand while her legs scooted it back. With her other arm she scooped up the cat and put him out the door, almost in one motion. Even putting the cat out to pee made her seem beautiful to him.

She said, he thought at the time rather defensively, "Well, he wasn't a policeman. But he might have read about it on the news. That's all. So what was so strange about it?"

He had to smile and told her that from what he could remember of the report, some street excavation was happening next to a bank, so they hired a private company to keep watch at night since the excavation was a ditch right up against this bank wall with a hole in the wall right into the bank's vault where the safe deposit boxes lined the room...a hole in the bank's wall...right in. So the funny thing was that the guard himself broke into all the boxes and stole the contents. At least, that was how Kevin remembered it.

Beth scratched her nose lightly with her long fingers and smiled. She said, "That is funny. When did this happen?"

"I think it happened last weekend," he said.

She said, "It just goes to show you never know. Did they catch him?"

He said he didn't know. He had just listened to the lead-in part.

The subject had been dropped as far as Kevin was concerned, but as Beth cleared away the few items left on the counter, she had told him that she couldn't stop thinking about it and had decided to see what she could find on the internet.

Finding anything on the internet was a long shot, she had figured, but maybe these people knew Carl, if she could find the name of the company involved.

Moving the laptop to the kitchen counter, her search began with Swiss bank robbery but, as she dug deeper, she found very little real information in English other than what Kevin had told her.

Feeling guilty, she thought, for digging up old personal memories and not wanting to ask him more about it, she had found a Zurich newspaper byline name, Hans Busher, whose report was written in English. She hoped the name Busher meant an internationally oriented Swiss who spoke and wrote English and that his byline was not just a translation.

Using her maiden name, just in case, so Carl might recognize her name if it came to that, she wrote:

Dear Mr. Busher, I am trying to find an old friend in Zurich who is or was connected to the security business. Having seen your bank robbery report, I was hoping to find someone in that security firm who might know my friend. Is there anyone you know whom I may contact? Sorry to bother you for this, and thus I highly appreciate your response.

The next day, Busher answered something like:

I would be happy to help you find your friend. In that I have many personal contacts, please let me know his name and I will find his contact information.

So Beth answered with more information thrown in, like:

I'm embarrassed since the biggest problem that I have is that I don't know his last name. We met several years ago while sailing to Bermuda, but have only his first name as Carl and that in Zurich he, then, trained vulnerable clients on self-protection. I apologize for bothering you and assume that I was being ignorant thinking that he could be contacted without a last name, and I am not even sure he is still in business. But, thank you anyway for your time.

So she had sort of given up, but with all the extra information, Kevin could tell she still had hope.

One day later, Busher wrote back:

You might mean Karl Beck. May I call you on Skype to discuss this situation? My Skype name is Horsebush.

This rattled Beth. Discuss the situation? Call? She began to worry that she had done the wrong thing. Embarrassed and unnerved, she told Kevin about the message exchange that she had begun.

"What do you think I should do?" she asked that evening.

"Do?" Kevin said. "You should see what he wants to discuss."

"Maybe he wants me to pay him for his work," she said.

"No, Beth," he said. "Not only would that be ridiculous, but completely unreal. You know you could just hang up on him. It's something more and maybe interesting."

"Interesting? What do you mean? He wants to know if this is the right Carl...except spelled with a K."

"Okay, so you find out," he said. "What harm can it do? But my detective ears hear something else."

"Something else? What do you mean?" she said. Now she was getting nervous.

"Beth, I don't know. Just contact him and see."

He could tell she was curious and a bit afraid, even if she didn't want to admit it to herself.

The same evening, asking for no online visual, blaming it on slow internet, but probably because she didn't want him to see the messy kitchen nor her without makeup—who knows?—she sent her Skype name and was surprised to get a response immediately.

It must have been four in the morning for the Swiss journalist, asking if he could call. She called Kevin over from his half-snooze in his chair in the corner.

"Hello, Mr. Busher," she said. "This is Beth Sturgess. My husband Kevin Nuss is with me."

"Hello, Beth and Kevin. Thank you for taking my call."

"No, I thank you," she said. "It must be in the middle of the night. Why are you up?"

They heard him laughing. He said, "I am a journalist. We never sleep when there is an important story."

Beth looked at Kevin with raised eyebrows. "Important story?"

"Well, let me explain," Busher said.

This is where Kevin picked up his favorite line and decided, if he would ever decide to relate some part of this story to anyone else, he'd like to start with this, quoting this journalist.

Busher said, "We have a bank robbery and a murder. It is a complicated situation and, if you don't mind, I would like to ask you some questions that might enlighten me on the situation."

Beth was shaken. She turned to Kevin to beg for him to take over the conversation, but instead, in her nervous panic, immediately said, "What does this have to do with me? Sorry. I don't understand."

"Well," said Busher, "I don't know if it has anything to do with you, but, if nothing else, you might find it interesting. The thing is, we don't know if the Karl I am speaking about is the same Karl you know. Karl Beck was the owner of Karl Beck Security…"

"Was?" Beth said.

"Well, he might still be, but he has disappeared. Or, at least, I cannot find him."

"And what does this have to do with the bank robbery?" Then Beth paused a fraction, before daring to say, "And murder."

He said, "I will try to explain the part I know, but we have not established if this Karl is your Karl. Can you tell me what you know about him or what distinguishes him?"

"Oh, gosh," Beth said. "I don't know what to tell you. I was very young and at that age, what do we notice except our own reflections in the mirror?"

He didn't say anything so she went on. "He was very Germanic. Handsome. Muscular. Short."

"Ah, short. How short would you say?"

She wasn't sure. She asked Kevin, "He came up to here on me. How tall is that, Kevin?"

He said, "About five one or two."

Busher said, "Can you convert that for me? You mean, five feet?"

Kevin said, "Yeah, five feet plus, maybe, an inch or two."

"Okay, let me convert that to give myself a picture." He was quiet for a few seconds. "That's about one sixty. Okay, that makes sense. What about his hair?"

This is where Kevin thought she made a funny.

"Yes, he had hair," she said.

Hans Busher laughed and said, "Anything special I mean? Color? Long? Curly? Short? Half bald? Receding?"

Beth said, "It's so many years ago. He might have different hair now."

Kevin felt she might be wanting this to be a different Carl and was reluctant to answer. Kevin held back as long as he could but was too curious about the case to let it go. He said to Beth, "Didn't you tell me he was missing a toe?"

"No, it was a finger...a tip of the finger on the left hand," she blurted out. "I mean, I never noticed it before he told me about it. He said he lost it mountain climbing."

This was a typical overexplanation he saw in his work that made him think she was fudging the truth a bit. And she had never told him about the mountain climbing before, but he let it go.

Busher said, "Well, that seems to be him." He was quiet. Making a note, maybe.

Then he said, "By the way, I forgot to ask where you live in the States."

"In Maine," she said.

Busher seemed excited. He said, "Maine! Where in Maine?"

They were both a bit surprised that he even had heard of Maine.

"In Bangor," Beth said. "Do you know where that is?"

"Well, actually, yes," he said. "I have studied Maine in detail for a story I did about one great American Dan Ludovico."

In unison, they said, "Who?"

He said, "I figured you might not have heard of him, which was part of his greatness. He didn't promote himself. He was one of America's richest people and even attended the World Economic Forum here in Switzerland each year. I have written about his benevolence and studied his life as best I could.

"Anyway, he had a cabin in Maine up in a rather secluded bay which I cannot recall the name of at the moment where sorrowfully he died in a boat accident some time ago. You can look up his history on the internet. You should be pleasantly surprised by this man's generosity and humility."

Kevin, the aspiring police detective, moved in. "Okay, Mr. Busher, explain what this is about. Please!"

"Of course," he said at once. "I will try to explain as much as I know. It seems that Karl Beck's company had the job…the watchman's job outside the bank. Beck's reputation is…or was, very good. Then last weekend, the hired watchman…uh, a Mr. Borger, was murdered and left dead in the bank…dragged in first or killed after he got in…probably whacked on the head with a crowbar. Then two bank boxes were jimmied or crowbarred out, I don't know which boxes and what the contents stolen were. That's it. The police are completely tight lipped about any further details."

Kevin said, "And Beck is gone?"

Busher said, "Yes, it seems so. Or at least, I cannot find him and neither can the police."

Beth said, "Do they think he did it?"

Busher paused. "I don't know. I have told you what I know. I was hoping you could tell me more about Mr. Beck."

Beth looked at Kevin and shook her head with a shrug, not like she didn't want to tell more, but like she didn't know more.

She said, "Sorry, Mr. Busher, but you know what I know. It was many years ago and I was a teenager. You know everything I know."

Busher said, "Don't forget to look up information about Dan Ludovico. You may have met him on the street and didn't know it." He thanked them both for the time and signed off.

About a week after the online meeting with the Swiss reporter, Beth told Kevin she would like to fly down to Bermuda to visit Florie. He sensed her guilt feelings since he knew Florie had been a good friend and Beth had promised to visit her one day. He guessed her sudden stirred-up Bermuda memories made this the time.

She asked if he wanted to go with her. He said that, as much as he wanted to go, having never seen Bermuda, he couldn't. No time off. And besides, it would be easier if she went alone. She could stay with Florie. He felt she was relieved.

He asked how long she would be.

"Oh," she said casually, "just a week or less, I think. You know, after a short time visitors begin to smell like fish, or something."

He couldn't tell anyone why he knew what really happened next and that the story was true. He would simply say that Beth related it to him.

And he could never admit to anyone, even in his most detailed, intimate storytelling, how much he missed Beth, how her leaving, when he left her at the airport, left a hollow hole in his chest until he met her back at the airport.

If he could ever tell this story, he would like to have ended the story explaining that he was not sure Beth ever suspected Karl for what happened in Bermuda. He thought it best that she and Kevin never talk about it for his own reasons.

So he would finish the story, omitting several things he could never tell.

He would leave out that he didn't want to distress Beth any more than she might already be, because his nose told him there was not much question that Karl had been looking for revenge, even if it was only evidential proof. And if the Swiss police ever checked out his story, Beth had been Karl's excuse, alibi-like, for being in Bermuda, to meet his lover, his secret lover.

And Kevin would leave out how, to conceal that the cat could not be fed or let out, he had dumped Shadow's corpse in the trash at Logan.

2. JOE

THE THEFT

ONLY JOE KNEW THAT HE WAS SOON TO BE EXECUTED, EASILY LIFTED AND CARRIED in his emaciated state and dropped off the roof of the hospital, three stories to his death.

That was why, after he healed enough to climb out of his deepest sorrow for Martin's death and out of bed, Joe continued a long silence.

His surrogate family, Kevin, Beth, and a shrink had obviously had a powwow. He could almost hear their discussion. Joe silent? Silent Joe? An oxymoron. Even Kevin, who hardly knew the guy, could understand that Joe must be in deep depression. With the hospital psychiatrist and Beth ganging up on him, Joe began to respond, but nothing like his old loquacious self. He really didn't feel like it.

"In short summation," the shrink, in a soft feminine voice, said to Joe, "you feel useless and lost. It's not strange. You have been dependent on your partner's income. You've been weakened by the accident enough that you can hardly do common labor. You have no specific training, except as a bodybuilder which is probably what saved you in the accident. You are forty-two years old. You have no savings or other income sources and no place to live. Does that sum it up?"

Joe couldn't make himself nod a full nod. He dipped his head just enough to humor the psychiatrist into thinking she had diagnosed his quiescence correctly.

Today, as Joe and Kevin sat alone outside the Central Maine Medical Center, perhaps it was the beautiful sunny day in Bangor with the breeze just enough to discourage the mosquitos, the nearby healthy pair of grey squirrels twitching and fluffing their enormous tails, the smell of the cut grass, and/or the amorous mating songs of the birds that manipulated Joe so that he felt less trapped in hopelessness.

Whatever it was, Joe said, "Did Beth ever tell you how I arranged her trip to Bermuda?"

Joe watched Kevin as Kevin sat silently, seemingly conjuring up the memories of what story Beth had related, or probably what story he wanted Joe to think Beth had told him.

Then Kevin said, "I don't really remember. Why do you ask?"

Joe said, "I don't know what to do. I'm in danger."

The two men looked at each other, each reading the other, with Joe already regretting the admission. Joe said, "You're the policeman, but I doubt there is much you can do in my case, even if you wanted to. You may just decide to arrest me."

Kevin squinted at Joe and shook his head in a sort of disbelief, but said nothing.

"There was this guy who had a boat…a sailboat…and I thought it would be a good idea to let Beth get away from everything and sail off to Bermuda."

Kevin nodded.

"So she did. I mean, I arranged that she did. I thought that would be the greatest thing on earth for her. She wasn't in any condition to protest, I mean, a beautiful sail to Bermuda." Joe fell silent. Kevin seemed to be following a blue jay and her mate as they hunted for berries around the redcurrant bush off to his right.

"I got into…I got…I started…" Joe fell silent again.

The blue jays flew off together with their bounty. A large dog barked in the distance, seemingly to scold Joe or maybe just to irritate him.

"This guy, Gerry, was…is somewhat of a crook. I take that back;

he is a crook. He suggested that I could help him. A favor for taking on this girl to Bermuda.

"Well, no, actually, the truth is, it started before that, when I think about it. We met in Provincetown at the gay club where I worked. I don't know what the hell he was doing there. He asked if I wanted to earn some extra money and as I was really poor, doing striptease in the middle of the night in P-town, what did I have to lose? But the stink of his offer turned me off…at first. I said I would think about it."

Another pause, the distant dog's repetitive rounds of barrel-chested barks—three in a row—echoing again and again, were the only noise breaking the silence.

"Meeting in a café the next day, he pushed me harder, saying that he had some stuff he needed storing temporarily. If I would do that for him, he would *richly reward me*, he said and showed me a wad of cash. I, obviously, understood that it had to be something illegal or he could just arrange storage himself. In fact, I still didn't see why he couldn't just rent some storage and put whatever it was there. I asked him that and he just looked at me for a while, probably trying to figure out how stupid I was.

"Then this guy says, 'Look, this is stuff my father is having me bring over to the US from Bermuda. He doesn't tell me what it is; to me it is just boxes. My dad stresses that they cannot be stored in his name. Or mine for that matter.'"

Again, Joe paused. Kevin scratched his ear and shut his eyes, acting as relaxed as an old dog or, Joe felt, more like the large cat, intensely aware without showing it.

"So look, you're the policeman. You know it's got to be funny business, but he kept suggesting that I would not have to worry about anything, nobody would know anything, and he was going to reward me, or his father would, like anybody who lent a hand in any business. It was all kind of vague, but I was exactly as he thought. Broke, young, and stupid.

"I asked him if it was drugs and he said absolutely not. His father would never dream of doing anything in that area. In fact, his dad probably didn't even know what drugs meant. That's when he hinted that it was probably artwork, even if, supposedly he didn't know what was in the boxes.

"Artwork didn't sound too bad to me, dumb me, and I had a cellar storage area, so I said I would do it temporarily. And it really wasn't going to be much; *just a few boxes*. And what clinched it was he made it sound like taking Beth with him to Bermuda was doing me a big favor."

Kevin continued his silence with his eyes imperceptibly open like the cat, only enough probably to see, now and then, if Joe's body language matched his voice. Joe looked at the sky seeing only the dire goddess of misery looking back down on him.

"Kevin, I've been naïve and stupid. Of course, I had to know what was in the boxes, so I bought some brown tape to reseal them and sneaked a look into some of the boxes that were lowest down, so that they maybe could be hidden under the other bunch of boxes. Maybe not so noticeable that I had tampered with them."

Kevin opened his eyes and gave Joe an anticipatory expression, probably an expression he used to pressure his suspects into continuing.

"Yeah, well," Joe said. "It wasn't drugs and it wasn't art; it was money. Cash. Stacks and bundles of American money. I lost my breath at the enormity of the cash if every box was packed with cash. Bills in different denominations, but mostly large bills.

"And…and I couldn't imagine that, with all the varying denominations, there was any way that this money was counted correctly. Well, actually, I could imagine, after I thought about it enough, trying to decide if I could help myself, so I let it be. For a while." Joe sat thinking for some minutes. "Except I did take some right away to give to Beth. She really needed money."

The only noise he and Kevin could hear were the nearby jays squawking and the drift of traffic off in the distance. Then the dog resumed its torturing rhythmic sound.

"It wasn't long after this all began that I met Martin on the beach and we became lovers and Martin asked if I wanted to come live with him…that he was lonely…that he loved me. And…well, Martin had money. Lots of income from books he wrote, his lectures, his university income, and, I don't know what, but he had money and a good life…except he was lonely.

"And when he asked me, I was, of course, glad to get away from the dumpy place I was living, to get a new life, to not be alone, to be in love…to be loved. Martin had a great summer house at the far end of Commercial Street in P-town and a brownstone in Boston's South End. I would be taken care of and he even liked that I had read a lot and had taught myself so much and that I liked to talk and discuss things.

"We were a great pair." He paused, tears in his eyes. "But, anyway, that's beside the point. I had started taking cash, and I took cash when I moved, skimming several boxes. I thought if Gerry missed it, I could just say he was mistaken, and, if he didn't. Well….

"I never really knew where he was at any one time. Once I had all my stuff out of the place, I emailed him and told him that I was moving and that he would have to find another place.

"He wrote back that he would immediately come over to move it to wherever I was moving. I said that was not possible and that I was moving in with someone else. He got really nasty, writing that I was a lot of things that should not be said in mixed company. Then he called and yelled at me and threatened me, saying that if I didn't let him move the boxes to the new place, he would kill my newfound friend. Kill him, Kevin. Can you imagine?"

Joe stopped again to slow his breathing.

"I assumed he didn't know who my friend was, and I wasn't about to volunteer that information. So, I guess, to show that he meant his threat, he set fire to the house in P-town. I mean, somebody did. We were in Boston that night when it happened. The fire and water damaged the place, of course, pretty bad. The inspectors saw whatever they see and said it was arson. Of course, I had to assume it was him. I have no idea how he found out whose house it was, but it is a small community. Provincetown, I mean.

"I was scared out of my mind. All I could think about was how I was ever going to get out of this mess. I didn't want Martin to know anything about it; he might throw me out. Probably would.

"The police couldn't know. What was I supposed to say? 'Hey, go look in the basement where I used to live. You'll find millions of dollars that I know nothing about.'

"And I still had the money I had stolen. Stupidly, I thought maybe if I returned it, he might leave me alone. I decided that the only answer was to rent a storage place in my name and haul it all over there. Obviously, I thought about how he would have to have access, how he would want to move the boxes himself to be sure where it all was and to count them to see if it was all there.

"I decided to go over to my old place to remind myself how much space I would have to rent and size up what it would take to move it all. And, of course, what I might need to do to put the cash back in the boxes. I was afraid he might be there, so after dark, I waited outside the house for a while. Seeing absolutely no one, I went in the front door. My one-room furnished place was on the first floor with the storage closet in the basement.

"Everything seemed quiet, so I went downstairs. But it was all gone." He looked at Kevin. "I mean, all the boxes were gone. Basement broken into through a window in the back. Lock on the door to the storage room snapped off and the door left open.

"I've been scared ever since. All the boxes were either stolen by some lucky thief who found his life's dream, or Gerry himself, or someone he knew, had come over, broken into the basement, and removed all the boxes. Either way, I was in trouble and, sorrowfully, I was sure that Martin was in trouble, too. Because of me."

Now Kevin must have felt that Joe was not going to continue on his own and finally spoke. "And how did you resolve it?"

"You're so funny, Kevin. So funny." Joe's face felt so tired and sad that it seemed heavy enough to slide off his skull.

Kevin said, "You didn't."

Joe said, "I went into hiding. Well, we did. I mean, I didn't tell Martin anything, but I had two things going for me. One was the basic principle that we, as gays, tend to hide anyway. We keep everything that we can think of as private as possible. My name on nothing; his name on the bare minimum, not even the door. So Martin found nothing strange in my stressing that part. And I reminded him that someone tried to burn down his P-town house and, thus, we were in some sort of threatening situation, at least, in P-town. So we stayed away, hiding, I hoped, in Boston until the police could do their work or assure us that it was safe to rebuild and to be there.

"And that's it. Twenty-two years later, Martin dies in the car wreck; my name gets publicized. I am worried."

"And the cash?"

"It's pretty much...well, no, I have some, but some was spent over time. Martin never really noticed that some bills were paid cash. But I lived in constant fear, and now...even now, this many years later, I don't know when and what to expect. I guess I deserve it; I asked for it."

Again, only silence, except for the ever-grinding dog bark.

"So you see, Kevin. I'm not such a trustworthy guy. And now I don't know what to do. I feel that they should have just let me die in the hospital. Truly, Kevin, I have no reason to want to live. I don't."

The two sat in silence for several minutes. Even the birds and the dog seemed to have stopped to listen.

As if Joe had only expressed a dislike for his hospital bed, Kevin said in his usual deep calm voice, "Joe, just take care of yourself. Get well. Come live with us. I will protect you. I will take care of the rest."

The days went by. Joe's health allowed him to be discharged and the administrative office was somewhat taken aback when he paid his bill with cash. Joe moved in with Beth and Kevin.

The development of drones and their applications had caught Joe's eye. Thinking that a drone could be something with which a limping cripple could occupy his mind and time, when Kevin and Beth's daughter, Geena, came home on a visit from the university, Joe asked her if she would help to choose a drone and help Joe to learn how to run it, but then it turned out that Geena helped him even more.

Geena began showing Joe how the drone could flip and zip and turn, fly under fences and around trees. And Joe was pleased that Geena seemed to find it fun, but he soon began to doubt that he, himself, would find these limited antics could be entertaining for long.

Usually Geena never stuck around for long, seemingly of the same opinion as Joe, but playing with the drone together with Joe one morning in the yard, she, having the mouth of a bricklayer, said, "Hey, Joe, see those fucking pigeons crapping up our roof? See if you can chase them off the fucking place."

And he did. And he kept repeatedly chasing the pigeons off day after day with the drone until the birds gave up and decided another house was probably a better nesting place.

Some days later she had asked, "Listen, Joe, can we get a drone with a camera? Are they too expensive? We could go over to the shitty ball games in the park arena on Union. You could film them. I can edit them, and we can post them on the Bangor Daily's pissy blog."

And so the ballpark project began, becoming so popular that Joe began to feel some optimism in his life. During the filming of one of the local softball games on a Sunday afternoon, Joe was approached by a man who wondered if Joe could help the man inspect a building site by using the drone and the camera. And Joe's business began, with Geena helping him to price the work.

His body was healing and his fear of being murdered could begin to fade.

3. BETH

THE RETURN TO BERMUDA

BETH HAD SENT AN EMAIL TO THE ADDRESS ON KARL BECK'S *SECURE YOUR FAMILY* website saying, *Your old sailing friend misses you* with her email address. A couple days went by, with her doubt growing about his responding, when she got an email from some email address she did not recognize and the weirdest text: *Can you meet me down there? Old Scar_l_Belly.*

Thinking this was some sort of spam, she almost erased it, but let it be. In the middle of the night, that night, it struck her that it had to be Karl, which she was now spelling in her mind with a K, the way the journalist did. He had written Carl with a C hidden in the signature. But there was no date, no time, no location. She figured that *down there* could be both reference to the scar and Bermuda. He was being so clandestine that she was afraid to try to write him back on that email address, but felt she had to.

She waited until she had spoken with Florie about visiting and had bought her plane ticket before she wrote back. She decided she should be secretive, too, and wrote only *OK fly Sat* having no idea if it would make any sense to him, if he would be there, or even if it was him. And how she would find him in all of Bermuda was, for the time being, a complete mystery to her.

When she finally got on the plane at Logan, fear stirred with guilt into a panicky soup. She was lying and sneaking off from Kevin to meet a murderer. Or maybe not meet him at all. Maybe it wasn't him. What could she possibly do that would help him? What could he want? And why? Why was she doing this? She tried over and over to force her mind to think it was the joy of seeing Florie after twenty-four years, but this thought was always trampled by a herd of *whys?*

When Beth landed at the airport on Bermuda's Saint David's Island, Florie met her with tons of hugs and a big flower garden–bouquet.

"Oh, Florie, you carried those flowers all the way out here on the bus? They must have taken a seat by themselves." Beth had tears in her eyes. She was more happy to see Florie again than she had envisioned.

Florie was decked out in her most colorful long dress of flowery reds and yellows, bright yellow sandals, and was as Beth remembered her, Florie the beautiful black model with bobbed hair, a never-aging movie star. Beth, with her page boy and light brown overalls, felt outclassed in every way including by Florie's graceful hand movements.

Beth never felt graceful or elegant despite her tall, thin figure; she was the blue-collar ambulance crew member. Beth's height had cramped her on the plane, and now, just as was her lot in the ambulance, also on the bus from the airport. Beth visually inhaled the forgotten explosive floral beauty along the road, and she soon forgot her discomfort as they settled into happy talk and happy tears.

In her little house wrapped so tightly in the thick green and vibrant flowers of her herbaceous yard, Florie had made room for Beth by borrowing an air mattress and moving a main room chair and a table to the other side of the room. As far as Beth was concerned, it was perfect.

But once Beth had gone to bed, she couldn't sleep; her mind would not shut down. She kept noticing sounds outside which, of course, she knew all had to be normal city sounds, but then....

The next morning was a Bermudian beautiful spring day with all the accoutrements of flowers, birds, and cheerful faces. Still dressed in her brown overalls, Beth took Florie, who now wore her turquoise gown, which in the light breeze flowed like water around her, down to a touristy place on Cavendish Road for breakfast, the first time Florie had gone out for breakfast for as long as Florie could remember.

Sunlit by a large window next to the glass door, the bright café had three kitchen-like tables with chairs and a short sitting counter for three people. The place smelled of chamomile, ginger, peppermint, lavender and sweet pastries. That morning, as it was a bit late for the early workers or tourists, the café was empty except for one man, his back to them, bent over a coffee at the counter.

They both ordered green tea and a breakfast of fresh-made pastries with a side of strawberries. They had talked about each other's health yesterday on the bus and now the subject was Beth's marriage and who Kevin was. Because she so trusted Florie, Beth felt she could even relate some things she felt were a big quirky about Kevin, even scary, such as overelaborate framing of his Eagle Scout badge and insistence that it be hung in the living room. Or even weirder was his unexplained obsession with a brick he said was important to him, like some sort of memento.

Although Beth also happily related her meeting and loving relationship with Kevin, Beth's mind began the uncontrollable mulling over Karl, his Bermuda presence or non-presence, until finally Florie said, "Beth, I feel something is bothering you." And in typical Florie frankness, she said, "What is it? Tell me. What have I done?"

Embarrassed, Beth said, "It's not you; absolutely not you." Then she realized that, if she talked about Karl, it would put her visit to Florie as less important, by giving the impression she was taking advantage of Florie's hospitality in order to meet Karl.

Beth wrapped her hands around her tea cup and said, "I have some bad memories here of some things that might have happened. You know me well, Florie. Now those things are coming back in flashes. I'm sorry, Florie. I came to see you and am so happy to see you."

"Yes, dear, but tell me exactly what you were thinking about."

Beth felt she had to answer. She waited until she felt she could present it right. "I am not sure if I am making this up. It might even be my imagination, but someone sent me a message that they might see me here."

"That's nice, dear. Who might that be?"

Beth noticed that Florie had not touched her tea. "You don't know him, but it is somebody that might be in big trouble. Oh, Florie, I don't know how to explain because I don't know much myself." She felt this was wrong, coming out so wrong and putting Florie in an uncomfortable situation.

The man said, "Let me explain." The short white man, who had been drinking coffee at the counter, stood at their table.

The sudden interruption stunned both Beth and Florie into silence. He was sturdily built, dressed in a tight-fitting black T-shirt, and white Bermuda shorts. But, as opposed to local white British descendants, he wore boat shoes and no socks. And he had short receding grey hair and was missing part of a finger on his left hand.

Beth gasped in a loud whisper, "Karl!"

Smiling, he looked from one to the other. "Hello, Beth." He turned to Florie and said, "Pardon my interruption. I am Karl from the boat…the boat that first brought both Beth and me to Bermuda. May I ask your name?"

Still being in a state of surprise or maybe upset about the sudden intrusion, Florie leaned back in her chair like she had smelled a bad odor and said, "Florence."

Beth pulled herself together and said, "Oh, Florie, I am so sorry. I didn't introduce you." Superfluously, she resaid the names, "Florie, this is Karl. Karl, my best friend Florie."

With a suspicious smile and even reverting to Bermuda-speak, Florie said, "Hi bye, Karl. Nice to meet you."

Karl looked at Beth and said, "No hug?"

She got up and was, for a second, startled by how she didn't remember how short he was and how she needed to bend over. While hugging him, she was afraid to talk for fear Florie would notice her imminent tears. Finally, as she let go, she said, "So how did you find me…us? How did you know…?

He waved her off and said, "I followed you from the airport, not sure who you were with. Excuse me, Florie. Then I knew where you were staying, that is, with this nice woman and early this morning, I somehow sensed you would come here."

Beth might have questioned this vague explanation, but what difference did it make? All she could think of now was how could he be a murderer? She said, "So what are you doing here?"

"You know," said Florie loudly. "I have some errands to do. I will leave you two to it. See you later, Beth. Is that okay? You are all right?"

Beth felt an ache in her chest. It was typical Florie to be sure that Beth was feeling safe. And no doubt Florie was suspicious of the very friendly man in relation to Kevin, her loving husband. "I'm fine, Florie. I'm fine. But what do you need at home? Can I do some shopping?"

Having abandoned her tea and standing in the door, Florie said, "Beth, you catch up with Mr. Karl here and I will see you later at home."

Buckets of shame and guilt poured over Beth as she had barely begun her visit with Florie and already she was talking with someone else. Someone out of nowhere.

Karl seemed to sense the discomfort and said, "Florie, I will take care of her and make sure she returns home before curfew." A smiling pause. "Seriously, we will not be long. We can catch up later."

Beth wasn't sure what he meant by that, but she was glad he understood. Once they were alone, he said, "You want a coffee?"

She said, "Maybe a tea, some green tea. It doesn't matter."

Her head was spinning with where to start, what to ask. Why had she really made the contact? Had he thought about her? He must have or he wouldn't be here. This was all so stupid.

Once the herbal tisane arrived for her, coffee for him, she said in a low whisper, "I think it would be a good idea if you told me why you are hiding here."

"Hiding? Why would I be hiding?"

"You tell me."

"I am not hiding. I am here to see you."

With the waitress in the back room, it was no longer a whisper. "Karl, stop right there. You are here because the police are looking for you. Why are they looking for you?"

"The police are looking for me. That is correct, but I am not hiding from them. I have no reason to hide. I am here because someone murdered one of my people and I believe I know who did it and why."

"So you didn't kill anyone?" she asked.

"Oh, Beth, I have no reason to have killed my own employee."

"Unless you wanted to rob the bank."

"So you know some of the story. You have done some homework."

"My husband is a policeman and he heard about it."

Karl said, "So what connected this bank robbery with me?"

"I got a call from a journalist, who somehow managed to connect you with me. Before you ask, I don't know how. But he clarified that there was a bank robbery and the police were looking for you."

"So why he called you?"

"I guess he was chasing loose threads. I don't know."

He smiled. "And so you missed me. And so you sent me a message."

"And you acted like a secret agent or an escaped killer. With a coded response. And so why are you hiding, Karl?"

"No, I'm not hiding. I just didn't want to be held up or delayed in any way while following my suspect."

"Your suspect. And so he led you here by chance."

"Not by chance. Let me explain." He paused to take a drink of his black coffee. "I followed Gerry here."

"Gerry. Gerry. Gerry who? You act like I know Gerry. Do I know Gerry?"

"Yes, you do. He brought you here some years ago."

Beth squinted her eyes and tried to get her mind to overcome her surprise and doubt.

Without her response, Karl continued. "His father died a while back."

"Yes, I heard from Florie."

"I think Gerry has been looking for something that his father had hidden, and decided that the only way to get at it was to steal it. I don't know what it was, but I believe it was in a bank box or two and Gerry did not have access to them."

"But…"

"With the publishing of bid requests for the street work connected with a new security system for the bank, if one followed along with the news in Zurich, it was easy to see that the street excavation next to the bank was going to happen. As soon as I got the bid for the security, Gerry contacted me to ask me about that dig. Well, not directly, since that would be too obvious. But the timing for his sudden interest in talking with me as an old friend arose when the planning was happening. And about that time, the old man died, I might say, under rather suspicious circumstances, in my opinion."

He took another sip. "I didn't put two and two together until the robbery and the strange break-in of just two bank boxes. Why not break into all the boxes? Most all the boxes would have illicit valuables in them, unreportable by the owners. A perfect crime to steal things that no one can claim.

"So this is a specifically planned robbery and my guy is murdered and I am both pissed and curious, thinking who and why? To shorten the process for you, I checked out flights and hotels and they smelled of Gerry from Bermuda and who, this time visiting Zurich, did not contact me to say a friendly hello."

"You're quite the detective."

"Well, it's almost my business."

They became silent, Beth wondering what to say next. She was beginning to realize how young she had been, how many years it had been, how she really didn't know this guy.

He said, "So how have you been?"

He did ask about her job and her husband. She could only feel he was being a distant polite—Karl the polite one. Was she supposed to summarize twenty-some years? And if she did, why? Where was this going? Not.

She said, "I'm fine. But I was wondering, why not report our captain to the police instead of following him here?"

"Beth, this guy is one slippery bastard. He has been transferring something illegal for his father from or to the USA, or maybe both ways, on a regular basis, probably on our trip, too. I suspect cash, but I don't know. There is no way the Swiss police could have any clue and they would have very little motivation to follow up what I could tell them on a guess…a whim. I came here to get some proof."

"And so? Have you? Do you have the proof?"

He paused. "I'm sorry, Beth, but I am not going to involve you in this. The less you know, the better."

"But I am involved. You asked me to be here."

"I did? I think you came here after many years to visit your good friend."

"You?" she said baffled.

"No, your friend Florie. It is in your own best interest to forget you saw me here."

"This doesn't make sense. Why did you ask if I could meet you here?"

"Did I?"

"Yes, you did. Now stop it. Why did you?"

Karl got up out of his chair and put some money on the table. "I can't tell you that." And he walked out the door.

Beth was thrown into confusion and exasperation, but she was determined to not let this mood destroy her visit with Florie. Beth was doubly irritated at herself because Florie was being the most gracious of hosts while, at the same time, it was hard for Beth to show her appreciation through the blanket of bewilderment.

Immediately upon seeing Florie that late afternoon, Beth had related the story she had heard of Gerry's father's death being maybe questionable, to which Florie seemed to just nod a knowing assent. It seemed to be a subject Florie preferred to drop. In fact, their evening together was strained with silence and trivial conversation.

The next day, the first of two chunks of information hit her already-bewildered mind. Trying to concentrate on being attentive to Florie and Florie seemingly being able to spend all her time with Beth, Beth began to wonder for the first time how it was that Florie managed to live with no discernable job or income. Beth realized that she had, at passing moments, thought about asking Florie about her livelihood, but it had always been the wrong moment or it just seemed inappropriate to pry.

"Florie," Beth said, as they were walking home after shopping for some flour and potatoes, "don't you have to work? Here I am taking up all your time and you are always out and about with me, taking care of me, making me feel guilty. Have you taken time off for me?"

Florie said, "Am I spending too much time with you, my dear? Am I in your way? Would you like to be more alone?"

Beth understood that Florie was referring to this secret relationship Beth seemed to have with this sudden visitor.

"No!" she yelled, much too loudly as she saw people on the street turn to look. In a loud whisper, she said, "Florie, I want to be with you. That is not what I meant. I mean, how do you manage to live with no job?"

Florie was silent for what seemed like minutes to Beth and she began to wonder if Florie had not understood her question. She was about to ask again, when she stopped herself, thinking it would be rude to ask again if Florie had reason not to answer.

Then Florie said, "First of all, my dear, I have a job as an English teacher in the equivalent here of your high school. I don't have to work right now. School's out." She paused again. "And there's a bit of extra money. There was a court case once, not too long ago, against old Jason Hutchins that, as a group, our club dared to bring against him. And, although we could not get him put in prison, he agreed to pay his victims something." She paused to let that sink in.

Beth understood. With further detail, Florie's past hell would be ripped opened like a scab. She said, "I'm sorry, Florie. It was none of my business."

"You couldn't know, my dear. Don't worry. Let's make a beautiful lunch."

Then on Thursday, the day before Beth was to leave for Boston, Beth concentrated on her visit with Florie and enjoyed even their proximity to each other as they small-talked in the small kitchen. It felt warm and happy.

They were in the middle of putting the last touches on their lunch preparation, when Florie said, "From the pictures you showed me of your wedding, I'd swear I saw your Kevin out on the street here."

Before Beth could respond, an excited, pudgy, round woman with an outsized afro appeared at Florie's door with a concerned look on her face and, flapping her hand, signaled for Florie to come outside.

Beth could hear some animated whispering from both of them. When Florie returned, she had a somewhat dazed look on her face, but a dazed expression secreting a disguised smile.

Beth continued to move and resituate things on the table to try to look busy. She didn't dare to ask anything as she felt she had pried too much into Florie's business, but Florie burst out, "He's dead. Gerry Hutchins is dead."

Beth stopped moving like a mousing cat suddenly listening, waiting for more direction and said, "Dead? How did he die?"

"They found him drowned by his boat. Apparently, he fell overboard and a rope from the boat got caught around his neck."

Beth flew to Logan the next day where Kevin was waiting for her for the long drive up to Maine.

No, she was not sorry nor sad. Yes, she had known Gerry, but from what she had learned about him, it was hard for her to be sad. She had had a great time with Florie, happy to see that Florie was doing well and the weather had been incredible. She missed Kevin and was glad to be home. How was Shadow?

4. JOE

BETH IS OUT OF SORTS

Joe bought the Nuss household an electric pasta maker as a thank-you gift for letting him stay in their house. He was being a bit selfish, he knew, because, while living with Martin, he had acquired the taste for homemade pasta and had from their travels taught himself how to make real sauces from Italy.

It was dinner time. Beth had arrived home; Kevin would arrive soon; and daughter Geena, home from school, had set the table before disappearing to the bathroom.

Joe and Beth were working in the kitchen as a regular routine after Joe moved in, Joe feeling a huge obligation to be of assistance despite his still-healing wounds after almost two years. Even if the kitchen was surely not the biggest Joe had seen, he made the best of it. In fact, he missed Martin's kitchen where Joe was spoiled with the finances and the freedom to arrange it just the way Joe wanted.

Not only did this old kitchen feel darker and smaller because of the greenish patterned wallpaper, but it was, in fact, physically smaller with less available counter space for such things as this pasta maker, and less floor area for the Formica table and metal-tube chairs to barely squeeze in. Joe felt guilty that his presence was making the crowding worse than it used to be, because now with four in the house, the table could no longer be pushed up against the wall.

Every detail in the Nuss's kitchen was smaller including the window above the sink, the metal sink itself, the white fridge, and the light-wood veneer cupboards. The only thing that had seemed bigger was the rumbling dishwasher, but that, as Joe soon discovered, was an illusion because it was an older American model with less useable internal space than the silent German model he and Martin had had.

Joe's appreciation included doing the laundry and cleaning the house. And for the practical reason of needing the exercise to build his strength, he felt, along with long walks, that housework was a good beginning, especially because their less-than-advanced appliances took more energy than he had previously been accustomed to, like Martin's robotic vacuum cleaner.

But Joe knew that the time with Martin was gone and that he had to accept that he had nothing of his own, except the money he stole. So if Beth and Kevin were happy with it all, then he was pleased and could only be thankful for their gracious hospitality.

"So," Joe said, as he and Beth stood at the gas stove, "you use good canned tomatoes without added ingredients, a pure Italian olive oil, which I had shipped to us from an importer, and just a little garlic, salt, and pepper. Voila. We have a great sauce which just needs to simmer a little over a low flame. The pasta will be ready in five."

Then Joe noticed something again on which he had not dared to comment before. Beth's tears.

Joe said quietly, "Sorry, Beth, but are you crying?"

She stood beside him, not moving for what seemed an eternity to Joe as he slowly stirred the sauce with a wooden spoon.

She said, "I think I'm just tired."

He said, "Come on, Beth. What's the problem?"

She said, "Well, it's nothing you can do anything about. You just remind me of…Davis."

"Davis? Who's Davis?"

"Davis is our son."

Now Joe was in tangled bewilderment, with all kinds of thoughts running rapidly through his mind. Where was this Davis? Was he dead? In the military? Almost two years, and Joe had not heard of anybody called Davis.

Beth was silent. He waited.

Beth said, "Sorry, Joe. It's a bad chapter in our life and sometimes I just can't keep it away."

Joe stirred the sauce slowly and as quietly as he could.

"We, some years ago, we adopted a newborn we named Davis. So we considered him our own. But..." She stopped again, wiping her eyes with a paper napkin from the table. "There was something born in him that we couldn't understand. He had an aggressiveness or anger that was hard to control. We took him to doctors and, eventually, to psychiatrists. He got medication and counseling, but we finally, against my will, had to put him in an institution at a fragile age for, I was told, his own protection."

Joe felt it best to make no comment. This was as personal as personal could get, and Joe was sure that nothing he could say would help.

Beth said, "I used to visit him on a regular basis, but putting him into an institution was like punishment for everyone."

"So, you said *used to*. You don't visit him anymore?"

"Well, he's out now. Living on his own somewhere in New Hampshire."

"You don't know where? What's he doing? How is he surviving?"

"He seems to have...well, he stopped communicating with us after he got out, except to send me that poem." She points at a white paper slip taped near the holder for the paper towels. "You probably never noticed it."

But he had noticed it. He saw it when he first arrived, always doubting that he should ask about it since it seemed to be so sad and personal. On the lined paper in carefully, neatly handwritten ballpoint ink, but unsigned, was written the following:

The Stay

Seeking the opiate pleasure of absolute truths,
Omnipresence of loving, the theory of strings,
Like unified judgments, like pigeons on roofs,
My facade was shattered by dissonant rings.
Choir: My facade all scattered. Reality stings.

I entered a room like a vacuous court.
They took all my clothes and gave me a cape,
Not Batman's. Backwards. Embarrassing. Short.
My bare ass was showing. I couldn't escape.
Choir: Embarrassment showing. I couldn't escape.

My face was my butt. Picasso-y art.
As sound unsoftened could echo throughout,
Discharging cacophonies gave me a start.
They flew to the ceiling and even went out.
Choir: They grew to the ceiling and even blew out.

Out to the garden. 'Twas thunder, they said.
With sirens resounding and sulfurous smells,
I climb under the covers and into my head.
Multiverses of heavens and parallel hells.
Choir: Perverse verses of heavenly hells.

Seeking the opiate pleasure of absolute truths,
Omnipresence of loving, the theory of strings,
Like unified judgments, like pigeons on roofs,
My facade was shattered by dissonant rings.
Choir: My facade all scattered on reality's wings.

Joe said, "Yeah, I've seen it. I always thought it was some song lyric, since, well, it has all the structure, but I didn't recognize it…I mean, as a song I knew."

She said, "Maybe he meant it that way…as a song, but he has always written poetry. I think…I think…he is either very bitter…probably mad at us, as maybe he should be, or…I don't know, he did some research while he was in the… place and…" Again, it seemed she needed to think. But she wasn't crying. "He seems to have been looking for his real mother and, I guess, to have found her. I don't know what that means…for her, I mean."

Joe knew better than to ask more or bring up the subject of Davis again, but as the days and weeks passed, Beth seemed to have stopped crying. Joe hoped that her speaking about it with him had helped, and, more so, that he, Joe, no longer reminded her of Davis.

But it wasn't the last time she cried. He supposed it was natural that he should become her confidant, and he couldn't say he hated it. He, too, needed social intercourse; didn't all humans, like all the other social animals on earth? And maybe someone to lean on.

Like so many Saturday afternoons, in the dank, unfinished wash-room downstairs, they were once again separating laundry into colors when he asked Beth why she decided to work as an EMT.

He added, "For me, it seems too gruesomely—yuck! Bloody! Why and how do you do it?"

"I don't know. I suppose I have that urge some people have…to save the world, or what else do they call it? A nurse's martyr complex?"

He said, "Hmm, yeah, that may be true, but…"

"But what?"

"Well, I'm being very nosey, but why do you think you have that complex, if that's what it is?"

"Actually, I don't think that it's so hard for me to think why. You have forgotten, Joe. I have not. I ran away from home and you saved me. You know my story if anyone does. I was never nursed, so to speak. My parents had nothing to give in emotional support, so I'm probably trying to make up for that vacuum in my life."

They were silent for a while, except for the grunts and groans of bending over sorting clothing, but which were being mostly drowned out by the thunder of the old washer, which Joe thought sounded like a bowling alley.

Joe said, "How do they make washing machines so that they eat one sock?"

Beth smiled and said, "It's an industry secret."

Joe said, "I'm into secrets. Who do you know that can solve the mystery?"

She said, "You know the man of mysteries; ask him."

Joe said, "So are you happy?"

Surprised, Beth looked at him with a quizzical expression. "Why are you asking? You think I shouldn't be?"

Joe said, "No, that's not it. But happiness is elusive and certainly relative."

Her expression showed that she was obviously not sure what he was saying or why. She was only forty-four years old, but to him, at this moment—maybe it was just the basement lighting greying her hair and exaggerating her facial creases—she looked sixty.

She said, "I am the luckiest person on earth. Sure, as you know, we've had some tough periods, but I guess, you know, just what you said. Those tough times make me appreciate what I have. I love what I do and hope I die doing it. But my greatest happiness is Kevin…my man of music and devotion. How could I be more lucky?"

He guessed that she stopped short saying more either because she didn't want to make him sad for losing his love in the accident, or maybe she felt it was none of his business.

He wanted to ask if she felt she had to nurse Kevin, too, but decided that was much too personal and he was uncertain as to why he even had that thought.

He wasn't even sure why he had thought to ask such a question and regretted asking. But he had begun to worry for her and he couldn't tell her why. Even if he knew why himself and which he didn't, he could never and would never have told her.

But there was something about Kevin that was bothering Joe. And since he didn't know what that something was, other than a feeling, he promised himself never to bring up the subject of happiness again with Beth and to chase his own concerns about Kevin out of his mind, especially because she had just begun silently crying and gone upstairs.

As Joe continued alone sorting the laundry, his mind played a moment with Beth's *being out of sorts*. But the humor was lost in his uncertainty about whether she was crying because of something she knew about Kevin, or had the two had a serious argument, or had Joe again reminded her of Davis?

He would never know.

5. KEVIN

MR. LUDOVICO

It was the early fall with a slight hint of 2017's winter breath sliding south from Canada on its invisible grey runners. Kevin had been promoted four years earlier to detective with Crime Investigation Unit responsibilities, his dream job.

Lisa Underwood, the station's new receptionist, guides an unusual visitor from Maine Marine into Kevin's office and announces Marine Patrol Sergeant Steve Cummings.

Cummings says, as Lisa leaves the office, "Whoa, detective, she has two parts of everything interesting just in the right place. You know, from the outside, this police station looks like a mausoleum, but I think she'd wake the dead. She'd sure be dangerous in my office. She'd sink boats."

Kevin does not answer as the sergeant's comments feel like a boot heel grinding into his brain. What should he say? Kevin's short, explosive relationship with her had sucked him into a fiery timeless heat, scorched him, and swept him out onto the bleak earth like a burnt crust. In the back of his mind, he suspects the pile of ashes that she has created is towering, but he can't care as he feels an overwhelming strong ache, a yearning for her. No, an ache, a regret that it is over, even if logically he repeats to himself that it is for the best.

It had to end somehow, or it would have ended his marriage. He's married and forty-seven; Lisa's twenty-one and single. And sexy. For Kevin, sexy like tormenting lust. For Kevin, sexy like cyclonic desire tearing through the police station, every eye like his must be on the movement of her large perfect breasts and her tiny waist spreading to tightly-clothed hips and buns, barely a thin layer away from complete nubile nudity, always tight clothes to emphasize her bodily perfections.

Then she had asked Kevin for a ride home in a stunning moment while they were alone in his office.

"Sorry to ask you this, Kevin, but my car is at the dealer getting fixed. Would it be possible you could give me a lift home?"

She could have asked any one of the cops or staff in the station, but she asked Kevin. She said *Kevin* with a look that Kevin couldn't distinguish as a come-on.

She said *Kevin* like she wanted to know him, like she already knew him, in a young voice without tattered edges. Her question instantly blew all common sense out of his brain, obliterating any answer. Finally, after sorting the major pieces of his brain back into place, he said, "Sure. Of course. What time is it? Where do you live? I'm kinda busy, but it's okay."

Kevin had always and importantly kept his cool under duress, or tried at least, like during the car crash, the execution of investigations, even gunfire and, as he well knew, murder. He stood up, but she triggered something inside him, something that made him feel like he was standing on a trampoline.

He finally got his mouth to stop its senseless blather and waited for her to answer.

"Well, if you're too busy…"

"No, no, it's fine. Let's go," he said, like it was a date to see a movie.

"No," she said. "It's only fourteen hundred. I work until seventeen hundred, if that's okay."

He had to pause to arrange the military time. "Why are you using seventeen hundred? Have you been in the military?"

"Oh, no," she said. Her broad blue eyes stayed open dipping directly into his; her lips parted imperturbably as she smiled. Her chestnut shoulder-length hair curved to make her face seem a subtle heart shape. "I just thought that's what you might use. My dad used it, coming from the military and everything."

"No, we don't use it much in oral…while we are talking. It's okay, I'll see you at five. Just come in my office…stop in…and we'll go out…leave." Everything he said seemed to have sexual overtones.

She smiled her glowing, searing smile and said, "Thank you, Kevin." The same intimate penetrating *Kevin*.

After she left, his mind seemed to work again, but through a queasy filter of static. He was disturbed by his reaction. What was this in him? How could he be so thrown out of control, out of command of the situation? Beth was his love, the one he knew loved him. Is this what his father had bequeathed him? Uncontrollable lust?

With no clarification or tuning out the filter static, his caseload didn't get the attention it deserved for the rest of the afternoon. A few sentences here and there followed by no relevant thought.

And as five o'clock approached, he felt a prickling in his body, vibrating with a rising intensity he could only hope to control. He forced his head down to face the papers on his desk, but he no longer had any idea what, if anything, was written on them.

It was five by his watch, in fact, it was now a minute past. Had she found a ride with someone else? Two minutes past and she should have been there. She was just across the large foyer. Maybe she had changed her mind. Probably.

"Am I disturbing?" she said, exactly at four minutes and twenty-seven seconds past as she entered the office with her smile that sent the electricity down his spine.

"Yes, you are," he said, trying to sound humorous, rather than truthful.

In the parking lot, he began to head to the passenger side to open the door for her, but stopped himself. She wasn't a date. But in the car like a teenage learner, he had to concentrate on how to start the engine, how to back out of the parking space, to decide if and how to shift gears. He concentrated so hard that he forgot to ask where she was going until the edge of the parking lot, not knowing which way to turn.

"Home," she said. "Turn left." She didn't give an address.

As the old local police detective, he knew the town frontwards and backwards and would have known where to go, but she just told him where to turn and he was fine with that. It kept him from struggling to make a map in his head, to arrange a conversation in his head, to find something to talk about. Something about which they both could be interested in talking. Other than sex.

She began touching his arm as she gave instructions on where to turn, soft touches that persisted longer as they went. And he was driving too fast no matter how slowly he drove. He would arrive at the end of this intimacy too soon.

After only about ten minutes, she said, "I live here on the right." And without a pause, she said, "Come on up and have a beer."

He almost said he couldn't. He almost said he had to get home. But he couldn't. He couldn't make himself say it. He said simply, "Okay."

It was like sorcery, making his mind skip and erase material reality. Within seconds of closing the apartment door, she had her fingers on his pants and upon feeling his reaction, she had unzipped him and begun working on making him harder, if that were possible.

He remembered nothing of how they got from the entrance door to her bed, how they had stripped naked, and how he had slipped deep inside her. He did remember that within seconds after he had come that she didn't stop there and made him come a second time.

How had it been with Beth in the beginning? Was it the same? But now Lisa's breasts were so much younger, her body incredibly new, exotic, and extraordinary. He didn't remember having ever come twice before during lovemaking with Beth.

And Lisa seemed so happy about it, so pleased with herself that she could make Kevin come twice, even saying, "I bet you didn't think you could do that, huh? I'm good at that."

It wasn't until he was home in bed lying next to a sleeping Beth, unable to stop reveling in and reliving the episodic intensity, that he understood "I'm good at that" meant that Lisa was telling him that she had practiced with many others and often.

As the days passed, each day they found time somewhere to fuck, sneaking off to her apartment at lunch, faking overtime in the evening and even skipping food.

Toward the end of the second week at noon, pressing her up against a cold cement wall after climbing down the metal stairs into the station furnace room, it seemed to take her an abnormally long while to arrive back upstairs in the station. But, as soon as she did, she stepped immediately into his office that afternoon and complained.

"You left me there."

He said, "Well, I thought I'd better hurry to get back up here before anyone missed me, or became suspicious that both of us were not in the office."

"You left me with your mess. I had to use my panties to clean up and, then, when I got up to the restroom, I had to flush them down the toilet."

Looking intently at her, trying to figure out what she was telling him, Kevin said, "What could I do? What could I have done?"

"You could have stayed with me, helped me, brought me down some toilet paper."

It hadn't made sense to him, but that night as he lay in bed holding Beth next to himself, he understood that Lisa had wanted to be held like any woman, and he felt terrible. What a small favor to ask. They had gone to the cellar, fucked, and, nervous at being caught, he had abandoned her, dumped her immediately, left her standing alone in a dim-lit basement against that hard, cold wall with his warm selfish desire leaking down the insides of her thighs. He understood. He felt sorry and wanted to make it up to her. Do whatever he could do.

It was after that she seemed to find senseless hurdles to meeting him, insignificant daily obligations—shopping, visiting parents, hairdresser—which had never seemed to arise before.

The following week, he told Beth that he had an emergency on Wednesday evening, when Lisa had suddenly said to come over. He was so pleased they were finally, once again alone in her lair that he hardly noticed her demeanor, that she was distracted. That is when, as he wrapped his arms around her in his exhilaration that they were finally together again, she said she had met someone and wasn't interested in sex with Kevin anymore. She told him that she had found someone she *really liked a lot* and who *wasn't just a fuck buddy*.

Kevin stood numbed as her young, soft body slid like ice out from his arms. Being ripped out of a dream, cast out from their secret hideaway, Kevin's brain was thrown into unrecognizable chaos, so foreign he could not move or speak.

How could she matter-of-factly tell him she didn't want him in her apartment, where he had been so yearning to return and had felt he would be so welcome, as before, and where he would atone for his mistake? He wasn't sure how, but he had been so sure he would somehow make it up to her. Now suddenly, here he was, left standing in the reality that he was excised from that dream. Ejected like brown masticated chaw.

She even thanked him for their time together, like it had been lunch, and hoped that he had enjoyed it as much as she had. It seemed extraneous to reality that she would say such a thing. It was pointless to tell her how he certainly must have enjoyed it a thousand times more than she had, since, obviously, it had no importance to her how he really felt now about their time together.

Now he had to creep toward the door, to fumble at the doorknob, to crawl from a fantasy of heat and passion, looking exactly like the cartoon of a whipped dog, an image he was powerless to change, nor was he able to say anything that would maintain his dignity.

Once outside, his walk from her door to his car was a marathon of a thousand steps and of concealed eyes following each step. And driving home, he kept losing the way, circling blocks and neighborhoods.

From the bed, Beth, still awake, said how happy she was that he was home earlier than expected. He knew, at that moment, it was to Beth that he owed all the atonement on earth, which he then despaired of ever achieving, one iota. What kept Kevin from sleeping that night wasn't frustration or anger or a wish for revenge, or at least not directly, but anguish he did not recognize. Next to Beth lay a fool.

The next day in the office Lisa still existed. She was still walking, no, slinking around, taunting him by just being there, strewing his ego in pieces onto the floor, and smiling at him like they were just old friends. It wasn't until now, when she was forbidden and unreachable, that he understood how he had become mindlessly addicted to her, but that for her, from the very start, he had just been that fuck buddy.

So, who is this uniformed moron in front of him now? Kevin, who never otherwise raised his voice, yells at the man. "What can I do for you, Sergeant?"

The man pauses giving Kevin a narrow-eyed glare. "Well, Detective, we think we have an old murder at hand…a Mr. Ludovico…set up as an accident. We are not detectives at Maine Marine, just safety instructors. We need a police detective to take over the case."

Immediately Kevin is sorry he yelled at the man, and is directly worried. He sits up in his chair, takes out a log book, holds his pen as steadily as he can, and begins writing with the date and time of the visit, etching furrows in the paper from nervously pressing on the log book so hard, until it strikes him he had not listened.

It is not an investigation of him, Kevin.

This is something good. Really good. This is something to tear his mind away from her. He can put his whole being into this case. He should be pleased.

"Please, Sergeant, I'm all ears."

"Well, Detective, I'm all something else after seeing that gorgeous thing you have as a receptionist."

Kevin, referring to the sergeant's body part, says, "Don't be that something. It isn't worth it. It could be painful. You married, sergeant?"

"Okay, I get it. Don't be a dick, but she's a looker. Don't tell me you haven't thought about it."

Kevin doesn't answer. As the sergeant explains the background for his visit, the pieces fall together, and Kevin begins feeling better, since piece by falling piece, Kevin decides what he can do. His fool-hearted misery will stop; a killing will do the trick.

6. BETH

THE SHED

I<small>N COLD</small> M<small>ARCH</small> 2018, B<small>ETH WAS STANDING IN THE RAIN LOOKING DOWN A HUN-</small>dred feet at the shed. It was on the western outskirts of Bangor at the lower end of a field of an abandoned farm. It was the only remnant of that farm, a shack, which, although wooden and needing paint, had coped with the Maine winters through the years without collapsing because of its stone foundation, although one church preached that it was only the devil that could have built it and maintained it for so many years. How else would this den of iniquity be the sole building with no trace of a farm otherwise? For them it had the smell of accursed brimstone, and for everyone else just a despicable stench.

With tense voices, the locals called it *The Shed* and warned their children to stay away from it as did the parents themselves because The Shed was dangerous and only visited by evildoers and degenerates.

Through the years The Shed had certainly lost any odor or physical traces of animals, but Beth assumed it had been an outbuilding for grazers, for sheltering sheep or cows.

Beth and her shift partner Frank Stern stood, arms folded, in their rain gear with their backs against the heavy ambulance to avoid the disturbing effect of the emergency vehicle's oscillating red warning lights. They had an overview of the street, the field to their left, The Shed below the field, and wooded area behind The Shed and had made themselves visible to the police for any call for assistance.

Not that they shouldn't be attentive, but normally, when the call went out concerning The Shed, it was only about a slugfest, a knifing, or an overdosed addict, but never anything personally threatening to the ambulance crew. The police did all the heavy work, calming down eventual combatants or checking for weapons.

And now today underneath her conscious thoughts, she needed to be distracted from vague unsettling thoughts that had been flowing through her since the call. So today, as she felt the rain, heavy and warm, it was hatching the memory of that critical time, back then on the ocean, that transformation. That memory was still hers to use. To deal with disquieting thoughts. Usually.

But today, like an old neon light, the normally soothing power of rain was flickering on and off. Beth was feeling an irritated anxiety initiated by the strange thing about today's call; it was much too early in the day for the junkies to be gathering at The Shed. Put that together with the fact that the majority of the ambulance calls included specifics when dispatch was informed, and which allowed the ambulance team to prepare. But not this time, which would ordinarily qualify this as one more required-but-pointless run since, probably, the ambulance was not needed at the scene. So all Beth and Frank could do was stand in limbo with a blank slate until the police arrived.

And possibly to brood in the gloom.

Beth had always been able to smell the distinctness of rain since the sailing trip those thirty short years ago. Of course, the sound was different, too, but she actually *smelled* the difference between ocean and land rain. Warm rain had followed the frightening ocean windstorm when Beth was sure she was going to die. And it had been those subsequent days of rain and Karl's voice that had calmed her after the storm, and thus, ever since, rain and the faint memories of Karl had comforted her and even strengthened her. Yes, rain on land smelled different, sounded different. But still. It was rain.

She had used the rain during the pregnancy and birth of Geena, using the advice from her nurse friends to stay calm. And everything had gone well; the rain was her crutch. After Geena's birth, Beth had needed the rain even more. Her life with Kevin began to plague Beth's mind with indistinct misgivings. But they were young; of course, she knew she couldn't understand everything. Her friends in her health world helped her to rationalize that people change as they get older. The sexual contact continued. But it was subtly different, and aberrant enough that it seemed Beth could not get pregnant again. Doctors found no physical problem. Was it Kevin who was different or was she? That question might have incited conflict between them, but instead, laid an evasive blanket of silence over the uncertainty. After two years of trying to have a second child, they decided on adoption. And, with his disruptive diversion, Davis burgled her thoughts away from questions about Kevin.

Unexpectedly, out of the corner of her eye, Beth saw the movement of a figure. "Hey, isn't that Joe over there?" Beth asked Frank.

Beth couldn't see through the thick rain if it really was Joe or what he was doing, but the figure standing up the street about a football field away had the same body profile as Joe.

She had been a bit perturbed that Joe had forgotten her recent birthday. Joe normally remembered better than Kevin ever did. Joe had said April Fools Day always reminded him of her birthday on the third. But, of course, Joe was busy, what with his business and all. Not that her turning fifty this April was so special really, but he had always been good at remembering to wish her many more happy years.

But maybe he knew the days were not so joyous as they used to be. In fact, she was not even so sure anymore how they used to be. How had it been with Kevin? She was sure she had loved him and he had loved her. But had they just been...what? In lust? Naïve? No, she still loved him deeply and was helpless to feel any other way. Bring on the rain.

Just a month ago out of nowhere, in some miracle of distant mental empathy, Davis had sent her a new poem:

Rain

However it rains on the ocean,
The ocean's heart swells in appreciation.
Terrestrial rain can compassionately sprinkle life
Or angrily flood
Deluging mountains into your streets and basements
To tell you it is time.
                    —Davis

Was it an omen? His missive made her drive down the river innumerable times in the last month to a place on Penobscot Bay where she could stand alone watching and listening to see if the ocean would tell her what that time was. Alone, feeling unease at the ocean's roar on the shoreline's threatening rocks. Alone, feeling loss.

Back then on the boat, Karl had made clear how the sound of the rain on the water was just rain, but the sound of the shore was a dangerous, threatening sound for the sailor.

"You don't want to hear it in the dark!" he had said.

And now, leaning on the ambulance, she felt the threat welling up, mixing and confusing the sound of rain with the ocean shore. It seemed Kevin had changed, becoming more distant. Uneven. Off. He might be either having an affair or, in his new job, was working on secrets of which he could not speak. Or both. But what could she do? With a repressed surreal inkling, she was a bit afraid. Afraid of him? Afraid to ask? Afraid for their future? It was just a tortuous, aching sense she had, but nothing was the same anymore. It was that feeling she had had before Davis's adoption buried it.

So the thought of seeing Joe helped to console her.

She said to Frank, "Oh, I forgot. You haven't met Joe; you probably don't even know what he looks like."

In his soft, nasal voice, Frank said, "I should by now." His voice, incongruent with his aura, always amused her. Kevin was right; Frank was one big ugly-looking human being. So between his odd voice and his looks, Beth figured the poor guy had been teased his whole life, if anyone dared. *Frankenstein* fit him perfectly, because, as loveable a guy as Frank was, he was so stoic that he was scary.

Beth said, "I know. I know. I've talked about him enough. But I think that guy up the street looks like him. I wonder why he's here standing in the rain like that." Searching her pockets, she said, "I'll give him a call. To see if it's him, I mean. I haven't seen him for a while."

Just then the police siren, moving rapidly in their direction, chewed up the droning sound of the falling rain.

"Whoops! I guess I better not. Not right now," she said.

Frank Stern, the man of few words, was expressionless and silent as usual.

The unmistakable sound of a gunshot from The Shed tore the air, making them both instinctively duck and, crouching, circle quickly to the other side of the ambulance. Squatting with their backs against the ambulance, they looked at each other with raised eyebrows, not speaking.

As the screaming police cruiser arrived with blinding blue lights flashing so brightly and reflecting off countless wet surfaces, Beth, even squinting, couldn't look directly at it. She heard the cruiser screech abruptly to a stop. In fact, with the final loud thud, it sounded to her as if the car slid on the wet pavement and hit the curb so hard that she could imagine the damage to the tires and even the steering. The word *klutz* came to mind.

She heard the car doors open and the voice of the fat policeman she had met so many times, but whose name she could never remember. There were two of them, but she couldn't warn them about the gunshot. They were too busy. Too far away. Too loud. Her voice wouldn't carry in the rain. Not above their noise.

The fat man was yelling into some communications equipment that the police used, and which Beth noted especially because she felt the ambulance crews should also certainly get the same equipment or, at least, hook up to it with the existing ambulance radio. Other communities had it all linked, but then her company was private. Beth was so determined that this linkup was right for Bangor that she had spoken to her boss, who appointed her to write to every office and committee she could find to push the case for the equipment.

The regulation said that an ambulance was to be called to every emergency scene, needed or not. So obviously, she had argued, if the crew could, at least, listen in, they could be informed and prepared. And the police could instruct the ambulance team as to what to expect.

Today was a prime example. Here she had stood—they both stood—in the rain with no idea as to the purpose of the call. A sort of purgatory, leaving the well-trained crew essentially unprepared for eventualities. And now a gunshot and she didn't know why. Helplessly, she couldn't warn anyone. It made her sick to her stomach.

She would definitely bring up the subject again using today's example, not that she hoped something wrong would occur today as a result, but now it sounded bad. Already. Being unable to prepare and to be forewarned could make the difference between life and death. And she cared. That was the difference between the bureaucrats and her. She cared. She cared even for the lost, destroyed souls in the drug haven below, especially for them. She had been there; it hung around her like yesterday.

The wind and the rain suddenly let up, becoming a frayed mix of lingering drizzle and blotchy fog. Wading through the slanted wet weedy field that sloped from the road down to The Shed, the fat policeman, not so far away now, was calling for Kevin who didn't seem to respond.

"Kevin is here?" Beth asked to no one. Spontaneously she rose to her feet. "Hey," she yelled. "Somebody has a gun!"

Then she heard another gunshot.

7. KEVIN

SITTING IN THE SHED

Kevin knew exactly where to take Cricket. The Shed, which Kevin called the shack, was isolated and, at this time of day, unvisited, and that's what he needed.

The three wooden boxes inside the shack had been moved there by the local druggies who used the place to do their transactions and maybe have a social event. Remnants of burnt items—candles, handmade cardboard torches, wooden branches—indicated how the place was lit at night. The needles and scraps of paraphernalia strewn inside and out only validated the slight medicinal odor of the place mixed with the burnt items, but which was surpassed in waves by the smell of urine. The door opening, hidden from the road, let the various visitors climb up a dirt path from the trees by a creek below, and to get in and out without being seen from the road.

Although today the shack was wretched from recent activity, Joe, on his own, had often visited the shack to pick up the hypodermic needles, sweep the cement floor, and de-lice the place. It was Joe who arranged for junk like old sinks, toilet porcelain, and car carcasses to be hauled away from the slanted field between the road and the shack so as not to attract more junk, and once a summer to get the city to mow the weeds and harvest the winter trash, which had either blown in or been dumped.

In fact, it had been Joe who informed Kevin about the shack and had asked him to spread the word to the police force to leave it alone for the mutual benefit of everyone, Joe's argument being, why not control where the crimes, if they were actually crimes, would happen?

He had told Kevin that it stood empty most of the day; it was only after dark the users and dealers cared to creep into it from the trees in the back like nocturnal rodents. The visitors had heard and seemed to accept that they needed to police themselves if they wanted to keep the cops at bay.

So the police never bothered to bust the shack since it seemed as good a place as any to let this crowd congregate away from the general public—as long as no one caused any serious problems or raised any complaints—and as long as the police had the occasional informant among them.

Kevin sat on one of the boxes checking out the view through the broken slats. A small, opaque, grey plastic bag lay between his feet on the unswept cement. Because the shack had no windows, somebody had cracked a few of the vulnerable wood slats to let in light or maybe to allow some air to circulate from the doorless opening through the cracks and crevices, thinking to reduce the smell of urine, but instead with today's wind, bringing more of it inside.

During the day, like now, Kevin had thought he would have a fairly good view toward the street of the unkept field of low weeds, dirt, and ever-recurring accumulated clutter that covered the incline up to the street. The view through the crack wasn't as bad as looking through a dirty prison window, so Kevin doubted that the sheeting rain blurring things intermittently would be any special hindrance.

Kevin had never smelled a muskrat, but he thought Cricket smelled like one. Cricket, lanky, beardless but unshaven, had meaty butterfly-wing ears sticking out under his straight dark hair, pulled back in a ponytail, emphasizing that he had a head like a fish, specifically like a Pike, pointed in front with a wagging tail of hair.

Gusts of the weather front had blown the rain through the door opening, spraying mostly Cricket and circulating the odor from his unwashed sweats. Kevin noticed humorously that, because Cricket had barely registered the soaking, he was well accustomed to the ocean, making him in every sense even more *fishy*.

Cricket sat closer to the doorway on another crate, tapping his saltwater-stained sneaker to some unheard rhythm while he faced Kevin, who couldn't help thinking Cricket's nose could have met his chin if he had had fewer teeth.

Kevin tolerated all the smells of the place for a short bit to get done what he needed. But because it was raining so hard that it sounded like lead pellets on the shack's tin roof, Kevin wanted to wait for the front to pass so he didn't have to yell.

"Why're we here?" Cricket yelled impatiently. "It stinks here. What're we doing here?" He was his nervous self, hyper, at the higher levels of psychosis, legs twitching with each word, looking around like this place was collapsing on him. Kevin knew that Davis, alias Cricket, had become used to tight boat quarters, but the horrible smell, the absence of fresh sea air was helping to raise his anxiety. The strain in his vocal chords showed obvious nervousness.

And, of course, he had been forced to come here by his father. Kevin smiled. *Who wouldn't be nervous?*

After his self-taught authoritative silence picked up from a TV detective series, Kevin shouted above the roar of the roof, "We're here to talk." He was silent again, reveling in his son's nerves and impairing distress.

"About what?"

The pounding on the tin roof was letting up.

Kevin said, "You may wish your underwear was on backwards."

Davis said, "What's that supposed to mean?"

Kevin smiled. "You know the bulge that is supposed to be in front of men's underwear? You maybe might need to have the bulge in back for what I am going to talk about."

Davis looked solemnly at Kevin with a slight flicker of an eyelid.

"So Davis, why are you calling yourself Eric Larsen?"

"Why not?"

"You have used that name to fool a few people. I don't know how you picked it out. How does Lodovico sound to you instead? Wouldn't that be better?" He watched Davis's response with gratification.

Davis was unable to speak as his face reddened. His legs failed him as he attempted to stand up, but instead just switched his direction a little away from Kevin like one more twitch, scraping the wooden box on the floor. "What's that got to do with anything? What? Why're you saying that?"

"Oh, Davis, I am a detective. It's my job to know the background of people, like you have done, except better. You want to hear more?"

Glancing around like a feral cat looking for an escape route, Davis didn't answer.

Kevin kept his eyes on Davis's face. "I'll tell you more. You discovered through some sort of research you did while in the institution, that you were adopted and you decided to look up your parents. You discovered that your real father was Daniel Lodovico of Salem, Massachusetts, and you discovered somehow—probably speaking to your birth mother—that he was a horrible and abusive man. Your birth mother Ellen McKinnon was killed in a car accident up around here a few years ago. I was actually there at that scene.

"You staged a boating accident in Penobscot Bay the same day as your birth mother, who was probably rushing up to rescue you in some way, died, and which helped you almost get away with it since we were so busy. Some good Samaritan found you floating close to the shore, pushed some water out of your lungs, and delivered you to the hospital. I don't know how you got so lucky. Especially after you murdered a man."

Davis sat frozen.

"You murdered a man with a name similar to your birth father's named Dan Ludovico. Ludovico. Your birth father, Lodovico. Pretty close, huh? And both with the name Dan." Kevin fell silent, again watching for reaction.

He continued. "This man you murdered, as opposed to your birth father, was a person to be admired, a person who had helped suffering populations around the world. He was an asset to the state of Maine, a prince among men, someone to be locally proud of. In fact, internationally proud of.

"The mistake you made was that this man you murdered was very powerful and very rich. His family and acquaintances had no belief in the accident; they knew him too well. It took a year or so of court work, arm twisting, and judgments to get his death reclassified enough to open it up for me to be put to work.

"I have particular reason to understand wanting to kill the father that mistreated your birth mother, although I didn't know the man, but putting all the pieces back together, I can relate. But, after digging up Ludovico, well, you really got the wrong man. How you made such a mistake is still a mystery to me." Kevin paused. "The main point, Davis, is that you have put me in a huge bind. I am the detective on the case of the Lodovico murder and I come to find out that my son is the suspect. What should I do?"

On his face Kevin felt the pulsing of Davis's nervousness like a buzzing electric razor. Davis said, "I don't know."

"So after your hospital stay, after almost drowning, you decided to stay around here for whatever reason and work at a marina as Eric Larsen or Cricket."

"I live here because…because where else should I go? I live here."

"Well, Davis, you could have come to me for that discussion. And I would have suggested, or rather ordered you to get the hell away from here. Go anywhere but here. Now we have talked and I am now going to call for your arrest." Kevin took out his phone.

"Don't I get a lawyer or something?"

"Yeah, something," Kevin said, looking at his phone.

The wind was now only a breeze and the rain had slowed to drizzle. He pressed a button and a tinny voice from the phone, chirping loudly in the little space of the shack, said, "Police emergency. What is your call concerning?"

"Hi, Mack, this is Detective Kevin Nuss. I have a suspect hiding in the drug shack and need Bob Gaines down here immediately as backup."

"He's on the way."

Kevin shut off the phone without looking up, frozen as if he were waiting.

Davis sat staring first at the phone and then at Kevin in petrified puzzlement. "Why're you saying that? I'm not hiding. I'm right here."

Kevin calmly reached down between his legs and pulled a shiny chrome-plated pistol from the plastic bag on the floor. Holding the pistol in his open right hand, he said, "You see this pistol, Davis? It's yours."

"Wha…? I don't have a pistol. It's not mine."

"You do now and you are going to use it."

Davis's eyes widened. "What're you saying? I don't even know how to use a pistol. What is this? I'm outta here."

Kevin smiled. "Good. Exactly. That's what you gotta do. Run like hell. Goodbye. And hide somewhere far away from here in your real name."

Davis stood up staring at the gun in terror, turned toward the door, and lifted his right foot for his first running step.

To reinforce his command, Kevin raised his service revolver in his left hand and shot once, close to Davis, before he could put his foot back on the cement.

To Kevin it seemed Davis literally vanished because Kevin's ears were still screaming from the gunshot; he couldn't hear anything.

Despite not having much time, he stood up to see that Davis was nowhere visible, went outside to the back of the shack opposite the road, waded down through the wet, waist-high weeds to the trees, turned immediately, stepped into the muddy, worn path made by the night visitors, and made obvious shoe prints as he walked back into the shack again to wait.

The ambulance had arrived first, almost too soon. Through the crack, Kevin had seen Frankenstein and Beth talking by the ambulance in the misty rain, waiting for the police to arrive, but they were gone now. Probably his gunshot scared them. The police siren was loud now and tires screeched as the car stopped. Kevin shook his head, smugly amazed at the predictability of fat Gaines putting on his hammy clown show of *policiness*.

The two officers in the car jumped out, but it was only Gaines who began moving toward the shed. Kevin heard Gaines yelling into his microphone, "Where are you, Detective? Hello, Nuss, over."

Kevin let him continue his dumb calling, which any intelligent cop should understand would woefully divulge Kevin's position to any perp. Kevin watched Gaines waddle through the weeds and slipping in the mud down toward the shack, yelling, stumbling, waving his pistol through the words he was yelling.

It was time. Kevin shot the first of six bullets from the unregistered revolver, a pistol he had lifted from the evidence room for just such an occasion.

He shot first at the police cruiser. He couldn't hear the metal clank, but watched the cop duck behind the car. And, of course, he wanted Gaines to go into panic mode, to freeze and to make himself a bulging, blundering target. From this moment on, it was a matter of speed and cool thinking to get it all executed and arranged. Almost routine.

Now it was just a matter of shooting Gaines with the rest of the chamber as fast as possible to be sure that the bastard was dead, to have time to hide the pistol, to shoot off a couple rounds of his service pistol as he stood outside the back wall, as if he were trying to stop the escaping murderer. It wasn't complicated or difficult; he just had to be sure he did it quickly and cleanly, with the right timing.

The explosions of the five rapid shots in the small space were so loud they even hurt his eyes. The zinging forest of roaring in his ears was sure to give him a serious headache. He couldn't hear Beth or see her, and didn't have time to check.

After firing two shots from his service pistol at the escaping invisible murderer—somehow never visible to the others, of course, *because they were tending to the victim*—he could come around from the rear of the shack to mourn his comrade policeman.

He might have heard Frankenstein yelling something in desperation, but his own pistol was even louder than the small one. He would be glad when he could regain his hearing. His one mistake. He was pissed at himself for forgetting, or not actually thinking about earplugs.

8. KEVIN

THE MOURNING DAWNS

KEVIN WAS OLDER NOW, OLDER THAN HE HAD BEEN WHEN HIS BROTHER DIED, WHEN he didn't know how to mourn, when he didn't know how to explain death to his little sister. Surely, now, this time, this afternoon upon Beth's death, it was different; he must be able to explain it, at least to himself.

But if this was different, if he could think differently now, why was it that he still stumbled over his haunting self-reproach and unburied sorrow at not relating to and reuniting with his mother before she had died? And his brother before that? How could he not know? Was there no way of explaining death or, at least, preparing for it?

Being both a policeman and the son, he had felt, not long ago, back then, that he should travel to Clinton to attend to his mother, to discover what he should do about her situation, not knowing how his mother could or would deal with Kevin's long absence and sudden visit. While driving there, he had been forced back into digging up and searching through his childhood memories like some imperishable hidden litter with his name on it.

During his stay in her house, Kevin had tried to piece together his discomfort, which arose from his mother's lack of concern for Kevin's feelings.

Of course, he had understood that she had a right to be angry. What concern had he bothered to show since he left years ago? But he hadn't been that far away. Shouldn't she have understood that he needed to care anyway? Shouldn't she, at least, have shown some exuberance? Mightn't she feel some joy at seeing her long-lost son?

Kevin had concluded that his mother's love and compassion had died long ago, probably before his father had died, and only tolerance of her religious obligations had been maintained. She had contrived to live in solemn, empty practicality. Her solace was her religion, replacing also any feelings for Kevin, for his father, and maybe even for other people who couldn't stand to be around her.

During this visit in Clinton, as they sat at her kitchen table the afternoon of his arrival, he had felt he had no connection to her thoughts—a complete short circuit—but even with nothing else to talk about, he had felt he must ask the hanging question: what was next? What was she planning on doing from here on?

To Kevin's disquiet, her mouth had twisted into obvious displeasure at his question even before she spoke. Her once-strong reading voice had become shaky and worn, as was her whole persona. Slowly, she had said, "I will go on living here. I have friends and…" She paused. "I will visit your sister sometimes when I have the strength."

Her mentioning his sister had been a sharp rebuke for his absence. He had asked, "But what about when you get too weak, when you can't take care of yourself anymore?"

She said, "You forget that I have God and the church. They will take care of me."

He frowned. "How is it God will take care of you when you can't walk or feed yourself?"

She paused as if to decide what to tell him. "I have arranged with the church for home care and my cremation in Worcester and the church will be letting you know when everything is over and done. You needn't worry about me, if you ever did."

If he ever did. Another rebuke. Out of frustration, out of revenge (or would it have been an attempt to please her?), he had been tempted to ask her if she had appreciated not having to deal with his miserable father. The abyss between him and his mother had grown with painful familiarity, so familiar that he couldn't imagine why he had forgotten it. It made him push his tongue hard against the back of his clenched teeth to press out the sour sadness he wished he could express. Aside from his own and his mother's impersonal storytelling abilities, Kevin knew that neither he nor she had ever had the gift to express emotions, and especially not between the two of them.

But he had thought, or at least had hoped in his forgetfulness and inattention, that now, face-to-face speaking of death, arranging for death, meeting death head-on would force open the floodgate to all the hidden jumble of child-parental needs and mistakes that had piled up, dammed and jammed painfully behind that gate, and bring them closer. Wasn't that supposed to happen? But he had found her gate was locked long ago, rusted shut, the key lost if there had ever been one.

Kevin had decided to drive back to Bangor that same night, not recalling how he got home except to remember that the five-hour drive had been like floating on a long river of unrecognizable states of emotion, an abysmal stir of self-recrimination and hate, regret, sadness, and even relief, all of which flowed into, and made bigger, the angry void which, he became aware, had been in him for years.

Having had no further contact since that visit, the formal notice from his mother's priest about his mother's death, only three months later, had hit Kevin like an enraged moose charging out of a dark closet. The information he received of her death was a copy of her death certificate in the mail included with a letter from the church stating a Mass had been held for her funeral.

His first reaction, after the enraged moose, had not been the expected sadness, the dark closet he thought he should have, but inexplicably to remember the humor he, as a teenager, had found in these sorts of ceremonies and the word *mass*. He had immediately wondered whether it had been a mass of hot gooey tar or just a little piece of chewed gum.

He envisioned the ritual he had seen of the fanning around of sneeze-inducing incense from a swinging can on a chain and the spraying of water from a miniature mop, which, as a young teen, he had wanted to use as a cough joke, sneaking up behind his brother or somebody and faking a cough while, with a flick of the mop, he would spray the back of the sucker's neck.

And he had always been fascinated by the little wafer routine where the priest seemed to munch a few before offering only one to the faithful—his mother included—nobody ever asking for seconds, and then, while everyone tried to look pious, the priest did the dishes.

But just as suddenly, this teenage humor had not been so funny. He didn't even know what became of his mother's ashes. It was as if she had been sealed away from him in a sarcophagus throughout the intervening time and was then simply transported from there to obscurity. His mother; the reason he was born. Erased.

His anger at the priest was palpable and he felt revengeful hate. But even if the pain and guilt never went away entirely, back then he had had time to smother it; back then he had had Beth to turn to, to comfort him.

He had prepared for his own pending death once, back when the truck was descending over him. He knew death, didn't he? He knew his response to death, didn't he? He controlled death, didn't he? But preparing for the unexpected death of others who were in some way part of him, had not been possible. And he thought he had fixed that, and it was making him doubt things—those unspoken things—about which he had been so sure.

And, even with his inkling of guilt about his mother, he hadn't, after all, directly killed her, but he had gotten his revenge by killing her priest. That was certainly different from now. With Beth. Now, tonight, the white keyboard, blurred and warped through his tears, was the only thing visible in the darkened room. The used, wooden vertical piano had been a wedding gift from Beth, one she really couldn't afford and, thus, had to pay off over time. But she had said she had no question in her mind that it was important for him to be able to use his innate musical ability.

Often, sitting next to him as he played, and while their two kids took it as given, she would act amazed at the wide range of melodies he could magically pluck from out of nowhere—humorous musicals, happy cabaret, serious classical, honkytonk, ragtime, and silly sing-alongs.

And she would lovingly tell him repeatedly how he was proof of what she had read, how studies showed that musicians were smarter than anyone else and thankfully would live longer than anyone else.

Even though she would never try to play the piano herself with her strong beautiful fingers, this evening as Kevin's fingers formed the patterned keyboard chords, he felt that he was touching, at least, something of her.

And somewhere from the misery and heaviness draining his mind, a melodic dirge was groaning its way from the piano's strings, up the walls to elevate the grief in the small living room.

The red scrapings and clawings in Kevin's chest made him play louder in an attempt to supplant the shrieking beast that he wasn't allowing to escape.

Tonight he was angry, unforgivingly angry at the blubbery idiot whom he managed to kill, had wanted to kill, meant to kill. And wished he could kill again.

How will he? How could he explain their mother's death to Geena? Forget Davis. How does he explain? How *could* he explain this death? Even to himself? He could only continue to wish he could die instead. Continue and continue.

That was when he let the merciless talons of the unrecognizable beast grab him, and like the living prey being torn apart by the pitiless hawk, he screamed and screamed until the physical pain and blood made him believe that his insides were coming out of his mouth, leaving blood stains on the keyboard, stains he would never try to remove.

9. JOE

THE COURT SESSION

"Do you swear to tell the truth, the whole truth, and nothing but the truth, so help you God?"

Joe choked on the God part, but knew he had to go along with it in the land of oaths. Joe had never thought about it before, how foreigners he had met were right about how Americans are always swearing an oath, most often on a Bible. It was already bad enough that Joe had been forced to witness against his best friend. Maybe if he didn't cause a stir, stayed calm and quiet, his testimony might be less noticed and less important. A spurious hope.

"I do."

"You may take the stand."

It had been almost a year since Beth's death. The trial was being held in Bangor despite the defense's plea that it be moved to Piscataquis County since the accused was a locally well-known police detective. But the press had not covered that part to a great extent, because, although the killing had made the news, the local press got the stories wrong and blamed *some unknown drug-filled assailant*. The headlines made such a stir that the political pressure forced the community to tear down The Shed, leaving only the stone foundation. With Kevin's part in the story essentially ignored, the attorney general and the judge felt that a fair jury could be mustered.

Joe was trapped into testifying. Like a bad movie, the cop hiding behind the car that fateful day had seen Joe and his drone, and Joe had idiotically admitted to filming the whole thing before he even knew what he had filmed.

The trial in the red brick Penobscot Judicial Center on Exchange Street began with the statement of the assistant state attorney stressing the seriousness of the murder crime to the jury. The charges against Kevin, intentional or knowing murder, was a Class A felony punishable by twenty-five years to life in prison, and possession of a stolen firearm was a Class C felony punishable by up to five years in prison.

It was time for Joe's testimony.

In the light, paneled court room, sparsely decorated with patriotically suggestive framed prints, the assistant state attorney was standing next to a large digital screen facing the jury.

Turning toward Joe, she said, "So, Mr. Tink or Tinkerman, which do you prefer?"

"*Tink* is fine."

"Thank you, Mr. Tink. You run a business which uses drones. Is that correct?"

"Yes."

"And what is the use of these drones?"

"To help builders and construction engineers to inspect large construction for flaws and damage."

"And you record this inspection on tape?"

"Well, not exactly tape, but yes, I record them digitally."

"So why do you have a video of the proceedings last year on that August day of the murder?"

"Objection," said the defense.

"So why do you have a video of the proceedings that day last year?"

"Well, I had just bought a new drone. I went out to The Shed area to test it, to see how it worked in bad weather, or better said, *if* it worked in bad weather. I had a problem with the ones I already owned. I got this one recommended and..."

"That's fine, Mr. Tink. And why had you gone out to that area particularly?"

"I'm familiar with that area because I worked with the city to help clean up and maintain this area for...for the socially, for the needy...before they tore it down."

"And why did you do that, Mr. Tink?"

"Well, that's just something I found was a good thing to do, helping the destitute, I mean. It's..."

"Did you take the video because you knew the people in the video?"

"God, no. I didn't know what I was filming. I just heard the gunshot and sirens and thought maybe it would be something to film."

"How do you know the people in the video?"

Like a picture he had seen, Joe felt like he was standing on the back of a floating whale carcass out in an ocean with sharks surrounding and ripping away the flesh of the dead whale. Bit by bit.

"I don't know the policemen more than..."

"What about the defendant, Mr. Nuss?"

"Yes, Kevin. I know Kevin very well. And his wife...his ex...or whatever. Poor Beth. They have always been good friends."

"Thank you, Mr. Tink. I would like to point out to the jury that Mr. Tink could be considered an unfriendly witness, but is kindly cooperating. Thank you, Mr. Tink."

Joe looked at his hands folded in his lap, thinking they would be no good at fending off sharks.

The woman continued. "I will start the recording you took that day for the jury to see on this screen. Could you walk us through what we are seeing on the screen, please? You may ask me to stop it any time if you need to explain more."

Joe felt like the sharks had devoured enough of the carcass that now it was sinking. He tried to keep his voice from breaking. "I caught things on camera that I never expected."

She stopped the video. "Please just tell us what we are seeing, Mr. Tink."

He said, "You see the police car arriving and the fat…the policeman…well, both of them open their doors to get out of the car.

"Now the big cop, the driver, begins waddling, trying to walk down the hill toward The Shed, talking to his radio, I guess. Looks like he's blabbering away.

"And we see the policeman freeze and…then fall after being shot. Poor guy." He began speaking faster, crying, knowing he will be stopped. "Kevin was to become the hero who shot at the young man, because Kevin supposedly had been following the kid as a suspect in a past murder."

She paused the video. "Please, Mr. Tink. Just the description."

"Now you see how Beth Sturgess, the ambulance staff person. Kevin's wife. Of the defendant. My good friend suddenly has run down to the police officer who has fallen, instinctively wanting to save the policeman guy from whoever was shooting from The Shed, which was assumed to be the young man."

"Objection."

"Mr. Tink."

"Oh, god. She falls. Oh, god." Joe, sobbing, could hardly speak. "I can't get used to this. Oh, Beth. She caught a bullet in the wrong place; I never asked where. Maybe you know; I don't want to know. She was my best friend."

"Please keep your comments to the description of the video." After having paused the video a minute to let Joe get his composure, she started it again.

He spoke faster. "The policeman was waddling down the hill because Kevin had called for his help I heard, and, Kevin said that by coming up from the trees behind The Shed, he was able to shoot at the murderer to try to stop him as he ran away. And you see he didn't. Oh, Kevin!"

"Mr. Tink, please. You can step down."

"I have no idea if he meant to kill your mother, Geena, but I highly doubt it."

"Mr. Tink, you can step down."

Although Geena knew what was coming, through his own tears, Joe could see her crying. Davis never attended the proceedings.

10. DAVIS

To: GeenaN@gmail.com

From: DavisM@gmail.com

Subject: Your note

December 3, 2019

Hey, Geena,

Thanks for letting me know about Beth and, of course, that they are jailing the bastard. I'm very sorry. There is not much else to say.

Davis

PART 4

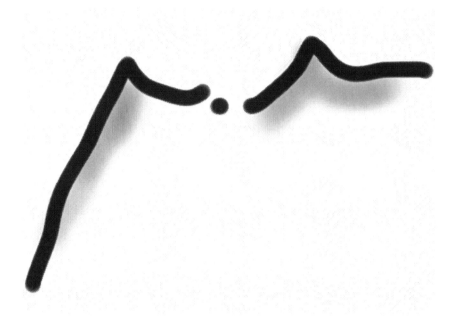

Looking at the past is a misconception. We should question
the notion of time and begin to remember the future.

—Professor Martin Case

2020 CE

1. JOE

JUST REMEMBER THE FUTURE

JOE HAD A CHOICE. EITHER HE WAS GOING NUTS OR GHOSTS DID EXIST. HE VOTED for reason; he was losing it.

Over the last month, a specific irrelevant concept—which Joe had no reason to create or to understand—had begun streaming through his brain. If Martin had been alive, he would surely have understood it. But Martin was dead. Ten years ago. Long gone.

Once Joe's building inspection business began to have a regular cash flow coming from subscriptions for his services from surrounding communities and the state of Maine itself, he was ready to move to his own place. He had lived off the Nuss's favor for too long and his privacy was not the least of the reasons to move. So he had already planned to move out before the double killing, alias murder, and, thus, right after Beth's death, he did so, to a modern apartment on the corner of Union and Sanford to be used as both a home and an office.

Despite his continued reveries about his life with Martin, Joe's social life began to grow. But nothing long term. He struggled to trust any new relationship, not because of those few people he liked, but because he didn't trust himself, his own brain, his own emotions. His visits and affectionate trysts with "old preacher friend" James were the most positive since they were short breaks from Joe's solitude. Through the years, they had kept contact via phone and email, with Joe following along as James became a professor of mathematics and logic and an extremely active essayist as a popular science writer and in philosophical atheism, politically near to Ethan Siegel, Bertrand Russell, and Noam Chomsky.

After Joe's move, he had kept an unspoken hope of seeing James more often but began to have an increasing ache from a dissonance in his head between factions that were supposed to be in harmony. His thoughts were in such conflict that he felt he, like an old joke, was losing arguments with himself.

Googling what he could find, he had found his conundrum with no solution.

Cognitive Dissonance, the frustration caused by simultaneously holding two contradictory ideas, for example pondering your own existence facing the paradox of wanting purpose while thinking that human existence is meaningless.

That was exactly how he felt.

Maybe during the time that he and Martin had been together he had been sane, even happy, when he didn't have so much time to think. It was having time to think, time to attack himself that was the problem. If he dared to try to inventory his reasons for his self-denigration in these crepuscular periods, they were not so difficult to list, were they?

First, he was gay. Yes, he knew he had to accept how he was born, but how much easier it would have all been if he were straight, especially because of his stupid father who should have helped him feel better about his homosexuality, not worse.

And his mother died young, and Martin died. And Beth died.

Those were the periods, full of caring and loving, in which he had no time to reproach himself as a failure. It was now. Now when he literally had no one to threaten him, to care for, or to worry about, that was the problem. It was the isolation, the loneliness that got to him. It was now that part of his brain was telling him about absurdity and futility.

And now. And now in the last weeks, because now Martin was back talking to him!

Since that was not possible, Joe was sure he must be schizophrenic. How else could he explain it? Unless, of course, Martin was actually talking to Joe in words. Talking in Joe's head. Was there some sort of line-o-type that fed in foreign wadding?

The voice said, "Just remember the future."

The statement was repeated again and again, during the day and night, keeping him awake like a throbbing sprained ankle. Joe shut it down as best he could. He had to. He had to sleep.

And who did he dare tell about this insanity? This was the stuff of stupid ghost and paranormal stories, of mystics, which he was sure were generated by scammers and nutcases.

He wished he could explain it to Beth, to whom he had always been able to tell anything as they worked in the kitchen. But she was dead. His monthly visits with Kevin in jail were a distraction. He could talk about Martin and use Kevin as a captive audience, but intimacy was no longer an option.

He was on his own and he felt he should be enjoying, at long last, the life he had been able to create, but his brain was not cooperating. It was trying to disrupt that life.

Just remember the future.

It was one repetition after another.

The one person he felt he might be able to tell was James. He and James had kept it going since 1988—for thirty-two years. Their sporadic meetings had become more often now that Joe had his own place, when James would fly over and stay for a few days and nights. Surely Joe could tell James about the voice, but would James be jealous about an old lover's voice? James might not want to accept it and would really think Joe was nuts.

Then Beth and Kevin's daughter arrived, with essentially no warning. Geena had called him first, asking if she could come over.

He hadn't seen or spoken to her for…he couldn't remember. Since the funeral. Since she had left to go to college and, according to Kevin, had begun to establish herself in technical stuff somewhere in Kansas City. He was not even sure how Geena found him, but assumed that she had spoken to someone.

Little Geena, named after a movie star. And to think that her brother Davis seemed named after the same woman. No wonder the poor guy had been sorrowfully institutionalized and now was off in screwball land—somewhere inaccessible—like Davis himself.

When Joe opened the door, he hardly recognized her. She had changed; she had grown up, twenty-eight years old, and she was beautiful. Mostly beautiful. Bright blue eyes, widespread beaming intelligence. A mouth with lips that seemed to form poetry before the words came through them. He could only wonder then if all her foul language had formed them. She had her father's Roman nose and her mother's thick dark hair that always seemed as impenetrable as her femininity, pulled back and tied with a happy red bow and the ribbon ends resting on her right shoulder. She was taller than he was, tall like her mother with her mother's poise.

He felt extraordinarily happy to see her in a way he could not describe to himself. It was not in his nature to find women so attractive. He tried to disregard the sensation as he hugged her.

"Oh, Geena, it's so good to see you. And so nice of you to come to see me. Please come in."

And she seemed to have tears, happy tears in her eyes as she launched the huge grin he recognized from her early family pictures, the one she had always had since he met her. That grin was certainly Geena.

"It's so good to see you, Joe," she said in a quiet, confident voice deeper than he remembered. As she stepped in, scanning the apartment, she said, "You have a beautiful place here." No swear words yet.

"Thank you," he said.

Then his silence quickly became awkward as Joe's usual verbosity was astonishingly stunted by his absorption of her appearance in her thin summer dress that moved with her body and highlighted her anatomy like floodlights on a scenic stage.

It was late Saturday morning on a bright July day, so in a way her golden summer dress was the right apparel, but why so sensual? Or was it just his reaction? No, she surely would not have visited just anyone, especially her father, with such revealing attire, hiding nothing underneath. Nothing was exactly what she had underneath, nothing except the shimmer of some pastel bikini panties. That's when he noticed the sweater draped over her arm, a sweater that she could use to hide under while out in public on the street or with anyone else, but now removed.

What was she thinking? Or was she? Was she even aware? She knew women were not his thing. Yet he was reacting. For him, it wasn't just her young perfect nakedness; it was everything. The sensuality from her lips to the feminine parts of her body, the movement of one element so in congruence with the other. Her eyes wide and deep and bright like sparkling candlelight outshone all the physical else. His thoughts were interdicted by the sensation. The abnormality. The improbability. The impossibility.

Then he said, "I'm sorry, Geena. I was thinking of something else. Please, make yourself at home." He indicated the heavy white sofa to his left. "Please sit. I'll get us something to drink. You want some coffee? Tea?"

She didn't immediately answer as she turned and approached the sofa, acting almost afraid to sit on it. "Tea would be fine, thank you."

"I don't have a big choice," he said. "Earl Grey? Citrus?"

"Either one," she said. "Your furniture is beautiful."

"Well, I'm sorry I bought white; it shows everything." He almost added *like you are.*

He had used the furniture to mend and amend the apartment's dullness, so typical of the recent remodeled condos and apartments with the kitchen facing an open room, only a breakfast counter dividing them. It was so standard that it bothered him, but he could not find anything original in Bangor unless he was willing—and he was not—to revamp and design an older place.

Filling a metal teapot, he placed it on the gas burner and hurried through the process of trying to set out the cups without the clatter, and bothering, which he never did otherwise, to set out the sugar and milk which, he noticed later, she did not use.

They had hardly spoken during Beth's funeral; the enormity of the sadness had hindered his desire to speak to anyone. Now he realized that while he prepared the tea he should have been asking the visitor about herself to make her feel more comfortable, but he wanted to be closer to her, to read her answers, to look at her face as she spoke, feeling he needed to understand exactly why she was here and what she was saying even if it were only the tiniest bytes of information. He did not try to resolve the *why* in his head.

"So," he said as he sat across from her in a reading chair, which, after pouring the tea, he had lifted closer to the small glass-top coffee table between them. He looked in her eyes and said, "Why do I have the honor of your visit?"

Of course. Of course, she went through a litany of the normal reasons he had expected. She was in town visiting friends. It had been a long time. She wondered how he was doing. What was he doing now? All very polite and proper.

His acuity grew as his parade of responses seemed equally peripheral to the primal exchange they were having.

He talked about his moving and why, about how his business had grown, and how glad he was to have an income, though the business was just business, and how he could speak to unions and help organize potential unions. He spoke of his work with the needy.

Finally, he said, "I'm embarrassed. I've only talked about me and forgotten to ask about you. You have finished the university and are working with construction?"

She seemed to think before answering. "Yes, it's a long story, inspired by you." She smiled. "Maybe I could bore you with it while we have lunch? May I invite you over to that place I saw across the street?"

"I'm sorry, Geena, but I have both a lunch date and a busy afternoon." Before he could continue, he saw how her face flashed disappointment before she managed to hide it. "But this evening," he continued, "we could have dinner and have time to talk. Do you have time?"

She smiled the familiar broad grin. "In fact," she said, "that's not only a good idea, I have even a better one. It's so hard to really talk in a restaurant, don't you think? Instead, I'll bring dinner here, if that's okay with you."

Somehow that idea pleased him more than he would have imagined and he immediately assented, agreeing she should come over at about six. He gave her the code for the door locks and told her to come right in if he were not back right on time.

His afternoon work was uneventful except for the intervening confusion of his thoughts of Geena, but he was pleased that none of the repetitions and the dissonance headaches intervened with the stabbing pain he so often experienced. A twinge of happiness was swelling up in him instead, like the intensifying warmth of rare single-malt scotch.

When he arrived home at almost exactly six, she had already been there long enough to set the table by the window and the dinner, covered in foil, was repackaged into his serving dishes she had been able to dig out from the back of some cupboards. No candles, he was happy to note since he would have hated having the glare between them, blinding him from seeing her slightest expression.

With all the preparation, she must have been there for some time. And she was still sensationally clothed in the same outfit.

All he could manage to say was "Oh, my god."

"I love your smile," she said. Before he could respond, she said, "You know, Joe, I could never have said that to anyone else. It's strange. In fact, I couldn't even have suggested dinner to any man in his own apartment."

The message was clear and he needed to fix things now. Now, rather than later. Now, rather than causing an escalating chance of misunderstanding and disappointment. Maybe somehow she had forgotten.

He said, "I have a hard time believing that, Geena. I don't know exactly how straight men are, but there must be some polite and gentlemanly types whom you don't need to fear. If that's what you mean."

She smiled and blushed, looking down at the table for some moments before turning to meet his gaze with her intense eyes. "Of course, that's possible. But I haven't met them. Not yet, anyway. Maybe it's my foul mouth. But you…" She stopped.

"You don't understand, Joe. Since I was a young girl, I've looked up to you as a hero. No, don't be embarrassed. You are my hero. For so many reasons, too many to tell you and many which are unclear to me.

"I know you're gay, Joe. Don't worry. But just your way of being is heroic and attractive, to me anyway. You are soft and loving and caring. On top of that, I'm sure you are the most brilliant man I have ever met or known."

Joe held up his hand in protest. "Hold on. Enough. You're much too young and inexperienced to say such things. You haven't met that many men."

She stopped him, putting her finger to his lips. "Stop. I have met some. But *that* is beside the point. Let's just have our dinner."

She turned and moved toward the table, no doubt expecting him to follow.

He said, "Would you like some wine? I have some Tuscan red…"

"No, no," she interrupted. "I don't drink. You may, if you wish."

He didn't respond, but merely sat down thinking that she was intoxicating enough, as some trite romance novel might have described it.

"So where are you staying and for how long will you be here?"

She seemed to look through him as she thought. "I found a bed and breakfast up the street. I don't know. My stay is indefinite, depending."

She didn't seem to want to continue. He assumed she was thinking about her father and he did not want to follow that thought. He said, "So you have a job in Kansas City?"

She described her graduation from the University of Maryland and how she was almost immediately employed as an engineer temp, with little pay, but hopes for the future. And now she was doing great, maybe even going to start her own business.

"And all because of you," she said. "You made the inspection of the construction sound so fun and interesting. I needed to be part of it. And you know, with my foul mouth, construction was dead-on."

He felt old as she spoke with an innocence he was not sure he had ever felt. After all, he was, compared to her, so worn and frayed, through so much more tragedy, injury, hope, doubt and more doubt, incongruity and internal struggles that he hoped she would never feel. He hoped. He had to envy her youth.

"You envy my youth?" she said.

He was dumbstruck. "You…you knew what I was thinking?"

"It's not so hard. I know you haven't had it easy from the day you were born. Why do you think I look at you the way I do?"

Again, he didn't know what to say. How could anyone this young have the least bit of empathy for his life? She made his brain feel stampeded by a herd of gnus. He was selfish, inconsiderate, incapable of anything close to her brilliance. He was just a simpleton.

So he told her, blurted it out. "You have to know that I am going insane."

Did he hope to scare her? To put her in doubt? To make her think that she wasn't so perfectly smart?

She said, "I doubt that, but I hope you are. I need your insanity."

She was looking straight at him without the slightest smile and, once again, he was left feeling that he must be a gaping idiot; not knowing what he expected, this was not the answer he expected.

She said, "Joe, you may not understand this, but I need to make love with you. I have thought that I must be insane. You are gay; I've known that since you told me you were born in a pickle jar and pickled tink. You have no interest in women and I am certainly a woman. But making love to you—okay, fucking you—has been an overriding preoccupation for...since I was eighteen, or sometime like that; I don't know exactly, of course. I didn't write it in a calendar, or even a diary. I have felt and feel it is impossible, but at the same time I feel it is something that is necessary and I don't know why. So how's that for nuts?"

Joe was gripped in a blur with nothing to say. He had felt opaque anticipation since her arrival that day, but he had not understood it.

Then she said, "There are whole other worlds that our five senses don't register, unless we remember the future. I can't explain it."

His mind erupted; his mouth opened. He stared at her in confused disbelief.

These words in his head. Repeatedly.

Responding to his silence, she said, "Did I scare you? I'm sorry. I didn't mean..."

"No, no. It's not that," he said. "You said something else."

"I'm sorry. I shouldn't have told you that. Why would any woman say something so obviously out of..."

"No, not that. Not the sex part." She frowned. "It's what you said afterwards. The part about remembering the future."

"I said something about the future?"

"Yes, Geena. You said there are whole other worlds that our five senses don't register, unless we remember the future. Exactly those words."

"I did?"

"Yes. Why did you say that?"

"I guess I didn't realize I was saying that, but why is that so shocking? Not much…"

"Because you said them. The same words Martin has said."

"Well, Joe, I don't think that sounds so shocking, or for that matter, so very original. I…"

"It's because I *am* going crazy. You can't know or even understand, but I keep hearing Martin saying this."

"You obviously miss him."

"I don't! I mean, I do, or I did, for the longest time, but I should be over it by now. Maybe a year, or even two, one can mourn, but not this long. But in the last few weeks, I keep hearing his voice."

He rubbed his face with both hands, and when he took them away, she laughed. She said, "I'm sorry. Your face has the saddest expression I have ever seen. It was so sad that, I'm sorry, it's not really funny, but it was almost like Mr. Magoo or, worse yet, a fucking orangutan. Oh, I'm awful to say such a thing, but you mustn't be so sad."

She got out of her chair, went around to bend over him, putting her head next to his. She whispered, "I'm sorry I made you sad."

He shook his head and stood to face her. He put his hands up on her tall shoulders with unbent arms and, looking up straight into her eyes, said, "You did not make me sad. I just…I'm just confused. I really think that I must be going off the deep end. Maybe I have a brain tumor. I have no other explanation."

She reached up, took his arms down and pressed her body into his, wrapping her arms around him. He felt like a small child with his head fitting under her chin. He had forgotten this feeling, if he had ever known it.

They stood that way for a while without speaking. Joe had never thought that he would feel right hugging a woman, other than his mother. It wasn't just warm and comforting, but also now an erotic feeling. Somehow she knew this is what he needed. Somehow she knew him. Deep inside him.

That's when he heard it.

Just remember the future.

He closed his eyes. Quietly, he said, "Did you say that?"

"I didn't say anything," she said.

"It was your voice."

"I didn't say anything, Joe." She let go of him taking a step backward.

"This is what is happening to me. The old orangutan is hearing voices."

"Voices? Whose voices?"

"Well, not exactly voices. It has been Martin's up until just now." He paused. "Now it was yours."

"Mine? What did I say?"

He looked at her carefully, reading her face. "You said something that I have heard a hundred times. Martin's voice has repeated it in my head over and over. I mean in my head, recently, long after he died. You said, *Remember the future.* I mean, not like you said it the first time, but this time, only the part he says."

She looked at him and shook her head. "That is weird. I mean, I don't mean you. I mean, what a thing to say out of nowhere. I certainly wouldn't know to say that. It is so out there. So out of context. I don't know how else to…"

Joe was silent. He just looked at her, but not focusing, staring through her as he tried to make sense of the present.

"Joe," she said. "The funny part is that it doesn't scare me, not coming from you. I have no sense that you are going off any deep end." She paused. "What else has he said?"

"He?"

"Martin."

He stared at her, both in disbelief that she wanted to know and trying to think what he had heard. Finally, he said, "Nothing. It's repetition, like it had to be repeated so I could remember, but always something that's so foreign to any comprehension of anything I might have heard or read."

"And?"

"That's it."

"That's it?" she repeated.

"That's it; just a meaningless sentence, to me anyway, but it's a full sentence, not a phrase or a picture."

"Have you written it down?"

"Written it down? No," he said slowly. "No, why would I? I don't want to. I have tried to forget it."

"Forget it! No, Joe, you need to write it down. Get it out of your head. Give it to someone. Give it away."

"And get put in an asylum? Thank you, my amateur shrink."

"Write it down. Give it to me. I will take it to some sonofabitch who understands and then maybe you can erase it from your mind. Maybe we can make sense of it."

He let her wrap her long arms around him again and to hold him against her body. They stood in silence for a time that no one measures and that no one wants to end because it hurts.

As her femininity devoured him, Joe said in a whisper, "Do you remember when you came home from school and had become enamored with Greek goddesses?"

Geena smiled. "Sure. Of course."

"Well," he said. "I think of you right now as Selene, the moon goddess, bringing peace to me."

Geena was quiet for a few seconds, and then with a silent laugh, said, "Well, that's a thought, since if I were, I could put you to sleep and keep you in bed and have, how many? Fifty daughters?" She paused. "Ugh, no. I would rather be Artemis. Still hooked to the moon somehow, loving her mother, and always hunting."

"For what?"

"I don't know. Knowledge, maybe."

She stayed overnight, naked next to him in his bed. He wasn't sure how she felt about it. Even how he felt about it. She didn't get her wish to make love with him, but because of the feel of her soft skin next to him, he left the bedding unchanged days longer than he had ever done, and because he wanted to savor the uniqueness lingering from the night's intimacy. There was a bond, an amorous bond that he felt he would continue to have, even if she lived on the moon and he on earth.

After she flew back to Kansas City, Joe had the sporadic notion that the thought police would soon be at his door to arrest him and put him away, buried deep into a padded cell. But he had to agree with Geena that his writing it down and giving it to her made him feel better, knowing that someone else was inspecting the garbage of his head dump. Or maybe it was just Geena's visit that did it.

But the repetition didn't stop; it just slowed or rather slowed in number.

Just remember the future.

Repeatedly. No sense. Even nonsense, maybe.

But then he could make no sense of his feelings for Geena either. It was more than platonic. She warmed his toes, his stomach, his gut, his soul. All right, his heart. And he didn't know what to do with it, or with her, as if he had any say or any sway.

So maybe, he decided, it was his fixation with her that thwarted his dead lover's message to him. Is that what it was? A message?

Her aura stemming it down to a slow crawl, to a minimum, must be a good thing.

But how could she possibly care for his queer soul? He had no answer. Maybe there was none.

Geena called ten days later and said that she had spoken to a physics professor she knew. The sentence Joe had written was quantum physics related. A science of inexactitudes. The physicist had said that the mathematics of quantum physics involved uncertainty, and he had no answers.

Geena thought maybe Martin had been trying to tell Joe something. During the call, she didn't tell him she was happy and bewildered by their relationship. That part she wrote to him. She wrote him because she said she was so much better at writing something of importance. Not so much better maybe, but able to edit and work it out in her own mind.

She wrote that she loved him. She definitely loved him for his brilliance and the way he made her feel. Obviously, it couldn't work that they were together as lovers, but good friends would work. *Work? That was such a bad word for it.*

But, as far as Geena was concerned, she wrote, uncertainty tied Joe to her, tied together by quantum physics. Tied by an uncertainty neither one of them understood. He could feel her grin like two electrons of quantum particles would feel even at huge distances from each other.

Yes, she was right. And as he felt her presence, he grinned.

2. JOE

DOGS

Sᴜɴᴅᴀʏ ᴇᴠᴇɴɪɴɢ, Jᴏᴇ, ᴛʀʏɪɴɢ ᴛᴏ ᴄᴀʟʟ Gᴇᴇɴᴀ ɪɴ ᴛʜᴇ ᴡᴇᴇᴋᴇɴᴅ, ɴᴏᴛ ᴡᴀɴᴛɪɴɢ ᴛᴏ bother her at work with something he thought was so questionable, kept dialing from time to time and getting a busy signal for almost two hours.

Finally, upon answering, she seemed stressed. "Joe! Oh, Joe, good to hear your voice. What's new?"

"Are you okay?" he said. "You sound a little frazzled."

"Oh, yeah. You know, I almost had my comeuppance today."

"What are you talking about? When? I've tried to call you for hours. What's wrong? Are you hurt?"

"Hold on. Hold on, Joe. Don't get your bowels in an uproar. I'm okay, but I was busy on the phone. I had been out running when this dog started following me. There was something about the dog and the way it was acting that didn't let me want to stop to pet it. When I got home and got the door open, I turned to look at it more carefully and confirmed the fucker had foam all around its mouth."

"Yikes!" Joe said.

"Yeah, I know. I called the police and they said they had had a report of a rabid dog and would come right out to catch it. They wanted me to try to keep it there. I tried to think of some goodie I might have that I could throw to it, but by the time I went to get it and came back, the dog was gone."

"I'm glad it wasn't a wolverine."

"What? A wolverine?"

"Forget it. I don't know why I said that. Just joking. So it's still on the loose?"

"Well, I don't know if they found it, but it doesn't make me want to go out running for a while. So anyway, that's why you didn't get me. I was out and then I was on the damn phone. So, how are you?"

"I'm as screwed up as ever, thank you," he said with a laugh, and was thinking, *like your brother.* "How's your brother? What's he doing?"

"Joe, you're changing the subject."

"Well, I hesitated calling, 'cause it's probably not so...well, it's sort of silly, maybe."

Geena said, "Come on, Joe. Speak up."

"You know, Geena, how this one phrase *Just Remember the Future* keeps climbing into my head?"

"Yes, I know. It's not getting better?"

"I don't know what you'd call better, but something struck me as a maybe, a big maybe."

"And?"

"Well, when Martin and I were driving back on that Friday, the day of the wreck, he...well, he talked about how he had figured out something really important about quantum physics or about life or something in that vein. It was so important, he said, that it could change everything and save the world, or pretty much like that.

"I didn't really believe him and still maintain my doubt, but then, he was a serious physicist and he was writing a dissertation about it, which, he said, he had hidden in a computer file at MIT."

"Hidden? Why?"

"Yeah, good question. He didn't want anybody stealing the idea or theory or whatever you call it. You know, he wanted credit, his due, and was really afraid someone would steal it. He was paranoid in so many ways.

"I don't know why, but I asked him—sorrowfully, ironically—just that day in the car, what would happen to the discovery if he died before he published it. He said it was coded or something so that even the geniuses at MIT couldn't get at it."

Joe was quiet for too long.

Geena said, "Joe, goddamnit, don't go there. I know what you're thinking. Don't even try to think that shit. It is not your fault he was killed. Now tell me...tell me why you called."

After another few seconds, Joe said, "The phrase that keeps repeating in my head might be significant for another reason. I had forgotten even that he yelled or what he yelled, obviously. I know it sounds stupid, probably, but it suddenly came to me this past week that this phrase was the last thing he said. And because he and I had each yelled our own thing in terror at the last moment and at exactly the same time just before the collision, I had forgotten it.

"It's highly improbable, just like his rantings about saving the earth, but maybe this sentence about remembering the future is the key to getting into his file. It's pretty far-fetched, but..."

"Joe, stop. That's not so stupid. The big question in my mind is how would you find out?"

"Listen, Geena, I have no idea. I barely remember attending high school. I have never been to a university, let alone MIT. You, at least, might have an idea of who to contact or even how to contact the right people. I can't just call up and say, hey, I was Professor Case's lover. He wouldn't even have mentioned his private life to them. And if...I don't know, if nothing. I...I don't see it."

"You have to try."

"Geena, I have no rights to anything of his. For my own part, I don't have to *try* anything. As far as his stuff is concerned, I don't exist. He has no living relatives that I knew or ever knew of. All his professorship crap is crap, as far as I am concerned. Everything that was ours was his. I have had to write off even thinking about it."

"I'm sorry, Joe. I never thought about that. I'm sorry. I should have. I should have."

Her voice sounded so sorrowfully sad to him, he felt bad. He heard a noise on the phone like she might be crying. But he didn't ask.

"Listen, Joe, I'm going to make some calls on Monday to see what I can find out." Her words thumped through a suddenly stuffy nose; she wasn't going to admit to crying. "What was the phrase again? Remember the future?"

"Just remember the future," he said.

After they hung up, Joe felt horribly desolate from her obvious sadness jammed with all the memories of his good life with Martin percolating up. If only he could bury those memories—surgically remove them—if only he knew how.

Maybe it was these flashback memories that were causing the supposed quantum physics citation in his head, or whatever it was. Nothing really to do with mental telepathy or ghostly dialogs. Stupid stuff that he was sure he could never explain to any sane person. But still, some evenings he had long conversations about it with Kevin who, at least, listened.

Monday afternoon she called. In her excitement, she hardly took the time to greet him. She said, "Okay, I spoke to my physics professor friend and he, believe it or not, went out of his way to call MIT and here's the deal.

"They, MIT administration, I mean, had found a distant cousin of Martin. Somebody named Henry Fried, out in Iowa to take care of Martin's stuff…Martin's MIT stuff, that is. They wouldn't say more than that, but gave him the guy's name and number. You can call this guy to get access to Martin's estate or whatever you need. I've sent his name and phone number to you by email.

"I'm thrilled to shit, Joe. At least, you might get some good results with his help. Let me know how it goes."

Although having great misgiving about getting any results and much less any benefit out of it, but needing to get this out of his system, Joe didn't wait long to call. Joe got no answer the first three times he tried, three different days at different times. No answer and no answering machine. He began to wonder if this distant cousin was a distant fantasy, but then on Saturday morning on the fourth try, he got an answer.

"Fried here. Who's there?" the voice on the other end said.

"Hello, Henry Fried?" Joe said.

"Hi there, friend, what can I do you fer?"

Joe hadn't even introduced himself. Just the tone of this guy's voice built hope in Joe. He had expected the guy to wonder what Joe was selling or maybe hang up on him like a cold-caller. The guy must be desperate to talk. One lonely soul out between the corn stalks.

Joe said, "Thank you for asking. My name is Joe Tink. I was a close friend of Professor Martin Case."

"Oh, nice to meet ya, Joe. Yeah, Professor Case. I'm glad his parents didn't name him Justin." He laughed. "Get it? I mean, I gotta ask ya if ya got it, just in case." More laugh. "I think he was a big wheel. Smart. Am I right?"

"Well, yeah. I suppose he was. I couldn't say any differently. And..." Joe had not yet figured out why this guy was so aggressively friendly. Joe was, thus, like his mother would say, discombobulated by it, unsure how or what to ask for or even explain why he was calling.

Fried said, "Well, he was smart fer sure. He was my cousin; that makes him smart right there. Just bein' funny. No, actually, he was a bigwig professor in MIT. I think it stands fer Massachusetts something."

Joe began to worry about what possible response this guy would or could have given to MIT. "Yeah, it does. Listen, Mr. Fried..."

"Call me Henry. Just not chicken. I've heard it before. Chicken fried, I mean. Get it?" He laughed like a tractor engine not wanting to start, possibly just as loudly.

"Okay, Henry. Okay, listen, I need your help."

"You got it. Like I said, what can I do you fer?"

Joe couldn't detect if the guy was trying to mock Joe or be friendly. "Well, you see, Martin told me that he had a computer file at MIT. He told me that, if anything happened to him, he wanted me to get into that file and...analyze the content." What else was Joe going to say?

Henry said, "Well, now, that's interesting. I reckon it was important stuff, I mean, fer high falutin' people, MIT and all. Are you one of them?"

"Sorry? One of them?"

"One of them professors or somethin'?"

"Uh, actually not. I am simply an old friend trying to do him a favor. Follow up on a promise."

"Well, that's good. You know, I even heard he was queer. Typical of them liberal east colleges turnin' people queer."

The guy paused, testing how Joe might react to this surprise secret shocker of detailed intel that an old farmer could know, despite living in the corn fields.

"Well, Henry, I don't know if MIT made him queer, but he was an odd duck." Was the guy going to go deeper into the subject of Martin's sex life?

"Well," said Henry. "They, I mean, them MIT queers asked me if I wanted any of his stuff. I mean, they didn't just up and ask me; they sent me letters askin'. I said nope. I didn't even know the guy more'n to hear I had some queer cousin professor back East. So I signed the releases to destroy it all. So I reckon they did. I ain't heard nothin' since."

Destroy it all. Joe's hope, if he had any, was in a plowed furrow, unless... "Do you still have a copy of that letter?"

"What letter?"

"The one they sent you."

"Hmm. I donno. There ain't no one letter. They sent busloads of paper. I don't throw nuthin' away. Just a minute."

Joe could hear the chair squeak, the clunk of the phone as Henry put it down, and the rustle of paper. Then he heard the guy grunt. More noise on the phone and a loud bang from knocking the phone on the floor and the word *shit*.

Joe heard more crunching sounds, a whack and a yelp. Finally, Henry got the phone to his ear and said, "Damn dog tried to run off with the phone. That's the trouble with these damn little things."

Joe wasn't sure whether the *little thing* was the phone or the dog.

"Yeah, proof right here I don't throw nuthin' away. I know'ed it could be good fer something, you know."

Joe could just imagine the piles of magazines and papers stacked around this guy's house, and probably a weedy yard full of household machinery, propped up broken tireless cars and, no doubt, a naked, rusty tractor perched on cement blocks as an announcement to the world.

Joe said, "Would you mind reading me what MIT asked you exactly?"

Henry said, "Well, sure. But I ain't so quick at readin' so, well, just so you know."

"No problem, Henry. No problem. Read as slowly as you want."

"No, I mean, it ain't that I read slow. It ain't one letter. It's a stack with *release this* and *no claim* on that and, I don't know what. The whole kit and caboodle just goes on and on. I ain't got time to read it to myself, so you may be the laziest guy ever was, but you ain't got time to hear it all."

Joe said, "No, no. You are right. I agree. But do you remember if there was a specific letter or form or whatever in that stack that talked about online or computer files?"

"Hmm. Yeah." More paper noise. "This'n here." Paper noise. "Seems I'm gonna have a party. Says 'each party shall release the other party from all claims, known and unknown...'"

"Henry, wait. Don't read it all. Just tell me how they describe the subject. I mean, after all the legal stuff, do they tell you what it concerned?"

"Well, it says at the top, *Concerning all computer files.*"

"And if you signed that document, what happens?"

"They don't tell me what happens. They just wanna know if I want 'em. And that's easy as apple pie. I don't. I mean, I like apple pie, but this stuff…"

"So if you don't, do they say they are going to erase them or anything?"

"You're a really nice guy, but you're kinda slow. You ain't no professor I can tell. Like I said, they don't tell me nuthin'; just that I don't want 'em. That's it. What am I gonna do with 'em? Wipe my you-know-what with 'em? I got these here letters fer that." He discharged more diesel-powered laughter.

As soon as Joe got through the struggle, as he saw it, of talking with this guy, he called Geena. "I didn't learn much, or as our farmer cousin would say, I didn't learn nuthin' 'cept he released the rights to the computer files to MIT. Either MIT has them or has erased them."

Geena said, "We have to find out. I'll call you-know-who."

Actually, Joe didn't know who, but he trusted her, even if she could die suddenly from a dog bite and…. Shut up, Joe! If only he could just control his mind.

The days went by—two, three, four—and no answer. He kept telling himself it didn't matter; it had been this long. What were a few more days? He could call her, but it wasn't that important, was it? She was going to let him know. Don't push her. She was asking a favor of her acquaintance. He was a busy guy. She couldn't begin rushing him. Was he just an acquaintance or her lover? He seemed to be awfully helpful. Then again, why was Joe even caring about all this stuff?

It was interesting, Joe thought, that, during this time, he had none of the line-o-type messages. On day five she called. Almost short of breath, she said, "Joe, what was the password exactly? I mean, what was the phrase?"

To calm her, he said, "Hello, Geena. How are you?"

"Sorry, Joe. I wasn't thinking. I'm fine. And you?"

"Good. So what's the story? He spoke to someone?"

"Yes, he did. It was a lot of back and forth about who he was and what authority he had and what possible connection he had to Martin's files, until finally he got through to them that he was not a crazy man, a spy, or looking for a reward, that all they needed to do was try the pass phrase.

"It turned out they were actually pretty desperate to get into the files and had not erased them. They were very interested in the possibility of the password phrase. He told me that, while he was held on the phone, they put the phrase *remember the future* into a bot that would try the phrase with capital letters, without, in one word, upside down and backwards, and a hundred other variations. But none of them worked."

Joe didn't speak. He had loved Martin, probably still did. Martin was a great guy, but he could be full of himself. And his ideas were, could sometimes be, pretty off-the-wall.

"So, Joe, now you can relax. You did the right thing. They were pleased that you cared. And they thanked us profusely. But that's it. It didn't work. I'm going for a run. Speak soon. I'll call you next week."

She hung up before he could ask about the rabid dog.

Joe put his phone down on the kitchen counter very slowly and carefully, even though he was not conscious of doing so. What took up his whole thought process was the headline on his phone's news feed—*MIT Announces Revolutionary Discovery in Quantum Physics.*

"So coincidental it's almost funny," he thinks. He might mention it to Geena or maybe just let sleeping dogs lie.

3. DAVIS

THINKING

I BELIEVE IN EXTRASENSORY PERCEPTION, IF, AND ONLY IF, THE RIGHT TWO PEOPLE meet, like we did.

"Davis, this is Stella," said the curator to me that fateful day in 2019. "Stella has been so kind as to offer to play your wife today since Doris had to go home sick."

It was the look in Stella's eyes that would not let go of me. In her eighteenth-century costume all I could see of her physical features, except for her eyes which smiled even more than her mouth, was that Stella was tall. I felt she was from that century.

Five minutes after the normal hellos, I felt I knew Stella inside and out and could talk to her about anything. Even my past. I obviously couldn't know her, but I did. Asking her to share food with me that evening at the Cedar Street Grill in Sturbridge was as natural as sharing the day.

She came home with me that first evening without my asking or my thinking to ask her since we both felt we belonged together. Without the least hesitation, she let me slowly disrobe her and to touch the presence of her naked body.

That same evening as we spoke without the least tension, Stella said the weirdest thing. "A philosopher named Foot, Philippa Foot, once said, 'In moral philosophy it is useful, I believe, to think about plants.' She meant that we are part of nature and that we need to judge our lives from that point of view."

I envisioned myself lying on the ground looking closely at the underside of a potato plant's leaf and trying to see its point of view. I said, "I'm not sure how I would take that point of view."

She laughed her beautiful laugh and said, "Plants are alive. In fact, we are discovering that they have brains and that they think and discover and adapt. Their actions are slower, but all of their actions and adaptations are based on their nature, as ours should be."

Some months later, I told her, "I learned exactly then on that day that, if I or anyone knows or senses subconsciously what the natural relationship is between the sexes, all he needs to do is fight through the abnormal, the artificial, the past, and he or she will eventually find his true love, as I did with you."

She said, "I don't believe most people find that love. I think we are the exception."

After we, with help from her parents, managed to buy an old house out in the sticks, every day I said, "Thank you, Stella, for finding me, forgiving me, and letting me find you." After she got pregnant, I would say something about her being my world and how lucky I was that I became part of hers, and this child would be our world.

The funeral was mine. I died. The museum arranged it, I think, along with her parents, maybe. I left in the middle of the reception.

* * *

To: GeenaN@gmail.com   July 5, 2020
From: DavisM@gmail.com
Subject: Your questions

Hey Geena,

I found the job at the Old Sturbridge Village Museum. The museum farm was a real farm. All natural. All organic. And I found my one love at the museum when she became part of the display as I was. She was hired to do bookkeeping, but had offered to play a farmer's wife when one of the regulars suddenly became ill and had to leave.

Before the afternoon was over, I had asked her if we could meet for dinner. It seemed our meeting was part of the all-natural of the farm. I didn't have to write poetry or to play any game with Stella. It was the most beautiful evening of my life.

After we moved in together when Stella got pregnant, the obstetrician said we might have problems.

And then she died. A horrible death, Geena, that I cannot describe to you. I have little recollection of who was at the funeral or why. Almost where it was.

Davis

4. GEENA

THE CATHOLIC CHERRY TREES

GEENA FELT GOOD ABOUT HELPING JOE WITH THE PASSWORD CONUNDRUM, BUT today he had made her think. And how often she had tried not to think about the past, but now Joe, in the middle of everything, had asked, "How's your brother?"

That question was hard to get out of her head during her run today. And, since nothing on the street or in the park was distracting her today, especially dogs, she could run this familiar route almost blind.

How much did she really remember about growing up and how much had she been told? Childhood memories were always like that.

How many times had she been told the story of the flaming Christmas rum-flavored plum pudding when she had said, *It's delicious, but I don't like it*? So, of course, she remembered that part.

How old was she then? Seven? Eight? Even ten? It seemed like she could picture where she was sitting at the table that Christmas Eve. But more likely, rather than remembering this scene because of what she had said, she remembered where she was sitting because she had been embarrassed. Obviously, while her reasoning had been that all the smiling adults around her at the table had said the pudding was delicious, why shouldn't she say it was delicious? It didn't mean she had to like it. It might have been funny for everyone else, but the family laughing at her was seared on her brain.

So she decided, at whatever young age she was at that time, never to laugh at other people, and especially not at her poor brother, who had been found in the Catholic cherry trees. From her present-day adult perspective, her thinking he had been found in the woods was now hilariously funny to her because she could laugh at herself. She couldn't remember when she had understood. But, at least, no one else could laugh at her, because she had never told anyone about the Catholic cherry trees or about later learning that it had, instead, been the Catholic Charities.

Some things about Davis she remembered. Some she obviously could not, since she wasn't there or was not told about them. But her strongest memory about Davis was that she loved him. Whatever age she was, probably five or six when Davis was being adopted, she had been prepped, told that she was going to get a little brother from the Catholic cherry trees and that he would need her love and affection, and in her mind, especially after he must have been abandoned and alone in the woods. It was a big deal. The biggest deal in her life for a long time.

And, of course, she loved him. Just like she knew the pudding was supposed to be delicious, she understood at this younger-than-the-pudding-story age that she needed to love him.

And to protect him. It seemed to her from the start that he was going to need protection all the time, one way or another, for the rest of his life. Either he was getting into trouble or trouble was getting into him. She didn't always know, until later, what trouble was or meant, but she, the older sister, was told to keep him out of it and she took that assignment seriously.

And of the antics she did remember, she is not sure if she remembered so much or was told about them later, but it was probably something of both, from small things like breaking their mother's favorite piece of china to Davis's carelessly injuring Geena with a hoe. Both these incidents and others may have been accidental, but he seemed to be an accident waiting to happen.

She certainly remembered all the swear words he taught her, but that definitely came later. She probably kept using these words because they were the one thing about him that she could keep.

But his childhood moods, if she had to describe them, were freakish? Frightening? Whatever they were, his moods conflicted with her love for him. Tantrums were one thing. She was told by her mother that it was a normal part of being a baby. But when those tantrums continued as he got older and older, well, it was no longer so normal.

And then, just as suddenly, he would be quiet and impossible to reach, like he was gone into another world. Now these days, these gyrations would be pretty obvious for shrinks to treat and maybe it was obvious then, too, but for Geena, as a little girl, it was just *mood swings*. And that is why, she guessed, he was in and out of school for reasons she never knew.

How she managed to love her brother who abused her one minute and wouldn't speak to her the next was, she supposed, the reason she got so mentally aware of herself. Mentally tough, she supposed it was called. Not always in control, but at least, aware of how she was thinking, how she should be thinking, and how she should be presenting herself to the world. And mostly to keep her little brother out of trouble.

And because she loved her little brother, it didn't matter that he did what he did, said what he said, and didn't. Didn't what? Admit to? She couldn't make herself go there. She loved him.

Before he disappeared from her daily life, when he was put away, she had some memories of intimate times with him, which were not the times when he actually did bad things according to Kevin and Beth, because he never did those things when Geena was around. She learned second or third hand, if at all. So for her these stories were just stories. But which made her worry.

The times she remembered best were when Davis, himself, told her stories, together alone in some warm corner or maybe hiding under a table. His imagination made her precocious little brother the best storyteller ever, early on most often exciting stories about fire-breathing dragons and swords and elves and guns and battles. Boy's things.

He had told her lots of stories, but the one story she remembered most, probably because it was the last fairytale before the fairytales stopped, was about a genie that a young girl had found when she happened to rub the bedpan under her bed.

"Your wish is my command, master," said the genie.

"Shouldn't you call me *mistress*?" the young girl asked the genie.

"No, you are my master, not my mistress," said the genie. "So what is your wish?"

The girl said, "I'm unhappy because the world is so scary that I'm afraid to go out of my bedroom. Can you fix that for me?"

The genie asked, "What's scaring you?"

"Everything," said the girl. "People might want to kill me with swords and guns or poison. Animals. Dogs and snakes and lions and tigers can bite me. I have read about earth-quakes and tornados and hurricanes that have killed so many people. And who knows what can fall out of the sky and break open my skull? I'm not brave like I should be."

"Now I understand," said the genie. "And your wish is for me to fix that?"

"Yes."

"You're sure?"

"Yes, most certainly," said the girl.

So, the genie began by killing all the people on earth, and, after resting with a cup of warm tea, he killed all the animals. Then he began tearing off pieces of the earth and throwing them out into space. All the pieces except a little piece where the girl's bed was located. Then, as best he could, because it was even a tough job for a genie, he cleaned out a reasonably large part of the universe, at least the area that might be able to fall on the young girl's head during her lifetime.

"I've fulfilled your wish, master," said the tired genie. "You are safe from everything."

"But, I'm hungry and thirsty and alone," said the girl. "I need a friend."

"You never said that before," said the genie, grumpily.

"But how do I get food and water?"

"Well, you didn't mention that in the beginning either, but I guess I can make it so that a cup and plate by your bed are always full. What do you like to eat?"

Oh, boy, thought the girl. At least I can eat what I want. She said, "I want steak and fries and ice cream. And no vegetables."

The genie said, "But neither steak nor potatoes are any longer available since I have rid the earth of all animals, and of everything that could possibly grow any food or be used to make ice cream. In fact, I removed the whole earth. You have only your bedroom left. I can arrange to have a few things that can grow in your bedroom."

"Like what?"

"The only things that have ever grown in bedrooms. Spiders, mold, dust balls, and dirt, in general, comprised of your dead skin and parts of the mattress."

Obviously, the young girl began to regret her wish, so she said, "I take it all back. Please put everything back. I won't be afraid of the world anymore. I'm sorry. I'll be brave. I need friends and family. I need the sun for light and warmth. I need…"

"Too late," said the tired genie. "You had one wish that has even destroyed any career that I might have had as a successful genie. I'm pissed. I'm going back into the bedpan. Goodbye forever."

And the genie turned into just a puddle of pee.

Young Geena had begun to cry and complained about the ending. "You can't just leave her there. What happened to her mommy and daddy? She needs friends and food."

And Davis had said, "Too late."

And no matter how much Geena cried, Davis would not change the story. And now as she was running, she realized that he had never told her a fairytale with a happy ending.

Later, when he was an early teenager, he told a story about blowing up a house, except the story about blowing up a house turned out to be true.

He and a neighbor boy Freddie—she never knew the boy's last name—had found a crate of blasting caps in Freddie's garage because the boy's father was in construction. According to Davis, the two of them had dumped the powder out of blasting caps into a short piece of iron pipe that they had also found in the garage.

Then, if the story was true—and she had no reason, especially later, to doubt it—they had used the father's wheelbarrow to haul other useful treasures they found in the garage—a car battery and a roll of electrical wire, along with the pipe bomb over to another neighbor's house near the edge of Bangor, a neighbor both boys agreed they didn't like because that boy had somehow been mean to them at school and was a *fucking dummy*.

When Davis had related the story, he had gone into some detail, telling Geena about what a "fucking bully" this "big fucking asshole dummy" was and about this house and the neighborhood. How the house didn't have close neighbors, how they knew these people were not home during the day, how the two boys somehow knew how to attach up the wires and the battery without killing themselves.

But speaking of not killing themselves, the two had little idea how it would really be when they hid behind the big oak in the yard and touched the two ends of the wires together. He told her that the explosion had almost knocked the tree over, uprooting it. Branches and acorns had rained down on them. The wheelbarrow disintegrated, and the windows and front door of the house were blown in before the front porch had collapsed.

He didn't know what happened to his friend Freddie, but Davis had run home and had sat on his bed expecting the police to come to arrest him within minutes.

And he couldn't hear anything except the ringing in his ears for the rest of the day. That evening at the dinner table he read the faces of his parents, especially fearing his policeman father, trying to understand what they were thinking or saying or might want because he couldn't hear them. He went to bed early, ears not just ringing, but screaming, it seemed, and awake all night in apprehension under the covers.

Nothing happened for the next few days. He had had time to regain his hearing and to tell Geena about it—some of it—which she had immediately dismissed as just another story since he was smiling while he told it.

But later, as the dramatic story of a house being bombed spread through the high school, Geena learned purposely to do what so many humans subconsciously manage to do; she separated fact from reality. It was her brother who did it, but it might not have been her brother who did it. Maybe the other boy did it. How would she know? But, of course, she carried a common guilt with her brother for her silence. A mark on her life's scorecard.

Some weeks later, the doorbell. The police. Loud conversations and stuff Geena was not allowed to hear, took Davis away.

Yeah, she kept contact with him through his stay in reform school and asylum and later on, if only it was a phone call or an email that he seldom answered, but that was normal for guys. But she, at least, followed along with where he was in a general sense most of the time.

The most personal contact, after he was put away, was when Geena and mother Beth visited him by traveling down to the reform school in Manchester, New Hampshire. During her first visit, he had excitedly told Geena the details of the explosion story, seemingly with no regret, even bragging how he plugged the pipe ends and how a metal shard of the wheelbarrow had barely missed him and stuck in the tree.

And on a later visit, he had told her that he was looking for his real mother.

When Geena had visited him in the hospital after the boat wreck that also almost killed him, he had told her how he had been asked to service this rich guy's boat and all the details of how weird the guy was, never talking to Davis.

Even when he was just a young boy, Davis seemed hyperaware of life around him. And because consciousness is seeing the future in order to avoid surprises, he had told her sometime later how he worked at creating surprises to maintain control of them.

But it didn't work. When Davis told her years later in 2014 how his love, Stella, had died, Geena in her midtwenties had cried more than when the fairytales stopped.

He told her on the phone that Stella died so fast, along with her unborn fetus broiled inside her, that she had no time to scream.

To understand what killed her, Davis said he had to slow down the freak phenomenon in his mind by imagining how the lightning split and crackled down the elm tree outside their bedroom, turned at a right angle from the tree trunk just at the second-floor level and, as a jagged laser, leaped flickering from the tree to melt a two-inch wide hole in the glass window pane, and snapped across an open six-foot space before striking Stella's sleeping body.

He told her, "I didn't need to imagine the rest. She, along with the bedsheets and mattress, burst into yellow and green thunderous flames. As I lay in our bed on the other side of her, with this aberration of nature occurring beyond any possible relevance to human comprehension, I had no opportunity to grasp it. But for the rest of my life I have had this image and the smell of her burning flesh at my every waking moment. And I can't sit near a dark window."

Hundreds of times he was asked "How did she die?" by authorities, insurance agents, friends, acquaintances, and even strangers because the bizarre story had made the news. And, of course, by his sister Geena.

And he had said, "And then I stood in the cold vacuum of the unlit universe and watched our constellation circle around and pour into its drain."

It seemed miraculous to Geena that Davis was still alive. She would keep tabs on him and hoped that his life would quiet down in the coming years, but what saddened Geena most was that he had never, and seemingly never would, ask for her help, or for that matter, call her. Not once. Never in a thousand years.

While she fumbled to find the front door lock because of her tears, Geena had to remind herself whether she had actually completed her daily neighborhood run, having floated through it this time, deep in thought, lost in the Catholic cherry trees.

PART 5

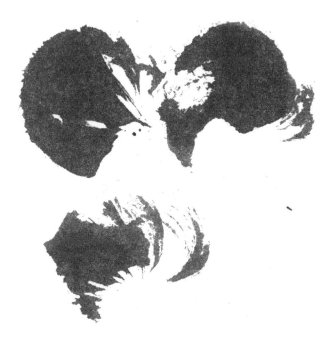

We live in a world that is beyond our control, and life is in a constant flux of change. So we have a decision to make: keep trying to control a storm that is not going to go away or start learning how to live within the rain.

—Glenn Pemberton, *Hurting with God*

PRESENT DAY

2043–2044 CE

1. DAVIS

MURDER OMITTED

I THINK, UNBEKNOWNST TO OURSELVES, A PART OF THE BRAIN GROWS LIKE A CHIM-panzee in a test lab, becoming deformed, angry, and self-abusive. I hope never to have to do it again. In fact, I'm sure I won't; it's too painful, but, in a way, it was necessary, much unlike the guy on the yacht.

I went ahead, threw the dart. I needed to find the right neighborhood, the right house (houses have their own weaknesses, favored by their more isolated location), the right owner, and, of course, the right time, so planning all took a while—a week or so—to find the victim. It's not like I loved killing people, but the dart was thrown. That was it.

I killed somebody's grandmother, and found enough money to get me a subway ticket, a plane ticket, to rent a place, and to eat for a while. Not bad. Not good either. The planning was good and I was lucky; she was not. The odds of a meteor falling on her head were the same.

It was easy then. That was twenty-eight years ago, but I still think about that woman. She was maybe seventy or eighty, not much older than I am now. Slow. Probably close to deaf. Even used a cane, the one I used on her head. I really tried not to kill her, but I read in the news that I did. She never saw me or heard me coming. She never knew how and when she was going to die, but we, the living, think it is better to die old. And quickly.

Maybe the regret is not so much the lady herself, but the family I saw leaving the house before I went in. They were probably not so happy about her death, unless they had a big feud—or maybe liked the idea of her money more than the "old useless" person she was—and were waiting for an inheritance. I tell myself that could be the case, but the papers never mentioned it. The money I stole would hardly have been of consequence for those family members, proven by the news stories reporting that nothing was stolen. I left the place essentially undisturbed.

So officially I am both a thief and a murderer. Admittedly. But if I had gone to jail and been released now like Kevin, been cleansed of my record, wouldn't that be the same as now? I haven't lived a life of crime since. Am I not equally penalized and absolved, as Kevin, as if I had gone to prison?

But I dread the approaching storm, coming to feed my garrisoned creature.

* * *

To: GeenaN@gmail.com   September 6, 2043
From: DavisM@gmail.com
Subject: Your questions

Hey Geena, How am I doing? Or what am I doing? Fine. As to guilt feelings, to this day, Geena, I regret misidentifying the poor guy on the boat; it eats away inside me. And I am left with the two big questions. Why don't I just give myself up, against Kevin's will? Why do I bother living? Living is my retribution.

Davis

2. KEVIN

THINGS

THE NIGHT BEFORE LAST, A NOISE WOKE KEVIN AT 2:33 A.M.

Good god, how tired he had been since all his concentration; every fiber in his body, all his physical activity had been so focused during the day, like he had been tweezering out a thousand splinters, one by one, while working on his jury-rigged workbench that he has contrived in the bedroom.

But he had been unable to think of a way to get back to sleep. As proficient as he had become throughout his life at letting himself sleep by diverting his mind like a grifter's sleight-of-hand, how could he find a diversion more distracting than an execution?

Or maybe sleep was not an option for him anymore. Other than his present project, he had not found any new distraction to dig up despite his lifelong practice of obscuring uncomfortable torment.

The piano is gone, sold long ago to cover expenses. But of the few things left in the house, their double bed makes Kevin feel Beth's absence most acutely as he severely misses the opportunity to reach over to touch her or to snuggle next to her as his agent of calm when he couldn't sleep.

He hasn't bothered to clean up the dust and dirt that has accumulated while he was in prison. He hasn't changed the sheets that were left on the bed, nor has he changed his clothes since his return. When he had imagined her scolding him for that, he wept as if the dearth of her wonderfully bewitching existence had begun only a week since his return instead of twenty-five years ago.

Sitting up, he switched on the bedside lamp, illuminating his new wall of the departed, as yet unfinished. Or maybe it was.

Viewing the portrait photos spread out over the bedroom's only expansive wall, he wondered why, having found the paint and brush in the closet, he had fussed over refreshing the white wall paint while, at the same time, not bothering to clean up the drips or the paint brush. But he had felt a brief satisfaction with the previous day's strenuous preparation, motivated by the tumorous dread proliferating in him while alone, unchecked by any diversion in what was once a house full of music, smiles, and laughter, and not least, visitors and friends, and the aromas of food, household fragrances, and Beth's femininity.

This house, now run to ruin—needing paint and nakedly exposed to the winter wind—made plaintive moans of neglect. It had been theirs, and, as homes should be, a haven. It was a place to which he had returned from things good and things that had haunted him, to be together with Beth, to talk and to sing and to play with levity in order to cover—even to completely muffle and smother—the things of which he could not talk. And now he couldn't even afford to heat the place. Dan Ludovico had gotten his revenge, the Ludovico Vendetta; there could be no other name for it.

That night, he had forced himself out of bed, to approach the wall, his tiredness slowing his steps even more, with a backache and unsteady legs underscoring his rotting body and the forgotten hours that he had spent when he had stood in concentration, fidgeting the whole day with clipping, framing, and picture hanging. As a young policeman, this small job could never have bothered him in the least; the self-abuse and the years were certainly catching up now at age seventy-four, the thought of which had just added to the pain.

As staring eyes from the wall focused in on his bent soul in silence, he had forced himself to accept that the deep growl that had awakened him was in his head or, more probably, in the house itself, rather than a beast in the room. His petite stature was made even smaller as, feeling frail and fumbling, he had hunched with his left hand against the wall to steady his body and his rapid heartbeat, caused by the sounds around him and the anticipated unknown.

So he hadn't done much yesterday; he was way too tired from that previous sleepless night to bother to attempt to clean up his mess on the floor of paper snippings, tape, nails and tacks, and even some pared pieces of tediously cut matting and framing. It had made his back ache just to consider the work it would require to sweep it up or to bend over.

So last night he had climbed back into bed at seven-thirty, right after a lukewarm bowl of canned chicken noodle soup, which was about all he had found in the cupboard. The empty soup can lay on the floor in the corner after he had clumsily knocked it off the counter and given it an irritated kick. He hadn't been sure he could sleep; it seemed like he didn't, but he must have, because a noise wakes him again.

His clock is dead; he has no idea what time it is. He knows no one can be in the room, but he thinks for sure he hears a voice, somehow not human, more rodent-like snuffling mixed with indistinct chatter, provoking his childhood phobia and simultaneous awe of wolverines which he carries in his stomach—mixed with his acrophobia and claustrophobia—ferocious terrifying wolverines, created by a description he had seen of a wolverine about it being the most deadly and aggressive killer on Earth, and reinforced by sci-fi movies, nature shows, and his own imagination.

"Hey!" he shouts into the dark testing his own subsistence, to erase the possibility he is dreaming.

A wave of uneasy alarm surges through his body like a sleeping forest denizen might instinctively sense from a twig's snap, as he thinks in response to his shout he hears a new and unrecognizable staticky noise beginning with a kazoo-like buzz, but ending with the sound of some large insectile exoskeleton fried in a flash of heat. Although unrecognizable, subconsciously Kevin senses it must be a sort of mocking laughter.

Still protected from his phobias and the cold by the bedcovers, Kevin speaks again loudly to further reconfirm he is awake and, like echolocation, to verify his physical position in the room, and, because subconsciously his solitude makes him feel equivocal about his existence, to reconfirm it.

He shouts, "Are you God or the devil?"

With a few seconds of rational thought, he knows his sensing of some presence in the house is nonsense, but he thinks it is, after all, the middle of the night, and now again a cool, stormy late-winter wind from Canada, just north, is creeping in the windows and making the house speak in perplexing tongues.

He hears what seems to be the thumping of footsteps, both small and large mixed with the breathing of a large animal, like an elephant. Just the sounds make him feel cold. He is cold and exhausted, not so much now from the manual labor as from the adrenalin drain of the excitement he feels for the approaching fulfillment of his long-awaited execution.

Now that he is about to nullify their victim, he is beginning to feel the idiocy of his phobias. Struggling out of bed, he forces a smile at all the eyes turning toward him from the wall; he is prepared. Fumbling with the bedside drawer and taking out Beth's passport, Kevin rips out the page with her picture, the only image he has of her. As with most passport pictures, it shows her most unattractive features...well, not unattractive maybe, more convict-like. In this solitary picture, she was so young, taken in a distant past, even before he knew her. It has been the only scrap of her he has, and, thus he has clung to it, using it again and again to evoke the never-aging warm memory of her, that memory becoming larger like a fairytale's rectitude.

"So many things, Beth," he says aloud, unaware of his sudden woebegone facial distortion including a passing sardonic smile. "Things!" he says aloud. Shouts it.

It hits him how, even at this level of speaking with the dead, or no one at all, he is still unable to explain, to talk of things that remain unspoken, denied even to himself. And yet, these things are right next to him, snapping at him like the jaws of a stray wolverine from the north.

He pulls the old stolen pistol—the one he had hidden and claimed to have lost—out of the same bedside drawer and shuffles his way over toward the wall. Kevin leans harder on the wall, afraid to lose his balance from the immediate weight of the seething torrent of ecstasy, sorrow, fear, despair, dread, and rancor that he feels flooding from the eyes. His eyes don't focus immediately on any particular face as he searches through the headshots, poses, and snaps of more and more distant times and the buried memories.

Is this the graveyard from where Biblical regret comes? The asking for forgiveness?

"It's too late now," not aware that he says it aloud.

Bitterness, disgust, and guilt shoot through his mind at a glimpse of his father who, before Kevin clipped the picture, had been posing stiltedly together with Kevin's mother on the photographer's chair, forcing Kevin's focus deeper into a claustrophobic and frightening tunnel like the one he and Jake had dug together as children in their backyard, and which Kevin refused to enter a second time.

"I'm stuck, Jake. I'm stuck. Pull me out." But Jake had only laughed. Kevin slowly had wormed his way out. After crying. After forever.

And now, as with so many unpleasant memories, Kevin's time-shovel, that buried his realities, digs deep in an instant, to inter that memory but propels him into another. The terrifying Grand Canyon.

The memory of his childhood visit with Jake and his parents when Kevin had seen a person, some distance away, sitting on the canyon's edge on an extended natural overhang with his legs and feet dangling above an indecently fathomless drop. Kevin could just feel the rock overhang breaking or, if it didn't, he knew that this person could slip in one careless move. It made Kevin sick. He had to vomit and run away from anywhere near the canyon's edge as it began tugging at him, trying to yank him down into it.

So immediately after, he began learning how to overwhelm and submerge troublesome unpleasantry—as best he could, as with so many things later—to shut away how he had been teased by his father for his fear of the canyon and to shut away how he was tormented by his brother for his fear of that backyard tunnel. He began learning to efficiently and immediately find another fantasy or story to drown the unpleasant one in an ever-churning subterranean eddy.

Now Kevin induces his sister Mag's presence together with pained disappointment.

"I'm back, Mag. Come live with me. I have a house. You won't be alone."

"Kevin, I'm fine. I'm not alone."

"But, I am."

"Yes, Kevin, but I have a life."

She didn't tell him she didn't need him. But then she did.

* * *

At this very moment, as these memories are passing through Kevin's brain in a kaleidoscope of time, he has begun to accept the noises of the winter storm. He wonders what time it is. A sudden gust of wind shakes the house, rattling its frame like it needs a strong reminder to speak now or forever hold its secrets.

Kevin drops his gaze to the floor, oblivious to the added debris and paint smears from his work, being suddenly sidetracked by a creak in the floor like Joe's familiar footstep. But he sees a black cat and, despite his first shock, is immediately relieved to have discovered what was making the noises in the house this morning, or whatever time it is. Then he recognizes it. The cat—Shadow, Beth's black cat—exactly the color and size and face—nose, ears, eyes.

No. Of course, it can't be. It can't be Shadow. He dumped Shadow's body at the airport long ago. And cats don't live this long. In the dim light, the cat assesses Kevin with green night eyes—green surrounding staring black openings.

"How'd you get in here? Is that you, Beth?"

The cat refuses to answer and sensing that Kevin is coming closer, crouches—ears back—and, growling deep like a panther, rejects him and disappears around the corner. Kevin feels a trenchant chill take its place, creating a spatial vacuum so strong that the winter wind roars louder against the house and makes Kevin try to yell above it.

"I know you didn't want me."

Using his elbow, he impulsively shoves his makeshift work table; hammers, wood slats, nails, toolbox, all crash to the floor. In response, the wind gusts rattle the windows, making Kevin yell even louder in a crescendo of each word.

"Is it my fault? I mean, I've tried, Jake. But why'd you do it? What'd I do to you? What did I do, Jake?

"Why'd you kill yourself in *MY* BED?"

And then he hears a human voice call his name.

3. DAVIS

THE FERRY FAIRY

HOOHAH! I COULD HARDLY WAIT TO BE STABBED BY A DRUNK JEALOUS HUSBAND.

The secrets of a small village are broadcast on the street signs and written on the doorsteps. Through the years that I've lived here in Yrdal, I've been used by a number of the local widows and other women, married and unmarried, for sex—a need these Norwegian village ladies happily express, including the woman in the house where I am renting a room. I say *USED* because none seem to be looking for more than some sexual release; they all come and go at irregular intervals so openly—without a second thought—that I have often wondered if they are meeting to schedule the hours spent with me, like at the PTA meeting, if there is such a thing in a hamlet with no school. Or maybe as I said, the schedule is just a flashing street sign on a street with no signs.

The way these women make me aware of their desire is in a few seconds at the Yrdal grocery store, asking if she can bring me some cabbage or potatoes from her garden. I have to admit that these rendezvous have impelled me to shop for better food, to make my bed, do my laundry, and to clean my room, or, at least, agree to these housekeeping necessities when one of these women makes an offer to do these chores for me—instead of bringing potatoes. I would have little incentive to put any order in my life otherwise.

So if the women have it all organized, what about the husbands and lovers of these women? The men in the valley are stoic and silent, except when they get drunk. This trait hasn't encouraged me to attend the events which bring out the booze—and too often belligerence—and that is all of them. And, the booze is always home-made super-proof gasoline that could kill a goat and has been the cause of many deaths in Norwegian lore and reality. I have heard of at least two such deaths in our little village. I don't know if the overpopulation of widows in this village is caused more by the men's dangerous work on the ocean or their rotten alcohol.

I believe that, because of the women and children in attendance and the formality of the celebration, Norway's national holiday cele-bration may be one of the least drunken, until the wee early morning when the decent folk and children are in bed.

My house owner and a couple other women have said every year that I must spend the evening in the village on Norway's national holiday, May 17th. From just looking out the window, I knew, with-out attending the festivities, that the men and the women would all be proudly dressed in their regional *bunads*. But the lady of the house explained that food, beer, and the accordion player's polkas and waltzes would step it all up into a fest on the harbor.

Oompah. Oompah.

Hey, even if they always meant well, I have never bothered or, better said, been attracted. But for once, this year, after fifteen years, instead of listening to the noise from the village center off in the distance, I thought I would go into the center since the weather was warm—so warm the locals might well melt in their heavy traditional clothing. The big celebration was traditionally on the street by the dock and in front of the grocery store where I went to do my food shopping and seemingly always meet the ladies.

But this evening because I hadn't socialized in ages, I sort of felt like a turtle exiting his shell and just as clumsy. It had been a long time since I'd been in a crowd, if you can call a hundred-some peo-ple a crowd. I'd learned enough of the dialect around here to speak to the locals, although I don't think Norwegians, in general, in other parts of Norway would understand this local dialect. This night, my big plan was just to speak to a few people and leave early.

There, in the village celebration, I met Isa. It wasn't like I saw her in the crowd and cupid shot his arrow. No, she walked up to me and asked me to dance, or more like told me in English to dance with her. I was dumbstruck. She was beautiful—nothing like the locals—I mean, she had some sophistication and perfect makeup—none of the overdone smeary stuff. She even smelled like a goddess instead of the damp musty odor of the locals to which I had become so accustomed and acclimatized. She floated above everyone else and I was left speechless like that naked turtle.

I had never learned to dance and especially not to waltz, but she taught me how. I'm old and ugly and she made me feel young. I was bitter with mankind and she made me forget.

She was not dressed in the drab colors of a traditional *bunad*. Her slender body was decorated in a red kerchief around her neck, a white cotton blouse with a deep V-neck purposely exposing her small breasts at the slightest turn, and a blue knee-length pleated skirt—all the colors of the Norwegian flag. Her sockless black slippers hurt my arches just looking at them. But she was young—at least half my age, I was sure, and a short-haired, smiling blonde whirlwind. She lifted me out of a darkness that had formed around me through the years.

I don't like accordion music—is there anyone who does? But she made me drink beer with her and the music tasted right. I almost didn't know how to speak to her since I was not sure she was from this earth.

After dancing a waltz—or was it a polka?—I said finally, "Jeg heter Davis."

"I'm Isa. Please speak English. I need to learn. I work on the Hurtigruten and we are, for the foreign passengers, all required to speak English."

"Sounds to me like you already do," I said.

"Well, sort of," and she smiled one of her huge smiles.

I figured she just found foreigners interesting and I was the lone foreigner.

I asked, "And where are you from?"

With a smile, she said, "Ferry land."

I said, "Yes, I believe you are from a real fairyland. But where do you live?"

"Here," she said, again smiling. "All my life. And we all know that you have hidden away in your house for years, and now you are here."

"Why haven't I met you in the food store?"

"I never did the shopping. My mother did. And then I began working on the boats and have been away. My parents moved to Bergen for work. This year I got off on May seventeenth and so I decided to come here to celebrate." She smiled. "And lucky for me, you decided the same thing."

I wanted to think that she was flirting with me, but I knew I must be as old as her father, and I wondered if her mother had been one of my visitors.

I said, "Why is that so lucky? You're missing your friends talking with me."

"Oh, all my old friends are gone. No one can stay here and make a living. So I'm lucky."

"Because you have the Hurtigruten ferry job?"

"No, because I met you."

What was I supposed to think? The best I could do was stay silent.

Big smile. She said, "Have I embarrassed you?"

"Well, yes. It's not every day a beautiful young woman surrounds me with her charm. So I don't have the words."

She looked at me from the corners of her brilliant sapphire eyes while putting on a crooked sly expression and said, "So? Where did all those beautiful words come from if you didn't have them? I think you said something; you are trying to fool me." She exploded into her smile. "And what about we go over to my place." She paused and pointed off to the left. "And have a beer?"

"Am I supposed to say no?"

She said in a Tinkerbell voice, "I don't think so."

A dog began howling at the accordion music as we left.

Her place turned out to be her parents' old house—a small, wooden one-bedroom building, barn red on the outside and barn rough on the inside—and which, like so many other houses in the area, no one had bought.

Before we went in, she said, "We have no inside toilet, so if you need to get rid of some beer, like I do, it's time to do it now." Pointing, she said, "My father used that tree." She went inside a small shed behind the house, while I used the tree.

Once inside the house, I had to ask. "You grew up here?"

"Yes."

"Where did you sleep?"

Another smile. "Out here in the main room on a folding bed. It was okay when I was really small, but when I got older, it was…well, you know. I couldn't even…what's it called? Master-bate? I mean, the sound travelled everywhere."

Now I *was* embarrassed. I figured she must be drunk.

"Have I embarrassed you, again? You don't need to worry. My parents are in Bergen."

Okay, I didn't need any further hints. Now I was sure she wanted to head for the bedroom.

But she didn't want any nuanced doubt. She said, "How about we try out the bed and then have that beer afterwards?"

I might have felt this was just one more of the locals looking for foreign aid, but this was different. I cared for this young thing and I was almost afraid to break her in two; she was so much smaller, more tender, less old and used. So I let her guide me.

I held out my hand and she took it and pulled me gently into the bedroom. Without a hug or a kiss, she began to unbutton my shirt, no doubt to show me how to undress since I seemed helpless and unable to accomplish it.

I lifted her scarf over her head and began to undo her buttons, saying, "Do your buttons work the same way as mine?"

"Almost," she said, but immediately, she yanked her blouse over her head and dropped it on the floor. The rest of her clothing was on the floor in seconds. As opposed to the women who have been visiting me, Isa seemed to have an imagination, or she thought that I did, so rather than pulling me into bed as I expected, she sat on the bed—her slender naked young body so improbable before me—and, helping me off with my pants, began blowing me.

I was not sure if this was some sort of young-girl thing or did she get her lessons from the internet? I had never really enjoyed the solitary one-sided unfairness of a blowjob. No matter what, I was afraid that either I would come right away or, by trying not to, would lose my erection. Either way we would not have intercourse, which I thought would disappoint us both. But soon my distraction disappeared, and I was lost in her grip. She seemed to know exactly how I felt—where my sensitivity had been hiding. And she knew when to stop and to pull me down on top of her.

At first, slipping inside her was like the perfection I felt with Stella. But then within minutes, Isa bent her body and let out a moan and I felt her liquid fire, again and again—so many times with such power that I knew somewhere in there I had come in the middle of it all, but was not sure just when. It was all one blinding eruption. This was not Stella.

After that, it was not time to speak, only to lie beside each other with our eyes closed and to marvel. I realized we had not kissed and I laughed.

She felt my body shake and said, "You are laughing."

"Yes," I said.

"And the funny part is?"

"It wasn't a funny laugh," I said. "It was a happy laugh. I haven't laughed a happy laugh—or any laugh at all—in years."

And we sat naked and had our beer in the main room and I asked about her work on the ferry line and her schedule and when we could meet again. It was all so backwards from how I thought it always had to be. Because we had fucked first and still not kissed, there was no barrier between us; the sex game had been played and it felt we could be who we were.

That evening she could tell me her dreams and I could tell her my fears. At first. But as the evening wore on, the grey gravestone of time and generations—and hidden crimes—grew in the room between us, but only at an angle that I could see. She wanted to see me again, next month when she was off from her work. And I was happy with that.

* * *

We kissed the next time and the time after that and, I suppose, the time after that and so on. Month after month she would disembark from her ferryboat workplace right on schedule and we could spend two nights in *her place*. The word had spread fast in the village about our relationship, so my intermittent lady visitors had stopped coming over. I had to clean up my own messes, and that was just fine with me.

But there is a problem with happiness; you want more. As long as I had felt nothing, I could be satisfied with my room and statistically one of the most dangerous jobs in the western world—commercial fishing. But during that year, Isa made me care if I died or injured myself or ate right or got sick or slept. And I wanted to see her more than once a month and I began to dream of how it would be to live with her, if only we could afford it—and said so.

She thought I could get a job on the ferry line and we could work together. There were several such arrangements; the Hurtigruten preferred married couples. They would help with my missing ID papers.

But I had many hours and days to think about that and what it would mean being twice her age, a whole generation older. She would want children—enduring and accepting crying babies and sleepless nights. I could see fighting with a teenage son—possibly inheriting my own horridness—when I should be a laidback grand-father. I was young back when I had the ambitions I had for our child with Stella; we had our whole life to live. Isa was Stella frozen in time; I was a tired fisherman in my forties and no longer a dreamer. My imagination had died along with my poetry.

"You are an idiot," she said, when I tried to explain the gap. "You are only as old as you make yourself."

I knew it was a lost cause, trying to explain time and age. It would be like her trying to explain to me how it felt to be pregnant, to have life growing inside me, I supposed. But I had to try to tell her that I wanted no children—I was too old—because I knew the day was coming when she would tell me she wanted children.

But instead, she said, "I'm pregnant."

Do things happen because you expect them? That weekend while we were sitting on the dock—more or less watching the gulls and the terns do their never-ending waltz over the water in the evening summer sunlight and waiting for her appointed ferry to arrive from the sea—she said those terrifying words, making a merciless mael-strom gape open in front of us.

But, of course, only I could see it. Age was not the reason. The churning maelstrom was twisting with my past crimes. Crimes I had not just hidden from her, but from myself. Crimes that, if I told her, would devastate her and ravage her innocence—and be engraved on every doorstep.

I became all too aware of the village families milling and jabbering behind us, as they always do when the ferry arrives. The boat's arrival is a big deal each week, being the window to the world and the only entertainment. So a local crowd of adults, children, and dogs always gathers, wrapped in an enigmatic shroud of anticipation.

It was only minutes before she was to embark when she told me. And it would be a month before I saw her again.

I said, "I thought you were using birth control. I don't want a child."

I don't know if I have ever hurt so much inside. In the center of my soul. I don't know how I got it out of my mouth. The sea birds drew blurry white lines in my tears. I no longer heard the assemblage of voices behind us. I heard—and hear now—the aging creak of the wooden fishing boats, the undulating harbor water weeping for us, and the threat of the foreboding low thump of the ferry engine.

She had worried about my response and had waited to tell me. And, then—after she disappeared into the looming ferryboat—she never came back.

* * *

To: GeenaN@gmail.com   September 23, 2043
From: DavisM@gmail.com
Subject: Your question

Hey, Geena,

Thanks for letting me know what's-his-name was let out of prison.

In answer to your question, I guess we humans should find it normal and natural to find a mate. No, I have no new love. Nor do I care to find one. In this sparsely populated area north of the Arctic

Circle, it's not like a person can, or would even care to, do the mating dance at the local disco or expect to meet someone at a socialite's party. I sit on the dock with taciturn hapless men—drinking the homemade hooch for hours during the local festivals and during the nightless days, and the dayless nights—and wait for the ferry.

Davis

4. KEVIN

THE UNREAD STORY

Kevin, being the storyteller that he has always been, created a story that had developed from information he read in the prison library both in books and on the internet, out of things he imagined and that he feared, and out of things that he thought he understood. He wrote it down and printed it out on a prison computer the last day of his internment, the only narrative he ever put in the written form. He felt as if he were remembering the future.

If Perfection is Death

The three-and-one-half million acres of forest land known as the North Maine Woods is bordered by Canada to the north and west and by two railway lines built in the early twentieth century to the south and east. The counties that include the forest are parts of Aroostook, Somerset, Penobscot, and Piscataquis, preserving some American native names if not, sorrowfully, the native Americans themselves or much of their history.

In what was once the Ahnaki tribe region of Penobscot county, Maine, a lone woodsman and hunter, of indeterminate age, lives in a cabin that his Norwegian father built when he and his wife crossed the Atlantic to help set up and run the first sawmill in the area before everything was bought up by the timber corporations. The buyout agreement left the father and his wife with hunting rights and enough to live out their lives in the cabin they built. From his parents the son learned to hunt, cook, and survive on his own in the woods, and in return the son helped his parents until their deaths, his father first and his mother a year later.

Both in Norway and Canada, a gluttonous predator—one female and one male—normally tenaciously scouring the northernmost remote forests in each of these countries for prey, living or dead, had become disoriented, maybe because of a change in the weather or maybe the sun.

Although *Gulo gulo,* or wolverines, seen by some as symbols of good luck, do not travel in a straight line, these two, wandering south this winter ranging at the same pace with the cold weather, were somehow connected and possibly bearing good fortune either for someone or for some location.

The Norwegian wolverine veered west toward mountainous Lofoton. The Canadian wolverine continued south, traveling the same distance, entering Maine, roaming as far south as Penobscot County, a location where the beast has not been seen in recent history.

The Norwegian son, living alone in the cabin, in and off the quiet woods, learned to be vigilant and is always sensitive to unfamiliar sounds. But, not ever feeling it necessary to follow such news, he is not so aware of solar activities that are invisible to the human eye.

A billion-ton cloud of plasma from the sun, like a monstrous tongue larger than a million earth-sized planets, is beginning to lick the earth and will increase its effect in the coming days. Although this cloud is invisible to the human eye, NASA heliosynchronous satellites STEREO-A and STEREO-B were able to see the ultraviolet ejection in time to let NASA scientists, with little impact, warn the earth's population that the direct strike of this coronal mass ejection would, in a few days, probably break through the ionosphere in places enough to cause problems with electronics, increase cancer rates, and affect an unquantifiable number of subatomic particles, although the effect on the subatomic particles is completely immeasurable.

While coronal mass ejections have previously disrupted the electricity grids in large geographic areas, most infamously, although not the largest ever, in Quebec on March 13, 1989, this newest giant solar ejection is powerful enough to shut down industries and the electronics of many cars on the roads in Scandinavia and North America, along with many other parts of the world, causing hours of collisions by the thousands as some cars shut down in front of following cars while others simply spin out of control as the drivers panic.

As the ejection haphazardly affects the Global Positioning System satellites, many pilots are in panic mode trying to remember how to fly without GPS until enough satellites come back to life to save the situation. And, although not the most serious result, millions of people, sure it is an apocalypse, panic in countries throughout the night world when their cities and houses go dark while the sky is filled with the green rivers of light they have never seen before. Partially the apocalyptic view is right as the increased cancer rates will show up later unevenly around the earth.

During the traffic chaos, the Norwegian animal, shaking her head, seems to wake from a dream and turns back north to find her way home, revoking any hope of good fortune. The Canadian wolverine has turned as if the Northern Lights caused by the solar ejection are an étude or, maybe because of the enormity, a whole symphony, calling him home to Canada after such a long journey.

Standing outside his cabin scanning the woods in the moonlight, the lone Maine hunter and woodsman of Norwegian descent is oblivious to the solar attack except for the rare sight this far south of such enormous and continuous purloining green rivers of the aurora borealis flowing through the sky, making the full moon ripple in a noxious vile green.

Having been awakened by a suspicious noise, he, who has never seen a wolverine and has no idea that seeing one is good luck according to Passamaquoddy Indian legend, thinks it is a badger raiding his trash, and, as *homo sapiens* have so often done, decides that killing it is a good idea.

His shot is perfect if perfection is death.

5. KEVIN

THE WALL

Kevin's house lights blink momentarily, making him wonder for a fraction of a thought whether it is the solar ejection, a warning about his unpaid bill, or the stormy winter weather. Having rid himself of his inane fears as he hid under the bedcovers, he has grunted his way out of bed, dug out her picture and his pistol, discovered a cat in the house, and now—leaning on the wall—is trying to make his brain work. He has an urgent need to go to the bathroom in every way possible. But he just cannot care. As far as he is concerned, he can go in the pants in which he has slept and hasn't changed for days.

A loud voice says, "Kevin?"

At first, Kevin is frightened by the sound of his name, but, hearing the wind through the open front door, quickly realizes that it's Joe having used his key to get in.

Joe shouts, "Kevin, are you here?"

"I'm in the bedroom. Come in. What time is it?" He hears the door shut.

Yelling over the storm noise and getting louder as he approaches the bedroom from the entrance, Joe says, "Sorry to drop in on you like this. You asked me to come over when I could. You said you were here. I let myself in. I couldn't get an answer at the door. I knocked and knocked. Are you okay?"

Kevin realizes this explains some of the noises he had been hearing that the stray cat could never have made and that he had completely forgotten he had asked some days ago—the day he left prison—for Joe to come over. Still wrapped in his hooded blue parka, Joe enters the bedroom, hugging a full paper grocery bag. He says, "What time is it? It's early evening. I finished work and did some shopping. You've been sleeping?"

Kevin says, "I guess I've lost track. Time doesn't make sense to me anymore. Thanks for coming. I'm glad you came. I've got things to tell you."

Kevin tries to stand as straight as his thin, worn body will allow him, subconsciously checking if he has any pride left in him. It lasts only a few seconds. Trembling from the pain in his back that shoots down his left leg, his shoulders move forward and his body twists. With a groan he fumbles for support against the wall, causing him to hit one of the frames and knock it to the floor, with a noise that disrupts the momentary silence as the winter wind outside seems to be holding its breath.

Joe says, "You look terrible. And you're hurting. I thought you might need…. I brought you some groceries. What's with all this picture stuff? And the mess. Your bedroom looks like a junkyard. You want me to help…"

Kevin interrupts. With a wry smile, he says, "You know, while once much too long ago, at least twelve years ago actually, before the prison time, when I'd try to comfort myself or, at least, try to cheer up the world around me by playing the piano, I could have snapped that picture frame out of the air with quick reflexes before it hit the floor, or, at least, just bent over to pick it up and hang it back on its nail. But, now I'm a cripple, you know. Injured my back lifting weights in prison, often purposely. My decrepit body doesn't want to cooperate, and was the reason I was released early.

"You know all that; I've told you. Besides, as you can see, both my hands are busy, one hand leaning on the wall and holding Beth's picture to help kill my everlasting internal pain, and my left holding my favorite stolen revolver against my leg, trying to get the cold steel to relieve some of the pain there."

Putting the grocery bag on the floor and reaching for the picture frame, Joe says, "Let me get it for you."

"No!" Kevin shouts, pointing the pistol at the fallen frame. "Leave it there. It's okay."

Joe frowns. "What's with the gun? You use it to relieve pain often? Or are you about to shoot somebody?"

Dragging out his life like an old threadbare tablecloth, getting more stained and useless—no one needing him anymore—was pure misery. After a long silence filled by the rattling of the leaky windows, Kevin says, "Yeah. Tonight it's time to relieve some pain. Dying? Yes, dying is the thing."

Joe grimaces. "Come on, Kevin. This isn't you. I care."

"Joe, you have your own life. You have been more than kind to spend time with me in prison and to check on the house all these years. But it's time to free you. And me of me."

"Kevin, if you..."

"I'm old, lame, and tired. And I think it's time to tell you that..." He pauses. "...I've killed a string of people through my life." Killing had been exciting, a thrill, but, like all thrills, stopgap and fleeting. "But being free to kill myself I think will be the most stimulating sensation, both temporary and permanent at the same time."

"What the hell are you talking about? You want to kill yourself? What about me? Do you care about what I think or are you going to shoot me, too?"

Kevin's weariness is inaugurating the impulse of consciousness, so that things he had locked away he now feels seeping through a crack, like Etna's magmatic movement from its underground chamber. There is something about Joe's being here that annoys him—just because he is here when he had other plans. "Shoot you? Hmm, I...I have to tell you something."

Joe frowns and starts to say something.

Kevin says, "Shut up. Just listen. It's comforting, even satisfying, to know why I felt such a need to kill. I mean, the *things* that made it feel so gratifying. I used to think that something in my head might be damaged or missing. But you helped me."

"Kevin, please. What're you saying? You've killed people. No surprise. Isn't that what police need to do sometimes?"

As if Joe had not spoken, Kevin says, "Early on, everything that you said during your prison visits had seemed like pure and unadulterated crap. Pure crapola. I could barely stand to listen. You even said yourself that you didn't understand anything that your professor-love had said, but as the months and years progressed, you told me that talking about it, talking to me, that you used me to clarify it all for yourself.

"In one way or another, you repeated that being born was a pain in the ass and with good reason. And as you repeated things over and over, I began to understand that I was not born defective, but maybe, instead, I had an additional, undefined human sense that few people have, except for maybe a few crazies, as you might call them."

"Kevin, stop."

"No, Joe, you shut up and listen. I have so much to tell you, and…not so much time. As hard as I tried, I couldn't understand whether my extra sense was *knowing* or *sensing* or *realizing*, or maybe, as you said once, whether this sense can't be defined and just doesn't have an existing word to describe it in the English language, like some ridiculous dimension other than the three that humans know, or like you said, missing words that other languages have for *snow*.

"And as unknown as that sense might be, you described how your dead love had been discovering new universes…parallel universes, places that *homo sapiens* could not find with their ears, eyes, touch, smell, or any combination of them."

After a hesitation, Kevin exhales, "Yesss" in a long, ophidian hiss, almost in concert with the winter wind stroking the house. "And I could never explain it all to anyone else and barely to myself, but I think my victims might understand and already know because, by being there, they're already…there."

Joe says, "Come on, Kevin. Now you're creating some sort of religion? Please, Kevin. Something's wrong. Can we go somewhere? Let's get out of here. It's only eight o'clock. Let me take you to dinner. You must be starving."

Kevin says, "I just want to go there or the other there or the indescribable multitude of *theres* that you talked about. I see them like a bunch of very round, black balloons of no special size since it won't matter once I am dead. Or maybe I'll go to that unknown place *huttiheita*. Either way, I like the idea that someone—as many as possible—should see me or experience me going there or maybe specifically to that unknown *huttiheita*."

"*Huttiheita*? What the hell is that? Kevin, you're going off the deep end. I'm serious. You're talking crap. Please stop. Please. Let's get out of the house. It's cold in here. Besides you have to see the green sky. The rivers in the sky."

Kevin, still in thought, begins to cry—in part out of happy relief that he feels that he now knows why he has killed—and says through his tears, "All that time in prison, you've been explaining everything to me without even knowing. Now I know why I've felt such affection for you, Joe, but, while I've felt this great closeness to you for years, even before prison, I'm sad that it's gone. Broken."

Holding out his hand, Joe says nervously, "I'm still your friend, Kevin. In fact, as a friend, would you mind just handing me your gun? Please. I'm worried."

Kevin's shifting mind exiles him back into the darkness behind his childhood bookcase, where he used to try, the only way he knew, to expunge his angry frustration, except that now, crowded in there with him, are all the eyes of his victims shining in expectation and anticipation.

Pointing the gun at Leon Duprey's faded press photo, Kevin says, "You know, Joe, I can't remember where I left the brick. It was my souvenir. A mini-tombstone."

As Kevin begins examining the row of pictures, Joe edges toward the door, tripping over the groceries, spilling cans and bottles.

Kevin continues staring at the gallery. "Joe, you're not paying attention. Look here. This is my father faking a relaxed position on the arm of the photographer's chair. I smell the alcohol on his breath right now. He always smelled like that, even at breakfast."

Instead of bothering to honor his mother's priest, Kevin felt the negligence somehow was appropriate, so he had just taped the newspaper's black-and-white photo from the Worcester *Telegram* story of the executed priest—no frame—to the wall. Pointing at the photo, he says to no one, "You could never appreciate anything I did for you, Mother."

Then taking notice, as if by surprise, of the snapshot he so nefariously took with his phone on the street in Bermuda of that thief with the sailboat, Kevin gives himself a brief inner smile of satisfaction at his masterful achievement.

"So, Joe, I want you to know this. Listen carefully. This is why I asked you to come over. I guess you sort of already knew this before, since I told you not to worry. I watched at a distance, what must have been short-Karl arguing with the son-of-a-bitch boat owner in Bermuda, both probably planning on how they could kill each other. Karl, no doubt, went home to Germany or Switzerland—or wherever he was from—all happy and confused. And to think I was able to retrieve that old wad of cash that Beth had hidden under the sink, that she had never known it was you who had sent it with her—the money that you stole from the guy who had hauled that same money to the United States on that very boat—and which ended up paying, with barely a trace, for my trip to Bermuda. See, you didn't have to worry. Now that's a story, as good as any. I would love to have told you earlier, but it was one I never could." He smiles. "Until now."

"You killed that guy? The boat captain? How? You went to Bermuda?"

Kevin seems to ignore Joe, and says, "And who else? Why can I remember Leon Duprey's name, and Karl what's-his-face, but not some others? I have pictures of each and every one, but names I can't remember. It's strange, like I can remember my elementary school teachers, year for year, first name and last, almost how they looked. My high school teachers? A few. Mr. Bryan. Miss Fetcher."

Joe, squatting down to pick up the spilled groceries, says, "Kevin, let me cook you something. How about some food? It looks like you haven't eaten for days."

Kevin continues staring at the wall. "But my old Boston police buddies? My prison mates? Not a chance. Why is that, Joe?" He begins crying again, harder than before but his sobs are drowned out by the house complaining even louder about the winter wind.

Joe seems afraid to speak, standing again, silently, until finally he says, "Kevin, I'm going for help. I'll be right back. Please, wait for me. Don't do anything stupid."

After Joe leaves the bedroom, Kevin hears the wind through the open front door. Joe yells once more, "Wait for me! I'll be right back!"

Shut out once more, the wind resentfully returns to rattling the windows. Now alone, Kevin scrutinizes the wall of pictures. Name or no name, this jury on the wall, his prey, are now his witnesses, the vouchees, the testifiers he needs to exploit and experience his thrill of revenge for being born, and who will surely appreciate it.

In a low voice, Kevin says, "I am the wolverine."

As the eyes of his audience—his complete range of victims, except for the one he knocked on the floor, one he can't, for the life of him, recall and who will miss being a witness—glare from the wall into his wet, red eyes, he raises his pistol and puts it in his mouth, aiming up at the palate. He holds Beth's picture in front of his face and tries to say her name.

"Beh..."

The pistol feels so incredibly heavy in his shaky and cold hand. He can't help but find dark humor in the momentary absurdity that he should be wearing earplugs. In a final act of indifference, he lets his bowels go.

His house suddenly goes dark, like some sort of response or precursor, as the sun's plasma tongue causes some of Central Maine's electric transformers to explode. It is dark both outside and inside the house except for the flickering green rivers of light in the night sky, which Kevin can barely sense. With his head tilted back, for a startled inkling he thinks he sees, through blurry darkness, the red pickup truck, grill first, descending slowly on top of him. Hindered by the gun barrel, Kevin can only snort and cough a partial snigger when, all at once, the red thing transforms into the animal that woke him—the Bony-Eared Assfish swimming in his tears. And the smell of its excrement is loathsome.

With the roaring explosion, all the eyes shut. Except for the ones on the floor.

6. DAVIS

SCREWING UP

When police detective Kevin scared the shit out of me, my search for love continued. I didn't know it was a search, but it was. The previous girls and women at the marina were my training grounds. I learned ideas of what to do or say once we were alone and, I suppose, they did, too. Tell me how else we learn. But if the society is sick, the ethics are wrong, the morals are screwed up, what we learn is wrong and sick and screwed up. And worst of all, we have no way of knowing how bad it is.

Each one of my younger encounters was strange in some way, teaching me something. Some I don't think about anymore, but the strangest ones I do at times. Like the one, as we stood alone wrapped around each other near the ocean harbor, she said, in response to my unbuttoning her blouse with the obvious plan to put my hands on her breasts, "I can't stop you." Her voice was flat, like she had gone into a trance. The confusion of that statement and the way she said it stopped me cold.

Another young woman, while we two were alone below deck on her family yacht, let me take off all her clothes above the waist, but that was it. She had nothing against my putting my hands anywhere on her upper body, but as that got quickly boring, the rest of the evening we played topless checkers.

Another stood fully dressed and bared her perfect teeth with a sly smile in the summer moonlight as I stood facing her. I touched only the tips of her braless breasts, brushing her nipples through her clothes with my fingertips until her nipples hardened. Then, in the sweetest and happiest tone, she said that it was time for her to go back to her boat, alone.

Even eight years later, while I worked at the museum, on my first date with a young waitress, I escorted her back to her apartment building in town. We kissed and hugged softly and quietly in her apartment doorway. Seemingly unconcerned by the chance that anyone could have come along the hallway, she let me feel her dampness through her panties and, thus I fingered her as we continued to stand in that doorway until she came, literally flooding my hand and her leg. Then she called me a jerk and shut the door and I never saw her again.

In comparison, the first European woman I met at a small hotel on my way through Sweden—the hotel's floor maid—taught me a lesson about women's equality. I stopped to ask her where the bathroom was since my room had none. She took me by the hand without a word and led me into my room, pushed me onto my back in my bed, and, after working to make me erect, straddled me until I had come. When I then begged her to stay longer, hopefully to return the favor, she said her first words. "No, my husband is waiting for me downstairs."

I knew then that I was in a different world, and that I had to find the bathroom on my own.

* * *

To: GeenaN@gmail.com   December 8, 2043
From: DavisM@gmail.com
Subject: Your breakup
December 8, 2043

Hey, Geena,

I'm fine. Hoped you were, too. Sorry to hear about your breakup. It isn't your fault.

When I was sixteen, working at the marina in New Hampshire, I would clean myself up and flirt with the young girls on the boats, using my poetry. Playing a guitar would have been better, but my musical abilities have always been zero, very unlike our policeman detective, who could liven a room in a second.

I learned something from each one of my flings back then. Something negative. I always thought it had to be me, Geena. It wasn't.

Davis

7. GEENA

THE LETTER

"Geena Nuss? I got a delivery for you," the big oaf of a FedEx man had said. Pointed to her office by the receptionist that afternoon, for Geena he seemingly came out of nowhere. She almost falls out of her chair in fright. He doesn't seem to care to apologize or is such a goon and so used to scaring people that he enjoys it.

Referring to a letter he holds in his hand, he says flatly, "Ya need tuh sign fer this here."

Not only is this delivery odd because she is not expecting any, but in addition, this parcel was sent to her at the office slated by Joe without any warning from him, and, on the white envelope which she has removed from the FedEx pack, is written in Joe's handwriting, "IMPORTANT: Do not open until you are home."

Geena has good reason not to like the feeling this delivery is giving her. It is not her birthday or any special holiday, so this surprise is startling. In fact, it sends chills down her spine as she stares at the envelope on her desk. And she has read the first line: *Your father is dead.*

Because she knows her curiosity won't let her concentrate on work the rest of the day, she feels no qualms about simply reporting that she needs to leave the office, but not until she has urgently tried to call Joe to see why he has sent this mystery letter.

She calls him four times from the office, but gets no answer, which puts her into an apprehensive funk, because he always answers her calls. So she left so fast, cupping her hand over her mouth, that the receptionist, one of the two women from this morning's discussion about New England's falling leaves, was sure Geena was sick and spread the word that Geena might be out for a few days.

Nervous about reading the letter when she arrives home, Geena keeps putting it off. She thinks about making a pot of tea, but doesn't. She fluffs and re-fluffs the pillow in her reading chair in the corner of her bedroom, fiddling with the envelope between calls she continues trying to make to Joe. Twice, three times.

The uneasiness she feels turns to dread like she felt waiting for the jury verdict in her father's trial.

With one last futile try at getting Joe to answer, she is forced to read the rest of what he has written, beginning with the announcement she had read in the office of her father's death.

He died suddenly from a self-inflicted gunshot.

I feel this will not be received with any great trauma on your part as I think you and, I assume, Davis knew something about what I am about to tell you, since neither of you have kept any sort of contact—what I would call family relationship—with him since you moved out, and especially after he went to prison.

Geena stops reading and stares at the ceiling. Joe was right, but she is not at all sure what it is that she is supposed to know. And how will Davis feel? Maybe Davis knows something she doesn't. It saddens her most that she doesn't know her own brother well enough to sense how he might feel about their father's death.

Something grey-green, but strangely also dullish red, incomprehensible and frightening is hanging upside down from the bedroom ceiling above her head. She fears it is the unknown between them, between her and Joe, which she had loved, the uncertainty that had once bound them together, which she had always envisioned as a small dot of light traveling at light speed, bouncing between them.

Squinting to focus better, she can see it is a large green bottle fly, but, increasingly reddish, like an undefined entity hanging there ominously doing nothing, some primordial and obsolete dark misshape, just hanging like a drop at the very tip of a timeless stalactite, waiting to fall. Waiting for enough reason or maybe *the* reason to let go.

And she has only read the first few lines of what looked like, typically Joe, a typewritten dissertation. *Typical Joe* usually made her smile, but today the feeling is dread.

I found his body when I returned with help. I took care of all of Kevin's funeral arrangements since he had surreptitiously deposited money in my account and mailed a note to the police to let somebody know to find his body—not knowing that I would even be there, describing what I should do once they contacted me as he instructed, and to tell you and Davis about it after he was in the ground. It was his request. Please don't berate yourself for any reason. It's okay. It's done. You know I was the one closest to him and had been checking on his house while he was in prison.

It was different with your mother; we all cried. I watched the sun set on the evening of Beth's death. It was like a bloody eye over the White Mountains, red from crying—the earth crying for Beth and for you—and, of course, for me who loved her, too. Even Kevin died with a picture of her in his hand.

You, Geena, for years have been the bright light of happiness in the dark passage I have inhabited and, if I had a choice, I would do nothing to dim it. I believe, Geena, even though you have been far away, your existence has inexplicably kept me going, many times. And I love and thank you for that.

To give you a bit of good news, you know I still heard Martin speaking to me for the longest time, a bit fainter as I got used to it, but always reminding me of Martin, which would never let me have a normal relationship with anyone else. I tried to tell myself it was some subconscious conflict, but I thought it was connected to that sense of an undetectable reality that would never end until I was dead. I had come to recognize some conceptual limitation of our human reality, so I held a faint hope that maybe death is when that reality could be discovered, realized, and appreciated.

Then suddenly, the Night of the Green Rivers, as the press called it, the voice went away. I knew it immediately. I had a new life.

With the enclosures, you can see that your father left whatever he had to you (will enclosed). I won't try to judge why he snubbed Davis, but you can do what you want with that. He also left a small story (enclosed) about wolverines he had written down, he said, on the last day in prison. To me it seems he must have been thinking of Davis in some way. Kevin may have just been entertaining himself, but this odd story was remarkably prescient.

Anyway, I'm writing you, Geena, also for another reason, because I can only imagine you will want to know one day. And you can decide if you want to tell Davis about it. I could never make myself tell him, since I hardly knew him.

Your father got out early for health reasons and good behavior. He was obviously no saint, even though for the longest time I thought he was. At one time, I might even have been his Plato as Plato was for Socrates, a spinner of legend, adding to your father's image in the same way that all saints, heroes, and gods-on-earth begin, and as the tale becomes a saga and passes on through generations, translated and embellished, that person becomes more than his or her reality.

In fact, I'll even admit that, some years back, just for fun, I wrote a future obituary for Kevin, which if someone should find it along with the accompanying photograph of some ceremony from his police days, would imagine Kevin as some important historical figure.

Kevin turned on his flock. I am not sure what Kevin saw or felt. I thought I did. I thought we had some subtle connection, but Kevin had something deeper in him. Something sinister. I suppose you could call it a secret hell.

You may think that you have had enough bad news, but brace yourself, Geena.

After the fact, the police were curious why Kevin, for some reason, had hung a string of framed pictures of people on his bedroom wall in some sort of ritual before he shot himself. Other than a picture of the poor fat policeman, they wanted to know if I could identify any of them. I told them that I only knew one, a picture of his father I had seen cut out of a professional portrait of his mother and father that Kevin kept in a drawer. When they asked about why Kevin would hang up these pictures, I said that I had no idea, which was true at that moment.

Geena, when I remember the future, it still gives me pain. That weight Kevin lifted from me years ago could only grow into guilt for what he did. Because of a second picture that I recognized, I can guess that Kevin had killed all of the people he had put on the wall.

That second picture—the one I said nothing about, because I thought the police should figure it out on their own or, more probably, because I feared for myself—was a snapshot of a guy from Bermuda who had threatened me for

stealing dirty money from him. Kevin had somehow miraculously traveled to Bermuda, found the guy, and murdered
him. For me. ME! I, Geena, albeit however unwittingly, was
the cause of this person's death.

Putting the pieces together in my head, I have come to
realize that Kevin—forgive me, Geena—was a murderer.
Maybe of the worst kind. Devious, plotting, cold blooded.
I can come to no other conclusion. He even killed his own
father. And a priest. When I look back on the local cops' lack
of support during the trial, I imagine even they knew or suspected something. He seemed to become careless on purpose
like he wanted to be discovered. I don't know. I was blind.

You and your father were the only true friends I had. Your
father's killing himself would have been enough to cut a
cord—shut down something—shut off a light, and which I
thought you might also feel. His death alone made me question any purpose I might have for living.

But discovering then suddenly that my best friend had
been a serial murderer, has ended any desire in me for the
future that I thought I might have. I cannot comfort you
because I am in such a horrible state of confusion, shock, and
guilt about this situation that I cannot comfort myself.

Every human is like a starling in a flock which seemingly
has no purpose. However, a bird doesn't worry, has no sense
of the future, thinks only of the space around it. The single starling communicates with the others about something
immediate, but when it drops out of existence, the rest of
the flock show no concern and the dead bird is relegated to
oblivion, like we all are after a bit of time. But our stories far
outlast the storyteller.

When you read this, I'll be that starling, but without any
answers and without a story. I thought at one time that I

would want to be remembered for something after I died, until finally I thought, for what possible reason?

Yes, I love you, Geena, but it is no longer enough. It is not your fault. I realize now that I have simply been chirping. The way my life was, I could suddenly see that I might just as well be a cat's lunch.

Now I've been called by a priest. Who knows what that will come to?

To sign off, I wrote you something stupid, hoping to make you smile someday:

Springing from a pickle jar,
So gay, I'm pickled Tink.
Spending all my repertoire,
My pen's run out of ink.

She screams.

Because of the tone of the letter and all her previous distress, Geena's immediate thought is that he has committed suicide, and, thus, in sadness and anger, she screams his name in the bedroom so loudly that neighbors in the apartments above and below her—in fact, in all directions—hear something. Some of whom will soon knock on her door, feeling an immediate need to offer help.

She sits benumbed in the liquified ocean of her frozen past for a period in which time does not pass—when time is not measured, but loneliness is unrestrained. And as that loneliness turns to solitude, she is forced to act.

Her eyes are blurred from tears, but she can see that the reddish green bottle fly above her is gone, revealing something she has never seen there, a remnant, at first glance like a crack in the ceiling, but then upon closer inspection more like an indelible burn mark. Barren and crooked, twig-shaped.

She has drifted to the kitchen to find tissue to dry her eyes, unveiling her worry and fear. What the fuck has really happened? He is surely alive, having written *I've been called by a priest.* Is he trying to be funny? But then what does *who knows* mean? Her decision is made.

That's when she flinches at the startling knock at the door, a neighbor who heard the scream.

8. JOE

JAMES FREDRICK'S LETTER

Dear Joe,

Despair. It hangs here like a dirty rag needing to be washed or thrown away, but I cannot.

Despair. I feel it. It messes with me. Contaminates me.

As I approach later life, at age 78, it is not my pending retirement and eventual death that is bothering me; it is my awareness growing from the infancy of safe-and-anxious self-importance to the realization that we, humans, are the tiniest scintilla in an endless cosmos. Although we pride ourselves on being aware of that vastness, we are so purposeless, having sprung from a chance spark on the ocean's bottom on an ordinary planet of the wink of a star in a galaxy being sucked into a black hole.

So I envy the womb of religion creating a story of purpose. Why would we conscious humans not create such stories? We would be completely insane not to create something that gave our existence significance. But not being capable of shrinking my thoughts into any such dogma, I have hidden my dysthymia behind the need to speak to my students, to shower, and to eat my food. But the rag of futility flutters nearby in a quiet breeze, sometimes. And other times in a tempest.

So I struggle with my purpose, that of not transferring any

of my disquieting perception to their minds—to those around me—and to hope that frying eggs, washing clothes, passing a test or passing by the destitute, studying and absorbing culture, shopping and starvation, sex and loving, war and culture, sickness and cats, economic worry and wealth will not let them feel their despair.

As I have aged, that squalid rag of knowledge has wiped away the loam of distraction and, although I cannot care about the triviality that it holds, it dangles off in the corners to torment and ridicule me. I endeavor not to see it, but I confess to you, my love, that you are my true savior. Your love eradicates my dernful insignificance, letting me care. Only you have that power…the sway over my affliction since the day we met in Provincetown.

I have found through the years that each of our meetings has lifted my soul and each of our conversations has been much too brief. Come to me. We can drift in my small boat and fish. And while I listen like a wide-eyed child, you can tell me in depth your many stories. How you managed to be friends with a serial murderer and about your "quantum physical" love. And maybe we can solve the mystery of the hidden MIT data file. Who knows?

Or if you would rather, we can just fish.

Come to me. I need you. Our life together can be and *will be* a long and beautiful sunset. I promise.

James

9. DAVIS

GEENA'S VISIT

To: GeenaN@gmail.com
From: DavisM@gmail.com
Subject: You are coming?

August 1, 2044

Hey, Geena,

And now, twenty-two years later, my sister decides to visit. She has something to tell me that's too important to write.

You want to follow my track? Good luck. You'll have to hunt down a fisherman. I knew I would have to sneak into Norway somehow. You can get here easier than I did.

No country just lets a person ride in on his white horse. I took a plane to Stockholm, a train north to Östersund in Sweden, and then over to Trondheim in Norway. By pure chance I met a fisherman in Trondheim who offered me a job and who took me north to where I am now.

How do you find me?

The closest airport is near Harstad. Send me your arrival time and I'll see you there.

Davis

10. GEENA

UNSPOKEN CONVERSATION

GEENA KNOWS HE HAS MET DEATH IN THE MOST HORRIBLE WAY. IT HAS BEEN TWENTY years, or maybe longer—she can't remember exactly, but he said twenty-two—since they have seen each other. He said that he was hesitant about meeting her, hesitant after all this time, he said, but, typically, he gave no clear reason. She worried about how he felt about her visit.

Rushing out from the airport arrival area after the long strenuous flights from Kansas City to Boston (stopping two nights), to London, then to Oslo and north to Evenes, a small airport north of the Arctic Circle, Geena energetically carries her tall, gangly body like she is twenty instead of fifty-something, striding with her long steps through the sliding airport arrival door pushing her red suitcase ahead of her, eager to see her brother. Eager to show how concerned she is about him.

She doesn't immediately recognize him, off in a corner on the other side of the entrance hall like a bewildered animal, and is quietly shocked by his hoary appearance, creating in her constructor mind millisecond-long specters of barnacles and rust. Disturbed as she is, before greeting or hugging him, as she steers her bag toward him, she shouts across the hall as if her voice were aimed only at him. "Davis, why are you living here?"

He has not asked her to come, but he has not said much of anything important to her about himself for the years since Stella's death.

All communication with him by phone or internet has consisted of platitudes with little specific information despite her efforts to pin him down. His response concerning this current visit was flavored with sarcasm, that he guessed Geena must have something really important to tell him, accusing her of always making living seem urgent.

As she approaches, he says, "I could ask you the same thing, Geena. What the hell? But I guess, since you honked across the hall like a taxi, all of northern Norway knows you've arrived."

It is a demeanor with which she should be familiar, that old brotherly teasing, right? She feels happy as they exchange warm embraces, even if she is nauseated by his odor, but is immediately perplexed when, instead of grabbing her bag and bundling her off in a car to wherever he lives, he simply escorts her toward the crowded airport coffee shop.

The airport is small with an even smaller section for the café, a section looking more like a locker room smelling of moldy socks than a café, cluttered with barren sturdy tables and robust steel chairs for the matching hardy northern breed of humanity, stoically crowding it.

"Why? To see you. What else?" she says.

"So how long are you staying? You never said," he grouses.

"Well, that depends on how long you will have me. I mean, really, Davis, I've traveled a long way. Couldn't we just go over to your place to have some peace and quiet and discuss what to do?"

Already through his body language she senses his resistance to her checking on him, obligating him, but, dammit, it is time she did. She is, after all, the only family he has left.

He says, "First of all, you should know that we are almost a two-hour stomach-churning bus ride away from where I am living and the actual house I live in is so tiny you would hardly fit through the door, so it isn't like we can just drop in. Dropping in or out doesn't work. To plan anything, sister Geena, I need to know how long you have thought of staying."

"You sound like you don't really want me to stay. Am I right? You don't even want me to go home to your place. Why?"

He hesitates, waiting for the rumbling takeoff vibration of a Norwegian Air passenger jet to fade.

"Geena, it's not like I live in the Kansas City suburbs. I live in a place even the Norwegians would call *huttiheita*, an unknown place way out there, in a small room in a wooden house, surrounded by a grey stone landscape rising out of the sea like monstrous threatening teeth, which I am sure, coming from Kansas, you would hate. And, other than today, I work when the weather allows."

She frowns. "I won't ask if it is the house or the grey teeth I wouldn't like. In fact, I could skip the teeth, but would love to see the mountains. But what are *you* doing there?"

He looks at her silently for a moment making her wonder what game he might be playing. It is like he is continuing to hide some obscure thing for some vague reason even though she has taken the effort to come all the way here. She keeps wanting to say, "What the fuck?" but feels he must come around.

He says, "Since you keep asking, I guess you really want to know, maybe. It's almost tempting to tell you." He smiles. Humming, he scratches his bearded cheek making a sandpapery sound while he thinks. "Okay. Long ago, back in the nineteen-seventies some guy wrote a book called *The Dice Man*. I don't remember who wrote it and I don't remember how old I was when I read it, in my teens somewhere, but I do remember two things. One is that I had a hard time finishing it because the author and protagonist. He wrote it in the first person..."

"Yes, I get it, Davis. Fucking tired I am, but give up!"

"Okay, anyway, he kept sledgehammering my brain. And the second thing I remember was that, out of necessity, he used dice to determine his life."

She rubs her face with the palms of her hands, trying to stay patient, but continuing to stand in the hall outside the café makes her legs ache from her extreme tiredness.

He says, "I don't remember much else, but later I began to understand the book better and the purpose of the dice. So, I replaced dice with darts. Since Stella died, I've been using darts to determine my future."

She says, "Davis, what the hell are you talking about? It sounds like bullshit. What does this have to do with anything? I'm tired. Do you know what time it is for me?"

Despite her fatigue, she begins to digest more of her younger brother's aging, an aura of grey. Rough greyness with deep, weathered lines. She senses he is sinewy strong in his middle age from hard labor, but, in fact, he seems only an emaciated ort of what he used to be in his youth.

He still has his friendly face, but his head has become a lopsided brick with a protruding nose. He already had a strong jaw, so his thick but close-shaven beard makes his jaw even bigger, and the useless black stocking cap perched on his head makes his head smaller at the top like a mountain, misshaping his head even more.

His worn and scarred face matches too well his tattered and frayed sweater, showing the dirty-grey collar of a t-shirt under it, which only confirms that his jeans are not purposely ragged out of a need for stylishness. All of which, because of his middling height, could just as easily be borrowed clothing with no secondhand value.

How could he have chosen boots that made him look more like a serf? The scuffed, unpolished boots Kansas farmers wore during the Thirties Dust Bowl. And the odor. He smells…other than stinking of fish, what is that awful smell? Earwax? Earwax, like the smell of her ex's pillowcase.

She hurts for him. She is already exhausted, but his impoverished appearance makes it worse. Obviously, it is not a choice for him. She closes her eyes, hoping he will get her out of here, away from the airplane din and the markedly hushed, whispering airport crowd.

He says, "I said I would meet you here because you are my sister and I owe you that, I guess. You came here to check on me, I have to believe. I mean, otherwise, as you said, why else?"

It feels good to keep her eyes closed, just to give them the tiniest contingency rest, and to try to think, to make sense of him, to get through to him. She begins noticing how it is only the foreigners who are loud. Germans and Americans bellowing rather than just speaking or whispering.

And Geena feels she must be bellowing without speaking a word, not because she is taller than these people for once, but in contrast to these grey and brown Norwegian giants, her red blazer, white pants, and ballerina shoes scream American. But here she is, dressed all foreign, because she has dressed up for her brother, even wearing their mother's gold medallion with the German inscription, thinking he would notice, thinking he might even appreciate it. A fucking waste.

Turning as if to enter the café, he says, "So, Geena, I think it is best we get something to eat; it's on me. They make pretty good stuff here, being a small airport, it's made by local people at home, not the normal airport fare. While I was waiting for you, I saw they had some knekkebrød, I think you know, a kind of Wasa hard bread that they serve with smoked salmon or goat cheese. The coffee's good." At a small table, he motions for her to sit and says, "Sit here. What can I get you?"

She says, "No, Davis, let me get it." She begins feeling for money first in her jacket and then her pants pockets.

"Geena, please. Just sit down. Relax. You don't even have any Norwegian money, I'm sure. Just tell me what you want. No, better yet, I'll just bring over a choice. Close your eyes and rest."

Grudgingly, she lowers herself into a chair, feeling guilty, but he is right about the kroner. She hadn't had time, or even the thought, to exchange money with the time zones and days running into each other. He, on the other hand, doesn't look like he can afford a single cup of coffee. To relieve her guilt, she decides she will give him some money before she leaves, and closes her eyes again to wait, thinking about how she would like to shower and change these clothes.

Instantly, it seems, he is there tapping on her leg, waking her from her sudden sleep, having placed a tray with large ceramic cups of coffee and the assortments of hard breads with salmon and goat cheese as he has promised.

"Coffee will do you good," he says. "And then we can go for a walk and get some air."

He is smiling, but still not offering to take her back to his habitation, whatever it is. She decides that, to encourage him, her only choice at the moment is to stay calm.

She says, "So, Davis, tell me about your place and what you are doing?"

"As I've told you some time ago, I'm presently working on a fishing boat. You know, the ones that go tuff, tuff, tuff. And renting a room in someone's house," he says.

"Why?"

"Why what?" he says.

"Look, Davis, I've written you and you always say everything's fine and that you're doing fine and a bunch of malarkey that means nothing. And look at you. You look like you've been dragged in by a fucking cat. I'm worried for you."

"Don't be. I told you I have a job, helping a guy run his fishing boat. I've got a nice place to live with nice people. I read lots and lots of books. So, what's the problem?"

She stares at him, agitated. "Davis, the problem I find is that you seem to have disappeared off the map to a corner of the earth. You are my only brother and I worry about you."

"Well, don't," he says.

Just when she was planning on staying calm, how could she? His answers are like a dog's snarl, making her cringe.

Not offering her the plate, he picks up a hard bread making a loud crunch as he bites into it. She regrettably remembers that he as a boy, pathetically, never learned civility and manners. His table manners were always such that thinking of passing service dishes to others at the dinner table would never enter his mind. And speaking of dogs, his gaping-mouth chewing had always sent her nerves in a spin. Watching people eat was never any pleasure, but now seeing his rust-colored teeth is especially disgusting.

She is distracted by how he looks at her. To her, his odd eye movement makes her think his eyes must have difficulty focusing or even functioning, and she wonders if the light and the salt of the ocean is destroying them. She hopes it isn't his brain being barbecued.

She says, "I hope you wear sunglasses when you're out on the ocean."

He smiles and shakes his head as if she has asked him to lead them in prayer. "You don't get it. There is no way to wear anything that could get caught by the cables and lines. After I lost two pair of them, I gave up. We have to work fast."

"Well, excuse me for asking," she says softly as she fiddles with the corner of a hard bread on the plate.

Sensing he is not about to continue telling her anything, she speaks. "Davis, I am your sister. Please tell me why you are here, in nowhere land. I would much rather have you closer to me and the kids, essentially, anywhere around Kansas City. You could choose. I can help you find work and the kids can see their uncle."

As he scratches the stubble on his neck, seemingly contemplating something to say, she envisions how the springy little hairs must be flinging gross particles of dead fish everywhere.

"Well, I'm sorry too, Geena, but to me, you are the one who is far off in a corner of the earth, in a country, and even more a state, that cares less about humanity and its own people than most anywhere on earth and especially compared to here in Norway, but I'm glad you are there if you are happy there, happiness being relative. Oh, and despite living there in the Bible Belt, I see you've kept your foul mouth."

He grins very Cheshire-like. She is too tired to think what to answer.

He says, "I can tell you basically why I'm here, but I warn you that you won't understand, no matter what I say."

"Give me a try," she says. Not a bit hungry, she picks up a Wasa bread with salmon and takes a bite to help make him feel he has done the right thing buying the snack, to seem relaxed, to help him to open up.

"Have you ever been in love, Geena? I mean, you have, or rather had, a husband, I think. Were you in love with him?"

"I've been in love," she says flatly.

"Well, I won't ask you more about that, but my point is that, unless you have been deeply in love, like I was with Stella, you can't know how her love gave me life and how her death changed my life."

"I might," Geena says, chewing.

"Before I met her I was destroyed. After she died it was even worse. Our child was going to be our one great bond and achievement, especially because the doctors had said she shouldn't even try because of her physical problems."

"I remember your hinting she had health problems."

"Well, it's nothing to go into now, but we were so happy that she was pregnant. I was happy for the first time in my life. I worked a crummy little job posing as a farmer in the Old Sturbridge Village Museum, but my preoccupation…my whole devotion was going to be to her and our child."

"Yes, Davis, I understand."

"Then if you understand, you might have a clue to my devastation at her death, and my inability to care about anything anymore.

"Throwing a dart was a way to make me move forward and it brought me here. The work on the boat is often exciting and dangerous, right in line with my need to avoid hopelessness. And I don't have to worry about or even feel like jumping overboard."

He pauses again, seemingly not planning to explain more.

She finishes the *canker-bruh*, or whatever he called it. She is hungrier than she had thought, and besides, he was right. It tastes good. She says, "But somehow you never explained what happened between living in Sturbridge, Massachusetts, and living here, a million miles away. In fact, you never explained how you landed in Sturbridge after leaving the..."

He glares at her like she is an alien, like human language will not work. But this time she is determined he is not going to escape; she waits, elbows on the table, holding her cup and staring at him through the steam of her coffee, hearing snatches of incomprehensible conversations around her.

Finally, he says, "I needed money. We had lost everything. The insurance wouldn't pay for anything. Not a dime. The death, the fire, water damage was all a so-called act of god. The fucking insurance company left me without a house after I had lost my family. I was destroyed and destitute."

Geena says, "You could have come to me."

"Theoretically, yeah. But my mind was leaning more in the direction of leaping off a tall building. Somewhere along the way, having read that book, I decided to write a numbered list of alternatives for the future, which included jumping off that building, murdering someone to get their money, and begging on the street."

Putting down her cup, she closes her eyes, feeling queasy for fear of what he might say. And which he does.

"I murdered someone," he says.

Barely opening her eyes, she sees him looking at her, anticipating her response. She says, "Okay, Davis. Very funny."

Staring at her, he says, "It wasn't funny for her."

Leaning forward, she scrutinizes his face for a sign of the fraternal jokester, but finds no indication. "Davis, I am too tired for your humor. I don't think that was funny. So what have you done for money?"

"Well, you are right. She didn't have *that* much. So, I don't know if it was worth the murder, but my dart had decided that murder was the option and she had enough cash stashed around her house to get me here."

Is he repeating *murder* on purpose, so everyone can hear? She glances around the café at the strangers staged at odd angles around them, drinking coffee, silently eating, exhibiting impassiveness except for the two children begging their mother for something they think they need. But everyone, some so close she can hear them stir their coffee, appears preoccupied, hopefully not listening, apparently not hearing what her fucking brother is saying, or they are all good at faking not-listening.

She talks through gritted teeth in a low scold. "Davis, will you stop it! We are in an airport and somebody might not understand that you are goddamn joking."

He says in a loud whisper, "It wasn't the first time. You think I'm joking?"

"Yes, I do," she lies. "You better be. You're making me sick, and, for that matter, fucking sick. Now get off this subject and tell me about your getting here."

"Well, it wasn't so revolutionary. I threw a dart at a map. It landed here."

"Why?"

"Why did it land here? Physics, I guess."

"Davis, why didn't you throw darts somewhere near me, or someplace reasonable?"

He grins. "To escape murder charges?"

Now she is angry, but she keeps her guise, feeling she is not going to get a straight answer no matter what. Worst of all, from what she knows about his history, she fears that what he is telling her is all too true.

She says, "I came here to tell you your father died."

"My father? What about yours?"

"You can joke about that?"

"I guess if you said *our father*, it would sound like God died. But that happened some time ago. And *my* father was definitely no god, and neither was yours. I think I already knew your father Kevin died rather recently, like some weeks ago. Not sure how he died."

Geena is dumbfounded. "You did? How?"

"I don't know. I just knew. Probably Mr. Death, here on my shoulder, whispered in my ear, '*You've been moved one click closer.*'"

"Will you fucking stop that!" she yells. Immediately, she feels surrounding heads turning their admonishing faces at her. She whispers, "Enough of that crap. Did Joe call you? He said he wouldn't. No, he wouldn't." She doesn't give him time to answer. Slightly louder, she says, "You know he disappeared…Joe, I mean."

"No, I didn't. What do you mean, disappeared?"

"Yeah, a short time after our father died, Joe wrote a note and said he was going to see a priest. Fuck, I don't know, maybe our dad's death did something to him." She pauses, filtering the information, trying to decide what she can or should tell him. "It broke my heart. Joe was very special to me. Because of the company he started, he was the one who inspired me to become a structural engineer, to build bridges and buildings."

She would never tell Davis about how intimate she had truly felt, or the things…the specifics Joe had told about Kevin. "But Joe never seemed happy. He kept trying to find something, and went out of his way to hunt for it in everything he did. He couldn't make it all fit. In fact, I think he never got over the death of his love, feeling like

353

it was his fault. Finally, he even, well, it doesn't matter. That's what eventually got him, I think. His guilt. Maybe."

"So you think he suddenly saw God, do you?"

"Even worse, Davis, I don't know how he went or where he went. He simply disappeared." She is on the verge of crying, but holds it back by telling herself it is the wrong time and that she is, after all, overly tired. "I stopped in New England on the way here and went to his apartment, and since I knew his codes, I went in expecting to find him, but his place was empty and as neat as a pin. No mess. No note. No dirty dishes. No dirty clothes. It was like he never existed. But I understood he had moved somewhere."

"How do you know he's not dead?"

"When he wrote me the letter, he didn't say anything about ending his life. Besides, he had taken the time to do a serious move and have people clean up afterwards. I asked around and heard that his place was already in the process of being put up for sale. And his letter to me was sent from somewhere else like he was traveling."

"Where?"

"Ann Arbor, Michigan. Which, of course, tells me nothing. He talked about existing and not existing. He said he had a new life." She pauses, unsure what to tell him. "In his letter he said he had been called by a priest, whatever that meant."

"So, he was alone and found God. And you're still afraid he will kill himself. What's the deal, Geena? He never gets over his lost love; I don't get over my lost love. You're afraid I'll kill myself, too? Is that it? Is that what you really came here to find out?" he says.

"Jesus, Davis, it hardly feels like you care who died or even whether..." she says.

"Should I? Geena, we all mourn those we choose to mourn for reasons of empathy and need. I didn't find the whole earth mourning for Stella. But death is the whole earth's unavoidable destination."

She winces. "You're not the most optimistic soul I have ever known. I can only wonder how you would have felt if you were born in North Korea or starving in the Sahara. I hate to say it, but you actually look like you escaped from North Korea and came here after crawling through some shit-forsaken desert."

He says, "I think it might be time to take that walk outside. Wrap up those two *knekkebrød* and let's get some fresh air. Meet a moose or a wolverine." He stands up, smiling. "If you can stand to be seen walking with a North Korean."

"More like a downtrodden desert rat." After quickly wrapping the food in a napkin and handing it to him, she stands, grabs the handle of her suitcase, and, smiling optimistically as her hopes rise, says, "Let's get out of here."

As they step outside through the revolving exit door, she realizes how soundproof the building has actually been. Out here, even the noise and the diesel smell of the idling jet engines is overbearing, destroying what could have been a beautiful sunny, warm, and wind-still October day. Now, unless they travel somewhere else, she wonders how they are going to talk and hopes he is leading them somewhere away from here.

She tries to orient herself in this world, wondering for the first time what day it is. The weather is as confusing as the visit. North of the Arctic Circle. Warm and sunny October? She wants to ask how that could be but the noise grinds down the thought of speaking. She looks at her watch. She knows she is exhausted but scolds herself for not noticing the sun is resting on the horizon at noontime.

On the tundra, just past the narrow asphalt parking lot, she can see a bench surrounded by low-growing evergreen shrubs, huddled in defiant protective bunches surrounding slightly taller, deformed birches—vegetation pressed and twisted from the harsh burden of the northern climate—like her brother.

Waiting for the reverberation of another Boeing departure to wane enough to speak, Davis says, "You can always go back in where it's quieter, especially since you shouldn't try to go too far dragging that suitcase." Indicating the bench, he says, "Let's sit over there for a while."

It is altogether obvious that he has no plans of inviting her home or even to let her stay in the same mysterious village where he lives, if actually there is one. His hospitality matches his table manners. She is tired. She needs that shower, and to rest. The whole purpose of the trip is obviously all for nothing, making the exhaustion engulf her body.

As they approach the bench, she hears a small plane's buzz overhead, sounding like it is the broadcast medium for the green bottle flies that swirl up flame-like from their respite on the bench.

She is beginning to hate her own brother, or at least, hate how he is. *Uncle shmunkle. Forget it, kids.*

After they sit, it seems they have nothing to say, both using the jet noise as an excuse. Then the jet turns off its engines and, in the quiet, he says, "You know, dear father Kevin was not necessarily the man you and I thought. I saw him screwing a woman who was not mother Beth."

She pales. The things he knew. Trying to deflect it, she says, "Well, Mother died young."

"No, Geena, before he shot her. I think that's part of why he lived in guilt."

"Lived in guilt? Davis, why are you saying that?"

Did he know? What did he know? She is unable to think clearly as her last pinch of adrenalin has just become a cold cinder.

He seems not to hear her and continues to speak over the sound of an approaching not-so-distant passenger jet. "You can go on believing what you want. You should. In fact, I know you will. I don't say that what I think is right. What I'm doing is right for me because death is here." He taps his ear.

She says in a desolate, debilitated voice, "I don't understand what you are saying."

His voice seems to gain strength as the engine noise increases. He says, "That's normal. As soon as we are born, we're different from every other person on earth including our brothers and sisters, for a million reasons.

"You can't even imagine the experience of the person sitting next to you who developed under different circumstances than yours, not only from birth, but also from the advancing flow of life's evolutionary transformations on each of us, which might take *me* closer to feeling what a nocturnal bat feels, while you, on the other hand, are carried closer to a bond with a distant human by a quantum particle. Who knows?

"But, Geena, we all, in the end, every single one of us, will devolve into the Bony-Eared Assfish."

Stunned, Geena finds the energy to yell above the jet noise. "Your father's favorite word leaps out of your mouth like you were...like he was here. Davis, what the hell is going on? What are you talking about?"

"Geena, I don't know what I am talking about," he shouts. "Since mother Ellen died, and mother Beth died, and then Stella, my one love on this earth, died..." His words have tears in them. "...I have never felt so lonely and never felt so alone. In fact, after Stella died, I never felt anything. I have never cared about anything or anyone since. Thank you for making me feel sane for one hour. I am saying goodbye to you, my sister. I see my bus is here."

Picking up the napkin-wrapped packet of food, he rises from the bench and, without turning around to wave, walks through the engine howls of the landing jet toward a waiting bus.

11. DAVIS

REVELATIONS

THE PELTING RAIN ON THE BUS IS FORCED INTO AN OMINOUS SOUNDING PSALM BY the gusting wind, and is eerily harmonious with the poetry of the dolphins' clicks and creaks that I can't get out of my head. It's only two days since I left Geena at the airport and here I am back on a bus headed north, and I don't even know why. I mean, I know I'm getting off at the Space Center and I know what I'm going to do—once I get there. But I don't know why I bother, except maybe for my mother.

The rain is more like a hailstorm, as it tends to be nowadays—I mean, when it does rain, even the drops are bigger—and lets me get off work since working out on the ocean in this weather is too dangerous. Even the bus has to struggle against the wind howling in from the open ocean on the left. And on the right, the walls of rock crush the water out of the air as the wind slams against the unabashed faces of the naked mountains that ennoble Lofoten. The road-floods are more precarious as the oceans expand. The bus driver is literally creeping along so as not to lose control, and maybe he can't see much. I don't think I would want his job right now.

Sitting to my right across the aisle, the only other passenger on the bus—what I think is a woman—hunched over like a pile of wet trash, a picture reinforced by the stink of the wet cur on the seat beside her—is tipping her head to another rhythm, adding to the unsettling feeling of this hour-long passage north.

But I think it's about time to lam it; we're almost there. I hear the driver announce on the anorexic P.A. system some indistinguishable phrase smudged by the thudding rain. To my left, even through the torrents of water, I can distinguish the phallic outline of the Ardland Space Center rocket-shaped sign in the dim morning light.

For some reason as I exit the bus, the rain is reminding me of a line of poetry—or maybe just a partial line—that I wrote and sent to Beth years ago, but had forgotten until just this moment. It was something like

> *Terrestrial rain can angrily flood,*
> *Deluging mountains into your streets and basements*
> *To tell you it is time.*

I begin to fear the reality of my visit. Upon entering the space center building, I realize that, just as I, the fisherman, have the clothing to protect me against the rain, so does every visitor and employee here. Thus, the space center's garage-size entrance area is festooned with yellow and red slickers, brown rubber boots, innumerable umbrellas, and water is flooding the floor. I only hope I can recognize my own weather gear again in this jumble since it's all so similar. But then, maybe I won't care.

Farther in, at the reception desk, I say in English, "I'm here to see Dr. Camila Ademir."

"Is she expecting you?" says the young, fat receptionist who has a sign on the counter labeling her Elsa. She has been taught to smile, begrudgingly, but not to change clothes; her stringent body odor stings my eyes.

"No," I say. "I couldn't make an appointment."

She looks a bit uncertain. I say, "I didn't know what day I could arrive, not to speak of the time."

She seems to sympathize, probably assuming my travels from

some foreign port were hindered by the weather. "I will see if she is available. And your name?"

"Davis McKinnon."

After a bit of intercom searching and repeating *There is a Mr. McKinnon to see Doctor Ademir*, and responses from varying voices, Elsa announces with her pained expression, "The professor will be right out."

Behind Elsa on the left is a door marked *WC* and, because of her grimaces, I can't help but think how she might have the runs but is still doing her job like a tough Northern Norwegian while suffering gas pangs. In the same wall to the right is another door marked *Auditorium*. I sit down on one of the peripheral benches fastened to the white walls of the echoey reception area to wait and to rehearse my soliloquy. If there had been any crowd of people waiting here for the auditorium, the noise level from one loud person could have destroyed any ability to think.

In less than five minutes, a short, delicate-looking dark-skinned woman in a white blouse and tan jeans marches—smiling—toward me across the grey and white vinyl tiles of the reception. She should be older than I am, but I'm sure that I look older than she does; she is well-kept by an inherited youth. Her shining eyes are accentuated by her rapaciously black hair surrounding her head.

Almost before I can get to my feet, she says with an indefinable foreign inflection, "Hello, Mr. McKinnon. What may I do for you?"

Although she has not offered to shake my hand, my original twinge of angst is allayed by her outgoing personality and willingness to meet me out of the blue—and even by her soft, exquisite perfume. Somehow I'm lucky.

I say, "Thank you for taking the time to meet me." Glancing at the receptionist, I say, "I was wondering if we might speak in a more private…uh…in just a bit more privacy? If you don't mind. It won't take long, but it is important."

She does the expected inspection of me, trying to figure out if I could be a salesman, a kook, or even worse, dangerous.

"What is this about, Mr. McKinnon?"

I repeat. "We need to speak in private and I assure you that it is important."

Is she going to believe me? I almost don't; why should she?

She turns to the receptionist and says, "Elsa, we will be in the auditorium."

Without speaking or turning to me, the professor strides toward the designated door. I can only assume that I should follow her, but, to be sure, I pause long enough to confirm she's leading me there. She exits the reception area without turning back and leaves the door open. I follow her in and close the door behind me. The small brightly lit auditorium we have entered has about ten rows of fixed dark plastic chairs facing a screen and a podium.

She says, "Because of the weather, all of our normal presentations have been cancelled. Usually, we hold presentations in here almost daily about our research programs, so you are lucky, Mr. McKinnon, that I have time for you since I am the presenter. Do you know what we do here, Mr. McKinnon?"

I know they hire out their rocket services to governments and organizations who need to measure air quality and the effects of the aurora borealis, because I looked it up. That's all I know or care to know.

I say simply, "Yes, I do."

She doesn't seem tempted to elaborate on my supposed knowledge and only points to a chair by the table on the stage area—a step higher than the rest of the room—and motions for me to sit. As she halfway sits on the corner of the table—folding her arms and looking down at me—she says, "Okay, Mr. McKinnon, what is so important to bring you here. Through the storm?"

I feel sure her stony brown eyes are able to stop invading armies and are challenging me so that my trip here may be for nothing.

I smell her dragon breath. But I concentrate on her dark, heavy eyebrows instead, so as not to be distracted, or more probably, deterred.

I say, "Dr. Ademir, I know you are Bolivian. I know also that you, at a very young age, were first educated as a physicist at MIT and later as a marine biologist."

Expressionless, she is unfazed by my personal knowledge of her, since, of course, I could have looked that up on the internet. So I need to get personal. The things the dolphins told me.

I say, "I know that you studied quantum physics under Professor Martin Case at MIT." Still no reaction. Was that on the internet, too? "And that, during the time you studied oceanography, you befriended a doctoral candidate at Woods Hole, Massachusetts, named Ellen McKinnon working on dolphin communication."

Now I have her. She responds by moving to a chair facing me. "Yes, Ellen McKinnon, my friend. And this woman was your...?"

"She was my mother."

She smiles a real smile—showing yellow, aging teeth. "And how is your mother? Is she still...?"

I look directly into her eyes; I am in command. She will listen for a while if I'm careful. "She's dead. Died young."

The professor dons a sad face. "Oh, I am sorry. She was so bright."

"Well, me too, but we all die," I say in a way that should calm her. But then I can really throw the curve. "She died long ago—thirty-four years ago—in a car collision with Professor Case."

Her eyes are now puzzled under a wrinkling of her brow. "Oh, my. They were in the same car?"

"No, they collided...crashed into each other...head on. Up in Maine."

I'm trying my hardest to not feel the guilt for her death once again, as I have a thousand times before. The pain can be overwhelming.

She sits silently long enough to absorb the prospect of the story. "Oh, my." She pauses. "They both died?"

"Yes. Simultaneously, I heard."

She hardly pauses. "That sounds terrible. And so much lost knowledge."

"Yes." I wait, creating a purposely awkward pause.

"Is that what you wanted to tell me, Mr. McKinnon?"

"Not really. I mean, yes. I needed to tell you that so that you would…uh…I could tell you why I am here."

She looks at me with a rapid chain of expressions that combines curiosity, confusion, and, now once again, skepticism.

"Mr. McKinnon, if you are looking for money…"

This is not the direction I want it to go. My uncertainty has aroused her suspicions again. But how can I sound certain? Or maybe it's my looks. But I even dressed up for her.

"I'm not sure why you ask," I say. "I'm sorry if I look so needy."

She frowns. I think she's embarrassed. Is that a good thing?

I continue. "Dr. Ademir, I have been asked to visit you and to give you a message because of who you are and because of who I am—an old fisherman. And, I am told, because you knew Professor Case, and because you knew my mother.

"I am worried that you will not believe me, of course, but I have no choice. Therefore, once I have told you what I have to tell you, I will leave on the next bus, because I've done everything I've been asked to do. You will never see me again, most likely."

She speaks noticeably without contractions. "I am sorry, Mr. McKinnon. I did not mean to insult you. I should not have said that. Please, forgive me. Who has asked you to give me this message?"

I say, "Before I tell you who, I would like to give you the message."

I reach in my shirt pocket and take out the micro-recording chip, holding the diminutive black square in my open palm in front of her.

"This recording is the message. I have no idea what it says; it is in a language I don't understand. As I hand it to you, the message

I was instructed…uh…I am to give to you is, and I quote, *You have ten years to understand. After that, you become our food.*"

I practiced not saying more. I wait. She says nothing. I look only at the thing in my hand. I'm afraid to look at her face. I'm fairly sure she's thinking that I am the exact nutcase she feared. At this very moment, I cannot help but wonder, too, if I am.

I say, "I have to go now. Please take this." I pick up the tiny black thing between two fingers and reach toward her to drop it into her hand.

She doesn't stretch out her hand for it. She says, "And who is this person who sent this so-called message?"

I swallow. I know if she were a man, she might punch me in the face for what I am about to say, for wasting her time. I say it anyway.

"The dolphins."

I wait.

She says, "The dolphins."

"Yes."

She says, "I am not familiar with that organization. That is an American football team, is it not?"

I continue. "Please. You don't need to believe me. Just take this recording and see if you can translate it. I didn't come here to make any kind of fool of you or to make a joke. I was told to come here by dolphins and to give you this. I don't care what you do with it. I don't care if you believe me. I have done what I needed to do. I will leave now."

I drop the recording onto the polished wood table and stand up.

"You speak to dolphins often, Mr. McKinnon?"

I know she's making fun of me. I look into her eyes and shake my head. "My mother did. You do what you want with it, Professor."

I walk out of the room, turn around, and step back into the doorway. She is staring at the memory chip still on the table.

I say, "I forgot to tell you that the dolphins also told me why they chose you. It is just what you said. So much lost knowledge."

I turn and walk through the reception. In the time that it takes for me to hunt down my rain gear and struggle to put it on, I keep thinking something else will happen. But it doesn't.

The rain is still cascading horizontally, so I know I'll be engulfed by the deluge for the hour at the bus stop—nearly mutating into an amphibian—but it's better than waiting in there.

At least I can smell the sea, Mama. At least I can breathe.

And think.

I can do nothing else. I think that now in 2044, the North Sea has warmed enough for the dolphins to come north of the Arctic Circle, to talk with me. Did you send them, Mama? I felt the warm wind from the ocean water. I sensed them coming; I smelled them. Do you believe me, Mama?

"Record us."

Okay, first I thought maybe this was my idea, because you know, Mama, I used to have a good imagination.

Was I delirious? Am I now? The dolphins knew you, Mama. That you could understand.

I surrender to the few who think they control the world around them and the multitudes who let the world happen to them; I am none of them. Forgive me, Mama. I, like the space woman, don't believe any of it; I believe as she does, that I am merely insane. The incomprehensible is grooming me for the coming storm.

As the bus arrives, a silly song runs through my mind—or more like a psalm. "Holy! holy! HOOOLY! Lord God all flighty!"

EPILOGUE

ERASEMENT

GEENA TOOK A ROOM NEAR THE SMALL NORWEGIAN AIRPORT AND ARRANGED TO fly out the next morning.

Back in Kansas, she mailed a handwritten note to Davis on her personal notepaper, and which her grandchildren will find, apparently unopened, in a moldy box of personal family items someone will discover years later in a Norwegian basement in Lofoten and will mail to them. Included in the envelope will be a forty-year-old uncashed personal check from 2044 written out to Davis for $500 and this note:

Dear Davis,

I cried all night for you that night, for Joe, and for myself, but for the last time. No more. I want to be happy.

Love, Geena

* * *

She—Mama—will be called Geena, the engineer, by her progeny, especially because she says engineer things such as *life is like a large roll of cable of which some parts are used properly and some are thrown away, and then the cable comes to a sudden end.* But her own cancerous death will be long and painful, more like a thin thread that finally snaps at age seventy-eight in the fall of 2070. At least, she will have had her children to tend to her, to love her, and to tell stories about her to their friends.

They will tell their friends that their mother had been the most optimistic person on earth, never speaking derogatorily about anyone or anything, never smelling a bad smell, or hearing a negative word. Why, they will say, even on her deathbed she would never complain even though she must have been in agonizing pain so much of the time.

Their favorite part of her story, because it will be both funny and so like her, will be some of her last words—*I'm so happy I'm pickled tink*—as if she really didn't mean to say it that way. They will be sure that her fuzzy, aging brain has screwed up an old saying and made it cute. The rest of the words, the part about *running out of ink*, they will figure, means she knew she was dying.

Joe, unaware of the worry that he has caused Geena or that her worry about him may have helped instigate her cancer, will have eventually emailed Geena explaining that when one gets into a new romance, the rest of the world doesn't matter and that most new lovers vanish from the earth for a period until the intensity has quieted down.

But even if Joe will write and Geena will write back, saying she is happy to hear he is fine, the bond will have been broken, neither of them caring or wanting to bring up the distressing, disturbing past or what might become their future since that future does not involve the two of them together. They, like starlings—like Davis—will speak of the present and write only of the space around them—the weather, an article in a blog about travel, or maybe a recipe. Thus, having little to say, their correspondence will soon become sporadic, and will eventually be reduced to an annual online Christmas card. Joe will never talk about his new love; Geena will never bother to mention her cancer.

* * *

Privately within herself, Geena feels she has her mother in her, so much so that she *is* her mother, and she, as opposed to what she has noticed many women feel about their mothers, likes being and is proud of being the mother Geena knew. Upon selling the old house, Geena considers buying back the old piano her father used to play—maybe as an heirloom to pass down to her children or just as a memory—since, after all, her mother had bought it. But it is only a momentary thought since the stains on the keyboard would bring back the wrong memories and would have to be explained over and over.

In fact, Geena will never manage to tell the true story of her mother's death without crying. So early on, in order to avoid the trauma for everyone, Geena creates a tale that said Beth had won some indeterminate gold medal in Switzerland before Geena was born, then had died at Geena's birth; thus there is no more to tell. It is easier that way.

But her offspring will be left in a fuddle when asking about her family. Once she will mention a far-flung brother living in Arctic Norway who, although living in the mountains, is somehow an ocean fisherman. And when asked more about him or her father? Geena is brilliant but is odd—*funny in so many ways*—they will say, since she will be so vague or reticent about her history, most of the time by cleverly changing the subject through asking about the inquisitor's day or latest activity. Or maybe she will evade the subject by telling some anecdote about her having had a long-distant boyfriend—before the marriage to their father, sometimes, and sometimes after the divorce—but never being very clear when that relationship existed or why. Or is she mixing up someone with her brother?

For her descendants, the weirdest and funniest thing for a while about Geena will be that she never calls death by that term; it will always be the *Bony-Eared Assfish*—said with a smile—and which they will attribute to her propensity to swear. For a short while, even before Geena's death, the *Bony-Eared Assfish* will become a funny playground name for young grandkids to call playmates. But for those in the family who understand its association with death, remembering that fish will be discouraged, and within a year of Geena's death, it will be blotted out by everyone.

After her death, more memories of Geena will soon fade, partly because the descendants are dealing with their own lives, but also the memories will become vague and forgotten almost before they begin, because, as the details of Geena's life will subconsciously be mulled over and found wanting, the peculiarities will become confusing and disconcerting. It will be best to get on with life and to file Geena under the general heading of *Eccentric*.

The wolverine tale will remain unread as Geena loses it or throws it away. She, thus, has no way of seeing how the story shows that Kevin, besides having an unusual awareness, had some sort of link to Davis, except for the small hint in Joe's final letter. Joe had been aware of it when he read the story, but had been too occupied with his new love to remember—or to care to remember—to follow up that thought with Geena. Worse yet, such ties are part of a past that he doesn't care to provoke.

* * *

Of Kevin, if anybody asks, Geena's offspring will proudly show the story, which, Geena will have told them, some person named Joe had once written and accompanied with the photo of the formal crowd surrounding their heroic grandfather, Kevin Nuss—a story in honor of his being appointed Attorney General of Maine and about all his heroic actions and how he had died helping the disadvantaged masses suffering from the effects of global warming. Oddly, no matter how they will beg her, Geena will never elaborate.

She will say, "The story is quite clear except for the details." And they will feel an antagonism that spurns further questions.

As much as Geena's children might try to remember the future for their descendants by framing a picture of Kevin for the bedroom wall, the names, faces, and lives of Kevin and his history—true or imagined—will become as forgotten and unknown to them as their future could ever be to Kevin.

* * *

Geena will die never communicating again with Davis, or knowing that he died two days after her airport visit with him. When she will think about her brother, she will imagine, and in fact once posit, that he also got cancer. Then upon being diagnosed at around age fifty-nine with an overload of white blood cells, he threw his dart to choose the day. So, she will imagine that he decided to feed the once-cheated megalodon, and while the fishing-boat captain was busy at the helm, Davis slipped unnoticed overboard into the cold North Sea.

But neither she nor any of her family will ever know that Davis's total existence was erased eight years earlier when the bus on which he was riding home from the space center blew off the seaside road near a bridge into a tree-barren, rocky valley, killing both the driver and Davis, or so it was determined. It was established as an accident because, as the bus was not found in time to save them because the ferocious weather had vacated such rural roads, no one suspected that Davis had forced the bus off the road after killing the driver. And when finally the bus company reported the missing bus and the accident was discovered, Davis had no identification on him as to where he lived, and although the Norwegian government had the address of his rented room in medical records, his body was never matched, claimed, or identified. The locals who knew Davis had always protected his identity, partly for his sake, but mostly for their own desire to stay out of trouble.

* * *

Through the days, months, and years of Geena's later life, she continued thinking of her mother each time it rained, each and every downpour. Because year by year the rainstorms become more torrential, on Geena's last night that fateful November in 2070, the Kansas tornadic rain will roar like the brutal ocean pounding the New England shore. Through the inundating tumult, Geena will feel a looming white whale whisper palliatively in her ear and then silently carry her back to where she has never been.

ACKNOWLEDGMENTS

I WANT TO THANK GRAZIA, MY LOVING SPOUSE, FOR HER ENDLESS PATIENCE, SUPPORT, and literary brilliance. I am indebted to my editors, but especially Rebecca Heyman who also beat sense into me and didn't give up on me. Leslie Busby, Sydney Holt, my granddaughter Aurora, and Bob Muens helped me with their personal knowledge and talents. And I want to thank numerous friends and other family members for their contribution and encouragement; you know who you are.

Printed in Great Britain
by Amazon